Forever

Forever

Natalie J. Case

Copyright (C) 2016 Natalie J. Case
Layout design and Copyright (C) 2016 Creativia
Published 2016 by Creativia
Edited by Donna Rich
Cover art by http://www.thecovercollection.com/
This book is a work of fiction. Names, characters, places, and incidents are the product of the author's imagination or are used fictitiously. Any resemblance to actual events, locales, or persons, living or dead, is purely coincidental.
All rights reserved. No part of this book may be reproduced or transmitted in any form or by any means, electronic or mechanical, including photocopying, recording, or by any information storage and retrieval system, without the author's permission.

Contents

Chapter 1 — 1

Chapter 2 — 26

Chapter 3 — 44

Chapter 4 — 66

Chapter 5 — 83

Chapter 6 — 98

Chapter 7 — 118

Chapter 8 — 142

Chapter 9 — 166

Chapter 10 — 187

Chapter 11	202
Chapter 12	219
Chapter 13	241
Chapter 14	261
Chapter 15	275
Chapter 16	290
Chapter 17	308
Chapter 18	331
Chapter 19	357
Chapter 20	383
Chapter 21	399
Chapter 22	426
Chapter 23	449
Chapter 24	466
Chapter 25	481

Chapter 26	501
About the Author	521

Chapter 1

I AM comfortable in the dark, when the moon slumbers and clouds dim the stars and the smell of the earth rises in the still air. Perhaps that still moment is the only place I am comfortable. My years have been long and have seen me travel nearly all of this world, often alone. I have given life and dealt death, but I offer no regrets. Regret is a waste of effort when justice brings the guilty no peace. I will see justice in the end, I am certain of that, for all that I have done, and all I have not.

So much has gone now and I am ill at ease with the time, the waiting, here at the end of my life. The ancient game is played out and three souls, born together in the lost pages of time are as they were meant to be ... but to tell that story, my story, I must go back to the beginning, before I came to be, before any of us had come to be.

It begins near to the birth of time, or man's keeping of it, when three brothers entered into an unholy bond, bound by blood to the night, trading the daylight for eternal life. The stories tell of their calling, the slaughter of their mortal families, and the beginning of what would be called The Family. The middle brother, a brutish man named Crenoral, chose my mother to be his first bride. She had been a farmer's wife, and was pregnant, only barely so, when Crenoral came and called her into the night. She followed him, bringing me with her, and leaving behind a mortal family of two sons to mourn her. It was some time after that when I came to be born.

Our existence and all of its dark burden was new to us then. There were no rules to our existence, save for the drinking of blood and the death that rose with each sunrise. The Family was small, those three brothers, their brides and the occasional other whom they adopted along the way. In all, there were no more than twelve in my earliest memories, aside from Crenoral and his brothers.

I was born in a dark, dank cave somewhere in the Caucasus to a mother who wasn't exactly beautiful. She learned early how to make use of what gifts she was given, and when she chose, could be dynamically attractive, terrifying and compelling at once. I can still see her long, angular face and hair as black as the night, which made her appear somehow harsh, unforgiving. Her green eyes burned eerily in the darkness and smoldered in the firelight.

There was little to our relationship but for the vague, distant kinship we all shared and the occasional moment of maternal gesture. Her life was securely coiled around her own hunger and little intruded upon her desire, save her duty to Crenoral. She did, however, take pleasure in telling me how long she was forced to carry me, and how I had maimed her in my infancy.

When I was first born, Mother fed me, returning from her own hunt to suckle me to her breast. My teeth and instinct combined to fill me with the blood that she brought for me. As I grew, ever so slowly, I was given to drink from her wrist, but the damage was done and both breasts bore scars from my years of feeding. As she complained, and grew bored with me, Crenoral would feed me, cradling me in his arms as he held his wrist to my lips. The day came, however, when it was no longer enough, the instincts born within me cried for release, the hunger needed to be appeased.

I waited in the dark of my nursery crypt, cold and hungry, the Change full upon me when Crenoral came. I caught him unaware, pouncing from my sleeping pallet and clawing my way up his chest to bite into the tender skin at his neck. When I was sated and pulled back from him, he was laughing, wiping at the still dripping wound. I was breathless and shaking as he pulled me to him and held me tightly, pride filling his words. "Amara, my little one, what a killer you shall be." He held me, caressing my wild, un-brushed hair and showering me with kisses until the Change subsided.

The next night was ours. He bathed me and dressed me, parading me before the gathered clan as his perfect little daughter. I was proud, walking beside him, knowing we were going out into the night together, and that not even my mother was afforded that honor. I was his protégé and he was my mentor, my father.

I might have even passed as his daughter, though I was born with skin purely white. My full head of black hair was thick like his and slightly wavy. The fangs that sliced through flesh so easily had cut my mother as I was born, though they were the only teeth in my head. Over the next decades, the rest of my teeth came in and the fangs became somewhat less noticeable, retracting until the Change came upon me. My eyes were so dark that they might not be discerned from the shadows and my vision was sharp in the dark without a moon or stars. There was little remarkable about my appearance, save these things. I did not possess the odd, translucent beauty of my brothers and sisters, nor the mysterious, gripping quality I would find later in humanity. I was, beside them all, rather plain.

That night, none my inadequacies mattered. I was glorious beside him, my tiny hand held in his thick one as we followed the night down from our mountain home, a slowly growing abode above the natural caves that hid us by day. I had never been outside the protective walls before that spring night, and I wanted to see everything. The crisp aroma of broken grass was punctuated with bursts of fennel and yarrow and underscored by the constant base of damp earth. There was a slight tang in the air that Crenoral said came from the sea that was nearly a whole night's journey away, even for us, to the east and slightly north. Sometimes, when the wind blew just right, it brought with it the scent of the water. Closer to us the aroma of blood faintly came to me. I was more familiar with this scent and my feet quickened their pace.

Two of the local tribes were at war and the call of blood and death rose higher in the air as we moved through the trees. My little body shook with excitement as we neared the battlefield and I felt my teeth biting into my lower lip. The scents grew sharper as the Change came over me, transforming my tender, child-like features into something far more terrifying.

As we paused in the shadows of the trees, Crenoral smiled down at me. His face was also distorted by the Change, his thick eyebrows thicker still and raised somewhat from his eyes, which seemed brighter. His smile revealed white teeth and deadly fangs. The pale light of the half moon reflected off his face, making him appear to glow. I wondered if I glowed too.

Yards away from us, a man walked a slow pattern through the field, pausing from time to time to examine a body. His wrapped feet scuffed on the stones and cold dirt of the bloodied field that had earlier been filled with living souls, but now held only the dead and the dying. The smell of him was nearly overpowering. I had never seen a mortal alive before.

He was smaller than I had imagined, in a rough spun cloth tunic girded with a leather belt. He wore a bag over one shoulder and he was collecting items from the bodies. His breath plumed on the chill air as he looked around him nervously. I licked my lips in anticipation, willing him closer. The hunger inside me was undeniable.

I held my breath, as Crenoral stole up behind the man, overpowering him quickly and pulling him to the ground, with one hand covering the man's mouth. Crenoral used that hand to pull the man's head away from his shoulder, exposing his neck and signaling me to come. I scrambled over a stiff body and slick grass. I could see then he was already bleeding from a small wound Crenoral had made with a blade secreted in his hand. I looked up at Crenoral expectantly.

"What are you waiting for? Drink."

I needed no further encouragement, clamping my small mouth over the bleeding, pulsing wound just below the man's ear. The taste was richer than what I was used to, thicker, sweeter. The echo of another heart called out to my own, even as I felt that other heart slowing. Images of his life filled my mind, thoughts of his brother, a child, his fear of death. For all my appetite, he was far more than my body could contain, and when I was full I pulled back, my face was wet with his blood. I pulled a corner of my tunic over my sticky chin and looked up at my teacher.

Crenoral laughed and dropped the man, leaving him to die alone where he fell. We made for the outskirts of the nearest camp then, and Crenoral feasted twice before we turned for home. As we walked through the night, he spoke of the people of the mountain, those closest to us. He warned me away from certain roads and told me stories of his early days, when he and Bestin raged through the nights.

Crenoral was a dark and sinister man. He had already reached his mid-thirties when his elder brother came to him and kissed him with immortality. He was short, as most men were in his time, dark of skin and hair, and he was possessed of deep, dark blue eyes, made all the deeper by the prominent brow that gave him a permanent scowl. Even the many years spent in the embrace of the night only slightly paled him. Dark hair, trimmed short, conferred on him an appearance of strength, even when the Change was not upon him, and he was charismatic and charming.

He doted upon me in those early days, lavishing me with gifts and praise. He made a show of honoring the day of my birth, though the others clearly despised me for the unnatural way I came to be. Crenoral fancied himself my father, and I the only daughter he would ever have. In turn, I adored him. He gave me anything and everything my heart desired and I followed him through the nights, emulating him.

From that first night on, I went out to hunt among the tribes of man, a child small, frail...fearsome, ferocious. Hand in hand we wandered through dark settlements, stealing through opened doors and crawling into open windows when we could find no wayward soul dealing death or attending to urgent private matters in the small hours of the night. In those days the hunger was more than I knew how to control, and I would fall upon my prey fiercely, leaving little behind.

Crenoral's pride in me was palpable, and the strength and rush that came with the blood was enthralling. I had known that we were stronger, faster than our mortal cousins, but was fascinated by the frailty of the human body, the ease with which death came to them. I was captivated as well by what I saw as we passed like wraiths through settlements and villages. Homes built of wood and stone, gathering places, shrines to gods and goddesses, tools with which they killed and worked the ground all would bring me to pause in my hunt, running my tiny hands over them until Crenoral's hunger dragged me away.

One night, in a village on the western slope of the mountain where the salty scents of the distant Black Sea would reach strongly if the sky was clear, I stole a small piece of burnished copper from the room of a young girl whose blood was sweet. Her things had enthralled me, and I settled on the reflective surface, slipping through the night back to my dark crypt to spend hours staring at my own face.

By candlelight I watched my face change from one not much different from that of the girl who had last owned the primitive mirror, to that of a monster. I had seen the others, my mother and Crenoral, as they Changed and wondered about my own face. I knew I was different, though I had little understanding of what that meant. The face that scowled out at me was not unlike Mother's, though my brow was not nearly as pronounced as hers or Crenoral's. My sunken eyes made my face seem far more sinister than any mortal child my size I had seen. My teeth, already slightly larger and more distinct than the humans I had encountered, lengthened just noticeably, their sharpness catching on my lip if I wasn't mindful of them.

Not all of the gifts of the Change can be found in a mirror though, and the truth of our differences from our mortal brethren can be found in those that cannot be seen.

Senses intensify as the Change comes and the speed of our stride can imply the notion of flight. Our eyes are not well suited for the harsh light of day, but are keen in the dark and shadow. We, small as we might have been, were the dark predators that hunted in the cold shadows and caused the preternatural fears among the early ancestors of today's man. Much of the uneducated mythology and barbaric belief dismissed so easily by modern scholars is, in its deepest core, the reality of who and what we were. There was no escaping our hunger. There was only death. It was all I knew in those days.

I was, however, quite alone. The Family despised me, even Mother who grew bored with me as Crenoral became enamored of me. He was my only companion, and when I was not with him I was alone, or bullied about by Arda and Vahe who despised me. Vahe was the oldest of Crenoral's clan, taken, on a whim when Crenoral needed company, from a sheep pasture. He had only been sixteen. Arda was little more than that, brought by Vahe to serve his lust. With my arrival, Crenoral left them to their own darkness. They hated me for that. My childhood was filled with torments, the hunger which haunted my day and night and their hatred, softened only by Crenoral's affection. I craved companionship, and after a time it was not that of a doting father that I needed.

Crenoral seemed to recognize it. I appeared as a human of six or so when he came to me, beaming and happy with himself. It was the night of my birth, three hundred and sixty-five years old as I recall, a night when he and I would celebrate and he would bring me incredibly tasty gifts. He had been away for many days, and I was expecting his return with something from a faraway land.

"I have brought you something, Amara," he said, slipping into the dark room, his teeth shining in the light of a single flame from the crude oil lamp beside my bed.

I looked up expectantly and saw the flush upon his face, the tiny telltale drops of red at the corners of his mouth. He sat beside me and gathered me into his arms. "What is it, Father?" I asked in a voice hushed with excitement.

He squeezed me once, then disappeared out the door. When he returned, a child walked beside him. A boy, no more than ten himself, beautiful as the night, with fair hair and skin. His face was vacant and I could smell the distinct aroma of death about him. This was no juicy morsel from the east or north. Crenoral brought him to me, sat him beside me. I could see the minute changes just barely begun in him, upon his once human face. His porcelain-smooth skin was paling, his lost eyes widening as the pain of death registered. The deed was already done, and the hunger was awakening. "What is he, Father?" I breathed, one hand grazing the surface of his skin.

"He is yours, darling, forever. Does he please you?"

I was enamored, watching him go from being human to being like me, seeing him die and be reborn. "Yes, Father, very much. Does he have a name?"

"Adan," the boy himself responded, his face turning to me, his eyes clear.

I clapped my hands with glee, so excited to have a new friend, a playmate. At last, a companion who would be devoted to me. Crenoral beamed with his own happiness. "Are you hungry then, my young ones?" he asked, after a time.

I was at his side instantly, Adan only slightly behind me. We went out together to hunt. That night, in the glory of the newborn of the night, we fed gluttonously on anything that crossed our path; deer, rabbits, and finally as the clouds closed in over the half-full moon, a teenager rising in the small hours of the morning to begin his chores. Adan and I frolicked in the shadows as Crenoral watched, beaming at us like a proud father. We slipped into the dark of our caves just minutes before the dawn, Adan and I falling together into my bed to sleep contentedly tangled together.

We were inseparable for a time after that, Adan and I, with Crenoral lagging along behind. Adan was an eager student, willing to learn all I could teach him. I taught him all that I knew; the names of stars, the stories of the Family, how far off we could travel in search of food and still have time to return before daylight, how to find shelter from the day when you've gone too far. Our hunts were punctuated with play as he taught me the games of his homeland north of the Black Sea.

There was a connection between us that made words nearly meaningless, as if we could read one another's thoughts. I knew when he needed to feed, and felt the pull of sleep dragging on him as dawn approached. Hunting was exhilarating beside him, my own excitement enhanced by his need. I was too young yet to understand the feelings that I felt, but I felt them fiercely.

Crenoral shadowed us, watching our play as any proud parent might, his eyes darting around us whenever we neared a place where people might be found. Adan and I found endless fascination in finding children out attending to bodily needs or setting to chores in the earliest hours of the dark, and seducing them into games. We would draw them further and further from their home, playing until it was obvious that the child wanted to go home, or until we were bored with the game. Then, we would fall on the child, leaving the body for the village to find with the sunlight. All the while, Crenoral watched, a strange smile on his face that made me wonder what pleasure he got from watching our nighttime games.

Adan and I were caught up in ourselves, in our union and the pleasure of being children free to roam the night. He was the companion that filled an ache inside me that Crenoral never could. It took some time, but eventually Crenoral became bored with our increasingly private world and left us to ourselves. Mother or one of the others was given the task to watch us while we fed, though we often slipped away unnoticed. I suppose it was inevitable that Crenoral should feel shut out of our lives, as we became increasingly more dependent upon one another than on him.

It was also inevitable that I would grow beyond my pet, bored with his limitations. He was, after all was said and done, a child, his mind and body stuck in the moment Crenoral stole him from the daylight. In truth, I had never thought about it before, that while I aged slowly, I did age, and none of the others did. I was constantly maturing. I noticed it as the dawn pulled him to sleep, while I, still excited from whatever fun we'd found in the night, lay awake beside him. I saw it as my head inched slowly passed his shoulder. I could see it in minute ways if I looked, my fingers lengthened, my hair grew longer, my appetite lessened ... and Adan remained the same. Our interests began to change as well.

Our play became increasingly violent and Adan's desire for blood intensified. I was generally sated easily, and sharing a meal with him was sufficient most nights for me. Many nights I had no need to feed, or chose not to as I saw nothing that interested me. As time passed, Adan desired more. His needs carried us miles from home, down the mountains to the shores of the Black Sea in search of towns and villages that had never heard of our kind, or felt the sting of our bite. On those nights we were forced into the mountain caves for shelter. As he fell into the deep sleep of the Family, I lay awake, listening to the strange sounds and smelling the odd odors and wondering what made me different.

It was becoming obvious that I was different, and my interest in our violent death games was waning. We fought over little things, and it would hurt me every time he would storm away in anger.

I wanted him to stay with me, so I would give in and do as he desired, but my heart wasn't in it. We began hunting separately from time to time, and I would find him returning with Arda and Vahe. I suppose it matters little which one of us stopped looking for the other first, but eventually I was alone again, and Adan was just another member of the Clan.

Occasionally after that I would hunt with Crenoral, but it never felt the same again. I was changing, realizing I was not like the others. I was not human either, and that left me to wonder where I fit in. Crenoral began to seem to me as the others did ... cold, distant, so unlike the father I had once adored. The night eventually arrived when I, in all my child-like wonder, truly saw him for the first time.

We were hunting together, alone in the quiet of the early night. Not far from the mountainside where we dwelled, we came upon a family of three, settling in to sleep beside their wagon. They were young, the mother could have been no more than seventeen or eighteen, the child barely three. Crenoral played with the man when he roused at our approach. Crenoral taunted them, the Change plain upon his face. Their fear only encouraged him. The child cried, perhaps sensing the coming death, and I found myself holding her, trying to quiet her. The hunger burned hot inside me as Crenoral joked with the man, earning uneasy laughter, then embarrassment and finally the man's anger. He lunged at Crenoral who only caught him and bent him to his pleasure.

Then, he tormented the woman, her dead husband's blood staining his face as he touched her breasts and kissed her. He flirted with the idea of bringing her into the Family, having grown bored with his latest fling, and not yet ready to go back to my mother, as he always did eventually, but in the end he killed her. I was still holding the child. He was sated, happy with himself ... a monster. He laughed at my revulsion of him and mocked the protective way I was holding the child.

I felt the hunger inside of me and clung to it, utterly revolted by what I had just witnessed. The child began to cry again as Crenoral grew angry with me. "What will you do, Amara? Leave it here to die slowly?" he asked, circling us. I felt hot tears sting my own skin as the Change transformed my face and the need to kill filled me.

"I will not kill it," I said, clutching the child tightly to me. "I will not."

"It is not a choice ... look at you." His voice was low, menacing. "I can feel how much you want her."

Small blond curls tumbled out from under her bonnet and big blue eyes opened to stare at the mask of evil on my face. I felt as if she was looking through me, touching some part of me that had never lived until that very moment. Yes, I wanted her. My heart pounded with it, wrapping around her own as if to squeeze it from her breast. "No, Father. I will not. She is–"

"What, Amara? What is she? What is she if not food to sustain you?" He crowded over me, his eyes dark. The pressure of him nearly broke me.

"A child. Innocent. I will not kill her." I repeated it like a mantra as I released her and set her in the grass beside the dead body of her mother.

Crenoral stared at me in disbelief, then looked to the child. She had ceased her crying, and only looked upon us, as if memorizing our faces. "Innocence is no protection," he said. "Innocence is only the absence of knowledge. Think how sweet she will taste, how hot her blood must be now."

"No." I turned my back and took the first steps away. He followed.

"Kill her now, or be punished."

I stopped and looked up at him. The Change had left his face, but in the dark his scowl was dangerous and his eyes glittered with anger. It frightened me, but I did not respond, only stepped away. He continued to follow, his fury almost palpable on the night air. I hoped he would continue following me, and forget the small child alone on the side of the road. I hurt inside with the unanswered hunger, I hadn't fed in several nights, and his displeasure with me cut deeply.

I kept moving until I was behind the closed door of my room, and even then I could feel him, hovering outside the door. I didn't sleep, and was up and out into the night almost as the sun went down. I had never before ventured out without at least Adan for company, but I could not bring myself to face him right then. I remember little of that night, but I hated myself. I hated what I was, where I came from. I fed to appease the hunger, but it left me morose and disgusted.

When I returned, he was waiting for me on the ground floor, just inside the door. His hard hand came down across my face with a force that knocked me over. I lay still for a moment, then felt his hand in my hair. He pulled me to my feet and dragged me to the place that would come to be known as the punishment closet. It was a storage hole, barely big enough to stand in, and I still wore the body of a child. The door shut and was barred behind him.

Time passed, I couldn't tell how much. My young body was unaccustomed to the starvation. It became harder and harder not to throw myself at the door, and to hold off the Change. Before Crenoral returned for me, I had spent more than twenty-four hours in the hold of the Change. I shook from head to toe, desperate to feed.

He brought to me a child then, when he knew I could not resist. Thankfully, it was not she whom I had already spared, but a boy about the same age, his eyes wide and red as though he had been crying. His tiny heart raced, his blood called me. I tore his neck open and swallowed his life, nearly ripping his head from his small body. Crenoral laughed. "That is more like it, Little One. Do not disobey me again."

I did not feed again until the hunger became unbearable, until it tore me from my sleep and dragged me into the night. Then, I did it quickly, leaving little sign of my deed. I would leave early in the night with the young ones, brought to the clan by the impatient Vahe and Arda. Their hunger drove them all night long and they were easily distracted, allowing me to slip away and wander alone. I avoided Mother and Crenoral, certain that they would sense that something was wrong with me and punish me again. Crenoral's attentions however had returned to his first bride, and they were rather absorbed in themselves, so it made little difference to them if I chose company other than theirs. Indeed, it seemed as if Crenoral were as disgusted with my actions as I was with his.

It appeared to all as if I fed as I had in the past, leaving early with the small group and returning several hours before dawn, but I fed little, hiding my starvation as best I could. I hovered near humanity, listening in on conversations of the world, of farming, hunting and children, love and desperation ... things I knew little of. The lure of them was strong, I wanted them desperately, craved the warm rush they alone could provide, the heated passion of approaching death.

More than that, I longed to be a part of their lives, their loves ... their light. I wanted to stand in daylight and feel the heat of it kiss my closed eyelids and work its way into my soul. I was utterly smitten with the mortals who had been my playthings and suppers for as long as I could recall.

Chapter 2

I FOUND that I loved to hear a voice sing, or watch children at play in the warm glow of a fire after supper. It brought a smile to my face, and made my heart shudder. The hunger filled me and I felt some great pleasure that rivaled the killing itself in the strain of holding myself still and silent and unchanged. I also found that I aged more rapidly when I went without feeding. In my infancy, my mother had counted decades as mortals do months, and the decades since Crenoral had brought Adan had seemed as years. I could, at long last, pass myself off among humanity as a young woman of fourteen or so.

It was then that my heart governed me most. Long nights I would walk alone, unwilling to take human life. I would feed every few nights on wildlife, sparingly. Once or twice fate conspired to leave in my path a wounded or sickly soul, who would not live whether I fed or not. Soon, even that left a bitter taste on my tongue. I would hold them and whisper things they could never understand. I tried to be gentle and take what I needed to survive. When I'd finish, laying them softly back as I had found them, I would cry, sometimes violently, sobbing in an anguish I was unable to put into words. Once or twice, I became overwrought by it and would vomit back what I had taken, leaving them in a puddle of their own blood.

I would hunt animals when the need grew to deafening volumes, falling upon deer, moose, whatever I could to feed the fire. Sometimes I would spot one of the others, watching me. In my most rational moments I knew the time had come to leave the Family all together, but I had yet to do more than think about it. Even then, I knew what my future life would be. Mathis, the old hermit who fancied himself a mystic saw it in me. He would whisper to all who would listen that I was the harbinger of their doom. He said the portents told that my unnatural creation was the omen of the end. Mother and the others had come from superstitious human stock, and easily believed him.

Crenoral, of course, would not listen. I was still, on some level, his beloved daughter, and in his eyes they were merely jealous of his obvious affection. I may have angered and disgusted him, but I was his child, and he would not show me anything but affection in front of them, lest they think him weak and easily influenced. He showed no signs of recognizing that I no longer returned the affection, or of the changes within me.

They knew. They watched me wander aimlessly all night and return no more sated than when I left. They could smell the bloodlust, the hunger I refused to feed. They taunted me; harassed me ... tormented me until I wanted to turn all of my needing upon them and feast better than I had in months, even years. Mother knew as well, I think, as mothers sometimes will, but she said nothing. I wanted to be free from them all. How they sickened me ... my stomach churning as they talked so trivially of death, to see blood dripping from open mouths as they fed. I hated them, despised them for what they were, what I was because of them ... for the ease with which they killed, with no remorse, no regret.

Time passed slowly, and I tried to make some sense of it, of my life. Mankind was growing and began to spread across the open spaces, building towns and villages where once wilderness reigned. I was still so young, so naïve, though my body had matured a great deal. I discovered that I could travel down the dark side of the mountain before the sun had completely set, covered in a heavy cloak and keeping to the shadows, allowing me to travel further away than I ever had before. I found a small village that I had never seen before, grown up several hours from my mountain home. Little stone and mud brick homes with closed roofs, wooden doors and windows clustered around a central gathering space with a fire pit and benches, all nestled in the shadow of the mountain.

There was something familiar in the patterns of their lives, comforting to me in some way. I watched from the shadowed trees as the men returned from hunting and from tending the grain fields and the women scurried children indoors or served dinners. I listened to their language, and learned the words hovering outside their windows. Their women were strong and led the family in their daily chores, while the men saw to the building and filling the needs of their village.

I learned that they had named the mountain on which I had lived my entire life. They called it Arakatz, and on certain nights they celebrated in ceremonies I could not comprehend. They had painted skin and chanted around a fire while one of their number performed some rite that invoked the great strength of the peak that overshadowed them and the grace of their god, Ar. Their lives were simple and I wanted, more than anything, to feel what they felt.

In all I spent a year or more watching them, learning to braid my hair in a style which emulated the women, and styling my clothing after theirs. Garments of wool, dyed brown with pigments found in the earth, the women wore long skirts that protected their legs from the cold, often in layers so that they could carry things and dry their hands on the outermost layer, while still keeping warm.

It was on a celebration night, early in the spring, when the irises and gladioli had not yet put out their first blooms, I stepped out of the shadows and followed the rumbling voices as the chant rose, into the village center where the holy man poured out an offering into a wooden bowl on the shrine. The smells of the wood fire, the sweaty bodies that danced in disarray near the fire, all swirled around me, intoxicatingly. There was expectancy on the air, as they made their pleas to Ar for their coming planting, and the hunt that would follow to supplement the remaining of their winter stores. The emotion was thrilling, and I let it sweep over me, wanting their happiness to be my own.

As the celebration came to an end, I was reluctant to leave. I knelt alone, warming my hands over the remains of a once roaring fire. There I felt calm, the glow of the hot coals bathing my hands in a ruddy color that made them look nearly human. The air around me grew quiet as I knelt there and the villagers scattered to their homes. The pounding of my heart quieted and I breathed deeply of the life that infused that place.

"You are not of our village," a voice said near me.

I jumped upwards, pulling my hands back away from the fire as if they might somehow give me away. "No. I am ... not," I said haltingly. I was frozen to my place, caught in uncertainty. Some part of me wanted to run, far and fast, and never return. The part of me that was drawn to them, bade me to stay and talk. I did not know what to say, and my grasp of their language was entirely theoretical. "I live ... with my family ... not far from here." I was too nervous to consider lying, but neither dare I tell the truth.

He nodded and poked a long stick into the fire. I recognized him as the holy man who spoke at these celebrations and prayed for the people. Up close he seemed much younger than I had anticipated. He had removed his ceremonial headdress and I could see he had short, curly hair that was lighter than most of those in the village, a soft blond-brown that was echoed in his beard.

"What brings you to us?" he asked, his voice clear and pleasant.

I was sure I could never articulate what had brought me to enter that village that night. "We, my family, have no village." I stopped, struggling for words. "We live alone, up on the mountain. I wanted to see."

His eyes were dark, but glittered in the dying light of the fire. "What did you see?" he asked.

"My people have no ... ceremonies, like yours. It was beautiful."

"Do you not have gods?" he asked, stirring the coals of the fire.

I shook my head. "No, not as such. My father would not approve." I tried to imagine Crenoral giving an offering to some faceless god, but could not.

"Where is your father?"

I looked up from the coals, slightly startled. "You are a young woman, and it is well past supper. Won't he worry for your safety?"

I knew I should leave, but couldn't bring my feet to move. I found myself speaking again. "My brothers and sisters are not far away, looking for one of our animals that broke loose. I came with them."

I was completely enamored of him in those few minutes, his voice, the gentle nature, the concern for my safety. "I am Amara." I said, almost breathlessly. I had never given my name to a mortal before.

"And I am Adroushan, priest of Ar for the people of this village."

Nearby I could sense one of the others, probably Arda. "I should go now." I said, moving away. I paused and turned back. "Could I ... come back, another time?" I held my breath.

He smiled and nodded and I exhaled in relief. That began my first friendship among mankind. Once every ten days or so I would appear in the little village in the shadow of Arakatz and seek him out. At first I asked questions, curious about his god, and the people. We would spend the early dark sitting outside his hut while he told me the stories of his people and of the great city more than a week's journey north. He showed me clay tablets with curious symbols on them that he said recorded the stories he taught me. As spring gave way to summer, I brought gifts of wild flowers and shiny stones I sometimes found in the caves. As summer gave way to autumn, I came with shells and smooth stones from the sea. When winter blanketed the valley in white and hunting was scarce, I brought rabbits and deer from parts of the mountain they would never reach in the snow.

I told him little of myself, and what I did say was vague. He seldom questioned me, though he often expressed worry about my traveling alone so often at night. I assured him that I was less alone than he might think. Indeed, I often felt one of them hovering nearby on the nights I tarried there with him, watching me. I didn't understand what drew me there to sit with him, or why I craved his company almost as much as I craved his blood. I knew somehow that it would be sweet, not quite like that of a child, but precious, delicious. Near him, the hunger was cooled, the need appeased by his calming nature.

His voice was almost magical, and the poetry he recited came to life with a beauty I had never experienced. His hands were large, soft. When they touched me, my heart raced and I ached with desires I didn't quite understand. When I saw those hands touch another, an irrational anger filled me. I guess one could say that I loved him, though this was different than the affection I had held for Crenoral or Adan. As we walked through his village, I imagined what it would be like to be a part of his world. Or, to make him a part of mine.

It was late spring of the following year when I arrived shortly after sundown and he took me by the hand, leading me out of the village, through the poplar trees, to a small clearing near a pond that sat still and dark beneath a starry sky. He had spread a woven wool blanket on the ground and prepared a small meal. I was terror struck. I had never eaten human food, and was unsure if I even could eat it. I searched for an excuse, a reason, anything to get me away from him, but the smell of him was strong and he seemed so pleased with himself. I was trapped by my own affection for him. If he noticed my reluctance, my terror, he said nothing. He was warm and gentle as he led me to that blanket and handed me a wooden goblet filled with wine.

I knew I would have to try it, despite my fear. Hesitantly I sipped, expecting to gag upon something that was decidedly not what my body wanted most. Instead, my mouth was filled with a warm, sweet rush of a delicate flavor that went beyond the mere taste. I swallowed quickly, feeling the heat of it flood through me. He smiled again and began setting out the food.

I was like a child tasting sweets for the first time, as he set out a smoky cheese and fruits, bread still warm from baking and roasted duck. I tasted each in turn, savoring each morsel, awakening to each new sensation, every change of texture, aroma, and flavor.

The cheese smelled and tasted of age, mellowed by smoke and lightly flavored. It crumbled on my tongue and stuck to my teeth as I chewed. There was a round fruit that seemed soft and fuzzy on the outside. When he cut it open, the inside was orange and juicy. The taste was somewhat tart, but not unpleasant. It was soft to the bite and the juices burned as they ran down my throat before I could swallow. He cut into the rind of a small melon, then broke it over his knee, scooping out the seeds before handing me half of the white flesh. This too was juicy, running down my chin as I devoured the soft, tenderly flavored meat.

Even the duck, the very thought of which turned my stomach, was truly delicious. Somehow the taste transcended even my hunger for the blood, cooling the fire without slaking it, and arousing me. He watched as I ate, sipping on his wine, smiling at the obviously unexpected pleasure I found in each rapturous bite. I was aroused by his nearness, by the flavors, by the feeling of filling and heat that the food produced. It was more than I had ever felt, more so than even the killing had ever produced in me. I was hungry for more, so much more. My appetite had only whetted upon the mortal food.

Adroushan touched my face in obvious affection and I could smell him, his life beating in those veins just beneath the skin. I turned to it, brushing my lips across the flesh, tasting the exquisite saltiness of his skin. He moaned and his arm slipped around me, bringing me in close as he kissed me. I knew I should resist, but the fire of his lips on mine burned away my resistance. I melted into him, my body hot with the wine and food and desire.

Somewhere deep inside I could hear my own voice warning me, cautioning my passion, but I paid it no heed. I wanted him, in more ways than that which he was offering. His kisses and touches were dizzying, as hungry as my own, or more so.

Frantically, we pulled at each other, lost in lust and passion, consummating our friendship in hasty desire. I never felt the coming of the Change, never realized my own error, until it was too late to recover. His heart roared in my ears, speaking to me as his poetry did, pulling at me. The hot touch of him upon my tongue was unlike anything I had ever tasted, so beautiful, so ... much ... more ... I was breathless and full, and he lay beneath me, naked and dead, one jagged wound in his neck. His blood coursed through me beside the fever of the food and I howled into the night in anguish.

I could hear the others, Arda and Vahe and the rest, laughing from the trees. They had been watching, knowing my long restrained hunger would bring this to an ugly conclusion. I flew at them in a rage, lashing out at them in anger at myself, at my inability to control my desires. They allowed me to vent my emotion, circling me and letting me spend the remainder of my energy before they gathered me up and took me home.

Crenoral paced around me, Mother hovering nearby as they relayed the incident, from the moment I had met Adroushan through that very night. I knelt where they had deposited me, on the floor of his room, still naked and shaking. It was silent a long while before he ushered them out.

"Do you see, Little One, what becomes of you? Do you see now?"

I didn't answer, just huddled further into myself.

He came to kneel beside me. His anger and disappointment hung in the air around me. "They are not pets. They are vulgar, vile beings. They are not like us. They are mortal, cattle ... nothing more. When will you accept this?"

He sighed and stood to resume his pacing. "I'm tempted to lock you in your room for the next two hundred years, see if that brings you back to your senses. I don't know, Illari, what do we do with her?"

Mother moved forward for the first time, her face paler than normal. Her dark hair cascaded over one shoulder and her dark eyes seemed to shimmer in the low light of the torches that lined the room. One hand lifted my chin almost gently and those eyes peered deeply into mine. It was more intimate than she had been with me in many years, though what she saw in my eyes I could not begin to know. So much about her was a mystery to me.

"Hmmm ... She is weak yet. So much of her is still like her father." Something in her voice made me realize she meant the mortal man who had been her husband before Crenoral had called her. This seemed to anger Crenoral further. "Do not hold it against her, Love. She will come around. So much of her is like me as well. It is the mortal heart in her that holds her to them."

At that instant, that mortal heart seemed to be thundering with a life of its own, I could smell the humanity with me, the very essence that each of us in the Family craves. Crenoral turned, a strange look on his face. "That can be remedied," he said, his voice low and menacing. The Change came upon him quickly and he flew at us. The air reverberated with his sudden fury. Mother stepped quickly between us, the Change taking what little humanity remained upon her face.

"No!" They stood, locked in a stare that might have melted any mortal and filled the room with a sense of dread. I was afraid to move, lest I precipitate some further argument. They stayed that way from a long, long time. "You took that from me, Crenoral. I'll not let you take that from her as well."

"Step aside, Illari."

"Not this time. Remember that she was not offered a choice in what she is. You and I made that choice for her on the night you made me. If she chooses to hold on to what remains of who I once was before you, it is her right. If you wish to rip it from her, you will do so at the cost of losing me forever."

For a while longer, they stood in a silent battle of wills, but for once in her life, Mother was the stronger. His need for her companionship must have exceeded his anger that night. So suddenly that the room itself seemed to sigh, he gave in and stormed away. She hung her head, as if the confrontation had taken all her strength, then turned to me and smiled. In that moment she was more maternal than I can recall her having been before or since.

"Mother?" I said softly, reaching a hand out to her. She came, kneeling beside me and taking my hand. I didn't understand what had just happened.

"Dovan was here," she said, as if that explained everything. She touched my cheek and smiled, then the moment was over. She stood and was once more the cold, distant stranger.

Chapter 3

MY MOTHER sacrificed a great deal that night, and neither of us would ever have the same relationship with Crenoral again. I knew that from that moment on I would be watched, more so than in the past. My activities were reported back to Crenoral as if I were some criminal. I was afraid to visit the village, though I heard through Arda that they cursed our kind and vowed vengeance. It was Adan upon whom that vengeance would fall, nearly a hundred years later, caught feeding on one the village's children; he was driven into the fire at the shrine and burned alive. It sent ripples of fear through the Clan and the village was declared off limits.

I wasn't allowed out alone for years after that. Crenoral was convinced that I had taught the people of the village how to kill us. No mortal had taken one of his children before. No one spoke to me for a long time, not even Mother, though I was forced to accompany Crenoral and the others and participate in their blood baths, to feed gluttonously when they felt I had not fed enough on my own.

Of course, there was a part of me that reveled in the killing, a part of me that was complete and whole only when feeling a human life fade beneath my touch. Otherwise it would have been rather difficult to force me to it. I am a stubborn creature and seldom submit to such coercion if my own nature is truly set against it. So it was that they drew me back to them, brought me to temporarily set aside my guilt and fit myself into the role they would have me play.

The time came however, when my thoughts returned to my previous plans of escape. It was the time of the Birth, when we celebrated the making of Bestin, the eldest of the brothers, into the monster he became. All I knew of Bestin was the stories told of his Birth, many of which had already transcended from truth to myth to legend by the time I heard them. It was said that he was sleeping beneath a tree, having set out on a journey to retrieve a stallion for stud, when the shaking of the earth awakened him. From the ground sprang a creature so vile that the scent of him caused plants to wilt and Bestin was said to have challenged him. They fought and Bestin held his own for several hours before the creature bit him and he fell to the ground dead, only to rise several hours later, changed forever. There were other variations of the story, none more believable. It was said that the tree still existed on the road leading up to the home Bestin now claimed for his clan.

It was Bestin who had brought it, the cursed gift of eternal life, to his brothers, Crenoral and Dovan. Each of the three had created Clans of their own, spreading out in the world to keep the feeding fields from depleting. I had seldom met either of the other brothers, but to celebrate the three thousandth year since the Birth, Bestin called the three Clans together at the ancestral home of the Family, three nights' journey to the north and two nights' journey east of Arakatz. This began the Great Hunt, seven nights of gathering hundreds of victims, from as far away as could be reached, including many gathered on the journey. They were held in a fortress built on the very ground where Bestin and his brothers had lived.

So it was, far from our home and all that I knew, I distanced myself from my Clan, trying to stay out of the way and planning a trip out with the hunters to disappear. I made my move the night before the celebration, slipping away and making good time into the dark, but it was not to be. Crenoral must have suspected or missed me. It matters little, what mattered was only that he found me, trying to find shelter against the coming day. His eyes were filled with an emotion I can only describe as disappointment as he brought me back to the fortress. I expected another lecture, a long day of his self-important criticism of my shortcomings. I was surprised then when he sank with a sigh beside me on the sleeping pallet. "What is it, Amara? Why are you not happy?" he asked softly.

I could almost believe he truly cared at that moment, that were my reasons good enough … he might let me go to seek out what happiness I might find. I too sighed. "I … don't know, Father."

I replied just as softly. "My heart is heavy within me. I do not wish to kill."

"You will die without it ... you know that?"

"I will die if I continue. I do not understand it." I stood and paced the little room. He looked so small, so defeated there on that bed, his head hung, his eyes closed. It made me pity him, to want to comfort him, to stay. That of course, was his charm. "Let me go, Father." I said it so softly, more whispered from my mind to his than actually spoken.

His head snapped up and suddenly the life returned to his eyes. I could feel him swell with anger. "Let you go? Go where? Ungrateful wench!" His hand snapped across my face, bringing tears to my eyes. "You embarrass me, and my Clan. How dare you behave like this now ... here? You will go nowhere! You are my daughter and you will stand with me tonight. I shall think of a suitable punishment for you when we have returned home."

He flew from the room, slamming the door behind him. I heard something heavy dragged in front of it and knew I was trapped. I was at his side then, as it began. Over a hundred men and women were led before the blood-hungry Family. Bestin stood before them and chose for himself a beautiful young lady. She was brought before him and held tightly. She shook; I could see it even from my place fifty or sixty yards away. Her fear was palpable, but it was nothing compared to what it would be in seconds. The Change swept through him, and his face became contorted with fury. He bared his teeth, hissing through his fangs as he bent to her neck. Her scream echoed through the great hall, bouncing off the walls and lifting on the night air, before it was cut short and he raised a bloody face from her and dropped her like an empty sack to the floor.

He lifted his arms and a cheer went up around us. As one the Family fell to it, with his encouragement in our ears, "Feed Children, Feed."

I was swept alongside Crenoral as he chose our victims, holding mine, a young man of perhaps fourteen, beautiful and trying to be brave. I hid his face as I did the deed, knowing I would never leave this place while he lived. My heart danced in dreadful rhythm with his, his fear coursing through me as his mind whispered images of his family and home to mine. The blood was hot and it burned as I swallowed, echoing the shame burning in my heart. I sent apologies after his soul as I felt him go and looked up to find Crenoral set upon his own victim.

I set my thoughts upon escape to a quieter place then, at least to getting out of the blood, the death, but Crenoral clamped one powerful hand over my arm and held me to the spot. I refused to participate further, closing my eyes against the sight of so much death, lest it entice me to feed again; trying to cover my ears and heart against the cries and screams of the dying, lest I come undone. The scent of blood around me was dizzying, and appealing to my body's desires. There was no blocking it out, no escape.

My eyes searched the hall almost frantically for something to divert me from the madness that surrounded me. I felt a tug upon my attention and found eyes locked upon me from across the room. I blinked to clear my vision, and found Dovan watching me, his lips red with blood, the Change completely gone from him. He seemed to nod in my direction, and I could feel something shared pass between us, something friendly and warm. I wanted suddenly to run to him, feel his arms wrap around me. Crenoral rose from his last victim, his eyes dancing between his brother and me. Then, he stepped in front of me, blocking me from Dovan. I don't remember ever seeing him as furious as he was just then.

When it was over, I spent the next day once again locked in the small room, before I was dragged from it by Crenoral and held by his side the entire trip home. The punishment was severe when at last we were home, and I somehow imagined it had more to do with that one moment with Dovan than with all the rest. The beating was bad enough to keep me well behaved for many long years after that.

He became my constant shadow, this Father who had taught me to kill. To avoid his wrath, I retreated into a world of relative quiet, teaching myself to read the symbols that Adroushan had first introduced me to, collecting the tablets and later scrolls as I hunted and killed, taking them from my victims, or their homes. I went out early to dine and returned quickly to secret myself away in my room far beneath the earth to read the words of mortal poets, prophets. and storytellers.

As I read and studied, I learned of the mortal world, and I watched. It would be nearly three centuries before my relationship with Crenoral eased again and he relinquished his control a degree or two. His attention was diverted by the plans of the latest members of the Clan, two brothers, Tova and Urel. They had come from the cities to the south, found by Crenoral asleep in the pass to the south. He had brought them into the Family after the older pleaded for the life of his brother and offered to build Crenoral a home like the powerful men of the mortal world possessed.

I knew I was still watched. I could feel the eyes and ears of them following me at night. For awhile, I was content to bide my time and wait. I played the dutiful daughter, obeying the house rules and never stepping over the line. Still, I made plans, those long nights shut up in my room. I had learned from careful conversations and silent observation which of the trinkets I stole from my victims were worth trade, and which to leave behind. I watched and waited, knowing that the time would present itself. I was right.

The manor was nearly complete, a dark, hulking house built of stone and wood. The main hall was nearly the size of the former building, standing empty and cold and all around it were mammoth rooms filled with furniture no one ever used. Three stories rose from the ground, covering the holes where we lived. The entrance to the caves where the clan still spent their days was hidden by a simple wooden door in a hallway behind the main hall. The Clan had grown to nearly a dozen, probably more than was wise considering the scattering population of the towns below us. Too many years of death from above had driven many away.

The exception to that was Adroushan's village, which had grown in recent years. They had long forgotten Adroushan, but their faith was still strong. Life in the town revolved around their god, and the rites to honor him. The Clan seldom ventured there, remembering Adan's death and Crenoral's decree, but the young members of the Clan knew nothing of either, and one of Vahe's children chose the holy man's daughter as his bride. The town rose up and made to assault the manor in retribution and to cleanse the mountain. With crude spears, pitchforks, and torches, they made their way up the mountain and set upon us.

The battle was utterly one sided, but the Clan relished it, throwing themselves into the fray with wild abandon. It was in the middle of this melee that I fled. I hoped that they would believe me dead in the fighting, lost in battle. With only a small leather satchel filled with the baubles and trinkets I had stolen and a few robes that I had traded Urel for, I slipped into the darkest shadows, clawing my way up into the highest, deepest crevices of the mountain. There I hid myself for close onto a year, surviving on the blood and occasionally, the flesh, of whatever animal happened my way.

When I at last allowed myself to believe that my Family would no longer look for me, I made my way down the other side of the mountain, putting as many miles between me and them as I could each night. I kept away from villages and towns, so much more prevalent than they had been before, keeping to the dark roads and treacherous paths.

I was hungry, and wanted blood. I knew that if the situation presented itself, I would kill, and the Family would somehow find me. With each passing night, I forced myself through an increasingly populated world, ever southward toward the cities I had heard rumored of in far off places I almost did not believe existed.

The forests and hills I was accustomed to slowly gave way to a fertile plain, alive with groves of fruit bearing trees and crops of grains. From the descriptions Tova and Urel had given, I was still more than five nights travel from the city they had called Tadmor. The green plain gave way to sand and the long walk across a desert. It fascinated me, sand for miles with no water in site. I had only known sand on the shores of the sea.

None I had ever known, but Tova and Urel had been this far south. It frightened me to think how alone I was, but it comforted me as well. I was free of Crenoral, and had only my own desires to contend with. To the south, across the desert with its black expanse of nothing, Tadmor rose from the sand, a city where rich men built opulent homes and, to hear the stories told by the brothers, anything could be yours for the right price. An oasis gave birth to fruit trees and greenery that harbored life, and the city reeked of it, of sweating bodies and animals, of birth and death and all the stages in between. It called to me, and repulsed me. The scents, the sounds, the air hummed with everything I wanted.

I was drawn in by the massive rows of homes and shops selling pottery and fabrics, all closed and shuttered as I flitted through the night streets. The people were fascinating, their lives so much different from those I had known. I wanted to fit myself inside their lives, to learn their secrets. The rich homes near the city's center were endlessly captivating, with walls painted in bright colors and beautiful shapes, and fountains of water in gardens of flowers and fragrant trees

Even amongst the poor I found things to entice, the scent of bread baking, the banter of children fighting sleep. It reminded me of those things that had brought me to Adroushan's village again and again, only on a much grander scale.

As much as I hungered for it, I fought myself, my nature, and my convictions. I fed little, when I had no choice, and what I did take made me ill. I found it hard to sleep with so many lives so close at hand, the hunger burning brightly inside me. The faces of those I had killed began to haunt my dreams when I did sleep, hidden in stable stalls or dark alleys. Mortal food did little for me, fueling the need for blood with its heat and the pleasure of its taste and texture. I fled Tadmor, ever west and away from my past. I was despondent, unable to wrench myself free, either of the driving desires that propelled me, or of the guilt for the things those perverse desires drove me to.

The other cities were the same, and I fled them each in turn. It was then that I was to meet the man who would change the course of my life forever. He had been a healer, a physician. He lived in a small home on the road into Abydus, and he found me in the dust beside that road, less than an hour until sunrise, defeated by my own hunger and the illness that came with feeding it. I was exhausted and ready to let it end. I saw him approaching, and felt the Change come over me, uncontrollably. He flinched a little, but squatted nearby. After a long moment, he held out his hand.

Hesitantly, I took it, but darkness consumed me before I could rise to my feet.

I awoke in a cool, darkened room of his home, the smell of blood and oil strong in my nostrils. He sat in a chair near the bed, holding a wooden goblet which he held out to me in offering. I took it in a shaky hand, sniffing before raising it to my lips. I drank deeply of something that tasted like the blood my body craved, and yet not, feeling the warmth of returning strength move through me.

"Easy now," he said, his soft voice thick with an accent I couldn't place. "I do not know how you will react to the formula." He took the goblet back and poured more of the dark pink fluid from a bottle on the table beside him. "You are very weak. We should wait."

"Who are you?" I asked, watching him rise and move to tinker with some jars in the soft light of an oil lamp.

"I am Damen, a simple physician. You are one of them."

The way he said it made me think he knew exactly what I was. I raised an eyebrow and crossed my arms. The liquid was stretching its fingers out into my body, and I craved more of it. "I've heard the rumors, the stories, but I've never believed them to be true. When I saw you, I knew," he said, one hand gesturing in my direction.

He turned to face me fully, his expression one of examination. "How do you feel?"

"I want more."

He smiled, and returned the goblet to my hand. I drank more slowly, running the liquid around my mouth to analyze it better. It was warm, not hot as I might have preferred, and slightly thick, like a heavy syrup. I could taste something of an animal blood in it, but it was unlike any animal I knew. "What is it?" I asked, handing him back the empty goblet once more.

"Let's call it an experiment," he responded. I stretched, feeling better than I had in weeks, months even.

"I'd like to know what is in it." I said, sitting up a little. I noticed he moved back away from me.

"A little of this, a little of that. I had hoped to be able to replace blood lost from wounds. It falls short of that."

Perhaps it did, but my body was fooled. It was the greatest blessing of my cursedly long life. I could feel it bringing life to my body, restoring the health my battle against myself had ravaged. I craved more, but thought it wise to pace myself. "I thank you, Damen. It seems to have done wonders for me." I shifted just a little for comfort and crossed my arms. "I have need of sleep, if I might trouble your hospitality a little more. I give you my word, no harm will come to you while I tarry here."

He nodded tightly. "It is not yet noon. Sleep. I will make more for when you wake. Perhaps then we can talk more."

He extinguished the lamp and ducked through the curtained doorway near the foot of the bed, and I got the briefest glimpse of sunlight streaming into the room beyond. In the dark left behind, my eyes adjusted quickly, sweeping over the mudbrick walls, the window, covered by a dark, thick cloth. Shelves lined one wall, crowded with jars and drying herbs and the table that dominated the center of the room held an assortment of animal hides, bones and teeth.

With a deep breath, I closed my eyes, listening to his movements in the next room as I let the fatigue pull me downward into sleep. It was not quite sunset when I woke again, instantly alert as the unfamiliar sounds of my surroundings registered and the memories of the morning shifted into place. Opening my eyes, I found the goblet on the corner of the table, beside a ceramic bottle. I rose slowly, sliding bare feet onto the cool earth and standing to reach across to the table. A sniff of the bottle's contents confirmed that it was the formula and I poured a goblet full and drank it quickly.

Not quite the rush of blood, but warm and fulfilling in its own way, the formula was satisfying, as nothing had been since Adroushan's death. I drank two more goblets full in rapid succession before I noticed that my host had also left a basin of water and a comb made of bone on the table, and on the end of the cot, a pile of cloth, that revealed itself to be a clean robe of a soft beige and a wrap as I picked it up.

It had been a long time since I had last bathed, and I took the opportunity gladly, rinsing weeks of dust from my skin and out of my hair before donning the fresh linen robe and sitting on the bed with the comb to detangle my long hair. I braided it then, to keep it from knotting up again before pulling the other length of cloth around my shoulders.

Peeking around the curtain, I could see the room beyond was mostly dark, with a ruddy glow in the far corner where the setting sun reached in through the window. My host was eating at a low wooden table, and looked up as I came through the door.

"Thank you, for the change of clothes," I said softly. "And the ... food. I feel much better now."

"Good." He set aside his bowl of a thick looking porridge and stood up, lighting a number of lamps to illuminate the room around us. It was a small home, but comfortable with a place to prepare food and to entertain guests. The door I had come through sat off toward the back of the main room and opposite another door that I imagined led to his private chambers. "May I examine you?" he asked, setting a lamp on the table near me. I nodded and sat as he gestured for me to come closer.

In the light of the lamp, I could see that he was older than I had first thought, probably closer to fifty than thirty. His fingers were stained a dark brown, darker even than the skin that stretched tightly across high cheekbones. His dark hair was shot through with gray and silver and his dark eyes glittered in the light of the oil lamps as he peered closely at my skin. He listened to my heart and tested my muscle tone with his fingers. When he was done, he invited me to sit with him among the soft pillows and talk of our lives.

He had come from a place called Epidaurus, where he was descended from a long line of healers, but had left them when his work was denounced. His first tries with the formula had led to the death of his patients and his fellow physicians had driven him out. The formula had changed and a second attempt followed, this time in Athens. More deaths had led to further exile, and so on, until he had given up and settled there, outside of Abydus. His life's work may have come to naught, if he had not heard the rumors of our kind, and thought to take one last chance on his formula when he saw me.

I told him of my journey, of my need to free myself of the demon within, and confirmed for him the rumors of the Clans. I did not know how many of Bestin's or Dovan's clans might have gone further west, but it was obvious that some had. I had seen no signs of the others since I had left them, indeed, hadn't thought to fear them finding me since I had left Tadmor, yet rumors of our kind had reached into Athens and beyond. I was not alone as I might have once assumed.

He never made a formal invitation for me to stay, nor did I ask. Yet, I spent the next ten years with him, learning to speak his native language and several others that he spoke, learning to make his formula for myself, learning to trust myself with people again. He taught me the care of the sick and the wounded, simple math and awakened in me a new hunger, the hunger to learn.

He was an old and happy man when he died, and I was more prepared to continue my journey, once again mindful of the voices on the night breezes, and the passing of others in the night. I set out to continue what had begun for me, learning.

Chapter 4

MY DESIRE to learn carried me from that little house near Abydus to Athens, to Mantinea, searching out knowledge. In Mantinea, I learned of an academy to the south across the waters of the Mediterranean, where scholars taught lessons in math and reading, and skills for careers in public service and the military. More than all of that was the library, rumored to be the largest of its kind in the known world, it was a collection of written words, clay tablets, beaten metal etched with symbols and animal skins, stretched thin and beaten into sheets to be marked with charcoal and plant dyes.

It was my love of the written word that drew me to that academy, and it was in that library where I would meet Jesse. He was young when we first met, not even twenty and handsome. Dark curly hair ringed his angelic face to make him appear so much younger than he was, and he had deep, caring eyes. I fell in love with him long before he even knew of me.

I slipped through the shadows in the night, haunting the narrow confines of the library's shelves after the students and scholars had withdrawn to sleep, with only a small oil lamp to read by. Long, low tables dominated the eastern side of the room, with lamps hung above them to light the space. Immediately closest to these were painted and decorated chests holding clay and stone tablets, most from the local area, some from the north and east. Arranged by origin, the chests stretched from the first table to the distant wall, and in that final chest lay the broken remains of tablets from the mountains of my homeland. Beyond the rows of chests came shelves of wood and stone, crowded tightly together and piled with fragments of stone and clay, and metal sheets with strange etchings on them, from the north. Seemingly randomly placed were freestanding stone monuments, carved with words boasting of victories and the reigns of kings already forgotten to most of the world. Most fascinating to me however were the shelves of parchment rolls, some nearly as tall as I, filled with words in Greek, Latin, and languages I had yet to learn.

Late one evening, long after everyone else had gone to supper, Jesse was still there, pouring over parchment and ancient clay tablets, haloed in a gentle circle of light from oil lamps scattered around the table. I watched him from a shadowed corner, keeping my distance, yet curiously interested in his reading. The materials he had gathered had a mystical nature to them, vague references to a creature of the night. Long into the night he read and studied, scribbling notes as he translated from Greek to his native language, and tried in vain to understand languages from as far away as the mountains of my home and beyond into the lands behind the setting sun. The next night was the same, and I simply observed him. Each night he set a frantic pace, setting up his table with new material, as the other students were pairing up for evening pursuits of less scholarly natures. Nearly a week passed like this, with me passing ever closer to him as my desires for him grew bolder, yet he hadn't even noticed me.

My boldness grew as I ventured into the library from my hiding place in the dank back buildings of the complex earlier than ever, and sat myself with a tablet of poetry at the table nearest the one he always filled with his work. As he sat, he looked my way at last. I nodded, a slight smile playing about my lips and he returned the gesture. That was all, but it sent a shiver of excitement through my heart ... his smile made me want him all the more.

He often worked nearly to morning, murmuring beneath his breath as he pieced together the stories of my Family from tales of ancient evils and demonic creatures. He believed in them, knew that they existed, and was determined to find proof there in that room full of words. I imagined, watching him as I did, when a certain haunted look would come across his face, that he must have at some point in his young life seen one of us, lost someone close to him to one of us ... and somehow lived to tell the tale. Only, he told nothing. He rarely spoke, and when he did it was only that polite conversation of society that said nothing of substance.

Around us, his society was rigid, structured. He was one of a community of Hebrews living and working at the schools, a passionate group of men that followed the laws of their god and remained separate from the other groups of men and women who studied there. I passed quietly among them, unseen, unknown, save by him. Their rites and rituals filled the air with their strange tongue, voices raised in prayer to the gods that I knew nothing of. Many of the scrolls and parchments contained in that library were merely long recitations of the rituals themselves, or their origins. Some were truly exquisite and beautiful in a way that transcended the ritual itself, but in a way I couldn't understand, only appreciate.

There came a time when I decided that I wanted him, in all the ways I can want. I was no longer content to watch from the shadows. I approached him, tantalized him with the ability to translate a text from my homeland, drew him close to me. It was a slow process of gaining his trust, of sharing ideas, thoughts. His belief was strong, but not entirely that of his people. Something had altered him significantly in his youth. He never did say what it was, but it was always there, somewhere beneath the conversation. He was charismatic, passionate, and argumentative. I started out trying to seduce him, but in the end, it was I who was seduced.

We would sit for long hours discussing some obscure text or a bit of poetry. Or, we would debate the nature of life, or evil, or gods. Other times we would each be caught up in ourselves and pay little attention to the other.

"Is it so difficult for you to believe that there is evil so dark that it cannot stand the light of day?" he asked, exasperated one evening when we had been debating around and around the subject.

"Of course not, Jesse, I only think you shouldn't hunt it so closely." The last rays of the sun had long since vanished, leaving heavy shadows hanging in the room where we debated, our table filled with texts of contradicting theories regarding the Clans. "There are some things better left to the night. Come, let me take you to dinner."

"No." He was sullen that night, not exactly depressed, but adamant in his refusal to be cheered. "I have more work to do."

"Let me help then. Where were we?" I shuffled through the gathered papers until I found the scroll he had been reading from when our discussion had erupted. It was a text from a land not far from the place where it all began, where Bestin created the first of the Family. It was not old, perhaps twenty years or less. "There is then, hidden by the darkness, an evil which drinks the very life of our people, stealing through the night and leaving in its wake a trail of death," I read to him.

I had seen the words before, though couldn't place where. "It was once as we are, but the demon rose within it, and changed it forever. It cannot die, it cannot be stopped."

I put the scroll down. "It sounds to me like the ramblings of a paranoid mind."

"Perhaps," he conceded. He was thoughtful, his handsome face almost blank as his thoughts swirled around the words. I found it fascinating to watch, I was holding my breath. "Perhaps the author was paranoid. Perhaps he was demented.

Does that make his words any less true? Slanted, maybe, but he must have seen something to make him write this. Here, what about this one?"

He pulled a much older clay tablet to him and tilted it to the flickering light. He licked his lips, and read haltingly, translating as he read. "I am Darious, priest and teacher. I serve his Highness Dukant . On this night, I have seen evil with my own eyes. He came from the mountain and fell to prey upon two men. He had eyes of coal staring out of the whitest face, and teeth that were long and sharp, cutting the skin on the necks of his victims easily to drink from their blood. When he was done, the demon raised his bloodied face and took to the skies. I pray I never see such evil again."

I shivered. Something in the words or his voice as he read them conjured the image of Crenoral. I willed it away, but my face betrayed me. "See, your heart knows the truth," he said, his dark blue eyes lighting up. "What would you say if I told you that I too had seen this demon, this blood feeder?"

I looked at him, and knew. His soul lay open briefly for me. I saw the reflection of that trauma of his youth. It was just a flash really, a white face, a screaming child. Then, just as quickly, it was gone and his face was once more closed to me. "I would say, enough for tonight. Let it rest, Jesse. Let it be." I rose and left him there, among his books and notes, but I would return. There was something in that young man that beckoned me.

It was on a night several months later, when both of us were about our own separate matters that my fate would find me, or us as it would turn out. It was nearing the time we both normally went to our separate beds, yet I was ensconced comfortably in a chair in a dark back corner, a single lamp shedding a dancing light across the tablet of poetry I was reading.

I felt him enter, long before I heard his footsteps. I sat up and put my reading aside, listening as he came closer, my senses filling the space between us, trying to identify him and his intent. It had been many years since any of my kin had been so close. His attention was on Jesse, who was bent over his notes, oblivious to the intruder. I stood and silently edged closer. The intruder didn't appear to know I was there, so intent was he on Jesse. Just as he came within arm's reach of him, I called out. "Jesse, is someone else here?"

Jesse's head came up and the other stepped back slightly. As he did, he moved into the light of a nearby oil lamp, and I started. The hair was longer, the face more drawn, but I couldn't mistake him for any other than my childhood tormentor, Vahe. I stepped out of the shadows, gathering my hard won confidence around me as his eyes widened in recognition.

"The young man and I were just preparing to retire for the night." I said, hoping he would accept that Jesse was my chosen prey for the night. He raised an eyebrow at me and smiled vaguely.

"As I recall, he isn't your type. Imagine Father's delight when I bring you home. We had nearly given you up for dead."

I moved closer, an old, familiar anger stirring within me. "I am not dead, nor do I plan to return with you to Crenoral." I was trying to remain calm enough to keep the Change from coming, to protect Jesse's fragile trust in me. His own growing discomfort triggered a need to protect him though. "You can tell him I said so when you go home to him. As I said, my friend and I are retiring for the evening."

"What, still playing with your food? Step aside, let me see how he suits my palette."

"Back off, Vahe." I was between him and Jesse now, and Vahe's face took on the look of the Hunt, his sharp teeth bared as he ran his tongue along them. Jesse swallowed hard, perhaps attempting to determine which of us was the bigger threat.

"What will you do? Will you fight me for him? I have feasted well this night, Little One, and by the smell of it, you have not. Step aside, lest I have to hurt you."

"Jesse, this would be a good time to leave," I said quietly, feeling the Change pulling at my features until they mirrored Vahe's.

"What's happening?" Jesse asked, as I pointedly kept my face turned from him.

"Leave now and don't look back." Vahe came at me then, and I lunged forward to meet him, hoping Jesse had listened, but not having the chance to be sure. Vahe had spoken true, he was strong with the blood of his night's victims, and his blows hit hard. I, on the other hand, had postponed my supper while I read. He pushed me and I fell against the table, scattering scrolls of parchment to the floor. I kicked out hard as he came closer, landing a solid blow to his stomach and sending him into a chest, which crushed beneath him, leaving him lying in a pile of wood and stone on the floor.

I backed away, moving under the overturned table, seeking some cover while I regained my composure. I hadn't much chance against my childhood tormentor, but I had an advantage knowing that he would not seek to kill me, only injure me and haul me back to Crenoral. Still, he would not be averse to inflicting as much pain as possible, without killing me. I pulled myself up and out from under the table, using it as a shield between us. After a little cat and mouse, Vahe grew angrier and flung the table, his teeth bared as he came for me. I ducked, coming up under him and pushing him into the nearest shelves. He howled in pain as he crashed to the floor and I moved for the dangling leg of the table.

I pounced, from across the room, and almost made good with the weapon, but he was stronger and tossed me aside like a rag. He roared his irritation and the building shook around us, threatening a landslide of tablets and scrolls off the nearest surfaces. He moved toward me, on hands and knees, warily climbing over debris as his eyes locked on mine.

We rose together and circled one another warily once more. He closed in, and I tripped over shards of a chest or shelf that lay scattered underfoot. He was on top of me in less than a heartbeat, his hands reaching for my head. I bucked beneath him, but was unable to throw him off, he had me pinned and was moving in, his teeth bared. I was unable even to prevent his bite.

His face suddenly changed, his eyes growing wide, the Change fading, his hands releasing to clutch at his chest where a broken table leg protruded from him. Hands pulled him off of me, pushed him to the side, then reached down for me. As they pulled me into a sitting position, Jesse took shape behind them. His face was drawn and pale as he looked upon my Changed face. I licked dry lips and willed the Change to leave me. "Thank you, Jesse." I said after a time. My voice sounded distant and cold in my ears.

Beside me Vahe was decomposing, his wide eyes staring at me in accusation. We watched silently as I came back to myself, then our eyes turned to one another. Everything had changed. "You should not have done that, my friend. One of them will surely come seeking revenge. You must leave this place. Go as far and fast as you can." I was already scanning around for signs of Arda. She and Vahe never traveled separately. She would miss him soon.

"What of you?" he asked gently, genuine concern coloring his eyes.

"I too must leave," I replied heavily. "They will know I was here, my scent is strong here, and seek to return me to Crenoral." I said it as if it explained all that he had just seen, when indeed, it told him nothing. I let him help me stand, and shakily crossed the debris strewn floor to my chair in the back where my oversized bag hid a bottle of my formula. There was precious little left, and the other bottle was nearly an hour's walk away, but I lifted it to my lips and drained it, letting it slip down the back of my throat, spreading some semblance of strength back into me.

Jesse's eyes were one me, watching closely. I held the empty bottle out for his inspection. "It isn't blood, only a pale imitation, something to get me through the long nights."

After only a moment's hesitation, he took it, sniffing at its mouth and shrugging. "I was only curious."

"I know." I took the bottle and dropped it back into the pack. "Now, we should both be on our separate ways. It won't take Arda long to find this place. I thank you again for saving my life." I shouldered my bag and headed for the door, but his hand on my arm stopped me.

I knew well enough from our conversations of the previous months that he had a fair understanding of what had gone on there, of what Vahe, and I, were. I saw something akin to sympathy in his eyes, and felt, for the first time, a small returning of emotion that I had held for him for so long.

"I should be thanking you. I could have been his dinner," he said somewhat uncomfortably.

"More likely dessert, he'd fed at least once already this evening." I said lightly, understanding his feelings and trying to ease the burden. "But, you are welcome. Perhaps then, we are even?"

I again started for the door, but his voice followed me. "Where will you go from here?"

I turned, a small smile on my face. It had been a long time since I had someone care where I was headed. "I don't know. Away, to some other quiet place. It isn't the first time, and won't be the last." I wanted to hold him, to comfort the turmoil of fear and affection and loneliness I felt from him. "You shouldn't tarry here, Jesse. If they find you, you are as good as dead … or worse."

"I have nowhere to go. They've found me before. I have nothing … I am here because I have nothing left."

I thought for a long moment, rationalizing my decision before I had even spoken it aloud. He was, after all, just a boy and he would need someone to defend him if they came. When they came. It was easy to surrender to the need to keep him with me. "Come along then, Jesse, let us leave this place."

He hesitated only a moment, his eyes reflecting something akin to desperation before he marshaled himself and nodded. He picked his way to my side over smashed tablets and ripped scrolls and I slid a comforting arm around him as we left. The night was largely gone, and together we were confined to travel only as fast as he could. I resigned myself to the slow journey, and did my best to settle him to the ways of the night. We would live in twilight and dark, daylight lost and dawn our enemy.

Chapter 5

THUS BEGAN our time together, our running. We hid near the outskirts of the city until midday when Jesse found us a merchant traveling the blue waters of the Mediterranean ocean to take us north, to Gela. I entrusted myself to him, though it terrified me, in a cart covered in oiled canvas, I rode alone as he pulled me to the docks. The streets were rutted and bumpy and I jostled about in silent anxiety. My fear grew as he lifted me from the cart, tucking the thick canvas around me in the hope that the sun would not reach me. As night fell we huddled together for warmth and comfort, a physical closeness we hadn't shared before. It made my heart race, the scent of him so strong, the feeling of him in my arms.

He seemed stunned, speaking little and clinging to me if I shifted too far away from him. Echoes of nightmares followed him from his sleep whenever he chanced to doze off, though I only caught the echoes, none of the images. That first night seemed to go on forever, sitting in the dark under the cover of nothing more than that canvas shroud, waiting for death or the morning tide to find us.

Finally, the boat began to move and I felt some relief. The trip was longer than I wanted it to be, imagining our pursuit closing in around us, and unable to feed. My formula was gone, and I needed supplies and space to make more. By the time we had landed in Gela, I was shaking in hunger and might have fallen to the need if I hadn't had Jesse beside me. It was there, in Gela, that the first of them came.

As I suspected, it was Arda who found us first. There was fury and anguish etched on her face and her strength was unbelievable as she chased us through narrow streets and into an alley. Jesse was hurt, his arm broken. I was weak from lack of food. She closed in on us trying to decide which made the better target. Arda lunged at Jesse's cowering form, getting past me easily. In turn I lunged at her, the Change snapping my face into a mask as I bit into her neck and clung to her back. I drank deeply, swallowing greedily as she screamed and tried to pull me off. We stumbled backwards, into a wall, but still I drank. She had fed well before coming after us, and had managed to bite Jesse at least briefly before I had taken her by surprise.

She collapsed beneath me, first to her knees, then face first into the dirt. As I drank the last of her, I could taste Jesse. It stirred me, aroused me. The blood coursing through me was more than I had tasted in years, and the heat of it filled me. I wanted more. The scent of Jesse's blood filled the air and called me. I was on my feet and moving toward him before I realized it. There was blood on his neck, the small wounds still oozing lightly. He was on his feet, cradling his arm, his face contorted in pain.

I might have taken him then and there, answering the need within, if he hadn't raised his eyes to mine, and I saw an image of myself in them. He smiled tentatively and I felt the Change fade from my face. Self-consciously I wiped at my mouth, though I was sure there was no blood left on it. I covered the wound with my hand as I reached him, my other hand gently touching the arm. "Let's get you inside," I said thickly. There were more of them about, but none close enough to worry me. Once we had found a place to hide ourselves, I tended his arm, and covered the wound in his neck. His blood stained my hand, taunting me, as the warmth of his body taunted me. I leaned closer, my clean hand brushing through his unruly curls. My first kiss was soft, my lips lingering over his briefly.

He didn't respond right away, but I was not going to be denied after so long waiting and after tasting him. My second kiss was more urgent, and drew him into my embrace. I tried to be mindful of his injury as my hands touched him, sliding down his body as my desire climbed. I felt him respond, after that moment's hesitation that seemed to be his trademark, and his hands found their way to my waist. He had to be invited to be bolder, but proved a quick study, and we found ways to please each other as the day passed. I kept myself vigilant in my passion, lest I lose myself and take him all the way, as I had Adroushan. As the daylight faded and the dark took hold, we rose, donned our clothes and set out.

Whether it had been Arda or some other member of the Clan that found Vahe's dust, the lingering scent which my extended stay left behind was reassurance that I was yet alive. Crenoral renewed the hunt for his lost daughter. He sent the clan after me, and after the one who had killed Vahe. I could hear them in the night air, their voices filled with anger as they tracked us.

We traveled from dusk through dawn, scrambling for shelter as daylight approached. I lost count of the number of them that found us, for they could travel so much faster than we, hampered by Jesse's endearing humanity. They died, one after another, whether by his hand or mine.

Jesse learned quickly, and displayed an incredible talent for being able to sense them, sometimes even before I had. He adapted well to life in the night, to living by firelight and moonlight. He was a fair warrior as well, a fact hidden by his slight physique and mild manner. More than once in that first year I owed my life to him.

We rarely spoke of the past, of things we had done or what we felt. My adoration of him expanded as he grew from the boy he had been into a dark, brooding man who was my brother, my lover, my protector, and my ward, all at once.

The woman in me who had been awakened all those years before in Adroushan's arms was realized in Jesse. His eyes alone could bring me to my knees with desire. His tears could rip my soul to shreds. His touch was the most sensual thing I have ever known, raising my passion to a dangerous level that might have damned us both. He was a gifted lover, given to romantic play and diversions most mortal men might not have survived with me. I was helpless beside him, more human than at any other time in my life. I could deny him nothing.

He was, however, a product of the society which had raised him, and he had clear-cut definitions of good and evil. He hated the evil, and he focused that hatred into hating the Family as the purest representation of all that he knew to be evil. He mostly overlooked the fact that I too was like them, forgiven by the grace of my birth. He was sympathetic, touched by my conflict. I adored him, nearly to the point of worship. I looked to him for compassion, love ... approval. Most of the time I received it. It was only when I was forced to my own nature that he withheld it, on a night in the forests south of Germania, nearly three years after our running began. We were set upon by three of Bestin's clan. We fought. He killed the first of them with the hand carved wooden dagger he had crafted. I was weak by the time I had killed the second, shaking with need and the draw of the scent of blood. I fed upon her and flew at the last of them who had Jesse's left arm and was attempting to close her mouth over the pulsing veins at his wrist. I took her down and fell upon her, draining her as well. When he pulled me from her, my face was sticky with cooling blood and I burned with the feeling of strength it gave me.

He looked upon me then with disapproval, with a reflection of that passionate hatred he reserved for them. I thought the look alone might kill me, his face contorted with anger and disappointment, the stiffness in his back as he walked away, the cold in his fingers when he touched me. Eventually he forgave me, but it changed us forever.

We discovered things about the Family in those early years, things I had long suspected but had been unable to prove. As the great religions of man were born, and everyday objects became regarded as holy, ground was sanctified, lives blessed, the Family's weakness was to become apparent. Jesse was the first to discover it, when we were set upon by two of them in a small town of a deeply abiding faith. His hands found a holy relic, a sacred stone of the people's faith, during the battle. He held it up, hoping to use it in some way to defend himself. The other reached for it, his hand closing around the smooth curves of it before the smell of burning flesh filled the air around us. The other screamed and dropped the stone, raising a burnt hand. He fled, and in the quiet he left behind, we paused. We speculated about the odd occurrence, tried touching it to my skin, but nothing happened. Even fully Changed the stone meant nothing to me, caused no pain, no burning. We moved on.

Several months passed, and often our discussions returned to this weakness. We developed theories and ideas, none of which were entirely brilliant or well balanced. Most were wild speculation based on various observances over time. We traveled through a region where the local folk had idols, small statues, some of which were carved of tiny stones and hung around their necks on leather strings. Each was said to possess the spirit of one of their myriad gods. We acquired one, which Jesse took to wearing.

That seems to be when our running away ended. We set out hunting, searching each long moment of the dark for our enemy. It didn't take us long to find one, a scrapper from Bestin's tribe who was strong, well fed and spoiling for a fight. Jesse and I cornered her deep in a wooded glen not far from Osijek and the battle began. It was, at the onset, purely physical, the two of us taking turns at her, until Jesse pulled out the amulet. At first it gave her no pause, but as he brought it closer she began to react. When he touched the hand that held me by the throat with it, the air was filled with the scent of scorching flesh. She screamed and withdrew, pulling away and warding us off with one hand. Jesse held her to her spot with the holy relic as I moved in for the kill. She died in much the same terror I imagine her victims felt as she released their souls. We had found a new weapon.

Over the next years we collected items held holy to myriad races and tribes, developed favorites among them, discovered which seemed to have more effect than others. We found that some items needed to be in contact with the skin of the unholy, as Jesse had come to call them, and other items, those that came from a strong, widespread faith, were often effective just by holding it before them. In all of this, the symbols of one faith would become an endearing beacon of all that mankind considers holy, and our greatest weapon.

Yet, in all of this, I was unaffected.

Time passed, sometimes slowly, sometimes not. Jesse aged before my very eyes, his dark hair alternately long and shaggy and nearly shaved from his head, depending on his mood. His face grew distant, cold, unreadable. His hair began to show the signs of gray, and the little lines around his eyes deepened with each setting of the sun. He was pale from a lack of sunlight, nearly as white as I. Quite a couple we must have made, should human eyes have ever truly seen us, but few ever did.

Stories told of a ghostly pair who wandered the night slaying demons, but little more than my dark hair and Jesse's wooden dagger resembled the truth.

He was changing in other ways too. He withdrew from me, into a deep inner place where he had only his hatred to keep him company. The nights grew quiet, restless. We moved from place to place, through the shadows of humanity, and all the while his feverish fear and anguish brewed within him. I was helpless in the face of it, sitting dumbfounded beside him as it colored his pale face and filled his eyes with a bright fire.

We found ourselves in a place not far from the Family's ancestral home, where Bestin still lived, and the people around them were cowering and afraid. Somehow this bothered Jesse more than I thought possible. It pulled him up out of that place where he hid from the world and from me. It brought words to his lips, words of charismatic hatred, of death. In the early hours of darkness, beside a bonfire to light the night sky, he stood before the people and proclaimed the evil of Bestin and his Family, of a purging, of the duty of these people.

They were caught up in it, as was I. I had been so long in his company, and was so lost in my love for him, that I had come to believe him nearly as much as he believed himself. Perhaps my need to believe in something beyond my own eternal existence led me to be swayed, or perhaps I knew our own brand of evil all too well ... I don't know, but I followed him.

It was not well planned, and I, of all those there, should have known better than to wait once the blood was boiled to that point. The smell of it filled the air, a virtual beacon to those who lived off death. Two nights after our arrival there, they came, Bestin and several others, drawn in by the scent of life and rage. Jesse and the townsfolk roared into the fight, but I held back, my heart pounding with fear, my hands tied by sudden doubt. The soft, intellectual man I had first known disappeared entirely that night, replaced by a monster of a different kind. He let a lifetime of emotion consume him, burning away the last of his reason, bringing him face to face with the maker of all that he knew of evil.

The small town was piling up with dead, and a few, incredibly were Family. Bestin roared in anger and pain from the center of the melee. Jesse and Bestin fought hand to hand and all else stopped, and all eyes fell upon them. Both fought madly, as if set against their equal.

Jesse held his own against the fury of the enraged Bestin, his dagger slicing through the air, and on occasion, the flesh of Bestin's arms or chest. Bestin clawed down Jesse's arm, leaving three trails of blood and nearly causing Jesse to lose his grip on the wooden blade.

Bestin's thoughts were free to the night, and I knew he equated Jesse with the tales being spread about us. I could almost taste his anger, his will. Then, without warning ... Bestin's teeth were bared, within striking distance, and Jesse, daring all, stepped even closer, wrapping his arms around Bestin, the dagger pressing into the heart cavity from the back ... Bestin slumped. Jesse raised his hand, the wood of the dagger stained nearly black ... and Bestin fell to the ground, his hands clenching vainly in the air. Jesse went to his knees beside him and all within the town fled into the night ... all but Jesse and me.

Bestin was dead. The maker of our kind was gone. I went to Jesse, but he pulled away from me. The corpse rotted away as we sat in silence beside it and the night melted. I left him there as the sun rose, seeking shelter for myself that he did not need. I sensed his disappointment, but could not place its source. I slept fitfully, awaiting his presence beside me. He never came. When I rose he was nowhere to be found, gone they said to make his peace with his deed.

I waited for him. Three more nights passed. Not a sound was heard in the breezes, it was as if the Family that remained had fled this spot in terror, spreading the word of Bestin's death to those scattered abroad. On the fourth night, Jesse returned.

The gray in his hair had multiplied, appearing silvery in the light of the nearly full moon. His face was whiter even than mine, and the lines had deepened to add nearly ten years to him. But, his eyes ... it was his eyes that spoke to me from across the ashes of the bonfire. Some of the sanity had returned to them, and they burned brightly with the reality of what he had done. There was pride and fear, shame and elation all fighting for supremacy there. For the first time since those first nights together he needed me. I held out my arms and he came, tears wetting my shoulder before his head touched it. I held him for a long time while he cried silently and when he was done, we gathered our belongings and left that cursed ground.

Chapter 6

I AM still unsure how we came to the decision, or whether or not we laid out our plans as one does before battle. I remember only the fluttering of fear in my heart, the images of death that filled my mind when I closed my eyes. I was so completely caught up in him, my being centered upon him, that my own voice was a distant sound I ignored. Then ... there we stood, in the early hours before the dawn, in the shadow of the home where I had been raised. It had grown in the years since I had last seen it, additions made as time moved and the Family grew. They were all within, locked behind dark doors before the coming of the light. We were silent and separate, as had become the normal for us. So much between us left so little to be said. At long last, I turned to him and we moved.

We found a place to hide ourselves, and protect me against the brightest light of the dawn, in an abandoned room that held the cast offs of those who had died or moved on. We hid far in the bowels of the room where daylight didn't dare. There we waited until the house around us settled and the sun was fully up. I wrapped myself in a dark woolen cloak and gloves and slipped with him through the shadows, skirting windows and the little pools of sunlight that would bring a lingering, painful death.

It was the beginning of the Great Hunt, and I could smell the gathering fear of the prisoners held against the night of the Birth. We made our way to the dark pits where the prisoners were kept, alive, but locked in terror and humiliation until the time of their death. Whispering to them to keep still and fear not, we slipped the bolt and released them. Jesse led them back out into the light of day and instructed them to run as far and fast as their feet would take them, but to be safely under a friendly roof by nightfall.

I, in the meantime, made my way through the halls and corridors of the mansion as if in some haunted dream, remembering my nights among them. I paused in a small, unobtrusive room where Crenoral put the pretty things taken from his victims. He was more likely than the others to take things of value. The chest had not moved in the years I had been gone. It came open easily in my hands and I stood before the treasures of a thousand years of plundering.

I filled my pockets and the leather satchel I had brought with the most easily carried baubles, rings and gems, easily sold and worth enough money for us to begin a life when this was done. In their place, I left the ring from my pinkie, one that Crenoral had given me when I was still small. I set out again, hoping to find Jesse nearby.

At length I found myself at the door to the lower levels. Floor after floor of the Family's sleeping vaults lay below me. It was bolted from within, lest an intruder open it and cast sunlight down below. There I waited for Jesse. When he arrived, after what seemed to my nervous heart hours, I was beginning to feel weary from lack of sleep. I fished through my pack to find the small flask I had brought to get me through until I could get back to my supply. I drained it in one long swallow, closing my eyes as it filled me, warmed me, pushed away some of the fatigue. "They sleep below." I said softly and he jumped at the sound of my voice.

"How many are there?"

I shrugged and sighed. "There is no way of knowing. When last I was here, less than twenty made this place their home, but much has changed since then. There could be more, or less, but it is definite that we will not get them all in one day, not without waking all the rest."

"So, what do we do?"

"We take those we can, the ones on the upper level. He makes the youngest of them sleep closer to the sun. They will be less prepared for us, and, there is an empty floor between them and the rest, or at least, there was."

He nodded and hefted the sack he carried full of wooden stakes. I turned and studied the door once more. I knew there was a release for the bolt on this side, in case of a straggler trying to get in ahead of the sun. I reached up to the door jamb, slipping a finger across the beam until I found it. I could feel the bolt release, and then pushed lightly on the door. It swung open noiselessly and I stepped into the cool blackness. "Let your eyes adjust, we dare not use a light." I whispered, pulling Jesse in and shutting the door and slipping the bolt. "Stay close, and tread lightly."

I led him down the darkened staircase, my heart pounding in my ears. I wasn't sure for a long time as we descended that I could actually go through with it. The scent of Jesse was so strong to me that I was sure the others would smell him and awaken. Eventually we reached the first floor, and cautiously rounded the bend, approaching the first door. "Remember, above all, they must not be awakened. If one comes aware of us, we are dead." He nodded tightly and I put my hand to the first door.

The brother within was young, from the smell he had only a few years with the Family. He slept atop a small bed, hands folded over his heart, his face serene and handsome. We crossed to him, I circling to his head, Jesse to his side, withdrawing a stake and hammer from his sack. I stood over the young man, my hands just above his face to thwart any sound if he should awake, and nodded to Jesse who gripped the stake tighter. He held it just above those folded hands and composed himself with a deep breath. With the swiftest of blows, he hit the head of the stake and sunk it through those hands and into the empty chest below it. The brother never even stirred. By the time we had reached the door, all that remained of him was a rotted corpse showing more bone than skin.

We made it through that upper level quickly, killing seven of them before my instincts told me that the sun was soon to set. We hurried together back up the stairs, carefully closing the door once more behind us, and just as quickly to the side door by which we had gained access the night before. Jesse threw a dark blanket over my head and scooped me up like a child, checking to make sure I had no skin showing, then opened the door and carried me off into the brilliant sunset. We reached the safety of our chosen hideaway, an abandoned cloister less than a mile away, just as the sun's last rays faded into the deepening dark of night. We sat in each other's arms listening to the sounds of the night.

I could feel the rage and fear welling up from that place as the Family rose and discovered its dead, its missing prisoners. The fury filled the night breezes as one by one they went out in search of the hunters who had killed within their own home. I stood guard as Jesse slept, my senses extended around me for any sign that we had been found. Only one came, and she was easily deceived, easily dispatched. I woke Jesse and left him long enough to discard the corpse far enough from our hideout to keep them searching elsewhere when she was found. Near dawn, I curled up beneath the blanket and dozed, leaving Jesse to watch. He would wake me if one came near, but I somehow knew none would.

I woke when the sun was not yet half way to its zenith and found Jesse pouring fresh formula into a bottle for me. The remains of his own breakfast lay around and he smiled. He handed me the bottle and waited while I filled my body's need. "We still live," he said softly, lying back with his head on my arm.

"For now," I answered, feeling some deep remorse, some lost pain within me. It told me that I was still one of them, still needed them, and somehow, that it was Crenoral's thoughts, not my own. "Come, the day slips away from us. We must see to the arrangements." I slipped away from him, turning away and walking dangerously close to that place where the sun was reflecting into the hall. Some part of me willed me to walk out into that light, to end my long existence. Then, Jesse's hand was on my arm, his voice in my ear, his lips on my cheek. I put my arms around him and clung to him, as if he were all that held me to this earth.

The moment passed and we released each other mutually, stepping away to fill our sack with weapons, to prepare for further death. We had decided through our vigil, that the place must be burned, that we lacked the strength to take them all one by one. Jesse brought lamp oil from forgotten stores in the temple once dedicated to some heathen god and we packed the oil in containers barely of a size to carry. All of this we did silently, even to the wrapping of myself in that stifling black cloth, and he carried me out to the small wagon we had loaded with our supplies. He pulled the wagon out to the road and along its muddy, rutted way, glancing back at me from time to time. I could feel him despite the darkness that separated us, sense his adoration and love for me, despite what I was. It brought me little comfort.

The house was quiet, sleeping when we arrived and we wasted little time getting inside. I tossed off the blanket and kept only the long black cloak against the occasional window as we passed through the building like wraiths, dripping fuel onto every burnable surface, marking long paths to be lit as we made our escape. At length, when the sun was high and only hours from setting, we stood once more at that door. I took the last jar of oil from Jesse's hand and smiled gently. "I'll see to it. Go and see if they brought in any prisoners last night."

He looked for a moment as if he might argue, might insist on accompanying me into the darkness below, but we were running out of time, and he obeyed. I opened the door as I had the night before, and began my descent, scattering the oil on the wood as I went. The whole first floor was empty, abandoned. My tread was soft on the wood, wincing as each splatter of oil splashed to the floor, sure that its tiny sound would wake someone below.

I made the turn at the far end of the corridor and slowly descended those steps. Before I even reached the bottom of them, I knew I was expected. I stopped, one foot still upon the stair and regarded him. Perhaps I had known all along that he would be waiting there for me, perhaps I even had wanted for him to be there. Now, a lump of fear and anguish rose in my throat as I met his eyes.

They were the cold eyes of a hardened killer that afternoon, deeper than I could ever recall having seen them before. I couldn't look away.

"Welcome home, Daughter." he said calmly, as if it were any other day, as if I was merely an errant girl, breaking curfew. "I have been waiting for you."

I didn't trust myself to speak, and I held myself very still, setting down the jar and crossing my arms to await his next words.

"I was disappointed that you took our prisoners, but I recall you never did enjoy the celebration. The others were, of course, outraged. I barely contained them until after the sunset. You and your friend are most fortunate that none of them found you last night. Speaking of your companion, where is he, Daughter?"

I could sense his thoughts searching lightly around to be sure that Jesse wasn't within striking distance and smiled a very small smile. "Elsewhere, Crenoral. I didn't bring him here for you. He belongs to me, a lesson Vahe was not willing to learn the easy way."

"Ah yes, poor, ill-fated Vahe. He never was very bright." Crenoral sat forward, his face ruddy in the red glow of my torch. "As for you, I always thought you smarter than this."

"Perhaps I am smarter than you thought. Or maybe I merely wish my tortured existence to end. What better way, what more brilliant a funeral pyre than an entire palace full of my family to burn beside me?"

"No, little one, not you. Your will to live is too strong within you. You have killed rather than die, you have abased yourself in the hands of mankind, rather than die. Even if you burn this place now, you will fight to escape its blaze. Therefore, your duty will never be fulfilled, for as long as you live, there is one of us left alive in you, and the possibility of passing along the affliction remains. Come now, abandon this foolishness and let us be a family once more."

His words stirred something deep inside of me, and I was breathing heavily when the shadows behind him stirred and my mother's face emerged over his shoulder. "Come back to Mama, darling." She held out her hand to me and I had to take a deep breath to steady my resolve.

"I am sorry, Mother." I said, gently knocking the jar of oil on its side. All three of us watched in the light of the torch as it spilled out in a gentle pool, slipping across the ancient wood to his feet. With my eyes closed, I dropped the torch and fled up the stairs, around the corner and up the next flight of stairs, bursting out the door and nearly knocking Jesse over. "Quickly, bar the door." We pushed a heavy hutch across the door and ran for our lives, already hearing the clawing of frantic nails at its wood.

The ancient home was ablaze, but we had taken too long and the sun, with its certain death for any who might somehow escape the flames, was setting. I knew then, looking back from the top of the hill, we were doomed. My eyes, sharper than his, saw the first of them, emerging on the shadowed side of the building, where the setting sun was hidden behind the distant mountains. With a cry of anguish, I pushed him and began running myself, madly, pulling off the confining cloak and tossing it aside as we made for the meager shelter of the ruined convent.

We armed ourselves with what was left of our weapons, several stakes and wooden daggers, sharpened table legs, and our own fear, then we took cover in what had once been a beautiful temple, beneath a dome of colored crystal. We didn't have long to wait, the first found us only minutes after the sun was fully down. She died quickly and quietly, a dagger shot off Jesse's crossbow straight into the heart. Next came the twins, two brothers taken in the prime of their youth. They didn't die quite as easily as the first, but they did die. After that, it became impossible to count them, or keep track of where they fell, whether they were dead or not.

We fought side by side with the calm and deadly accuracy of those who know they will shortly be dead. Then came the inevitable, we ran out of ready weapons. "Split up," Jesse said, putting the last of the stakes into my hands. "Find whatever you can. I saw more wood to the east. Go!" He pushed me away, then himself ran off to the west, drawing at least half of our enemy with him. The rest came my way and I let the Change rage through me, a cold, passionate anger filling me.

The fight was glorious, and I reveled in it, in the sheer excitement and violent joy of it. This was what that part of me which was like them lived for. I managed to use the stake to some advantage before using it for its intended purpose. It lodged in the rib cage of a young man, and ripped from my hands as he fell away. Then I merely fought, as those of their kind do, nails and teeth lunging for those soft spots where instant death beats. It had been many years since that night in the woods when I had last tasted real blood, especially in such quantity, and even as the thought repulsed me, the taste and the strength it offered drew me.

Eventually my opponents lay around me, dead or nearly so, and I picked my way out of the ruined little temple and headed toward what might once have been the sleeping quarters of the luckless souls who had occupied the cloister. I went quietly through the night, as only one who is comfortable and at home in the dark can, my eyes seeing easily the world around me. I gathered what I could of weapons as I went, knowing that more of them hovered just outside my awareness, waiting only for the proper moment to strike.

I was prepared when it happened, if somewhat trapped. I had bent to break the legs off the frame of a table when I felt his approach behind me through the door of the tiny bedroom. I waited until he was just lunging at me, then dropped to the floor and rolled away, coming up with the wooden leg. He grinned, his teeth flashing in the light of the moon streaming in through a small window. I brandished the make-do stake like a sword, tossing it from hand to hand as I tried to decide my best course of action. I knew he had me trapped in the room and would try to finish me here if he could.

So, I lunged at him, hoping to take him by surprise, to bury my stake deeply into his chest. The surprise was my own however when he used my own move to evade me, then grabbed the arm that held my weapon. He pounded it against the brick wall until I was forced to drop it, then pushed my whole body into the same wall. My head was ringing with the force of the blow, my body responding sluggishly as he pulled me now away from the wall and tossed me into the opposite corner.

I caught him, one hand on his chest, one foot in his groin, and with all my will pushed him away, far enough at least to climb shakily to my feet before he was upon me again. His nails raked across my cheek, drawing blood and raising the level of my anger. I broke the hold he had on my arm, pushing him aside and pulling every ounce of strength in me up from the bottom of my being. With a power I didn't know I still possessed, I pounced on top of him from behind, my teeth bared as I dove for his neck. He writhed beneath me, his hands trying to pry me loose as he stumbled around the room. I hung on, even when his nails dug deep into the fleshy part of my thigh.

His blood was flowing swiftly, pouring his life out of him and into me and yet I clung to him, feeding not just to kill, but to fill myself with sustenance as I hadn't in over fifty years.

I had to pull his hand out of my leg when I was done, and I knew that the wound would hamper me. I paused long enough to bandage it with a piece of his tunic, and to wipe my face clean. With returning strength, I knocked the other three legs off the table and headed out to find Jesse. The convent was eerily quiet, my heart pounded in my ears in the stillness. My senses extended around me, watching for attack and searching for my companion. The building was empty.

I found my way out the back of what had once been a kitchen, and into a garden gone wild. Roses, half-dead in the cold mountain fall lined the walkways, and arched over the paths. I could smell the dead Jesse had left in his wake as he fled through this place, and one who was not yet. My pace quickened as my ears picked up the sounds, and I was nearly flying as I rounded the corner, and came to a crashing stop, my heart plunging into my toes at the sickening sight of Crenoral leaning over my Jesse.

Jesse was sprawled on the ground beside a trampled rose, blood red petals covering his chest, his hands grasping at the air weakly. For an instant my fear was that this being who thought himself my father meant to take away the one remaining thing that mattered to me. Then, in the space of a heartbeat, I realized that he meant, not to take Jesse away from me, but to give him to me, for eternity, as he had once given me Adan. I was seized by unimaginable sorrow, panic, my breath robbed from me by horror.

I screamed and flew at them, the jagged table leg in my hand, my aim steady. I knew Crenoral could not move to defend himself until his task was complete. He would stay, hoping to finish his task before I reached him, before my blow struck home. I plunged the rough wooden stake swiftly through his back, through the cavity where once, centuries before, a human heart had beat, and still he stuck to Jesse. In my haste and anguish, the blow was not straight, deadly enough, but slow to kill.

I cried in anguish and pulled him free, tossing him aside to die alone while I knelt beside my love. I was too late. I could see the awakening, the quickening of this new life, deep in the depths of his eyes, like I had seen in Adan's eyes all those years before. In fact, he looked like Adan at that moment, or what Adan might have looked like had he lived to Jesse's age. I could sense the changes within his body, even as his hand clung to me and he whispered my name over and over like a chant. The tears stung my slashed face as I brushed his dark hair out of his eyes and whispered to him that it would be all right.

Behind me Crenoral moaned, and I jumped. "You bastard!" I said, turning to face him. His eyes alone were alive in his ancient face, his hands had slumped where they had been pulling to dislodge the stake, his gaunt body was bent at an uncommon angle. "You should have killed him. It would have been kinder."

Crenoral smiled a bloody smile. "When I tasted him I knew ... have you ... I've given him to you again. Adan. Now, he can be yours forever." He tried to shift his position, but the stake prevented him from moving. "I only ... wanted you ... to come home," he said slowly, his eyes half closed and a shadow of remorse on his pale unchanged face.

I never said another word to him, simply sat there and watched him die, holding Jesse in my arms while the pain of the change racked his body. I couldn't fathom his words, his mention of Adan. Jesse was nothing like Adan. Jesse was ... I couldn't think past the feeling of him dying in my arms, past Crenoral's vengeance. When he could finally walk again it was nearly dawn. I don't know how we found shelter that morning, but we did, in an unmarked, unused tomb in the unkempt graveyard of the abbey. I held him while he slept, but I don't think my eyes closed once all day. I thought about killing him before he could fully understand what had happened to him, but somehow couldn't bring myself to do it. In truth, some small part of me took some pleasure in knowing that finally something I loved would live as long as I did. That thought vanished however at sunset when Jesse woke and I looked into his eyes.

Chapter 7

HE KNEW, perhaps better than I, what had happened the night before, he was acutely aware of the need growing inside him, and, at levels deeper than I could guess, he was horrified. We spoke nothing of it as we returned to the convent to claim what was left of our things, and began the long journey to somewhere far, far away from this place. We shared what was left in my bottle of formula, and stopped several hours before daylight to make more. The next night we set out again, and so it went for many days, putting time and distance between us and this thing we had done.

Each night when we rose I could feel the hunger in him, could sense the growing need that would have to be answered. I knew that the formula I survived on was not filling him, was barely keeping him alive, and that soon he would have to kill.

He, I think, knew it as well. It drove him deeper into his depression, pulling him further from me, and at the same time it pulled at the very animal core of his soul. Hatred and hunger found some synchrony in him and despair hung upon his very shoulders.

We were walking along a wooded road, who knows how long after that horrendous night, and we passed a small camp where a young man was kneeling beside a fire, and the scent of stew filled the night air. He called out cordial hellos and we stopped to warm ourselves by the fire. The small talk was pleasant and the sound of another voice strange to my ears.

"Do you mind sharing your fire?" I asked as we approached. Jesse's eyes were glazed over and I could feel his need.

The young man gestured for us to sit. "Please, come. Hungry? I've got plenty to share."

"Yes, thank you." I watched it come over Jesse, saw his resistance die. I sat near the young man, flirted. All the while Jesse just watched, hardly moved at all. I let the Change come, knowing the instincts newly born in my love would respond.

Gently I pulled the man's head to my shoulder, smoothing the long hair from his neck. The vein there pulsed at us. He squirmed a little, but I kissed his neck and my hand carefully stroked his inner thigh to ease him. "Come, Jesse." I whispered. "Come, feed." I bit gently, releasing the intoxicating scent of his blood into the air. I knew that without it, Jesse would starve. It was startling to see him like that, the Change taking away all that might have remained of my beloved Jesse. He fed, and when it was done, he cried. I held him, but could find no words to comfort him. When the tears subsided, we resumed our journey.

I'm not sure anymore how far we got, or where we went, or what happened when we got there. I know that Jesse killed twice more, and with each death he grew more despondent, and less my Jesse. We went days without speaking at all, and when we did it was little, one-word noises with no meaning. I longed to have him hold me as he did before, to feel him around me, to talk until one or the other fell asleep, and, I feared what we might say. The days and nights all began to run together, and still in my memory there is little definition. Only one remaining morning stands out in my mind.

We had found an empty mausoleum and bunked down in it for the day, even though there was still nearly an hour until dawn. I was preparing more of my formula and he was pacing around me. He had killed early in the night and was still full of its energy. Finally, he came to kneel beside me and took my hand. "I cannot do this," he said, his voice heavy and full. He was deeply in despair, worse yet than I had ever seen him.

"You will grow accustomed to it," I said, clinging to his hand.

"You never did." And, he was right. "I do not want to. I cannot stand this ... thing ... that I have become. I am now that which I have hated and feared all of these years we have been together."

"I love you," I said, as if that would make a difference.

"How? How can you love this ... thing that I am?"

I looked at him, and marveled again at the years we had been together. I was never sure if my passionate love for him was returned the same way, but it hadn't mattered. His handsome face was creased with the years, his hair more gray now than black. He must have been close unto sixty. "I have loved you always, and will forever." I reached up to touch him and felt him stiffen.

"I cannot live this life forever. I can barely stand myself now, and I have taken only three lives. Can you imagine what I would be like in a year, or five, or a hundred? I will no longer be that person that you love." He withdrew from me to pace around the small chamber, then came suddenly back beside me, his face so close to mine I could feel his anguish, feel his whispered words in my soul. "They are so warm, so inviting. Their fear titillates me, arouses me in ways even your touch never could. The blood is so sweet, so wonderfully sweet that I might explode merely from the pleasure of its taste, if the very experience of such passion didn't repulse me in ways I have never before felt. It tears at me, the loathing of the very thing which gives my body pleasure, and yet it can never stop me."

I wanted to kiss him, to stop his words, to stop the reaction he had begun in my own body, the longing, the hunger, but I found myself trapped by them, unable even to breathe as he went on. "I am afraid, even of myself, but even that serves only to make the desire stronger. I find that with each death, with each sweet taste of blood, the revulsion grows weaker and the need stronger. My body finds increasing pleasure in their terror and their pain. It nearly hurts. And yet, as it is finally done and I release them, I am brought to tears to know what I have done. If I could never remember it, their faces, their whimpering cries, I might survive. But each day, as we sleep, shut up in the dark, I see them, I hear them, and it drives me insane."

I knew then, I think, what was going to happen. I knew, and there was nothing that I could say or do to stop him. "What are you going to do?"

"The only thing left to me, all that is left of my own will." He stood opposite me, his back to me, and he was crying. I went to him, wrapped my arms around him, tried in vain to comfort him.

"I will follow you," I said, and for the moment, I meant it.

He didn't look at me, only touched my hand where it wrapped around him. "I love you," he whispered, saying his good-bye. He disentangled himself from me and went to the door. Beyond it the sunrise awaited its cue. I think I called out to him once as he opened the door and slipped away from me, but he never looked back. I started twice for the door myself, even crossing into the path of the light.

The pain was excruciating, the burning unbearable. I tried, oh how I tried to stand there and die with honor, but Crenoral was right about my will to live, I threw the door shut, collapsing beside it and crying myself to sleep.

I was found several days later, cried out, burned, and deep in shock. I was barely conscious of the second burning as they carried me out into the bright sunlight and carried me by horseback to a nearby hospital that had once been a temple to the healing god Asclepius. My hands were blackened and my face blistered where the dark cascade of my hair had failed to cover me.

With Jesse's death, and the trauma of my own injuries, I withdrew from the world. There was no conscious decision to it, no definitive moment when I chose to cease to function. My mind froze upon the final sight of him, and refused then to yield it. I paid little attention to what mankind chose to do to me, withdrawing within myself.

It was not a pleasant time and the backward nature of medicine in those days did little to improve my lot. I bear the scars even today of the burnings as I was moved from place to place, though I have no memory of how they came to be. I have glimpses of moments, of being fed, of being bathed. I do not know how many years passed there as I healed, as I became less and less involved in the outside world. I was uncaring of myself, or anyone else. Those there were nice enough, doing as medicine of the day could to ease my pain and help me to heal, but I seldom saw them. My eyes had turned inward and would not return.

When my body at long length recovered from the ordeal, they removed me from the spacious and clean clinic where I had first been brought and deposited me relatively unaware in a dank, misbegotten place for society's lost and forgotten. Some of those people there given charge of the inmates were truly caring, and several made attempts to reach through to me, all of which I either didn't hear, or chose to ignore.

I suppose you might say that I wallowed in my self-pity and grief for my lost love. You might be right. The truth of my actions, of the death of my mother, and her Kindred, Crenoral's final sin, my ultimate loss...all of this contributed to my condition. In some way, I felt as though I were paying some sort of penance for what I was and what I had done. The time came, however, when the need and hunger drew me back, brought me up from that dark, withdrawn place and set me about the reclaiming of my life.

Instinct brought me up from within as a hand passed too close to my face. My teeth clamped down and I bit, drawing blood, despite the fact that the Change had not come upon me. The taste of it was unexpected and invigorating and it cut through the walls behind which I had withdrawn. My eyes blinked as I realized what had happened, I saw for the first time.

Even then, I sought some manner of punishment. They kept me isolated for a while, as I spoke the truth about myself and they were afraid I might act out again on what they saw as my delusions. Eventually, my good behavior eased those tensions, and I ceased to talk about who and what I really was. By then, the staff had come and gone and there was no one there who really remembered the circumstances of my arrival, nor were records well kept. I had grown weak, unable to feed on anything more than the occasional rat or snake. Even that did little to warm me. I was hungry, but still unwilling to leave the shelter of the dismal little place.

It was, by and large, the depository of the ills of society, those sins and misdeeds no proper soul would admit to, nor dispose of neatly, and so, they congregated there, milling about in ugliness, dying slowly, each soul alone in its private hell, chased by demons no one but they could see. Children as young as eight or ten slept curled up in small balls of tender flesh, with faces so dirty and hearts so broken it tore even at my merciless soul. Whores used up by the very life that created them, and tossed aside when no longer suited for their profession. Men and women, begotten in sin and never given the opportunity for life, clung to the shadows and curled up in the dark. Criminals made up a large portion of those held there, the poor, whose crimes had won them the wrath of society, and debtors, unable to pay their way out. Then, there were the others, mental misfits whose only crime was not being able to hide their madness from the world.

The place reeked of human waste of every manner, and the deeper, subtler smells of mildew and stagnant water. It was perhaps the first true thing I remember upon regaining something of myself there. That, and the unbelievable gloom, a darkness deeper than my native night, and unable to be dispelled with any manner of light. I kept to myself, feeding as I could on rats and mice and devouring the putrid mortal meals provided. I watched the staff, the prisoners, the occasional visitors, hoping for one that would be perfect and suited to my needs. The choices were few and the opportunity never came. I was growing distraught as my hunger grew. Then, I found Moira.

She had been a prostitute, a used woman. She had withdrawn from the world and the world had disposed of her. She wasn't as old as she looked, all frail and alone. Her eyes were sunken and hollow, as if she could no longer see outside herself, and whatever she saw within was terrifying. I was drawn to her, inexplicably, uncontrollably. She was beautiful, breathtakingly so, underneath all of the dirt and depression. I thought to myself that this was a woman no one would miss, including herself.

For many long months after her arrival, I sat across the room from her, feeling her pain, her hunger for more than life had unfairly dealt her, her desire to end. It was that, perhaps, which drew me most of all. I needed her badly, and far beyond my own needs were her own. I wanted to ease her suffering, to offer her the comfort of a warm embrace before the end, which she truly sought with all her heart.

I found my way to her in the common cell we all shared. She sat in a far corner where it was dark and shadowed. I stood before her for a small eternity, looking down as a mother might upon a pouting child. Slowly, I sank to the floor beside her, put an arm around her and gathered her close. All around us people milled about, each held within their own despair and unnoticing of the dark danger in my touch.

She turned vacant eyes to me and almost robbed me of my resolution. I gently pressed her head to rest on my shoulder, and lifted her arm, stroking her hair with my free hand. My heart was racing with anticipation and I had to force myself to go slowly, lest I bring attention to our little corner. Her arm was slack and pliant, her pulse slow and faint in the veins there at her wrist. I closed my eyes and let the Change come over me, pulling the wrist closer and lowering my face to hide. She made no sound as I bit deeply and drank harshly of her.

The taste was so scintillating after so long and the rush of returning strength and vigor was dizzying. I was near to finishing her when she raised her head from my shoulder, her eyes showing a spark of life that had not been there before. I found myself releasing her, covering the wound with my hand, trying to hide what I had done. She looked at me as if she could see through to my soul and brushed my face with her free hand. I knew I had to finish the job, but found I could not. She smiled gently and I came undone, crying as her arms folded around me.

I fled from the corner, knowing I would cause those around me to scream and flutter and that I would be restrained. Anything, I thought, anything to be away from her, from those eyes, that touch. Time passed, and I searched for another victim whom I could kill without question, but again, no opportunity presented itself.

The hunger was only stronger for having tasted of her, and I would prowl the cell by night, craving more, needing more. Finally, I once again acquiesced to it, and determined this time to finish my work.

I found her, as before, in the corner of the common cell, not quite as lifeless as before, yet listlessly awaiting me. As I came to sit beside her, she leaned toward me, as if for comfort, her head on my chest as my breathing became light and quick. The pulse in that wrist beat faster than before, calling to me. I could feel the Change come, quickly, nearly uncontrolled. I drank swiftly, lest I lose my resolve once more. I drank deep, listening to the rapid fluttering of her heart and the hypnotic rhythm of her breathing. I pulled her to the very brink of death, reveling in the warmth and comfort of my returning strength.

I was nearly done with my work, holding her head lest she look up at me and destroy me again. I had only to take those final reserves and she would be no more. As I drew breath and prepared to end her life, approaching voices caused me to pause and glance around me. I had taken too long. The day's meal was being served, guards entering the room and separating us into groups easier to handle. I had no desire to be caught there with blood on my lips and a lifeless body in my arms. Gently, I lifted her off of me, settling her against the wall, as she had been when I arrived. She looked up at me with sleepy eyes, and I knew I could never finish this which I had started.

It was worse after that, the aching inside of me, the needing ... the wanting, like some addiction to a drug. I could hold off from her for days, sometimes weeks before my need and the hunger got the better of me. Always, she was there, waiting for me in our dark corner, offering up her life for the taking, and for all my desire to end her torment, I found I could not.

She grew more and more lovely as the months passed, and yet it did not occur to me what I had done, what I was doing with each taking. The youth returned to her face, the shine to her hair. Still, she sat alone in the darkness, the strength still lacking, her soul still shadowed by her past. More than a year passed from the day I first took from her until it finally became clear to me that I had done the unthinkable, created that which I had once set out to destroy.

I finally saw it in her one late evening, while sitting dully by the cell door and preparing my plans for escape. She sat, as always, in our dark corner, her eyes bright and set upon me. A guard had noticed her, a brute of a man, not given to the finer points of courtly behavior. She never looked at him, but when he bent to kiss her, his hands on those private places a woman guards, she bit him, clung to his neck, not truly drinking of him, but he drew back with alarm and had her removed from the cell.

I knew then that I had to remove us from the asylum before she too came to understand herself and begin the rest of her transformation. I chose a stormy night, when even the dullest of souls would keep themselves inside. Most of the others in our common cell were sleeping, and it took a moment to get the attention of the guard. I had never used my body to entice a lover, and it seemed strange to me. He must not have thought it strange though, entering the cell and following me to the quiet shadows where Moira waited. I let the Change come full upon me as I kissed his neck, pulling him deeper into the shadows. I drank deeply, silencing him, then called for Moira. She seemed eager, maybe too much so, as she knelt beside me and did as I told her.

When she had finished her first meal, the last months came to life in her eyes, and finally, she knew. "I shall live now?" she asked.

I had never before heard her speak. She had a deep, musky voice that lilted lightly and filled the room though she barely spoke above a whisper. I nodded slowly, one hand brushing her cheek. "Yes, love, I believe you shall. But, come, we mustn't wait long."

I took her by the hand and led her out into the wild night. The flashes of lightning showed me the way back to the cemetery where they had found me that horrid day after Jesse had left me. I pried open the door of the tomb where I had spent that awful day and night, where all my worldly possessions remained. The leather bag lay untouched in the dark, cob-webbed corner where I had left it, its pieces covering the bottles and trinkets I had carried with me. My formula was, of course, gone, long since turned to dust, but my meager equipment was whole, and still hidden in the bottom of that bag was a little bit of money and jewels to see us through the next months. A hundred years had passed since I had last stood in that tomb and for a moment it felt as if none of it had happened.

"What is this place?" she asked, looking around her in awe.

Spiders crawled away from us as we moved. There was an old ache in my heart and I imagined I could still hear the echo of Jesse's final words to me. There was also the tinge of guilt at my final lie to him, that I still lived. "It is a place to protect us, Moira, nothing more."

"Tell me of him." I was taken by surprise, but she came to me, taking my hand in her own and

I saw an echo of my own face in her eyes. It had long been my observation that those gifts given to mortal man become enhanced when immortality graces them, strengthened, changed of course, but still there. Obviously she had been something of an empathic soul, which could have done her well in her former line of work. Now, those empathic skills were blossoming into near prescience.

"He was a mortal when I first knew him, as you were. He died here, in this tomb."

"How did he die?" We sank as one to the floor, wrapped in each other's arms. If I closed my eyes I could see him walk across that floor to that door and the death that awaited him beyond it.

"He was changed, made the same as you. He could not adjust to it."

"He took his own life," she said. "He left you, in the daylight." She held me as I felt the hurt return. "I shall not leave you."

It was like the promise of a small child, spoken to ease a pain, but with no real conviction to back it. I took it for what it was, accepting her acknowledgment of our shared course, and trying to remember my duty now to her which exceeded that of my dead and gone Jesse. "Nor I, you. Rest now. The sun will be up soon, and when it is gone we will have a long journey ahead of us."

We spent the remainder of the night and all the next day in that tomb, Moira in my arms and Jesse haunting my dreams. The next night we journeyed away from the sleepy little village where we might be seen, and to the south. By night we walked, by day we hid. She fed ravenously on anything we encountered; deer, rabbits, even a stray goat that happened across our path. There was precious little living in the country we walked, and almost no humanity to speak of. I knew she wasn't getting enough, and I knew she had to feed well. She was like the young ones I had hunted with in my youth, so empty and in need. I altered our route then, and we made for the cities of Europe. Eventually I aimed to take us north to the places I had never seen. It was Rome however, on the cold streets of the city that we would meet Leonard. Moira adjusted well to hunting in the teeming pools of Rome's lower classes. She seemed, of her own free will, to be drawn to those who needed the release of death, those sick beyond the ability of medicine to aid them, those whose crimes exceeded the ability of mankind to punish. I was like a mothering hen, haunting her steps, watching over her, ready, at a moment's notice to jump in to save her. She had little need of my saving, however. Her former profession served her well, bringing exactly the right instincts for this new life I had inadvertently given her.

I was watching Moira stalking her dinner when I first spotted Leonard, stalking the same man. Even I could read the sickness that had drawn her, an illness of the mind that turned him to prey on women and children to service his baser needs. She reached him first, flirting a little and drawing him into the alley. Leonard followed them, and I was only slightly behind him, ready to defend my child if I was needed. Moira already had the man in her arms, her lips red with his blood when we arrived. She simply looked up and offered Leonard the man's arm, which he took. When they had finished, they turned to me. I nodded greeting to the young man, and reached for Moira's hand.

"I am Leonard Leros," he responded with a courtly little bow. He was young, and I could tell

Moira was taken with him instantly. He was only an inch or two taller than myself, his face partially hidden behind a thick black mustache and beard. His eyes were a deep blue, filled with flecks of light that made them sparkle when he laughed, which was often. He was a man filled with ease and grace, and a natural joy that seemed to somehow belay his true nature.

Moira offered him her free hand, which he took, and together we left that alley, the three of us. We walked awhile, eventually coming to a place where we could sit and rest. "Where are you from, Leonard?" I asked, watching Moira flirt with him, her eyes flitting to his, then away as a small smile played on her lips.

"Originally, I am from a small county not far from here, but I've traveled a bit." He set his hat beside me and ran one white hand through thick black locks of hair.

"And, your Sire?" I asked, more curious than anything.

"Ah … Elizabeth … she was … beautiful. I knew her as a mortal, pursued her vigorously. Then, she disappeared, and when she returned, it was she who pursued me."

"So, you came willingly?" I meant it not as an accusation, for I know how hard an invitation it can be to resist, particularly if there is love involved.

"Don't we all?" he asked, his brows knotting together.

"No, I'm afraid not. You must not have known many of our kind. They often bring those they want by force or without asking. Such it is with Moira, I'm afraid." I patted her hand, but she seemed completely enthralled with him and didn't even take notice. "Not by force, mind you, but against her will nonetheless."

"No," she said, much to my surprise. "Not, exactly. I would have said yes, if you asked." I looked at her, but she looked away, suddenly shy. "You gave me a second chance to mean something. I never did before."

"Ah, but you do now." He kissed her hand, touched her face. "You are the very meaning of this night."

It cut at me to see them together, hurt me more deeply than I could have guessed. Yet, it was so completely natural for them, as if they had been destined from before their births. Instantly we were companions, sharing our daytime hiding and our nighttime prowling. We traveled Europe, the three of us together, exploring all that the night world had to offer. We seldom met others of our kind, and those we did left us to our own lives, mostly passing without even acknowledging our presence. If Leonard knew of my past sins, he said nothing, accepting me into his life as a mortal does his wife's mother.

Chapter 8

I TAUGHT them all I knew of the places we visited, as if I were their teacher, as well as showing them the more practical things that go with our longevity and dark nature. The world was growing increasingly dependent upon religion, as sickness and famine spread. That made our lives more difficult, more for them than for me. The night was a place of great superstition and fear, hunting was scarce even in the cities. They had to learn to hunt early, just as the sun was gone, to be invisible to the eyes of man until their prey was all but in their hands.

I was reminded of Crenoral as I floated with them, coaching as we went. "Moira, see how Leonard avoids the light, without appearing to avoid it? It makes it appear that the shadows follow him and not the other way around." We were in Greece, dancing in the shadows of ruins nearly as old as myself. "Come, watch. I will walk among them." Together they perched on a rotting wall and I slipped into the stream of humanity that passed by us in the evening. No one chanced to even look up, taking no notice of the wraith that passed them. When I returned, Moira smiled.

"You have had many more years to practice that," she said, taking her hand from Leonard's. "But, I think I might understand it now." She mimicked my every move as she did the same, moving into the closing marketplace to pluck an apple from a stall and return to us unnoticed.

"What think you, Leonard?" I asked, taking the apple and biting into it. "How did she do?"

"Beautifully, as always," he responded, kissing her hand. "But, you brushed too closely to that one man." He pointed at a young man who was looking puzzled at the faces of those around him. "He nearly saw you."

We watched as the man in question glanced around him, dazed and unsure that he had seen anything. Eventually he faded into the thinning crowd. "Come, children, it is time we were off about more private matters." We withdrew then, as the mortals did, into the privacy of what passed as a home for us. There were more lessons, quiet time spent lost in the journals I kept as a youth, or in ancient manuscripts that modern archeologists would salivate over today. I pressed upon them the need to know and understand what went before in order to be prepared for what lay ahead.

As the time moved by us, I could feel them growing closer to one another, and distant to me. It hurt me, and yet, I could feel a sort of maternal pride as I watched them blossom into intelligent and beautiful creatures. Perhaps it might have been better for all of us concerned if I had chosen to leave them once their lessons had been learned. Yet, I clung to Moira, my child, my treasure. I loved them both as I had no other creatures in my life.

To this day, I do not know which of us let go first, or if it happened all at once. One night I simply gathered my belongings and emerged from my room to find that they had gone. Only a note was left behind, like that of a child telling her mother she had run off to elope. "Amara," it read, "please forgive us. We are unable to say goodbye.

We will hold you fondly in our thoughts and hope to see you again one day. Until then ... Moira and Leonard."

I was, of course, heartbroken, though I myself had set my sights on leaving them. I moped awhile, hanging around the places we had loved together. Then, I gathered my wounded pride and my belongings and took to the night. I wandered alone after that, visiting London and Paris, Madrid and Cairo. Occasionally I would come across one who knew me, or of me. Once or twice it came to blows and I was forced, as with Vahe, to defend myself. It left me cold and empty, for I no longer believed my actions were justified, I no longer had my Jesse to convince me. Yet, I was unwilling to pay the price for those actions, to allow myself to die for those deeds. My will to live was too great, which brought me back to the same crime, dealing death to those who were so much like me.

I changed a great deal in those years, maturing beyond my reliance upon others for approval, for the conviction of the reality of life. I grew to like myself, to be aware of myself and my own desires. The world was an open playground to those like me, spreading its arms in welcome of the cold and hungry, offering sanctuary and kindness to those in need. The night was a thing to be escaped, which left it empty for my pleasure, barren of those who might come to know the true nature of the darkness. I traveled unmolested and quite alone, save for those times I required company. Then, I would don my most human expressions, and walk among them again. I found a certain comfortable existence in myself, moving from place to place, making friends, taking lovers, finding the person I had always desired to be. I was strong in myself at that moment in time. I needed no one and nothing, but the formula, which sustained my life, and the dark which held it.

There is something to be said for the children of the night, those newborn to the darkness, filled with the wonder and awe at her beauty that we who are more familiar with her shortcomings have forgotten. Thus it was when I found her, and I was instantly taken in by her joy, her trust, her lust for all things. I had forgotten what it was to feel such passion, such desires. I was mesmerized, hypnotized in the shadows of the moon, watching her as if entranced as she moved with fluid grace reminiscent of an earlier age through the streets, a wraith, a shadow, barely there and yet so fully alive that without her the world would grow pale.

She had been a child, barely seventeen, made in the heat of passion by another too young to understand what he had done, what evil would transpire to rob her of the innocent beauty he loved. He had been Maurice, a gentle soul with scarcely a year of night within him when he loved her, and a careless killer who found the truth of immortality two seconds too late to save himself from the fiery death of divine retribution. She was alone then, when I came across her path, alone and wandering her new world with the eyes of a child and the beauty of a girl on the verge of womanhood.

I shadowed her for several nights, content, at least at first, to watch her as she tasted the night air, stole silently upon the unsuspecting, laughed easily at the jokes of those around her, and fed with an insatiable hunger only those young children of the night can know. I felt a sudden kinship when at last she spotted me, sensed me, came to me. Her dark eyes sought out mine as if for explanation of herself, of myself, of the world. We stood silent upon the street, regarding each other. She saw in me the dark, ancient reflection of my life, the weariness in my soul, the forever beating of my heart. I saw ... love ... and life, beauty beyond the ability of the spoken word ... everything I had ever aspired to, and everything I had ultimately lost. It seemed I had known her forever, that I had loved her since I had drawn breath.

She sensed the need, the hunger in me, the weakness of my body, and in a simple gesture of faith and trust unearned and unasked for, she offered me her wrist. She had fed well, I had watched her, and she seemed, in that moment of meeting, to understand my moral bindings, my ethical dilemmas. She offered her wrist, her face open and inviting, the rush of her supper's blood calling out to me. I took her hand, drew her with me to the shadows, away from the glare of the street lamps and the sounds of the night people. The Change came quickly, easily and I drank of her, tasting the sweet, lingering pieces of the mortal she had been, and the warm, musky thickness of the foreigner she had dined on. I pulled back, licking my lips to savor the remaining drops. She smiled, her own sharp teeth white and shiny in the pale illumination of the moon.

"Hello," she said then, wiping daintily at the tiny pools of blood that were already closing at her wrist.

I smiled and took the hand she offered. We walked into the night, instantly at home with each other, minutely connected on levels that went beyond the physical act of sharing her dinner. So it began. We scarcely spoke, though we spent hours in the company of each other. I watched her hunt, kill... then savored it through her, feeding as I had never been able to.

We were a study of opposites, always walking closely together; she in her pale blond hair and fair white skin, her blue eyes dark and sparkling, I brooding and darker than the night from which I was born, my hair black and straight and long, so that it might not be told from the black of my clothes. Men were entranced by her, as was I, falling upon themselves the moment we entered a room and nearly throwing themselves into her embrace, even when they knew her kiss would bring only death.

She was beautiful in a way I cannot begin to make you understand, even with all these years I have lived and the fifteen modern languages I speak, there are simply no words. It transcends the ability of words. She was innocent, and a killer, child-like in her need for approval, her desire to please and her demanding for what her body required. Yet, she was a woman, filled with a woman's longing and able to use that beauty she possessed to her advantage. She took from the world what she needed, and did it with an awe and wonderment that left me aching when she had fed and come to me. Her ethereal grace and agility displayed all that was good about the curse of our lives, and yet something of her former human beauty clung to her as well.

She did not hunt as others did, as I had in the past. She wooed, she flirted, often for nights on end before she drew one into her final trap. Always a man, usually young, sometimes not. They were helpless in the end to resist her, many of them succumbing without scarcely a trace of fear. I was spellbound, caught up in her mystical nature, unable to see anything beyond. I would find myself breathless as she danced, played, flirted; aching for the very taste of her, the scent of her beside me, the sound of her voice, deep and musical. I was never far from her side, and whatever mystical strings bound us brought her inside of me. As she fed I could feel the warmth of the blood filling her, rushing to her cheeks until she looked like an excited girl flushed with the first kiss of love. My body craved what she brought to me, the release, the desire. Always I wanted more.

I bought us a home on the distant outskirts of the city, close enough to walk to and from each night, and far enough from the center of things to be left largely alone when we chose. We had no need of servants or aides of any kind, we had each other, and little else mattered in our lives at the time. I withdrew again from the world, seeing it only through her eyes, touching it only through her skin. I savored the newness of it all through her, tasting the familiar as if I had never known it before. I scarcely breathed in her presence, barely knew the needs of my own body, beyond the exhilarating rush of feeding from her and the exquisite pleasure of simply gazing at her.

She remembered little, if anything of her life before Maurice. Indeed, she scarcely recalled Maurice. All that seemed to matter to her was the moment. The nights stretched out in eternity from us. I held her in my arms as I might have once held Jesse, whispering to her of her beauty, of the secrets we had to share. I was utterly spellbound, held to her by the basest of needs. There was nothing hidden between us, our thoughts were free to the night air, easily read by the other.

She was, perhaps more than Moira ever could have been, my child. She depended upon me for everything, leaning upon my arm as we walked, looking to me for approval as she chose her prey. She mimicked my mannerisms, my style of speech, she bought us matching clothing. At times she was more a little child than a woman, giggling at things only she saw, withdrawing behind a wall of silence when reprimanded. She hated to be away from me for long, save for at feeding. Then, she would rush to me, as to a lover she hadn't seen in months, and melt in my arms as she offered herself to me. I wondered if this was how she had been with Maurice. I could not resist her, withhold anything from her. She was my angel, my cherub-faced child of death.

I was unprepared then, for what would befall us. I could not see the horror that was coming upon us, I could not know what cruel blow the world would fell me with, what terror would follow me the rest of my days. I am told now that it began somewhere in France, when one inscrutable monster killed in a spree unrivaled in all of history, awakening modern man to the presence of our kind, kindling a fire of vengeance that would spread across time, burning hot and low and dangerous. In that fire was born a new monster, perhaps more bloodthirsty than Crenoral's entire clan could ever have been. They were commissioned by the Church, blessed and sent out on their crusade to save mankind from the devil of the darkness.

Before then we had been creatures of myth and legend, a thing whispered of and feared, but never truly believed in by the light of day. As long as it had been kept that way, humanity was never truly a threat. Suddenly, we became the focus of great religious conviction, beyond that of those first early centuries. We were given a name... Vampyre.

I knew nothing of them, or the events which had conspired in their creation, but that did not keep them from finding me... or more accurately, from finding Rebeka, with me beside her. I understand now that even mortals ran from them, for they were said to be ruthless in their pursuit of their enemy, and uncaring of the innocence of any who stood between them and their chosen prey. They had their blessing from the Holy Mother Church, and the freedom and authority to condemn any that they saw fit to condemn.

They came in the early spring, wearing their white robes and crosses. I saw them arrive, watched them, my eyes flickering occasionally to the place where Rebeka flirted with her evening's choice, as they dismounted their horses beside the church. Two of them remained with the horses and the others went inside. A twinge of prescience touched me, but I assumed them to be simple clerics, traveling through and seeking shelter for the night. I ignored them, and the sense of doom that seemed to hang in the very air about them, returning to my nightly entertainment. It would be my mistake, one that haunts me still today.

Two nights later I saw them again, mingling among the night people, asking private questions, and heads turned our way. I grew nervous, I have never much liked attention. I sought out Rebeka. "Come, it is a good time to be away." I took her hand and drew her from the lighted windows of the pub where she had been flirting.

"I am not done," she said, pulling away.

My eyes jumped to one of the priests who was looking our way. Her eyes followed, and I felt her make the connection between the man and the apprehension she felt building within me. "What is it?" she asked, her eyes growing wide as fear knotted in my stomach.

"I do not know, exactly, but it feels like trouble." We watched a moment as the priest spoke with another, his eyes still upon us. "Please, Rebeka, humor me. Let us away."

She was resistant, but my apprehension echoed in her and she followed me like a reticent child. Once within the relative safety of our home, where there was no need to pretend, I actually shook with some tremor of unrealized fear. I should have known then. I should have seen it coming. Had Moira been with me I might have.

"Who is Moira?" she asked suddenly, pulling me from my introspection. In the time we had been together we had never discussed my past.

I smiled and sat beside the fire. "Moira is my daughter, as you are Maurice's daughter. I made her."

"Where is she now?" She settled into a little ball at my feet, her head resting upon my knee.

"She is with one called Leonard. They belong together."

"As we do?"

She seemed so innocent at that moment, so unaware of the world, of herself. "Aye, Rebeka, as we do." I brushed her blond locks absently, listening to the sounds of the night and the gentle crackling of the fire.

"And you, who made you?"

I was quiet a moment, gazing into the fire and seeing the faces of my Family, now gone. "An ancient one, one of the first three. Only, not in the same way you were made. He made my mother, and I was brought with her."

"Did he love you?"

"I suppose he did, in some way. Not all are made out of love though, Rebeka."

"So Maurice told me, before he was gone. I cannot understand that. How do you give such a gift to one you do not love?"

"I don't know, my love, I don't know." I smiled and contented myself with her presence, with her affection. The apprehension left me. The fire was warm and the night still young. I picked up a book of poetry we had been reading from and opened it to the marker. When she read from it to me, something in her voice reminded me of Adroushan and the softness of her hands soothed me. The priests and the foreboding of trouble were forgotten.

The streets were chilled, quiet the next night, as a late frost settled over us and we made our way to the tavern where we often spent the early evening. Very few folks were there, and those brave souls were huddled around the fire, casting fevered looks in our direction, as if blaming us for some hideous crime. I was too uncomfortable to enjoy my normal meal, and Rebeka pouted while I made a show of finishing my supper, for there was no one to flirt and toy with. She agreed easily when I suggested we leave, put off our usual evening stroll until another night when the air was less chill. As we emerged from the tavern we spoke of moving on to another town, of leaving behind the uneasy feeling this evening had placed in our souls. She was excited at the prospect of seeing big cities, of traveling the wide reaches of civilization. We were near to the edge of town, making quiet plans for the following night when she saw a man she had been courting.

She glanced aside at me, and I could feel an echo of the hunger inside her, the stirring of what she was, of the need which brings us all to feed. If it warmed inside of me, it must have been a raging flame to her. I nodded and busied myself at a shop window while she hurried along to catch him. I watched furtively, my nervous stomach urging me to keep a close eye on her. I was so busy in my watching that I failed to notice the approach of the clerics. A young one, no more than twenty-five spoke a greeting to me, "Greetings, Milady."

"Father." I smiled gently in his direction, hoping Rebeka wise enough to see them and move her supper elsewhere to dine.

"Might I speak with you?"

"If that is your wish." He made me nervous, a flittering in my stomach I couldn't place.

"What is your name, Daughter?"

"I am called Amara," I said, fighting my instincts to push him aside and head for Rebeka.

"And your family name?"

"Is older than anyone remembers. In my homeland, sir, we are called by only one name."

"Where would that be?"

"A very long way from here." I began walking in the general direction where I had last seen Rebeka. "I am sure you would not know it."

"Are you very good friends with the young woman I saw you with before, the pretty blonde?"

"She is like a daughter to me. Why do you ask?"

"The people of this town say she is cursed, that death follows her. Many men have died."

I stopped and turned to look at him, my face filled with a cold indifference. "There are many things that make men die, Father. Do you have a meaning to these annoying questions?"

"Do you and she live together in a state of sin?"

He was perfectly serious, and I had to keep myself from ripping into his neck. I knew then that they had suspected the truth about us, about her. I strained my neck to look for Rebeka. She had disappeared down an alley and been gone far too long. "Excuse me, Father, but I really must be going." I said, and headed toward her, but he touched my arm and continued his questions.

"Does she serve the devil? Does she drink the blood of the men she kills? Do you protect her?"

I grew angry and more than a little afraid. He kept slowing my steps, getting between me and the alley, deliberately delaying my arrival. When at last I made it to the corner of the nearer building, I could hear the low growl of a wounded animal, trapped, afraid, hurting. She was cornered against a wall, the dead man at her feet, four of the hunters holding her to her spot with crosses that gleamed gold in the moonlight. Her eyes met mine and I read in them her silent pleading. My heart stopped, my breath ceased. I felt fear and hatred welling up within me and I longed to tear these men to shreds.

I broke free of the hold the priest now had on my arm and began to go to her. I ran, feeling the Change begin and welcoming it. I was nearly upon them when I felt the blow to my head and neck. I fell in a pile of skirts and hair and limbs, the Change faded before it had fully come and my eyes rolled closed upon the sight of my frightened woman-child.

I awoke in a dungeon cell in what I assumed to be the local lord's castle. It was nearly dawn and the high window just above my reach would soon let in enough light to kill. Through the bars I heard her crying, a sound that broke my heart, tore at my soul. I called her name softly and she came, crouching beside me, kept apart by the cold steel.

Her beautiful face was smeared with blood, and her feet were bare, and bloodied as well. Her dress was torn, her hair in disarray ... still she stirred something inside me. I reached through the bars and held her, whispering sweet nothings to reassure her, to make her believe that I would take care of her. My head was pounding with the after-effects of the blow to my head, and I could feel blood crusted there when I reached up to touch it. The wound had already healed, but the blood had dried in my hair, matting it to my neck. Her wounds had likewise healed, but she was frightened and skittish. God only knew what they had done to her while I was unconscious. For the first time her mind was closed to me. I didn't press, I simply held her and tried to calm her.

I watched the approach of sunlight as it crept down the wall, spilling in a puddle of light that slowly moved toward us until I had to release her. We moved away, each into the dark corners where we couldn't see each other, but where the light didn't reach. I held my breath and tried not to listen to her fear beating wildly with the last of her supper, tried not to think about what might be in store for us both. Fear was not an emotion I had been intimate with before, although I had been occasionally afraid, never before had fear gripped my insides as it did at that moment, paralyzing me. I had no idea what was meant for us, but I knew it would not be pleasant. I felt the Change coming, and with it the strength of my birthright, a chance for freedom. But, there was nowhere to go. The day was full upon us, and even if I could get free of the cell, there would be nowhere for me to take Rebeka.

The sounds of men approaching drew me out of my inner thoughts, brought me from my crouch in the corner to my feet. Keys in the heavy iron doors and several men entered each of the cells, moving to stand in the center of the sunlight. They were "armed" with great gold crucifixes and I could hear the sounds of fear and anguish coming from Rebeka. I tried to maintain a cool demeanor, somewhat indignant at the treatment. "I demand to know what is going on! Why have we been caged like animals?" I was slapped hard across the face for my trouble, a stinging blow that nearly knocked me into the wall. The cross was shoved in my face then, as if that would hold me to my place, keep me from attacking them. I almost lost control of myself, I could feel the Change roaring to be released, but I bit my tongue and willed the fire to subside. It would serve no purpose at that moment.

Rebeka hissed loudly, and I looked sharply her way. The men were attempting to drag her into the sunlight. Her face was contorted by the Change and her fear, her eyes blazed as she fought them. But, ultimately, we were outnumbered and I could smell the flesh of her hand that they held in the direct line of the late afternoon sun. She screamed in absolute terror and agony and I felt my stomach twinge in echo of what she must surely feel. I rubbed a hand along the scars on my right arm from my own experience and shivered. I could hear her calling my name in my head, repeating it like a mantra that would save her. I wanted to go to her, hold her, calm her, avenge her. I could feel the need for the kill, the hunger growing inside me, and for the first time in years I wanted to release it, indulge it. I spoke her name softly, across the air where the mortal cannot hear. It seemed to calm her, or perhaps it calmed me.

They were coming at me now, their crosses and holy water used as weapons. They seemed disconcerted that I ignored them, and their relics, intent instead upon my lovely Rebeka. The lukewarm water splashed in my face, drawing my attention back to them, but not in the manner they expected. My eyes flashed angrily and I wanted to lash out at them, but I inhaled sharply and calmly wiped my face with one sleeve. "You're wasting your time." I said calmly. "Those trivial symbols mean nothing to me."

It mattered little what the reason for that truth might be ... it was enough that the fact of this disconcerted them more than the reality of Rebeka's dark, unnatural nature. They were certain that I too was a demon masquerading in human clothing, a truth only verified by the burning of my flesh as they dragged me into sunlight, but none of their "normal" purifying rituals affected any response but anger from me. That did not keep them from trying however, until the flood of sunlight falling through the windows faded, and they withdrew, afraid perhaps that our powers might increase with the dark.

Chapter 9

A FULL moon lit the cells that night, bathing my wounded Rebeka in the softest of lights. I held her through the bars, whispering to her. "Stay with me a while longer, Rebeka. I will get us through this. Rest now, tomorrow they will come again." I fed her then from my own wrist. I thought only of keeping her alive, and what new torment the morning would bring. She was weakened by her fight, her hands burned by sunlight, her face red with her tears of fear and pain. I told her stories of the ancient times, before the coming of the Church, of the hunters. I told her of my Jesse, of Moira and Leonard. Near to dawn she slept some, falling into the near comatose sleep of our kind. I drifted too, unable to truly sleep, but riding a nightmare out of that cell for a moment or two.

Then came the dawn, awakening me with a distant pain and the knowledge that Rebeka needed me.

I rose to standing, pulling instinctively away from the light and looked wildly around me to find Rebeka crouched in the dark corner of her cell, in full Change. One of the hunters held a cross tightly to her raised forehead, burning the flesh there as he murmured some Latin phrases beneath his breath. She screamed in agony, clawing at the man until he backed off into the pool of light. I lunged for the bars, forgetting the daylight for the moment, intent on wrapping my arms around him as he came close enough.

Disembodied arms pulled me away from the bars, dragged me to the dirt floor in the center of the light and held me there until I ceased my struggling. Then I was dragged to my feet, doused again with holy water and the great incantations began. I did my best to ignore them, concentrating instead on Rebeka, sending my thoughts of strength and hope, which only served to anger them more. Once the hunter who had detained me in the streets came close enough and I felt the Change come swiftly. I reached for him and came close to getting my teeth into his neck before a hard blow to my stomach knocked me backwards. That brought on more crosses and holy water and Latin prayers. I forced myself to calm, willed away the Change. My insides twisted around me as I listened to Rebeka's torment in the next cell. I was trapped, and there was nothing I could do to help her, or myself.

At some point that day they decided that they could not treat me as they had the others of my kind, that I was some different manner of demon beyond the ability of their rituals and crosses to purify, and instead chose to torment me as they would a mortal in hopes of obtaining my confession. They filled my cell, five of them and the interrogator. They chanted, effectively blocking my perception of what occurred in the next cell. He read to me the charges, many of them lies. He asked me if I would confess my sins so that he might recommend mercy. I was silent.

My dress was torn to the waist to lay bare my back. I was chained to the wall, my breasts and cheek held against the cold rock wall. They whipped me with a cat-o-nine-tails until my back lay in bloody shreds and I drifted in and out of consciousness. All the while they chanted their ridiculous Latin phrases. My mind stuck on them, struggling to translate them in an effort to block out the interrogator's words. "Delictum meum cognitum tibi feci et iniustitiam meum non abscondi."

As they unchained me, my knees buckled and I fell to the floor. My head swam and I am sure I must have been babbling back the translations of their words. "I have acknowledged my sin to Thee, and my guilt I have not concealed...."

More water was splashed in my face to rouse me from my disorientation. "Do you repent? Do you confess your sins?"

I shook my head, not really in answer to his questions, but in an attempt to clear it. I heard a scream and jumped. "Rebeka!" I am sure it was little more than a croaked word, but I felt her respond. She was alive. I turned my attention back to the priest who was now regarding me with a look of disdain.

"Forget the girl," he said. "Your concern now is your soul. Mercy is in your hands. You have only to confess yourself and you will be cleansed. This can all stop now. It can be over."

I held my tongue and he nodded to one of the men standing beside me. A wooden cup was lifted to my mouth, and I could smell a sour wine. I clamped my jaw shut and it took two of them to pry it open. I managed to spit out the first mouthful, but then I was forced to swallow lest they drown me in it. Before it had passed my tongue I could taste the poison, a drug which would shortly bring fever and violent, racking pains. "I can see you are familiar with this method," he said, a smile on his face. "Perhaps then, you know what will follow? Are you prepared to cooperate?"

The chanting renewed, "Domine, ne in furore tuo arguas me, neque in ira tua corripias me." I covered my ears. The drug had begun to spread its fingers through me, creating images in my mind and causing muscles to contract onto themselves. "Are there others like yourself?" he asked. "Like her? Where are they? How many are there?"

I don't know if I answered him, to tell the truth I can't remember many of the questions at all. I know the kind though, aiming to brand other innocents as Vampyre or witches, to release me of my guilt by laying it at the feet of the others. When the pains reached my stomach I began retching, vomiting out an odd mixture of formula and food and wine in a puddle at their feet. I fainted once or twice, welcoming the cool of the blackness in my mind.

With each waking I could hear Rebeka screaming or crying and pleading, and the ever-present chanting, each time the sound ripped my heart and filled my being with rage, each time I would reach inside me to the Change and some new torment would begin. It was as if they knew exactly which moment to start something new, and which of their bloody implements would best suit the purpose laid before them.

I was tied to my chair when I could no longer hold myself upright. I was hurting from a hundred wounds that seemed to no longer be healing. I was hungry. How long had I been there? When had my last meal been? Where was Rebeka? I couldn't concentrate more than a moment or two on any one thought, my mind rambling haphazardly until I felt the stinging blow across my face. "Why do you insist? Why do you make us treat you this way?" He leaned in close to me, his face in mine. His breath smelled of wine. I forced my eyes to focus on his face. "Make your confession, I will make it all end."

I squinted up at him, taken suddenly with the thought that I had no idea what it was I was meant to confess. I started to laugh.

It seemed to anger them more. He moved away and one of the others took his place, an odd looking instrument in its hand. I could smell the blood on it from its last victim. He approached slowly, his eyes intent upon me. Two others came from behind, one pulling my head back against the high back of the chair, the other holding my right arm tightly. I saw then what the instrument was for and my fingers clenched into a ball instinctively. Patiently the one with the tool pried my fingers open, laying claim to one and setting the instrument to the nail. I held my breath and tried not to feel the tormenting pain as he slowly and deliberately pulled the fingernail from its bed. He held up his prize for me to see, then dropped it in my lap and proceeded to the next.

Tears streamed down my face and I believe I screamed, but little sound was made. My hand was on fire, a thing alive. I wanted to shake it, to run from the pain. Never in my life had I felt anything to compare to that. He released me and moved back, blanching only slightly as the Change took over my face. I no longer controlled it, and it responded to the pain freely. The smell of blood only intensified the needs that compelled the Change. But I hadn't any strength, I had only the pain, and as swiftly as it came upon me, the Change left again. The next day they repeated the process on my left hand ... and shortly after that they began on my feet.

Whenever I became too disoriented, too distant they would splash me with their holy water. After the fingernails I lost the true sequence of the things which followed. The torment continued forever. My head was dunked in a barrel of cool rainwater and held under until my lungs would explode in agony and my heart pounded in my chest as if it would follow. I was subjected to things that even the darkest of our kind would never imagine. All the while they demanded I repent of my sins that I might be cleansed of my demons and my soul released clean. I have no idea how long it went on, I lost all sense of time and place as I drifted in and out, withdrawing into the preternatural sleep of my mother's people when the pain was too intense, all the while whispering Rebeka's name. Days and nights blurred together, the faces of the priests became one, their voices drowning all rational thought.

I lost myself at some point, calling out to Rebeka, to Moira, to Jesse ... anyone who might somehow hear me. I thought once that Jesse came, Crenoral lurking in the shadows behind him, then I felt the cold slap of leather against my bare thigh and he was gone. The others came and went as well, Mother and Adan, the small child I had left on the roadway. Reality withdrew and there was only the pain, the terror, and the need to find Rebeka.

When at last it was quiet, and my senses told me I was alone, I opened my eyes. It was daylight. I had crawled into the dark corner purely by instinct in my sleep. I held myself very, very still and listened intently. Somewhere very far away I heard faint music. It must be Sunday morning,

I told myself, and my tormentors have gone off to church to praise their god and themselves. My broken body howled its pain at me, and I could do nothing to ease it. I wondered if Rebeka too were in such a way. I lay still and listened for the sounds of any left behind to tend to us should we awaken, then, in growing alarm, for Rebeka. There was nothing, no sound to tell me she still lived. I squinted through the glare of the puddle of light, but couldn't make out anything. I climbed slowly to my feet, shuffled in painful steps to the very edge of the light.

Still, there was nothing. I called her name in a voice gone hoarse from my screams of pain. Nothing. My heart sank into my toes; my mouth went dry. I forced myself into the light and over to the bars, clinging to them as the heat found its way past the already present pain. I held to the bars as my sensitive eyes adjusted and slowly focused on the cell.

She lay nearly naked, her clothes ripped in her struggles for freedom, her face calm, the Change gone from it, the fury leaving behind only the peace of common death. A three-foot long wooden stake, nearly six inches in diameter impaled her heart, as if they meant to kill a man three times her size. Her hands were curled around it, as if she had been attempting to keep it from her or welcome it to her chest. I whimpered, reaching through the bars as if I might touch her, then backpedaling into the darkened corner as the sunlight became more than I could bear.

I huddled into myself, crying her name, and trying to find some shred of strength. I was tired, wounded ... hungry. I looked up, my eyes just making out her form now that I knew where it was. Something was born inside me. The thoughts in my head were not pleasant ones, but it was a method of survival. I knew I had to survive, more than that, I wanted to survive, to wreak my vengeance upon these Hunters.

I let the Change come, sweeping over my weary form, offering me some respite from the pain of my wounds. I let the anger and pain and fear that had been building in the time of my captivity spill out from my soul, infecting my entire being. I didn't think about my plan, or what it would mean, how I would deal with myself later ... or that I might yet die at their hands. I let the Change come, reveling in the feeling, baring my teeth, and breathing deep, invigorating breaths of the stale air.

When I moved, with the speed of the Change, I took a rat. It wasn't much, but it would start me in the right direction. Then I challenged the sun again, braving the fire to force the bars enough to squeeze through into Rebeka. I knelt beside her, touching her pale skin, her soft, blonde hair. Even in death she was beautiful, her body only beginning to decompose. I kissed her cold cheek, then pressed my lips to her neck. It was truly unthinkable ... to drink from one so long cold, and one with so little really to offer. Her last real meal had been days before, and what I had given hadn't mattered in the end. So much of herself had been spent in her efforts to live.

I bit gently, as if she might somehow yet feel it, and drank in small, garish sips, pulling back as the cold, thick fluid touched my lips. It sat cold and hard in my stomach, small comfort, but enough. I sat back against the wall and let it warm inside me, felt it spreading slowly, giving me some semblance of strength. As I waited for the rush of energy, I trapped two more rats. The more I fed the louder the hunger within me growled. I stood and squinted up into the sun. It was close to noon I guessed. I stooped and picked up the limp, lifeless form of my Rebeka.

The anger surged then, fueled by my snack and the feel of her light frame in my arms. I roared in anguish as I forced the iron door open and emerged into the darkened hallway. The guard died with a broken neck before he was fully aware I was there. I pulled him to me and drank deeply, feeling the warmth return to my body, my wounds beginning to heal.

Up the stairs, hundreds of stone steps carved from the very earth. At the top, servants stopped and stared, but stayed a great distance from me. I reached out for one and drew her very close to me, where there was no denying the demon I am. "Fetch me two dark cloaks and I shall not kill you today." My voice was harsh, filled with fury. She shook from head to toe and nodded fearfully. She returned with the requested garments and I donned one, then draped the other over Rebeka.

"Leave this place, all of you, and tell the others as well. Anyone found alive here tonight will die."

I burst out into the sunlight, pausing only long enough to allow my eyes some semblance of adjustment. We were indeed at the local lord's house, on a hilltop overlooking the village. I hid my face deep in the cowl of the cloak and set off down the hill, my eyes on the small church, gleaming white and bright in the day. I walked with great purpose and dignity, though the sun brought back the searing pain. Down the hill I went, through the town and up into the church. I pushed open the doors of the sanctuary and the Hunter in the pulpit, my friend from the street, turned somewhat pale. I locked the doors behind me and he seemed somewhat green.

The entire congregation, some sixty people or more, not counting the children, looked at me in horror. I must have been something of a sight to be truthful, my borrowed cloak thrown back to reveal my long black hair filled with mud and blood, my face contorted with the Change and rage, the dead Rebeka in my arms. I laid her gently upon the altar and looked up at the Hunter. He was the one

I wanted first, the one who I would hold responsible. The hunger within me was insatiable, fueled by grief and anguish and anger.

Two of them came at me, I suppose in hopes of containing me. The first died when my hand wrapped in his hair and brought his bulging jugular vein within reach of my mouth. I bit viciously, drank harshly, and dropped him, still very much alive and bleeding to death slowly. The second actually took a shot at me, swinging his dagger at my throat. My knee in his groin and a fist to his face sent him to his knees and I fell on him, opening his throat as I had the other's and letting him bleed to death.

The white marble altar was already stained red when I pulled the stake from Rebeka and faced my new enemy. He paled further yet and backed away from the altar. "I might have left this place in peace," I said as I approached him, the sound of my own voice cold and hissing through the fangs. "I might have gone anywhere and left these people to live out their lives in ignorance. Now ... now I cannot. You have taken my Rebeka from me and for that you will pay." I held the stake between us, prepared, it seemed, to use it to end his life.

Instead, I took his shaking hand and held it up between us, turned it over and slowly licked his wrist. It was salty with his fearful sweat. I could feel my heart speed up, keeping pace with his. I took my time, savoring his fear, that of the entire room. They were helpless, watching me. I bit slowly, watching his face, at first afraid, then pain, then the dizzying ecstasy of that kiss as I drained his life away, and, against the flow of blood, forced something of myself back into him. So caught up in the moment was I that his memories, his life passed with little notice, save for the briefest image, a child, a familiar face. It seemed disconnected somehow and more my memory than his, but it passed quickly and I saw only his face as it was now.

I watched that closely, the look in his eyes as he became aware of his dying body, as his heart slowly stopped its beating … as the blood went cold in his veins and the hunger was born in his gut. I pulled away from the bloody wrist as it filled him, and the first Change, uncontrollably strong, took him. I could taste his hunger and his revulsion at it. I grabbed a young girl from the first pew and brought her to him, baring her breasts and holding her lithe body tightly against his. He was awakened to the scent of her, the smell of her flesh, her blood ... the sound of it rushing through her frightened body. I bent her neck and bit it tenderly, opening the wound and pressing it toward him. It was more than he could resist, with the Change so newly upon him, and to his own dismay he found himself drinking hungrily from her, draining her life as I had his and dropping her from numb fingers when he was done.

"There is nowhere for you to go now," I said. "The sun is high outside and you will die if you step into it. Feed now, and feed well, for tonight you must run, far and wide, for I will find you. And I will kill you then."

I watched him fall to his knees and begin praying, an odd thing for one with blood across his face and clothes and the Change so full upon him. I left him to it and returned my attention to the people. They were dumbstruck, or crying, looking at me as though I were a monster, which I was that day.

I dropped my cloak to the floor and beckoned a young boy to me. He came hesitantly, his mother clinging to him. He bowed nicely, but I could taste the fear in him.

"What is your name, boy?"

"Nathan, I am Nathan."

"You have no reason to fear me, Nathan. I shall not hold you accountable. Tell me, who else here deserves this fate?" I asked him. He shook his head.

"No one, ma'am."

"Come now, child, surely other men have done the things this one has, or condoned them, urged them on. Tell me who."

His eyes stole to the lord, an earl if I recall, by the name of Sardone. His eyes grew wide as he realized I was looking at him, but I wasn't prepared to make such a pompous ass into an immortal ass. No, I had a better plan for him. Beside him his young daughter sat, a lass of perhaps sixteen, with beautiful brunette curls and green eyes, a smattering of freckles across her tiny nose. She was nowhere near as hauntingly, achingly beautiful as my Rebeka, but she was a pretty thing. I pointed to her and gestured for her to come to me.

The earl shook his head no, tried to talk me out of my course of action. I smiled, which must have been a frightening sight. "Sit down, my lord. I wasn't speaking to you. Come here, child." She seemed more frightened than the boy, but came, slowly, resigned to her fate, or at least faking it well. I had her sit beside me on the cold marble steps, laid her across my lap and covered her face with one hand as I bent to my task. In minutes, she too was enjoying her first meal as a child of the night, her own father.

I was cold, calculating, starving. I fed greedily, and created monsters of the children of the town. Anyone older than fifteen might be made immortal or taken as food, whichever suited me. The room was filled with the stench of blood and dying. It overwhelmed even my reluctant demon-priest, and I found him feeding most voraciously as the day wore on. All in all, that day I created nearly twenty new children and I fed on more than I ever had since the days I celebrated the festival with Crenoral's clan. I was strong, terrible, and evil, and

I reveled in the release of it, in the heart of my true being allowed at last to be free.

By the time the sun began its descent, the only thing living in the church were my prodigies and myself, and the three or four young children that even in my debauchery, I wouldn't kill. As night fell I gathered them to me, inhaling the bloody scent of the new made. Then, I pulled the priest to me, the Change still upon me, the anger gone cold in my stomach. "Go now, Hunter. Run into the night. Go far and hide well for the time will come when I will hunt for you. On that night, when I find you once more, I will do to you as you have done to me and mine." Somehow I had no doubts that he would somehow survive, despite his hatred for what he now was. I knew we would meet again.

The Change drained out of him. He left that place a ruined man and disappeared into the night, leaving us to finish what I had begun. In the center of all the death, Rebeka lay, her body gone nearly to skeleton, upon the altar. I kissed what had been her cheek tenderly and bid her farewell, then we set fire to the building and my new children and I left.

We swept through the deserted town, cleaning house, so to speak of those who remained, those who had somehow escaped the church that day. It was the darkest of nights I can ever recall. No stars, no moon to light the sky, only the burning of the church behind us as we made our way to the former seat of the earl. Most of that night was spent in the blind fury that had brought me to such deeds. We took possession of the town, of the manor house, of whatever we desired. Come the dawn, we made our bed together, in the very dungeon cell where Rebeka had died.

Chapter 10

I SENT my children out into the next nights to find any hunters we might have missed. For several nights we cleansed the surrounding area of those who would defy us, or who could bring the wrath of the Church back to haunt us. It was cold, harsh. I lost myself in it, in the mind-numbing fever of killing. I took comfort in the days, wrapped in the arms of my children, hidden in the darkness of the dungeon where once I had been prisoner.

I lived darkly in those days, reining in the bloody horror of my dark children, who would become heartless monsters beneath my tutelage. My sin in their creation held me a long while. I let my own self-pity and anguish for my two lost loves drive me deeper into that side of me which Crenoral had loved, partaking in an evil far greater than even my former Brethren had been guilty of. Unwittingly, I had been cause for a transgression beyond even Bestin's at the time of the Birth. Born in that dark, auspicious moment, upon holy ground where even the most innocent of my kin would dare not step foot, but which offers me little detriment, they were robbed of the very nature of their own being, and lost those few bindings of their predecessors. I loosed then, upon the foul night air, a creature unstoppable by the means of modern man to know. Gone were the afflictions of holy water, crosses and whatever other relics might hinder those more naturally made.

This I was to learn shortly after it began, when they brought to me a Hunter, come looking for his lost brothers, clad in his holy armor and holding his mighty golden crucifix as if it alone might save him. They gathered around him, some twenty strong, youthful monsters with the Change full upon them to affect terror in the old man. He hurled great and mighty curses at us, beckoned his god to look upon his situation and deliver him as he had Daniel in the lion's den. I smiled from the small earldom throne, for I knew his efforts were wasted upon me. For many, many long moments, it did not occur to me that they were wasted upon my children as well.

Marie and Édouard, the oldest among them and the instigators of most activities taunted the man, leering in his face as he recited his long prayers. Then he took the crucifix from the man like it was no more than the metal it was formed of. A fight ensued then, and the bunch of them fell upon the Hunter, each wanting some souvenir to claim as their own. Marie and Édouard withdrew, the crucifix held between them, watching as their siblings tore the Hunter apart. They huddled together, conspiring between themselves in the unspoken tongue of their kind until the man was dead, the ornaments of his faith scattered among the faster of them, or the stronger. It is an odd thing indeed, to see one still caught up in the Change and the gleam of a golden cross lighting his face from where it lay upon his chest. Perhaps that was the moment when I saw myself, my transgression. Perhaps that was the moment I began to pull away, unnoticeably for certain, for I was still quite enamored of them, and they needed so much from me at first.

"Come now, children, there is no need to fight." I rose from the small throne and came among them. "The night is young." I put my arms around Marie and Édouard, wrapping my will and thought around them as well. "There are plenty more trinkets to be found. Let us go out into the dark." And, we did.

The beauty of the night graced them tenderly, turning barely mature features to perfect imitations of themselves, molding them forever in that place of absolute beauty between childhood and adulthood. They seemed so fragile and frail when absorbed in some task, or asleep in our family tomb, almost angelic ... and demonic. The knowledge of death shone in their eyes, and their love of life lit up a room. It is hard, even now, not to smile when I picture their faces, especially in those first years when they were young, and so inspired by the night.

They were, however, adolescents, children with the bodies of adults, forever locked in a state of selfish denial of the rest of the world, consumed only by their own lives and needs. Many nights I was forced to reconcile some petty argument, which had grown to a death struggle. There was no line they would not cross, no page of their former mortality they would not turn. Each developed into someone other than who they might have been, all perhaps but the small, shy daughter of the earl.

Maryse was her name, a frail thing with no real will of her own, she often withdrew from the killing, and spent long nights alone in her old rooms. She alone retained some bit of humanity, some calm of her nobility. Occasionally, she would extend that influence upon her brothers and sisters. More often, she simply sat out in quiet protest, her eyes alone speaking of her shame. Always, however, she could be pulled into the fray, pulled along by the desires she despised, convinced by the others to partake.

"Are we devils?" she asked me once, when we were alone in the dungeon bedroom we shared.

"Devils? What makes you say so?" I asked, brushing out my hair. Her question brought back a twinge of myself, a piece of my conscience emerging.

"We kill. We live in darkness and revel in our sins. Are we the devils the Hunters name us?"

"I know no more devils, Maryse. They are all gone."

"Ah, then there were devils once. And we are all that is left of them."

"Yes, the progeny of evil. That is what we all are ... us, and the humans as well. The good and the evil are no longer."

"Then may we all reap the rewards of our fathers." She left then, and I sat pondering her, pondering all of them. She was, of course, right. Reward would come.

I held them to me, my immortal children, I proved to be a poor mother, unable to give myself completely to them, once I had begun to recognize the evil of my deeds. I ruled harshly, imposing strict rules upon them to keep them and the small earldom we dwelled in, safe from the outside dangers and to keep them all well fed. They came quickly to despise my rules, and eventually, me. My dark side slowly released me, and the guilt of my actions drove me back to my formula and away from the gluttonous feedings we had shared in the beginning. I took my meals alone in the dark shadowed halls of our home while my children slept below me.

My dark children derided me for my hypocrisy, much more entitled to it than my immortal brethren had been, and far, far crueler in it. They hunted the dark and increasingly unpopulated area surrounding us, occasionally bringing their victims back to taunt and tempt me. They despised me for who and what I was, what I refused to be, what I had made them into ... and I deserved it all, accepted it all. It is common for one made to the night to despise his or her creator, to hate the one who gave them the cursed gift, for the nature of the gift itself lends it to such things. Mortal men were not made for immortal lives, nor the sacrifices required of it, and eventually, if even for a short time, all who are thus hate themselves for it, and that hate easily transfers to the true villain.

The worst for it was René and his twin sister Racelle. They took greatest offense at all that had transpired and greatest joy in throwing their evil in my face. One night, closer to morning than was prudent for any of them to be about, they returned from a hunt with blood on their faces and clothes. They reeked of their dinners, a mixture of human and animal. They were loud and rowdy, like mortals after an all-night drinking binge. They woke me from my light slumber near the fire as they came in. Behind them the others gathered. Racelle laughed raucously as René stole the book from my hand.

"I am given to believe in the absolute of evil, and thereby, of good. There is evidence enough of such matters as to make them seem beyond discussion. The existence of the Demons of the Hill is tolerated by civilized man simply by virtue of their opposites among us." He snorted and tossed the book to one of the others. "Really, Mother. What dribble you read these days! What happened to those glorious accounts of the Family? The bloodbaths ... the killing? Now, there is something worth reading." He leaned over me and the smell of the blood upon him stirred the cravings I had been fighting. "Do you smell her, Mother? She was so sweet ... a new bride, seduced from the arms of her groom."

"Enough, René. It is late. You should all be off to bed."

"We are not babies to be hastened off with the rising sun, Mother," Racelle countered, joining René in front of me. "You surely must see that we are not children anymore."

I could smell the distinct scent of a man about her ... the groom I imagined. "I hope you enjoyed him," I said, seeking to rise and move away from the tantalizing scent. They followed me, knowing the struggle going on within and hoping to drive me back to the ways of their youth. I reached for my bottle, hoping to stave off the worst of it, but Racelle grabbed it and danced away.

"I did, Mother ... I enjoyed him immensely, so much more than you will this ... dribble."

"I enjoy my dribble just fine, Racelle," I replied, attempting to avoid getting angry. I reached for the bottle, but she tossed it to René.

"Come now, Mother, don't you crave the taste of the real thing? I can smell it in you ... if there were a human among us now, you would kill."

The anger was rising in me now, and the hunger had grown with their teasing. "I said enough! You are making me angry. Leave now!" I stopped chasing the bottle and stood still in the center of the room. They too stopped their dizzying dance around me. I was breathing in heavy gulps, trying to keep down the fury that lay just beneath the surface, the sudden desire to teach the insolent creatures just who was in control. They stared for a long, long moment, then Racelle started to laugh. As René joined her, he dumped the contents of the bottle, creating a strange red puddle on the priceless rug beneath his feet. It was enough to send me over the edge.

In one swift movement I grabbed René and pulled him to me, my fangs flashing in the dim light of the fire. The laughing stopped as I opened his wrist with those teeth and quicker than he could have imagined drained him to the point of collapse. He was right about one thing ... she had been a sweet thing. I dropped him in a heap on the floor and caught Racelle as she would have fled. "Now, have we had enough games, or shall we play some more?" I asked. She quivered in my hand, no match for the strength of my years, my fury.

"Enough, Mother, enough," she whispered.

I dropped her beside her brother. "Good, then get him downstairs before I change my mind. The rest of you clean up this mess and get to bed." I walked away in silence, the heat of anger and the blood agitating me beyond the ability to rest. Daylight was only moments away, but I could not sleep.

Of course, I, so much like Crenoral I see now, refused to see the truth of it, choosing instead to believe that I was loved, as I, in my twisted maternal need, loved them. They were the replacement for the brief, burning torch of Rebeka's company, and I was willing to overlook their transgressions for a time in order to keep them beside me. Perhaps I fooled only myself, perhaps I was the biggest fool of all.

As caught up as I was in them, even I could see our sanctuary could not last. The lords of the lands would come, the Church would send more priests, people would search out their lost relatives. The time would come that we would need to leave the place. I tried to tell them of the dangers that existed outside, of the Hunters who would torment them until they wished I had killed them on that day, of the others like us who drink from the chalice of human flesh but might not recognize them as Kin and take their lives. They listened, but heard nothing, as is often the case with adolescent children.

The creatures I had created would leave me slowly, finding their way out into the night, for this is the way of children. I felt very much alone and uncertain how to end it. Eventually, between my conscience and my pride came the day when I at last realized the full extent of my evil, the day when I would, at last, relinquish them to the night.

I left them quietly, slipping off into the cold of a winter night, knowing they would not miss me, probably not even mark my absence for many nights to come. I gave thought to ending my abomination, to burning them out as I had my Brethren, but I could not bring myself to it. There was no conviction to the thought, no need to punish and extinguish, and no Jesse to provide it. They were not prepared for what would follow, but I knew that those who were strong and still able to adapt would survive the coming months and years as they adjusted to life beyond the confines of the guardianship of their mother. I didn't journey far, hovering just outside of their awareness, hidden by their own blindness.

I watched and waited as they felt the first thrill of freedom from parental constraints, as they grew to realize I wasn't coming back, as they stretched their wings out around them. The world grew black. They killed with abandon, flinging themselves upon their prey and drawing the attention of the outside world I had done so much to keep at bay. They would discover that the world they had abandoned hadn't yet forgotten the evil that lurks in the dark. Their bloody terror spread outward from the place, stretching dark, cold fingers into the neighboring lands.

Eventually, Hunters came, and Hunters died. A few of my children died with them, their heads sliced clean, their bodies burned. Still, I waited, praying they learned their lessons before it was too late. They did not. For each death of their own, they repaid humanity tenfold, nearly eliminating the population of the small earldom. The Church returned then with a vengeance, bringing the human king with them. I fought with myself nightly, wanting to go to them, to help them escape what was meant to be, and knowing I could not. If they were to survive, it would have to be on their own.

Several more died in the following months, as they battled the inevitable tide of humanity, and the superior resources of the Church. One by one they vanished, dead or simply gone into the night, until only Maryse remained. I was near at hand, pressing my presence into her mind, ready to go to her, on the night when she emerged from the castle. The armies of the king and his Church stood circling the place where she approached the small regal human to whom she would offer her life. Her eyes found mine where I hid and I could feel her resignation, her near relief. She would seek no help from me.

In all the pomp and circumstance to which she had been born, looking more a pale, frightened child, than the monster she had become, she knelt before the man her father had served, and for the sins of her Clan she surrendered the lands, the castle, and her life. One swift blow from a giant broadsword severed her head cleanly from her body and she was gone.

A great cheer rose up from the gathered men and the order given for them to take the castle. I stood alone as they rushed inside to root out any who might be hidden within. The castle was burned, cleansed of the evil that had burrowed into it. In those days the Church had turned itself to lesser demons, or demonizing those who dared believe differently, but returned its attention to us with a vengeance. A great exorcism was performed in the town, and the process of cleansing the memory of the people began. Hunters were sent out once more, in vast numbers to hunt down my children and my brethren. Those who remained of the elder Family turned to hunting my children as well, for bringing back the terror. It was a cold time for us all.

Chapter 11

THERE WAS no trusting among the Family that remained, and we avoided each other as we avoided the Hunters. Mankind was perhaps safest then, in those years when our thoughts were on self-preservation, feeding only when the need grew too strong and abandoning rich hunting grounds for fear of attack. I returned to my wandering ways, avoiding friendships and distractions. I heard tales of the Vampyre, many of them greatly exaggerated or straight out lies. From time to time I could hear the Voices of my children, warning each other of dangerous towns and cities, or advising each other of quiet, peaceful places to rest. Simple, cold-blooded killing was nearly impossible for them then, but they learned that they could take a little, leaving a victim alive, but satisfying their needs. I heard rumors that some of them had made alliances with a human or two, enchanting them with the glamour of the night, or purchasing them with extravagant gifts, keeping them as companions to satisfy their hunger.

As for myself, I was weary of it all and chose a place to rest high in the mountains near the lands of my birth, where the snow caressed the jagged peaks year round. There I had hidden in years past, there I would return from time to time throughout my life. In this place I had discovered a cavern, deep and dry and I filled it with my most valuable treasures, those items I would not, or could not, part with. There was room enough to make a home of sorts, a sleeping chamber made comfortable enough with furs and blankets and a place for cooking and such. I had, in my first running from the family, hidden there, gathering animal skins and in later years supplying it with oil for light and other needs. The cave was placed high up on a mountain face with only a treacherous path leading down to it from above and possessed of the singularly most beautiful vista I have ever or will ever see.

It was almost as if you could see the entire world from that one spot, especially if gifted with the preternatural vision of the Family. It was cold and silent, existing in the space between mankind's domains, undiscovered, save by me. The heights were, perhaps, too much for the human frame, the air too light. I was alone. Over a year I worked at preparing the cave for my sojourn, my time away from the world at large. I carried and dragged supplies up the mountainside, through trees and meadows to the rocky crevice that hid the path.

I craved the silence I remembered from the days of my first escape, the solitude, after all the killing. Those first years I scarcely left the cavern, except for food and even that was a desire that seemed to have left me. I savored the silence, the lack of anything, anyone. I read by oil light and candles from those volumes I could carry with me from the towns several days' journey down the mountain. I tried my hand at painting and poetry and writing down the deeds I had done.

I suppose in some fashion I lost my senses, reliving so much pain over and over until the words fell to the page in perfect pieces. I laughed and cried alone, until the sounds faded into the distant hills. I spoke to myself or to no one in particular, or to the ghosts of those I had loved or lost or killed.

After a time, several years at least, I began wandering further from the cave, nowhere near civilization, but far enough to hear once more the whisperings of my kind on the breezes. Never did I acknowledge them, or call to them, but I would sit in a grassy meadow where the Voices were the strongest and listen for hours at a time. Other times I would explore the deep ravines and caverns of the mountains, taking great perverse pleasure in leaving some mystical mark upon walls so deep within the earth, that should mankind ever find them they would puzzle for centuries over how the marking came to be.

It was inevitable I suppose, for them to find me, for my life to pull me away from the childish pleasure I had found in my retreat. I had decided I was hungry, after a long time without mortal food or blood or formula. Days and nights were as a blur of time to me, there was little distinction. When I was hungry, I searched for food. It was late in the night, in the early summertime and I wandered aimlessly from berry bush to fruit tree, following the scents and eating as I chose. I felt her, long before she exploded into the grove where I sat awaiting her.

She was dirty as if she had crawled from an earthen grave without pausing to bathe. She was breathless and terrified, flushed with fear. A pale faced and quiet young man accompanied her. She fell to her knees in front of me, her eyes wide as if disbelieving of my existence. "Hello, Racelle," I said, leaning forward to cup a hand to her cheek. "What brings you to my solitude?"

"Mother, he has come. He killed René. He's not far behind me. You must help us."

"Who is darling?" It was all surreal to me, as if I were watching it from a distance somehow.

"The Hunter."

Something in me woke at that moment, and the months and years faded. In my mind I saw him as he had last been, crazed with the blood and self-loathing. I had promised to find him one day. It seemed he was no longer content to wait. I pulled Racelle to me then, probing her mind sharply to understand what had transpired to bring her to me. I saw René and their human companions burned at the stake, while Racelle watched from her hiding place, unable to stop it. "Come, child, quickly." I stood and gathered her in my arms, bustling her up the mountainside to the cave.

I could feel him coming, though still a good distance away. He doubled his pace as he felt me, and I had to reach behind me for the mortal boy who could not travel as fast. There was still an hour's journey up the mountain at a pace the boy wouldn't keep. "A long way up this hill is a crevice. Hidden in that crevice is a trail. It will lead you further up, then turn as if going off the cliff. Follow it. Watch your step. It will take you to safety. I will deal with the Hunter." I pushed them and turned. She was terrified enough to follow my directions without question. The Hunter was coming fast. I stopped and stood my ground, waiting for him to come.

I could almost taste him, the Change upon me before he had even appeared. He too was in full Change, blood across his face and across the red cross emblazoned upon his chest. His eyes were wild, flashing with first anger, then joy, then fear and back to anger. "What have you done, Hunter?" I said coldly.

"Only what I was created for, Mother." He spat the word contemptuously at me and began pacing furiously.

"I have left you to your own life, Hunter, when I could have come to you and finished what was begun when you killed my Rebeka. Go, and I'll not take your life now."

"I don't think so. Would that you had ended my life long ago. Now, you must contend with what you made." He moved closer and I could smell the madness which had blossomed within him in the years since I had last seen him. He was quite insane, and I had done this to him. It struck me as ironic and I chuckled.

"You kill your own kind, Hunter. You don't seem to understand yourself."

"I understand perfectly. I am the dark avenging angel, the touch of God himself, sent and empowered to cleanse the evil of your kind." He stopped and cocked his head to one side as if something about me seemed odd to him. "You should know that Mother, He sent you to make me."

"You are what you are because you took Rebeka from me, Hunter. It was my way of punishing you for your sins."

His teeth flashed in the moonlight. "Sins ... *my* sins? You are one to talk about such things, aren't you? So self-righteous, so pious. Remember, I was there that day. I know exactly what you are."

With that he flew at me, knocking me over backward into the cold, hard ground. We grappled for a few minutes before I was able to rise again and back off a few paces. It was odd, but the old anger and anguish seemed dimmed, and I felt no overwhelming desire to kill. He was right in one respect, I was not one to judge him, not after all I had done. I moved away, trying to draw him away from the trail where Racelle and her companion had withdrawn. He followed, intent now upon his new prey, and the old forgotten.

He tackled me once more, driving me to the grass, his teeth bared as he dove in for the kill. I pushed him off and rolled free, his teeth just grazing one shoulder. Before I could regain my feet he had his teeth buried in the fleshy part of my calf, his jaws locked. I screamed as I felt the burn of the wound, and the warmth of the blood being drawn through it. My hand closed on a rock and I cracked it against his head until he released me. My nails raked across one cheek, drawing bloody welts down his face, stark contrast to the pale glow of his skin. I limped away, trying to regain some composure and prepare for his next attack.

He was lost in his rage, no longer was there any resemblance to sanity in him. He fought like an animal, wounded and fighting for its life. It was all I could do to protect myself. I pushed him away each time he got close enough to bite me, grunting with the effort. His own voice was reduced to growls of anger and low moans of pain, punctuated with a wordless yelling that shook the trees around us. Finally, he wrapped his arms around me and I felt his teeth clamp down on my shoulder. In pure instinct I bit down as well, finding his bulging jugular with ease. The bitter taste repulsed me, the blood infested with whatever disease had ravaged his mind. His blood was cold, thick, bitter. It only served to madden me further. I drank as quickly as I could, trying not to taste the illness that coursed through him, infecting him fully, wanting only to finally kill this man who had been a monster long before he had met me. My stomach churned with disgust as the blood hit it, lying cold in the pit of my belly.

I closed my thoughts to it and drank rapidly. His thoughts however were open to me, like I had peeled back the canvas of a gypsy's tent. What I saw there repulsed me more than the blood, and educated me as well. In a flash of insight, or omniscience or shared memory, I saw into his sickened mind, uncontrolled, governed only by lunacy. I saw flashes of his childhood in an orphanage, his days in the seminary where he was first touched by the fever. Then, an image of Rebeka as he had seen her, a cold, calculating killer, a demon. It sent a shudder through me. Then, the dark image beside her, the protector, the true demon, and I was startled to see her wearing my face. I watched our torture and torment from his eyes outside the cells, I heard his voice ask shakily for mercy from his superiors. I heard him argue, not for our lives, but for the end of the torture, the swift mercy of death. I felt him being pushed into the cell, the stake in his hand, the absolute horror at the act filled me suddenly and I shrank away from his thoughts.

I realized as I watched through his eyes that he had not been the true villain. He had killed Rebeka, to be sure, but he had been ordered to the act, in order to prove that he had not softened in his resolve to the cause. He had become violently ill after, and was rewarded by his superiors with the privilege of the Sunday morning service where I found him.

I saw myself then, much younger, my face wet with tears. I heard my own voice say "I will follow you." Jesse's voice whispered "I love you." It startled me and I would have pulled away if I could. Then I saw myself as a child, at play in the night as I had with Adan. Memories of lives connected somehow to this man … this Hunter … memories he could not possess. The images grew chaotic, emotions spilling out that confused me, faces he couldn't possibly have known. Crenoral, Vahe, a reflection of Jesse's face.

The bitterness gave way then to something more gentle, more plain and I knew I was drinking back what he had already taken from me. It could go on for hours that way. My hands released him first, then my teeth, blood spilling from his open neck. Still, he clung to me, drinking greedily. I fought, pulling hard to escape him. Eventually, I won, and I backed away, feeling the skin tear where his teeth had lodged, the blood draining from the wound. He screamed in inhuman rage, the sound echoing eerily in the mountains around us, returning on the soft night breeze. Once more he came at me and we fell together, moving further and further down the side of the mountain.

I was dazed by what I had seen, weakened with my blood loss, but I knew he was weakened as well, despite the strength of his anger. I hoped to outlast him, to keep him from killing me, but no longer desiring to kill him instead. What I would do next, I didn't know, hadn't even thought about. It was foolish I admit, but I wasn't thinking very clearly. The blood had clouded my mind. I had taken so much of his infection inside of me. I could feel it working its way into my body, taste it in my mouth. I feared I might never escape it.

At that moment I felt the Presence of another. One old in the night, a member of the Family I had known in my childhood. It startled us both and we pulled free of each other, blood covering us as we turned and looked for him. I stepped away from the Hunter trying to find my bearings. Then, the earth beneath me gave way and I watched the sky grow distant. I reached up, and saw the briefest glimpse of a pale white face, half-familiar. "I will come for you." I heard vaguely, whispered in my mind.

I flailed about in the air, grasping about for something to catch a hold of and stop my headlong drop. I turned so that I could watch the ground coming to me. I don't remember screaming, but I must have. It seemed an eternity. I hung, suspended in air forever. I looked up again, for the Hunter, wondering if he had fallen too, and briefly, who the Other was. The ground reached up to embrace me, wrapping cold arms of solid rock around a body suddenly limp and frail. My heart froze as my breath exploded out of me and I felt as if my lungs had followed it. I lay suspended in that moment for longer than seemed possible, at the very brink of death, looking into it with eyes frozen open. Then, quite impossibly, I landed without notice, no sensation, no pain, only a cool blackness that separated me from the world.

I held to the blackness as though it would keep me from the pain, but woke soon enough with the knowledge that I was laying broken upon the ground. It came slowly, each tiny piece of shattered bone calling out its injury in its own tiny voice until my body shook with the chorus. Blood seeped into the ground below me, my blood, his blood ... though I couldn't identify its source or the depth of the injury. My eyes were open, but there was precious little within my range of vision, a few stars, a sliver of the forgotten moon. At times that faded and there was nothing at all. I could feel my lungs struggling to breathe, to take in some measure of air, but they seemed to be crushed by the incredible weight of my ribs which lay in pieces in my chest. I couldn't speak, though all I wanted to do was scream out in agony. I would have been crying if I could only have figured out how.

My thoughts flickered to the Hunter, and I tried to sense his presence, to lift my thoughts from the rocky ground where they seemed mired. There was nothing. I thought I heard sounds, like people approaching. No one came. I drifted in and out of conscious thought, and further and further away from reality. Time seemed to have stopped as I struggled against the agony.

I heard someone coming. I tried to make some sound to bring them to me, but nothing came. After a small eternity a face came close to mine. It startled me, so close, right above my face. Who? Who could this be? It wasn't Rebeka. That seemed somehow wrong. It was a young boy, with a pale face and dusty brown hair cut short above his ears. He seemed stunned. I thought I moved my hand to touch him, but it never moved. His hand floated above my nose and mouth, his head pressed against my chest. "She's breathing," he said. There was someone else hovering nearby. It must have been Racelle. No, the voice was deeper.

"There isn't time to get her to safety, it's nearly dawn. Cover her, and we'll come back for her tonight." The boy covered me with a dark, heavy cloth, blocking out my limited vision. Then they both withdrew. I felt them leaving and wanted to scream out to them to return.

I spent the day there, beneath that stifling cloth, staring through it into the bright summer sky, unable to even feel the material against my skin, save as a heavy weight. The pain, never fully registered, was gone, or more to the point, it had become so intense that I could no longer consciously feel it. I thought to myself that I must be dead, at long last dead. It didn't occur to me at that moment that were I dead, I would not possess such thoughts. My mind wandered.

I wanted to know where the Hunter had gone, if he too was dead, broken upon the stones. I worried for Racelle and the boy, alone with one of the old ones. Where had that Other gone? Why had he come there? Oh, yes, the Hunter. He must have come for the Hunter. But why? And, who was he? I had sensed no malice from him toward me or Racelle, but who can know another's mind? What had he meant with those final thoughts from the precipice?

I think somewhere through the day I came to understand that I was indeed alive, but only barely so. The heat of the sun registered through the dark cloth as a distant, half-felt memory that couldn't quite reach me. I saw Jesse, felt him nearby. I reached for him, but he stayed just out touch, his face floating in my delusion. It occurs to me now that I was quite insane, driven there by my own guilt and hatred and the unfathomable pain of my fall. Insanity would be my companion awhile, perhaps saving me in the end.

Chapter 12

WITH THE setting of the sun they came, the boy and the Other, lifting my broken body from the stones of the ravine floor and beginning a long trek to some unknown place. The pain rushed back as if my body had suddenly remembered it. In absolute anguish I felt each jarring step up the trail. I concentrated on the pain of it, hoping it would give me just enough of something to make some sound they might hear. I couldn't read the Other, he was distant, closed to me, but I could hear his soft voice as he spoke to the boy, instructed him to wash me and brush out my wild hair. I was being prepared for my burial. The thought terrified me, amplified by the remembered ordeals of a lifetime.

I needed to tell them that I was alive. I screamed inside, but no sound came. My heart beat so sluggishly even I was uncertain at times I lived. I lay upon some rock as the boy slowly bathed me in cool water from the spring near the place where I had fallen, my eyes open and staring into the night sky. The stars were bright and sparkling above us. Occasionally I could see a glimpse of one or the other. Each touch of their gentle ministrations brought back new reminders of the pain until it filled me and I could almost feel nothing at all. I thought of all the times I had wished for death, willed it to come, wanted it ... and now, here, truly facing it perhaps for the first time, I wanted nothing more than to escape the icy grip of its greedy hands. "Careful boy, she'll not thank you for greater injury," the voice said as my leg slipped from the boy's hands.

"I don't know if you can hear me, Amara," that voice said, hovering just over me. He was very close. "I must hide you now, while I see to it that the Hunter and his friends are gone. You will recover, and I will return for you."

Then, unexpectedly, I felt a warm flow of liquid on my lip, blood, slipping across my tongue, dripping into my throat. I could only taste the lingering flat taste of one who has been dead, but it heartened me that he would feed me before consigning me to my grave.

Once more I was lifted, and they wrapped me in a dark cloth, winding it around me, blocking out what little I could see. I was carried to the grave, which had already been dug, and lowered into it. Roughhewn timber scraped my raw skin. Each shovel full of dirt hit the close plank of wood above me, like lead as it struck. I was barely alive, scarcely breathing, and yet I could feel that little bit of air being robbed from me. My heart suddenly resumed its beating, roaring in my ears, the blood pounding through me so that I wondered if they couldn't hear it. Then, quite suddenly, it was quiet. I heard no more.

For a long time, I had little or no awareness save for the beating of my heart and the furious anger of my broken body. I couldn't count the days, months, years that passed. I was alternately on fire and frozen. I felt my limbs swell and contract and swell again. I felt the weight of the dirt pressed coldly against me. My conscious thought drifted from memory to memory. The absolute quiet overwhelmed me, and I prayed for some small sound.

When the silence became too great, I would try to make some noise, but for a long time my voice still failed me. When at last it returned it was small, weak, and I would talk to myself aloud until it became little more than a whisper. I babbled incoherently.

In one moment of lucid thought I realized my eyelids had finally closed and I spent a great deal of time exploring that little wonder, opening and closing them as if they had never before moved. In another moment I felt the light kiss of air, small and nearly unnoticeable, across my cheek. At times I did nothing more than laugh hysterically at the unbelievable horror of my situation, unable to do more. My thought processes were slow and cumbersome, and more and more what true thoughts I had formed around the fiery hunger building within me. I had not fed in a very long time, and what I had taken from the Hunter had soured and burned inside me, contributing perhaps to the madness that held me. The little that the Other had offered was small comfort against the desire. The hunger went beyond the mere physical need at times, and there were moments when I felt sure I could claw my way up out of the ground if only a hot blooded creature would simply pass overhead.

Other times I lay quietly and accepted my fate, but never for long. I would sleep, long dreamless sleep where the blackness claimed me for its own. Eventually something, anything would touch my consciousness and bring me back to the fear, the pain, the desperation. At some point I discovered that the sides of my tomb were shored up with wood, and wood kept the cold earth from smothering me. Somewhere near my face a thin, hollow reed channeled outside air to my desperate lungs. I would weep for days on end, scream until my voice and thoughts abandoned me, whisper to myself deliriously.

More than once I caught myself talking to those I had known as if they were there beside me in my mountain grave. I heard them from time to time as well, the sounds of children laughing, the chanting of religious rites, Crenoral's cold and unforgiving tones, Rebeka's voice crying out for vengeance. I saw Jesse's face repeatedly, as the Change came over him for the first time and he fully realized what he had become.

Sometimes the faces blurred and Adan was Jesse, Jesse was the Hunter, Rebeka became Adroushan, Adroushan became Damen until I was spinning trying to sort it out. I saw the gestures and expressions on Rebeka's face that I found so enduring on Adroushan's. I heard Crenoral's words about Jesse, how he'd given him to me again, and I began to wonder if it might somehow be true. If Jesse was Adan returned to me, and the Hunter was Jesse come back for revenge, could Rebeka have been Adroushan come back? Were such things possible?

Through it all my body healed. Slowly, achingly, until the overwhelming pain was largely gone. I did not know how long I lay there, how many years passed by. It was many, many years however. This I did know. With the pain went much of the insanity, and in its place was left only the hunger. It burned like a thing alive and apart, until I felt that it alone would drive me from the remainder of my senses.

Then, he came. I felt him for days before he came close enough that he might hear me, screaming with all of my inhuman rage and strength, calling him to me, directing him to the unmarked spot where I lay. I couldn't know who he was, or why he had come this way. I doubt there was any conscious thought on my part at all. My body had healed as far as it would without nutrition, without blood. The hunger controlled me. It was the hunger that called him, that brought him to me. It was the hunger which brought me to begin clawing at my prison walls, even as he began to dig down to me.

How delicious was the air that first kissed me through my dark shroud ... how warm the breezes that caressed me as he lifted me from that grave ... how sweet the blood pounding through the little vein in his neck as he loosed me from my burial cloth. My own heart echoed the flow of that blood in perfect rhythm, the hunger roaring, demanding. The Change slipped over me almost unnoticed and I could not help myself had I chosen to. I fell upon him and drank, all the years of starvation pulling me into the dizzying dance of death.

I tasted one older than myself when finally, I did more than swallow greedily. He lay beneath me, patient, trusting me to stop. He was the same as the one who had come on the night of my death, who had buried me here all those years before. I stopped and pulled back, licking at the blood that clung to my lips. I looked at him in astonishment, not truly recognizing him, but taken by his age and faith. He was dressed simply, not quite elegantly, the darkness of his clothes interrupted by the splashes of dirt and mud. He sat quietly, regarding me with something of a smile on his face.

And what I sight I must have been that night, my body covered in dirt and mud, my hair gone long and wild around me, reaching nearly to the ground; dirty, broken fingernails far longer than seemed possible. My face must have been kissed with madness, the last vestiges of the Hunter within, caressed by my own turn at lunacy. I stared back at him for a long, long time. "Dovan," I finally said, my voice hoarse and hardly recognizable as my own.

"Amara," he responded, the small smile growing slightly.

I could feel the blood ... his blood ... flooding through my weak body, and calling out for more. It was all I could do not to fall upon him and drink again. I was shaking with shock and need, my heart thundering in my chest. Dovan. The last of the three brothers who had begun us all, a memory from my childhood. I sat back away from him, as if his presence was a harbinger of my end, an omen of my past sins returned to haunt me.

"Don't be frightened child," he said softly, lifting one hand to me. "I came for you, as I said I would." He stood, brushing the dirt from him with a single swipe of one hand. "Come. We should find you some food, you must surely be starving." He scooped me from the ground into his arms like a small child. "I doubt you can walk yet, and if you can, it won't be for long. I've prepared us a place."

He didn't speak again, carrying me through the dark mountain night in silence until his keen, nocturnal senses located a nearby stag. He laid me gently on the ground, and disappeared. He wasn't gone very long, but to my depraved mind it seemed an eternity, and I began to fear his absence as much as I feared his presence. When at last he returned, the deer was with him, docile in his hands. Two small puncture wounds adorned its neck. It was full-grown, but still young, full of life. I all but sprang from the ground to wrap myself around it, riding it to the ground as I drank away that life. My stomach growled, even as the hunger cooled some. My sharp, raised teeth tore at the meat between them, ripping bloody ribbons of it to chew and swallow. I was like some animal feeding in a frenzy, unable to stop myself even when my stomach was filled.

Dovan pulled me from the animal's carcass and held me tightly as I shook with excitement and hunger and finally tears. I could not make the Change leave me, my face remained that of the monster I had tried to control and never fully had. When the tremors ceased at last, Dovan gathered me up once more and we journeyed further down the mountain. Half the night we went, and I was nearly asleep on his shoulder when he stopped, stooping to enter a cave not unlike my former residence, although with much more elegant appointments.

The outer cave was small, unremarkable and bare. Further inside was a larger chamber, with a plush rug and hand-carved furniture, strange lamps that burned with a soft glow and lit the room like the sun. Beyond that was yet another room, a bedchamber fit for royalty. The bed was hand-carved as well, its four posters rising up to support the black velvet drapes and canopy. Black lace adorned the mattress and pillows. Upon that mattress he laid me, with the softest movements and a gentle kiss on my raised brow. "Are you still hungry?" he asked and I nodded.

"I shall bring you something. Rest. Your body still has much healing to do."

I had a thousand questions to ask of him, of myself. I wanted to know why he had rescued me, where he had been all those years ... what had happened to the Hunter, and to Racelle ... but sleep beckoned me and almost before he was gone from the room, I slept.

I was disoriented when I woke, half believing his coming had been a dream and that I was still in my grave. I could hear him nearby, and I could smell ... food. I sat up quickly, too quickly I judged by the way my vision swam and pain I had forgotten registered in my head. He steadied me with one hand and offered me a bottle in the other.

"I doubt I'm as good at it as you must be by now, but it should be passable," he said as I raised it to my lips, barely hearing his words. The flat, not-quite right taste of the formula ran past my tongue and down my throat as I guzzled quickly. I drained the bottle completely and handed it back.

"Not bad, actually," I managed to say, already reaching for the next bottle he was uncorking. I drank that half way, then paused to catch my breath. On the tray beside the bed was a bowl of dark, rich looking broth and a half a loaf of bread. He saw my eyes on it and handed it to me.

"You might want to take it easy, child. You don't want to make yourself ill." I drained the broth, and sat back with the bread cradled to me like a baby.

I could feel the combination of meals working the magic of healing inside of me, and knew from the feeling that it would be awhile yet before I was up to my own hunting. "Why?" I asked, gnawing on the bread.

"Which why?" he asked, sitting almost hesitantly on the chair beside the bed. "Why did I come for you? Why did I leave you there? Why did I return? There are many questions. I have some of the answers." He watched me, his dark eyes veiled beneath his thick lashes as he thought about his words. "For now, let me answer the questions I see in your eyes, the rest will work itself out later."

"I came that night to warn you of your child's activities, the one you call the Hunter. His name is Daniel, if that matters to you. I knew he was coming for you. Don't ask me how, I knew. I would have reached you before him, or even before Racelle, but I ran into some of his mortal brethren. When I arrived, it was too late. You were gone." He shifted in his seat and I thought I sensed something of apprehension about him. "I chased him, but he got away. Racelle was hysterical when I returned. It was her companion and I who covered you to protect you from the sun, and who buried you."

I set the bread on the bed and raised the bottle, draining the remainder in one swallow. "Why? If you knew I was alive, how could you bury me there?"

"To protect you. Daniel was still in the area, so I didn't want to hide you in a cave where he or anyone else might find you. In the ground he wouldn't be able to sense you, he might think you dead. You needed the time to recover. It was all I could think of. Perhaps it was cruel."

"Perhaps? *Perhaps* it was cruel?" My voice was harsh, more so than I meant it to be. I tried to remind myself that he had come back for me. "How long?"

"Is it important?"

"How long did you leave me there, Dovan?"

"Seventy-two years."

I felt like he had kicked me in the stomach. "Seventy-two...?" I tried to imagine all that might have taken place in those years, of where Moira might be.

"She is safe," he said. "I saw her only a year ago. She is quite well."

"How dare you?" I spat the words out, sitting forward, trying to read him as easily as he had just read me. I was furious, but I wasn't really sure if it was anger at being buried in the ground for so long, or for the way he read me, or his presumption to interfere at all. "What gives you the right?"

"Would you rather I left you to him? He was winning that night you know. If I hadn't shown up when I did ... you would have died anyway." He stood and paced away. He was agitated, but I couldn't tell by what. To make matters worse, I couldn't tell myself how I felt. "I came because I had reason. I meant to find you, protect you. I've tried before, but you were never very open to assistance." He kept his back to me, his thoughts and emotions shuttered tightly against me. "You should rest. It will be quite some time before you are well enough to take care of yourself again."

He was gone before I could respond. I simmered in my mix of emotions, the hurt anger, the appreciation for his generosity, the outrage at his presumption. He was right, my body was not yet strong enough to support me, and was already pulling me back to sleep.

When next I woke there was a woman in the room, quietly cleaning. A new bottle sat on the table beside the bed. The smell of her filled the room, wakening the part of me that wanted her. I sat up slowly, reaching for the bottle though I wanted to be reaching for her. I took a long, slow drink and when I was done she was looking at me. "Are you feeling better?" she asked, just a hint of an accent in her voice.

I nodded, hoping she wouldn't come too close, lest I lose myself to the hunger building inside me again. "Good. Dovan went out for awhile. He should be back shortly. Would you care for something to eat?"

"That would be nice," I said.

She curtsied so politely and withdrew, returning moments later with a tray. The same rich broth and more bread was joined by some fruit and cheeses. "I do hope it's to your liking. I'm rather out of practice," she said as she set it on the bed beside me. Her hand brushed against my leg, and sudden pain rushed to the place. I must have paled for she leaned closer, concern flooding her face. "Are you all right?"

"Yes, please, step back." I said, my eyes closed as I battled the demon I carry inside. I drank again from the bottle and the delicate balance returned. "Thank you. I'm sure the food is just fine."

"I am Justine. Dovan is my friend."

I raised an eyebrow, as I bit into the yellow cheese. "Indeed?" I looked at her, and could see suddenly that she was neither as young as she appeared, nor quite as human either. Her face was abnormally pale beneath the blush, her eyes more sparkling than was allowed by nature. She reminded me somewhat of Moira, before the Change had come to her fully. She knew what Dovan was, and somehow she loved him. She smiled at me, and there was some manner of knowledge there, something she knew about me that even I was unaware of.

"Indeed. I think I hear him. Excuse me a moment?" She left and I turned my attention to the food, devouring it quickly and washing it down with the remainder of the formula. It did little to dull the aching of need inside me.

"I hear you've met Justine," Dovan's voice said. I looked up, somewhat surprised that he could enter without my hearing him. "I do still have a trick or two up my sleeve, Amara. Don't be so surprised by me."

"Well, Dovan, what can I say? Your entire person surprises me. I don't know who you are."

"I can change that … if you're ready to hear it. I have much to tell you." He sat beside me and his face softened. "I have wanted to tell you for so long. At first it was Crenoral who got in the way. Then it was Jesse. Now, you're here and you're all mine." He smiled and moved away. "What do you think of Justine? She's wonderful if you ask me. I adore her."

"Is that why you give her just enough to keep her young and beautiful, but do not bring her to you fully?"

His face dimmed some. "Aye. I love her and would not take away all of her humanity to make her one of us. But, neither can I bear to let her go. I must have her. She gives to me, so I give back."

"It is not fair to her, you know," I said, thinking of the distant shell Moira had always been until I brought her completely to me.

"I know," He said. "I know all too well." He was quiet a moment, then returned to sit in the chair beside me. "Now then, I was going to tell you about me." He leaned back, lifting his feet to rest them on the bedside table. He seemed more mortal than most I had known sitting there, as if we were sitting in the bedchamber of some manor house. I settled in to listen, unsure of what to expect, but with the surety that my perception of this man was soon to change.

"I was the youngest of my mortal brothers, as you know. I was twenty-eight when Bestin came. He didn't offer me a choice, as he had Crenoral. He knew me well enough to know that I would not come. He took me by force. In those first nights I was lost in my grief and newborn hunger. I gave myself to them, followed them as I had all my life. However, unlike my brothers, I refused to turn on my mortal family. I had a wife and three sons. I walked away from them, because even in that twisted place that comes with the gift, I loved them."

His face grew distant, visiting that time as if it were spread out in front of us to witness. "I watched from the distance as the boys grew, as my wife aged. She knew what had happened, but she wouldn't tell the boys. She kept the secret from them, told them I had gone to help Bestin and died.

They became men, good men. They married and had sons and daughters of their own. Eventually Crenoral took interest in what it was that drew me back to them. He too began to watch their lives. He became enamored of them. Maybe it was how much they resembled his own family which he had destroyed. I don't know."

He sighed and I could almost feel the weight the years had been to him. "She was the wife of my youngest son. She was a good mother, a good wife. From the moment they married Crenoral watched her. Then, he wasn't content to watch anymore. He went to her. She loved her family, but her love was no match for his charm. She went with him."

"Mother." I saw it in his eyes, the torment of that moment, of the night when Crenoral brought home his chosen bride.

"Yes. She didn't know me, of course, I had been gone for many years before she became a part of their lives, but he knew. He had always been a jealous man. I never thought he would go so far. I hated him for it. For the rest of his days I hated him for it."

We sat in silence for a long moment, and in that silence not only did my perception of Dovan change, but my perception of myself did as well. Suddenly there was more to my life than what I had always known. There were mortal ties within that immortal family I had known. Here before me sat my mortal grandfather, spilling forth the sordid family history that had brought us to this cavern on the side of a mountain thousands of years from the beginning of it. "What became of them?" I asked, for the first time in my years curious of the mortal family she had left behind.

"Your father?" He sat up and seemed to draw from deeply hidden memories. "He took another bride eventually, he had little choice. Your brothers were hellions and needed a mother's touch. She was not beautiful, but a strong woman. She raised them to be good men. Your mother never looked back."

"I know." I yawned involuntarily, my wounds pulling at me in a sweep of tired and pain. I wanted to stay awake and talk more, but the healing process would not be denied.

"We have years to remember, and many years to do it in," he said, rising. "I'm not going anywhere. Justine and I will not be far away. Sleep, recover. There will be time enough for talking another night."

Chapter 13

I RECOVERED in time, graduating from my sick bed to short walks in the wooded area around our cave. Justine proved to be a good woman, and a fair cook. Dovan was entirely a different man than I had supposed him to be. He was wholly paternal, giving and caring. He often carried me back to my bed when my ambitions took me further away than I had strength to return.

In those nights and weeks of nights we talked, often at great length about his brothers, about history, the people we had known. I found he had paid attention to my life, followed it as it were. He knew my children, those who had survived and had taken time to look in on each of them before returning to claim me from my grave. He told me of the descendants of my mortal family, the sons of his loins. They had grown far and wide, spreading across the continent to make homes for themselves. I could see pride in his eyes when he spoke of them, and when he looked at me. Part of me withdrew when I saw it.

Of his own dark children there were few left. His clan had been the smallest, even in the days I walked among them and over the years it had been hardest hit by mankind and other tragedies. "In all the world there can be no more than fifty anymore," he told me one night as we sat beside a cold mountain stream. "Fifty too many." He was dark, and had been for several nights, pulled into himself as if hiding from his own shadow.

"What is it, Dovan? What chases you?"

His sigh was heavy and almost painful. He didn't answer. I felt such a kinship with him, and yet his mind was closed to me. We had become so much like father and daughter that I reached out a hand to him. He didn't move to accept the gesture or to move away from it. He simply sat, staring into the murky water, brooding in silence. After a long time, I left him to it, limping away into the woods in the general direction of the cave. "He hurts." I heard Justine say before I could see her. Slowly her form separated from the trees. "I can feel it. His soul aches at what his heart can no longer feel."

"What is it that tears at him so, Justine?" I asked, truly concerned.

"If he were mortal I would say his conscience, but since he isn't it must be something else." We both turned and I could just make out his form in the silvery moonlight. He was bent over himself, making himself as small as possible. "He weeps."

I looked at her strangely for never had I seen one of them truly weep. "When we sleep, I hold him while he cries. He dreams of his life and it wounds him every day. I do not know how to heal such pain."

"Nor do I, Justine." I looked again and it almost appeared his shoulders shook, as one would while crying. I closed my eyes and turned away.

"He wanted to have this time with you," she said, taking my arm. Together we began walking back toward the cavern. "For the last fifty years he made this place for you, filled it with gifts for you, spoke of you. He wanted you to know the truth about your birth, about your mortal father. It was very important to him that he tell you."

"You make it sound as though he never intends to leave this place," I said.

She raised an eyebrow and shrugged. "I don't know that he will. He came to make his final peace with the missing part of his life. He has resolved all the rest."

"He came here then to die?"

"I cannot know his mind, but his actions speak loudly of his desires. He is tired, more than you can see with your eyes, and sickened by his life." We were nearly back to the cave and as we entered, it were as if I was seeing it for the first time. The entire place was dressed in things that had pleased me over the centuries, paintings by my favorite artists, furniture in my favorite colors, even things that resembled those I had kept in my room all those years before. In the farthest reaches of the string of chambers was a library, filled with scrolls and parchments and books of poetry and legend in languages as old as myself. It was as if the entire place had been built from my imagination.

"I have a gift for you as well," Justine said, lifting a small stack of books from a trunk in their room.

"He isn't ready for you to have them, but I think it is time. They might help you understand."

I withdrew then with the books, Dovan's own journals, written in his native language, one I had nearly forgotten, and reaching back to a time when he was still mortal, though the writing indicated they were less journals and more remembrances captured in words. "On that night I had found the woman I would marry. Her name was Justa, and she was as the very air," it began, once I had figured out the translation. It came back to me quickly enough from there and I was drawn into the incredible tale of one man's journey from contented bliss to the nightmare of hell.

"Bestin disappeared. No one seemed to know where. He was last seen at dinner, in a monstrous mood, terrorizing his children. Crenoral was furious for they were to travel to town on the morrow to sell that damned stud of his. Now I supposed he would bully me into going. I would much rather remain with Justa. She was due any day now, and the witch assured us of a son."

There were descriptions then of Bestin's family, the boys who tried to fill their father's shoes and two daughters not yet walking, and their brutal deaths. "Bestin was not gone. His family lay in bloody shreds on the funeral pyre. Only he could be so cruel. Only he would demand such sacrifice. I knew not what manner of demon this was, but I liked it not at all and wanted to have no part in it."

I lit the candles and soft oil lamps in my bedroom and fell across my bed, enchanted and appalled as I read. "Crenoral was gone. Nearly ten years passed since Bestin's departure and I could still feel his hand upon me. It was as if his shadow followed me into the day. I could only count the nights until they came for me as well. I tried to warn Crenoral's family. They would not listen to me. The boys were too young to remember Bestin and what he did. They wept and wailed for Crenoral's return, but I feared it greatly. I feared the death that would come when he returned."

There was a long gap in dates then, such as his dates were written, and I knew simply by the minutest of changes in his hand writing that the next entry was made in a rush of memory regarding the night when Bestin came for him. It was almost as though I could hear him in a hushed whisper in my mind as I read those words. "I am no longer. I am changed from what I was. They came to me in the middle of the night, drawing me from my home into the trees. There they fell upon me. Bestin was beautiful and terrible as he took my hand to bring me to him. Somehow I was helpless to resist them, unable to express my loathing of what they were. He kissed me, then I felt the first touch of my death. His teeth were sharp and he showed no remorse as he drank from me. There was little pain, only thoughts of my family, my children, regret. I felt myself going, dying I suppose. It was as though I watched the whole affair from some other place. Bestin held me as we fell to the ground and Crenoral hovered over us. Then, just as my thoughts began to fail me and I lacked the strength to care beyond the end of it, I felt something between us change. I tried to speak, to scream out. I did not want it. I did not choose. In the end, that mattered not at all. Something passed from him into me and the change began."

"I do not know how to describe this thing that has happened. My heartbeat slowed within me, my breathing quickened and then stopped. The blood ceased moving. My eyes closed, and yet I could clearly see my brethren waiting and watching, pacing in circles around my dying body. I felt each limb go numb and then contract on itself, as though the blood had been a swelling and with its departure my skin could return to its rightful place. My stomach churned with something beyond hunger. My heart stopped its beating. I died. Then it was born, this thing I am now. My breath returned in a rush, my brow fevered with desires too base to name. My conscious thought failed and in its place was only blood."

I shivered and pulled a blanket closer around me. The air in the cave seemed chill and I could almost feel Bestin's eyes upon me. That was, of course impossible, but I felt it none the less. It had never occurred to me what it must feel like to die that way, to be made. My heart seemed loud in the silence of the chamber, and my breathing seemed out of place. I read on, and it was as if Dovan sat beside me reading his pained and twisted narrative. At times he was remorseful, anguished by his new nature. At times he reveled in himself, losing the remorse of man in the thrill of delivering death.

So much like myself, I realized after a time, connecting my earliest battles with my humanity with his early battles with the monster he'd become.

He spared his own family, a thing he described as the most difficult to do. "You see ... it is those we love best that we desire the most." He wrote regarding a passionate visit to his wife's bedchamber. She saw him as a spirit returned to take her with him. He had been nearly undone by her pleading. "Physical attraction alone is hard to ignore in this state of being. The well-turned body, the dusty curls of her hair are enough to make my body scream in agony for a taste of her. Add to that my adoration for her person, the passion of our bed together ... the sight of her on her knees before me, her pale skin bare in the light of the fire. That part that stirs a mortal man to sin in such moments stirs me to much more passionate a thing and the hunger in my stomach echoes it so loudly that I could scarcely hear her words. I fell to my knees with the Change upon me, ready to take her in the only way I was able to at that moment. I was weak, intoxicated by her scent ... the blood pounding in her body ... her lips touching the cold, smooth surface of my unearthly skin. She seduced me into weakness, and I would have been helpless to save her had it not been for Gregan. He had heard the noise and come to see. The sight of my youngest son in his nightclothes, startled at the sight of me and crying in his fear pulled me to myself and I fled."

I don't know how many days and nights went by as I read. I hid in my bedchamber, wrapped in quilts and furs against the chill that had taken me. I read of his feud with Bestin over his making and over the nature of what they had become, and of his inability to disobey either of them for long. His clan was built in protest, bringing to him those Bestin thought not suited to the night. He relished in providing immortality to those with the talents to affect the world ... poets, prophets, musicians ... all were welcomed by him with open arms. Unlike his brothers, he explained in great detail what would take place once the deed was done, before he laid a finger upon them. He had a talent for picking those who could handle the influx of power inherent in the gift, those who would understand and use their power wisely. Somehow this angered Crenoral especially, for he was prone to those who had no gift for the dark and who often extinguished themselves before mankind had opportunity to do it for them. There was so much hatred between the three of them, and yet they were bound together forever.

"Crenoral brought home his bride. He has made his final insult, I have taken my Clan and gone. I could no longer bear to be there with him. She is my Gregan's wife. She does not know me ... us, but I have often seen her. It is unforgivable."

Dovan and his Clan left the Family then, moving far enough away that Crenoral's jealousy and Bestin's control was not so absolute. They were not far enough away, however, that they should not hear the next extraordinary news Crenoral announced to the night. "It was not possible, and yet all reports said that it is true. This woman whom my brother stole from my son's hearth was with child. Somehow it survived the death of its mother. What manner of monster will this child be? Will it bear resemblance to its human father? What will Crenoral do with it? I fear for its life and yet I fear its existence as well."

"Amara?" I sat up as if guilty, looking to the doorway where Dovan stood. Somehow he contradicted the image his words had created in my mind. "Are you well?"

"Yes. I am quite well, Dovan. Please, come in."

"You've been in here so long, I was afraid something was wrong."

He came to sit beside me, picking up one of the discarded journals I had already devoured. "Justine told me she had given these to you. I always meant for you to have them, I didn't think you were ready."

"You write beautifully. I don't know how to put them down."

"Thank you. Where are you?" He gestured to the leather bound journal in my hand.

I blushed, a little embarrassed, as if I had been caught reading a hidden diary. "Crenoral has just announced Mother's pregnancy."

"Ah, yes. Well, the next pages are full of reports of predictions by the eldest of the Family that you will be the end of us all. Even Bestin told Crenoral he should kill you as soon as you were born."

"Which he didn't do."

"He never was very good at taking orders. No, he was enamored of you, right from the beginning, as he had always been of Justa, my wife. You look very much like her, you know ... except you ended up with your mother's hair."

"My grandmother ... now there's a thought I haven't ever entertained. I always assumed I was simply born, and Mother and Crenoral were all I knew of Family for so long that I forgot to wonder about the rest. Tell me about her." I tried to imagine what she would look like, what my life might have been like had Crenoral never come for my mother.

He stretched and sighed. "She was a good woman, strong, healthy. She knew how to get the best from the people around her. Her parents died when she was only eleven. I married her four years later. I would have married her before that, but she kept refusing me, said she couldn't leave her brothers until they'd all married their own wives."

He looked at the floor, and I saw the reflection of an old pain in his eyes. "She lived a long life for the time ... long indeed. She saw our grandchildren born ... all but one." He smiled and looked up at me. "She would have liked you, Child. You have her strength of will."

I smiled too and set the journal aside, pleased somehow that he would think so. His presence was soothing, and a part of me marveled at how comfortable I had come to be with him. "It is odd, to read of one's birth like this, through the eyes of someone you've never known." If I closed my eyes I could almost picture them, the three brothers and Mother, with Mother's belly round with me. "I wish I had known you then, Dovan. I wish I could have grown up with you around."

"I was forbidden. Once Crenoral realized that you would be my granddaughter, he forbade me from ever coming near you. His damned jealousy. I guess he thought I would steal you away."

"And you probably would have, at least once I started to realize I was different from them." I suppressed a yawn, suddenly taken with the need to sleep. "Does she haunt you yet, Dovan? Justa, I mean? Can you still see her face when you sleep? Do you see her in Justine?"

"Aye, sometimes when she smiles, she is Justa, just as she was when we were both young."

"Could it be that she truly is Justa?" I lay back, sliding down to find a comfortable position.

There was a sadness in his eyes as he shrugged. "I have heard of such things, though I have seen no proof. I miss her often, and perhaps that is why I see her in Justine."

I nodded at the logic. My limbs felt heavy with the fatigue. I sighed and he stood to leave. "She will be there for you when it's over," I said, already half asleep. "Are you ready to be with her?"

He sat beside me on the bed, brushing my cheek in a fatherly gesture. "Aye, I am. I'm tired, Amara. Tired of myself." He seemed old and frail, though his appearance hadn't changed. It was as if all of the years had come to sit on his shoulders. I caught his hand and pressed it to my lips. I felt a warmth between us I had never felt before, a love that wasn't caught up in bodily passions or the need to please or impress.

I didn't have the words to express it though, and the simple gesture was enough, as he returned it and rose from the bed. "You should sleep. I can see it in your eyes."

I yawned and struggled against the pull of sleep, but it was stronger than I and eventually my resistance proved futile. I woke through the day once, long enough to drink from the bottle Justine had left by the bed, then fell into the deep sleep of my kind. The next weeks are somewhat hazy, filled with long bouts of sleep and hours of reading, hunger, and feeding.

Nearly a year after he pulled me from that grave, I went out to hunt alone for the first time. I fed that night insatiably, taking a deer, a boar, and more rabbits than I could count. I was beginning to feel whole and myself again. My reason had returned, my desire to live and my strength came with it. I was no longer a shell of myself. I was ready to leave.

It was several months before I could broach the subject with them, but when at last I did, Dovan already knew. "I was hoping we would have longer together." Was all he said in way of changing my mind. "But, I knew it would come to this."

"I'll be back this way again one day," I said, and I truly meant it. I had learned a great deal in that place, my perceptions of myself had changed and so had my understanding of my history, my place in the flow of time.

"The world is not as it once was, Child. Take it slow and easy." Dovan's smile was soft, conveying both his affection and his sadness at my departure.

"Don't worry about me, Grandfather. I have a talent for surviving."

"I've noticed. Still, I've given you a little to help you along," he said handing me a leather satchel filled with the things I would need. "Just promise me you'll stay away from those Hunters and keep a low profile."

"I will."

"And should you need us, we'll be here," Justine said. She kissed my cheek, and he my forehead as I shouldered my satchel and began the long trek down the mountain.

It was a long journey into civilization, and when at last I reached a village, I kept my distance for a week of nights, observing the life there. Things had indeed changed. I tried to remind myself that it had been well on to eighty years since I had last been among man. The streets there were paved with some manner of stone, looking almost like brickwork. Men and women passed through those streets in odd-looking dress. I passed as a shadow, unseen at least until I passed a still pond and caught my own reflection.

I was dressed fashionably enough, in a dress gifted to me by Justine, but I looked strange, even to myself. My hair hung to my knees like a black blanket. My eyes were sunken, my face long and ashen. Like the specter of death. As I stood gazing at the image I saw my mother in my eyes. I tried to see the person Dovan saw when he looked at me, but couldn't. I could only see the monster I had been when last I wandered in civilized company. I shook off the feeling and moved on, ambling north and east, toward the cities I had known, the places familiar enough for comfort. I was to find that the religious fervor that had swept the European countryside before my fall had left off of Vampyres for the time, concentrating on more human deviants and the governing of countries.

Those nations that had begun carving up the lands of Europe were becoming more established, ruled over by royal houses that fought over tiny strips of land and traded their daughters in marriage for peace and prestige. As I neared the place of my darkest deeds, war raged between the various nobilities of France and England. It was said that a woman led the French troops in victory over the English at Orléans. I knew little of the political causes, but the battlefields were easy to find, the smell of blood and fear called to me.

It was not far from Orléans that I found myself missing Dovan, and the solitude of the mountain. I had found a place to sleep in a half ruined stable, where the debris had fallen to create a space just big enough for lying in where the walls blocked the light of the sun. From my satchel I pulled the small book Dovan had given me, words he had written while I was with him, poetry and thoughts he had said he needed to share with me. I could still smell him on the paper as I opened it. It was too dark to read in my hideaway, but I held the book to me and listened to the sound of his voice in my head.

It seemed odd to be so alone again, though I had spent more time that way than I had with Dovan. I had grown accustomed to feeling him near me, comfortable with him as I had never been before, even with Adroushan or Jesse. There was no need to fight myself, no desire to kill. With Dovan I was simply myself. Perhaps that is what it was to have family, not in the sense that we were all Family, but the physical relation that came of sharing the same blood.

As I moved to put the book away, a creased parchment fell from its pages. I unfolded it, but couldn't see in the dark. Carefully, I inched forward, closer to the deadly light that beat down on the ground just a few feet away. Eventually I was close enough to read. It was in Dovan's hand, a letter of credit, giving me access to accounts he held at a bank in Paris, and another in Barcelona.

I changed my plans then, for I had seen Paris, but had never ventured to Barcelona before. A city was a place I could find myself again, with a little money to spend, I could find a room, buy clothing, and re-enter the world of man.

Chapter 14

My first night in Barcelona I was forced to kill a man. It was well after midnight and I presumed most would be fast asleep, affording me the city streets so that I might learn my way around unmolested. Unfortunately, this man was not asleep, but prowling the streets. I have no clue as to his business before he crossed my path, but upon seeing me, he ran at me with a blade in his hand, screaming obscenities. Seeing as my understanding of the local dialect was primitive at best, nothing I said had any effect on him and I backed off slowly, into the passage between a tavern and a dark stone building.

He sliced my hand as I sought to disarm him, and I turned my ankle as he lunged at me. I willed the Change to come as I fell beneath him, my hands abandoning the knife in favor of turning his head to free up his neck. He bucked above me as I bit and drank. When I felt him relax, his weight pressing me into the dirty ground, I stopped, short of killing him and wiggled my way out from under him. I took the knife from him and bent to retrieve my satchel, torn from my shoulder. I was bleeding, and wearing a fair amount of his blood. The ankle was swelling, and it was likely that I had sprained it. As I limped toward the tavern, I heard the man rise and come at me again. This time I didn't hesitate, riding him to the ground and drinking until I felt the heart stop beating. I was shaking as I finished, both from the rush of blood and from the deed itself. It had been a long time since I had taken a human life.

Thus it was that I presented myself to that tavern, my clothes torn and bloody, limping, my hand wrapped in cloth I had torn off my own skirt. The barmaid came to me as soon as I opened the door and I made great show of my injuries. I needed a place to stay and help getting around, and I figured that this was one way to get both. "I was attacked." I said, as she sat me in a chair near the fire and started to tend my wounds. "I just came into town. I have nowhere to go. He took everything."

I spoke haltingly with my faltering grasp of their language, letting myself shake, as she checked my hand. "Settle now, child," she said with a soft smile. "These streets are no place for a young woman at this hour. Luís, make up a bed." She finished pulling off my hurried bandage and winced. The smell of blood filled the air around us, and I started shaking anew. The earlier taste of blood only whetted my appetite for more. "Let me get some water and bandages. Then, you can rest. Tomorrow we'll see to getting you taken care of."

I thanked her, and when she had finished winding clean linen bandages around my hand, followed her to a dark back room with a cot. I was grateful when the door closed and collapsed onto the bed. I was weak with desire, but forced myself to lay down on that bed and close my eyes. I didn't sleep, wouldn't trust myself to leave the room, so I lay, waiting for the dawn and the return of the woman.

The only window in the room faced south, and was further blocked from the sun by the walls of the building behind it, rising up three stories and shuttered. I was quite safe from the dangers of the sun, but something about the growing light outside that window reminded me of the dungeon where Rebeka died. I found myself moving involuntarily into a corner of the room, my eyes fixated on the pale light visible through the cracks around the shutters.

I jumped when the door opened, startled out of my corner. The woman who entered was not the same as the one the night before. She was much younger, though the similar features marked her as a relative, likely a daughter. She dipped in a light curtsey. "Morning, ma'am. I'm Brana. My father sent me to see if you need anything."

I inclined my head in return. "Thank you, Brana. I'm grateful for the hospitality." I moved closer. She was little more than a child, perhaps fifteen. She smelled of the earth, fresh turned soil and the greenery of a garden. "I find myself with little left to my name, but what I managed to keep in my bag. I have a letter to a banker here in town however. I wonder if you might be able to fetch someone for me? I'm afraid I would only get lost."

She nodded. "I can send my brother, Phillípe. In the meantime, would you care for breakfast?"

I would indeed, but not the kind she was offering. Still, I needed to feed, if I were ever to remove the specter of death from my face. "That would be lovely, Brana, thank you."

That day passed slowly, and it was well past midday that the banker finally arrived. He was an older man, with gray hair at his temples and wrinkles around his eyes. We spoke briefly, and I was startled to discover he knew Dovan personally. "I understand you suffer the same affliction as your Father," he said, squinting at me. "Sensitive to the sunlight? A shame, really."

"Y-Yes, it is. Family trait though. We all suffer with it."

"That won't get in your way too much, once you set yourself up with some servants to take care of things for you. Will you be purchasing a house?"

I felt a little overwhelmed, trying to fathom just what Dovan had given me. "I wouldn't expect to be, no," I said. "I'm only stopping here for a time. I will be moving on soon."

"Well then, let me see to some arrangements. I can get you a room, a maid, and set you an evening appointment with a dress maker. That should get you started."

"And some compensation for the family here," I added. "They took me in when I was wounded. They should be compensated."

He nodded and handed me something to sign, then he was gone again, promising to return after sundown. By the next evening I was comfortably ensconced in a bigger room, with windows shuttered tightly from both the outside and the inside. There was a young maid to handle the things I needed but could not attend to myself, and five dresses being made by a local dressmaker. I was able to set up my equipment and send the maid for the supplies I would need to make the formula again. I realized it wouldn't be enough to bring back the appearance of health to my face, but it would be a start.

I knew I would have to hunt eventually, and the thought repulsed me. I was afraid of what I might become again if I allowed myself blood. The taste of the attacker was still strong in my mind, the frantic beating of his heart as I fed dancing about inside me.

I made furtive forays into the streets, long after the maid had gone to her bed, in the hours when only those with foul plans would be about. For many of these nights I did nothing but watch them, feeling the desire to feed, yet unable to act upon it. Finally, as spring was beginning to become summer, I chanced upon a drunkard stumbling along in the dark. He was a rough looking sort, with a few days' growth upon his face, his brown coat covered in dirt and his breeches torn in more than one place. At his belt was a small purse and a dagger, though his sword's sheath was empty. He had been injured and reeked of the blood oozing from a wound I couldn't see. I fell on him like a starved animal and left him just as the brooding clouds began their deluge, taking his purse with me.

It was easier after that. I would eat an early supper in my rooms, brought in by the maid before she left for the evening, and drink formula until the night was dark enough to hide me. Then I would venture out and feed, returning long before dawn and falling deeply asleep. In several months, the woman in my mirror looked less like death and more like a mortal woman in her early twenties. The feeding became less frequent after that, only once a week, then once a month. Eventually it stopped all together.

I was, however, growing restless and determined it time to journey. Staying in one place too long had been my mistake with Rebeka. I didn't want to make it again. After settling my accounts with the banker, and my landlord, I purchased a small carriage and fitted it with heavy curtains. I hired a driver who desired passage into France. From France, I headed to Austria. I was restive, and the idea of visiting places I hadn't yet seen interested me.

I didn't care for Venice much, and headed northward, into what had been Germania, to see Berlin. From Berlin, I ventured west. In London I heard that ships had crossed the ocean and found a "New World," a place filled with wonders and freedom. I considered it wild speculation when first I heard of it, for how could there be land across that vast sea, beyond who knew what manner of monsters?

Still, the stories continued, and grew to be far more convincing than the extravagant fairytales being told about the Vampyre.

News of a more violent purging of any who were deemed to oppose the Roman church curtailed my plans to travel south to Castile where I was told the stories of the New World originated. I had no desire to find myself face to face with Hunters again so soon. Instead I returned to Greece.

I traveled lightly, with one servant and a few precious belongings. Nothing seemed to hold my interest for any time, and I was feeling uncomfortable with myself. I kept away from the most populated places, fearing my unease would bring me to feed. It was back in France, in the nightlife of Paris, where I met a man who had plans to journey there himself. It was said that settlements were rising all over the New World, and that the hands of the church were not so deep into the affairs of the people there.

I determined to see for myself if what they were saying was true, if the New World was indeed free, if the hold of the Holy Mother Church truly did not extend so far, if even one such as myself could find peace there.

The logistics of it were easy enough, but required a more passable appearance than I seemed to possess. I made a pilgrimage of sorts back to my mountain hideaway, gathering items that would fetch a fair price, and would travel well. I paused long enough to call on Dovan and Justine, spending a few weeks with them before I began making my way to Portsmouth where my long journey would begin. As I went, I sold off some of the Family jewels, and various things I had collected over the years. By the time I arrived in Portsmouth, I had a small fortune with which to prepare myself.

I made the arrangements myself then upon my arrival, quietly, with extreme amounts of money to assure myself the solitude I would need to make such a journey safely. After all, I couldn't afford to have people stumbling into my room in the middle of the day, burning me with the bright sun. It was then a simple matter of waiting for the appointed day. September 13, a Friday as I recall, I boarded the ship with a small entourage of personal aides, a maid, a valet and a man to handle any arrangements that might be necessary. I had spent money on exquisite clothing and other necessities as well.

I purported myself to be a lady of some bearing, of some noble house or other, and kept quietly within my rooms, sending the maid or valet out for anything I might need, and paying them well enough for their services to ensure their silence about my peculiar habits. The journey was long, excruciatingly so, cramped in so small a space with so much temptation all around me. The closeness led me to weakness. As I slept by day I dreamed of the hot blood of the crew, or the sweet, young blood of the children in the cabin near mine. By night as I sat in my room with my servants asleep around me it was all I could do not to sink my teeth into their open and trusting necks. Perhaps the confinement intensified the need, or the nearness of them, the strong, unwashed scent of them.

The air aboard that vessel grew stale and unwelcome, choking in my throat. I wanted the freedom of the open sea, to wander in the salty air above deck, but couldn't bring myself to trust myself in my weakened state, lest I lose control of my frayed reins and bring down the wrath of whatever gods hold sway at sea. I even gave way to rats, feasting quite well upon them for the ship was overrun. It was little comfort though, and brought back the dreams of that day ... that awful day of my greatest evil ... and with that all the memories after, the Hunter, the fall ... I feared I might revert to that madness which had drawn me up that mountain to begin with.

I was greatly appreciative then, when at last came the sounds of the crew preparing for landfall, and the distant, but distinct sounds of a harbor town, bustling with activity could be heard. It was late afternoon, the sun still hours from setting completely. I composed myself to wait patiently for the dark, to disembark in my new home, to finally see this New World for myself. I sent my servants on ahead, to find rooms and a carriage. Alone in my cabin I trapped several rats, feeding hungrily from them, and draining two bottles of formula before I was content enough. Then, with the sun barely hidden by the far horizon, I emerged, clad all in blue velvet and feeling nearly regal.

Even from the view of the dirty wharves and piers, it was a beautiful sight. Not quite a city, grown up from nothing in a few short years, Charles Town shores were crowded with various manners of people from all over the known world. It was small by the standards of the cities I had known, but when seen through eyes as old as mine, it was easily seen as a growing, thriving place that would one day dwarf those in the Old Countries. The night air was cool, refreshing, clean. There was no scent of old death hanging in it, no signs of others of my kind. I closed my eyes and savored the sensation. Then, the crew was urging me to disembark, gently prodding me toward the pier and the young maid who I could see waving to me from in front of the hired carriage.

It felt comfortable, peaceful. Even the hunger began to subside as we rode into the city and came to a stop before a graceful inn, with a warm and welcome fire on the hearth, and the smell of baked bread filling the air. My servants had arranged a room, with shuttered windows, in the back of the place, where I would be less likely to be disturbed. I settled in, immediately releasing the two male servants, paying them more than adequately enough to find them new lives there. The maid I retained a while longer, having grown quite accustomed to her company and feeling the need to maintain the front of ladyship. Therefore, she was quite required, as no lady was to be known to be alone in such a place.

Chapter 15

HER NAME was Lianna, a simple minded, but well-meaning and decent woman. She was by no means pretty, but neither was she unpleasant to look at. She was well trained to her duties, having spent ten years in the service of a family in London, and even when in the service of such an eccentric lady as myself, and she never questioned my rare "illness" which prevented me from going out in the day time, nor my odd habits and strange equipment. She was all of twenty-five when I first employed her after her mistress had dismissed her for what she insisted were only perceptions of impropriety. She had balked at first at the idea of leaving her homeland, but her reputation was sullied and finding other employment was difficult at best. I grew to like her in the following years as I made a place for myself in this New World.

I look back upon her now and count her as one of the true friends in my life. A woman who was neither afraid nor enamored of me, a gentle soul who managed somehow to only see the goodness in me, and find ways to redirect me toward it. Eventually, she came to know the truth about me, accepting it as she did all else about me. She became my companion, my conscience, my friend. We spent nearly a year in that first port town, growing used to the differences between the Old World and the New, making friends and establishing accounts to finance the coming years. I had brought with me the most easily disposable of my goods, jewels and such that would translate into a great deal of wealth. Some of it we sold, some of it we hid away for another time. Then, as a new spring brought an air of excitement to me, we began our journey.

At first I was content to travel the established roads between the colonies, visiting the various and varied towns and villages that represented the civilized half of this new place. We stayed nowhere more than a few months, save for the place where I told her my life story. We had found our way to a place called Andover, as we traveled north with an aim to visit the colony at Pennsylvania. The climate in Andover was not much to our liking, and the townsfolk were far from friendly. Indeed, they seemed intensely fearful and suspicious of outsiders among them. The religion that prevailed there was stricter perhaps than that of the Church I had come here seeking solace from, ruling even the minute lives of its people. I was uncomfortable and made no plans to stay there beyond a day's rest. Unfortunately, on our way out of town, the carriage we traveled in broke a wheel and we were forced to return to have it repaired.

We stayed to ourselves, holing up in the small boarding house and coming out only at supper. It was nearly two days' time we had to wait for the repair work, made all the worse for their holy day falling in the middle, forcing us to wait yet another day. I stood at the window of our room and watched as the town became a ghostly shadow with the coming of the night. No one was about once the sun had gone down. I was afraid to leave the room, huddling beneath blankets by day, pacing like a caged animal by night. By sunset of that third day, I was most anxious to be gone from there, and I myself went to fetch the carriage from the smith's shop. He looked at me strangely as I paid him, and asked him to harness the horses, that I would return soon with my maid and we would be on our way. I bustled Lianna about, hurrying her in an attempt to avoid what I already could feel building.

When we returned for the carriage, several of the town's men had gathered, including their religious leaders. My heart began to pound in my chest and visions of Rebeka's tattered body filled my mind. I could feel what little color could occupy my cheeks drain as they approached us.

"It is a strange hour to be leaving town," one of them said.

"Perhaps, but I do not wish to stay here another night." I replied, accepting Lianna's help into the carriage.

"It would be better to leave with the daylight to guide you. The roads are not safe at night."

"We will be safe enough, I assure you. Come, Lianna."

One of them held Lianna's arm, preventing her from joining me. "Maybe you do not understand."

"I understand you plenty, sir. Unhand the lady and let us be on our way." I was getting scared. I had heard tales of the so-called "witch" trials that had been occurring in the area, and though I could never be considered a witch, these men had enough similarities to the Hunters of my past to frighten me beyond rational thought. My breath came raggedly, my heart pounded so loudly I thought it might beat a hole in my chest. Flashes of those horrible days and nights blurred past them and faces of those past tormenters appeared among them.

"Please, sir. Unhand me," Lianna said, in that soothing, almost enchanting tone she had. "The lady is right ... we really must be on our way. We've overstayed our welcome already." I don't know if she realized what was going on in my mind, if she could sense the remnants of terror that filled me at that precise moment. She did, however, not relish the tenor of threat in the men's voices. "The Lady's father is close on to death, and still three day's ride from here. She hopes to reach his bed before his passing. Stand aside and let us be gone from here." She spoke the lie with so much truth in her voice that no one said a word in response. With that, she climbed up beside me, gathered the reigns of the horses and released the brake. The men moved aside hesitantly and we began our departure.

I was shaking from head to toe when she finally stopped the carriage an hour outside of town. "Are you all right?" she asked gently, touching a hand to my face in concern.

"Don't stop. Keep going," I whispered, struck with images of them following and attacking us in the night.

She drove us on, stopping only once to relieve herself and once to allow me to crawl inside the dark carriage to hide from the sun. When I woke later we were well away from the scary little town. We found a place the next night, a small town with friendly, open people. There, once safely inside our rented rooms, I sat with Lianna in the early morning hours and told her about the Hunters, about Rebeka, about what I was.

She took it well enough, listening silently, sipping on her tea. It was almost as if she had known all along that there must be an explanation such as this for my oddities, and upon hearing it had all her questions about me answered. It overwhelmed me, the events of my not so distant past, of the last days, the terror in my heart still beating loudly. She held me as I cried it out, stroking nimble fingers through my hair to calm me. When I was done, she quietly got me settled into bed, mothering me to sleep. It was a restless sleep, haunted by the dark men of Andover and the white-coated Hunters of years past. Whenever I woke she was nearby, humming a soft tune or unpacking our belongings. It was a comforting feeling.

In that small town we rested, talked, and made plans. She asked me what I meant to do with my life, a question I couldn't answer. She seemed to see everything so clearly. She spoke with ease of destiny and fate, as if she could see them.

We spoke at length about the people in my life, and I told her about the time I spent beneath the earth, and the strange thoughts about Adan and Jesse and the Hunter all being the same person.

"I have heard that in some places the people believe that when we die our soul does not necessarily pass straight on to God, but that we return to live again and again."

I looked at her closely. I too had heard such things, but as with most mortal beliefs, I dismissed them. "Do you think such a thing is possible?" I asked, my head swimming with the possibilities.

She shrugged and smiled. "I would not know. If I were to have lived before, I do not think I would like to know. Once is hard enough, I think, without living forever or coming back again."

With that she rose and left me to go make tea. I had to agree with her, once was hard enough. How many lifetimes had I prowled the nights? How many times had I longed for the peace of death? What would be the point then of death, if we were only to return and start again?

It was meant to be like so many other towns, a stop on the journey, but before either of us took notice of the passing time, we had spent nearly a year there. With spring almost upon us, we set our plans into motion, to follow this new land to its edges, to journey beyond the civilized places into the wild openness we had heard tales of, and perhaps make a place for ourselves out there.

Thus it was that in early May we purchased a wagon and loaded it with all of our precious belongings and set out into the new world. Our first plan was to continue on to Philadelphia as we had originally set out to do. From there, we followed the wagon trails, moving ever westward. Through the last vestiges of mankind's holdings in this world, out into the rolling hills and waterways, into a land of vast open spaces, tall, waving grasses and animals. Occasionally we would happen across a settlement or small clusters of them that would one day become a town. We kept moving, watching as a new country grew around us.

Once a year we would make our way to the nearest city, sometimes requiring a month of travel. There we would take in the news of the world, stock up on supplies, purchase new clothing and relax in the relative luxury of rented rooms. As Lianna grew older and it was more difficult for her to get around, we stayed closer to civilization, making a home in Philadelphia.

It was a time of great enjoyment in my life. I enjoyed her company, the journey, the simplicity of our lives. When she died, at the ripe old age of seventy-nine, I stood at her grave and cried. It was not the gut-wrenching loss I felt as Jesse left me, or that I felt when I found Rebeka dead, but a dull-aching pain that buried itself deep inside of me and would not leave. I miss her still today. Fifty years passed, as she followed me from town to city to country road, never complaining or questioning. I laid her to rest in the town she had come to call home. She had liked it there, where the summer was warm, and the spring brought bouquets of beautiful flowers. I laid her there and wept for her, then I moved on.

I traveled alone after that, by night, on foot, taking my time to go in no particular direction for any particular reason. I still had no idea what I wanted to do with my life, my gifts as Lianna had called them. I enjoyed making company of mortal souls, especially those with a calmness of spirit. It seemed to compliment my chaotic one. Often I spent only short times with them, leaving them with some trinket or gift to remind them of me, to thank them for their friendship, to ease my own conscience.

Then came the night when the uneasiness of my life returned. I walked in the city where I had laid Lianna, returned there for the anniversary of her passing, and I felt it ... an old, familiar Presence on the breeze that told me that Brethren were near. He kept his distance, acknowledging my presence with a light mental touch before moving on. My private world was private no longer and the New World wasn't so new. I left town quickly, lest anymore of them be passing that way as well and less inclined to ignore me. I had come to love my peace and had no need of the battles such meetings could evolve into. Better to live solitary in the night than to spend each darkened moment fighting for life.

Of course, it isn't easy to do, to live alone, to avoid confrontations. Sooner or later they would come. It was in a city of those New World colonies where I was the most at ease, at the base of a mountain in the Carolinas, where the people were outwardly friendly souls. It was there that I would return again and again, to rest from my journeys and decide where I would go next. The town grew each time I went away, emerging out of the ground, with long, muddy streets lined with hotels and saloons, restaurants and shops that sold a fascinating array of goods.

I found my way back to it once the war between the colonists and the British had ended. I had no desire for the temptation of that much bloodshed, though I was perhaps more at ease with my own nature then than at any other time in my life. I spent the bulk of the war staying away from the battles, which largely meant staying away from civilization. It felt good to be among people again. There was a new opera house set to open, and a theater for the traveling bands of actors I had frequently encountered on my journey.

I found a place where a little liberal cash bought me a quiet room, darkened against the daylight to ease my "affliction" and a manager who knew how important the comfort of his guests was. There I settled in to be awhile, comfortable among the vibrant, growing city and her people. It was in this southern, humid city that Joshua came to me. He was young, scarcely two nights since he was born to the night, and filled with a hunger that I could feel echoing in the air around me. His creator had abandoned him without even a word to explain what he now was, or how to survive. He stumbled through the nights half blind with the need and terrorized by what his body craved him to do.

He found me outside a restaurant just after dark. I was in need of company, of a friend. He seemed as logical a choice as any, more so perhaps than many others in my life. He was so much like me, so human still, so scared, and uneducated in what he had become. He too needed, I could tell he had not fed since his creation. I took him to me, fed him from my formula, giving him enough to sustain him until we found something more substantial for him.

I found myself in the rather peculiar position that night, of actually having to teach him how to kill, how to fill the new needs. In truth, it was I who finally did the killing, slipping up on a drunken old man and pulling him into the shadows of an alley, silencing him with a hand across his mouth. I showed the young one where to bite and held his victim while he fed. When he was full, the man still breathed, so I slit his throat with a small knife

I kept for necessities, leaving him in a small puddle of his own blood. When I looked up from my task, Joshua was shaking with shock and fear. I smiled a small, weak little smile and stood, taking him into my arms, resting his head on my chest. "Shh, little one, it's all right. Calm yourself." I played with his hair, brushing it out of his face as his turmoil subsided.

As he straightened, his cheek brushed mine, awakening feelings I had thought buried with Jesse. When his lips, still warm with his dinner, pressed to mine, I pulled him closer, almost imagining it was Jesse himself I kissed. When I finally pulled away almost breathlessly, I took his hand and silently led him back to my rooms at the hotel. Dark, heavy drapes pulled tightly across the windows, and a bed draped in black guarded me against the daylight, but I wasn't sure it would be enough to protect my new friend. I settled him into the closet for the day, wrapped in the heaviest cloak I owned, promising to find better accommodations for the following day, then I settled into my bed.

I didn't sleep much, his touch had awakened me and my almost human body could not forget so easily. I burned with a hunger I had thought forgotten, tossing restlessly most of the day and slipping into an uneasy sleep near dusk. I dreamed of Jesse and the passionate years we had spent together. I woke with the sunset, calling out his name.

My first duty, after checking on the safety of my companion, was to find the manager and arrange a second room with darkened windows for my friend, who suffered a more severe case of the same affliction as myself. With a liberal amount of cash, the request was no problem, and he set about having the room prepared.

Chapter 16

JOSHUA MOVED into the new room and I set about the young one's education. We exchanged the pleasantries of names and backgrounds, vague and incomplete to be sure, then settled in to the task at hand. I found him a quick study, eager to learn from my centuries of experience and an ardent lover. He adjusted well, once the transformation was explained to him. He had not known his maker, had only happened upon him on the road into town. He said they had walked a ways together, conversing about the nature of good and evil. The man had been smooth, handsome, and rather nervous. He had talked of powers beyond the ability of mortal man to understand, and the great duty that came with it, of wanting to be rid of it, to hand it off to another. I suppose Joshua was his chosen recipient.

Joshua said that they had stopped on the side of the road to rest, and the man fell on him, subduing him quickly and draining him of life. He had passed out, and when he came to the stranger was gone, leaving a new made vampire to face the coming of the fiery dawn. Somehow, Joshua had found cover that first night and made his way into town the next. He fought the needs of his new body with the ignorance of one who did not know he had been changed. He had been appalled and afraid.

That was his beginning, dark and difficult to be sure, and I set about making the next years pleasant and filled with all the beauty our life could offer. I found he was a fun-loving man who had spent his mortal life with little material wealth and a smile as his calling card. Little about that changed. He brought light and inspiration to the night we shared, restoring my faith in myself, my own sense of humor and adventure. We grew comfortable with ourselves, with each other, with the semblance of a normal life which we built, even with the growing society around us. That society had grown increasingly night oriented, and we found ourselves happily attending masquerade balls and operas, ballets and concerts, making distant friends among the city's elite and endearing ourselves to its poor with generous gifts. The money was fairly easy to come by, with a few, well-placed investments and the occasional business trip to distant banks with forgotten accounts, or the sale of some rare and antique gem, and of course there was always purses and jewelry of those victims Joshua took in the dark.

We had little need of the money ourselves, aside for the paying for our rooms and clothes and the purchase of good servants who knew how to keep their tongues.

Shortly, we bought a house at the far edge of town, nestled back into a grove of trees, with a long, stately lane down to the main road, where we were safe from prying eyes and curious glances. Our servants maintained the house by day, and left us to ourselves by night, paid well enough to never question the idiosyncrasies of their employers. We lived well, and were known among the society of the day as well-bred, European nobility with generous hearts and pleasant manners. We played on as man and wife, adopting his mortal name and enjoying our game.

It seems odd now, the way we lived, but it was perfectly normal to us then. He would rise first, early in the evening, as the last rays of daylight kissed the distant horizon farewell, leaving me sleeping while he went out for his meal, and returning filled with the warmth and passion of it. When we rose together we would dress, drive into town and take our evening stroll, nodding in greeting to those we passed and pausing to speak to those we knew. We would join friends at some after dinner place to sip wine and make small talk, or take in a show at the local opera house where we maintained a box. The nights stretched on around us, the darkness was alive with bright lights and festive celebrations. We attended charity balls and ballets, had intimate dinner parties at our manor, a trick for poor Joshua whose immortal stomach could no longer tolerate mortal food, but a delicious time for me.

I was happy, pleasantly content, and only distantly disturbed by Joshua's nightly killing. He had sworn to me early on to only kill those who deserved death, those who killed, maimed, stole. That appeased my conscience somewhat, and I simply ignored the rest. I wanted happiness, and was willing to forgive much to maintain it. He remained much the same as the carefree mortal soul he had once been. He loved to play games and dress up in the finest clothes, something I don't think he had much of a chance to do as a mortal. He was not the most handsome of the men in that society, but he had a quiet charm that beamed when he laughed or smiled, and he was a loving being that always seemed to know exactly what to say. In retrospect, I didn't love him, but I was happy, or I pretended to be.

Looking back now, I should have seen the signs, heard the hushed voices, known the strange looks on the faces of those around us. Perhaps I saw and simply chose to ignore them, hoping that this time it would pass me by. In my happiness with my life, I was blind, caught again unaware. No matter which way I turn it in my head, even now, I still do not see how it came to pass, what it was that gave us away, or how they came to know us for what we were.

It was a night like so many others in our time together, we had plans to attend a ball at the Lady Shannon McKendric's home at the outskirts of town. We rose, a little later than was usual, and I bathed and began dressing while Joshua went out for his meal. When he returned he was excited, flushed. He told me that he had nearly been caught. He had nearly finished when he heard approaching footsteps and voices. They seemed to know exactly where he was. He hid in the trees along the river, leaving the poor, nearly dead whore in the grass beside the path where he had dropped her. He swore he hadn't been seen, that surely she was dead. He was petrified, agitated, pacing around me in circles as he spoke. His face wore the same horrified look it had that night when I had first found him. Again and again he repeated that she was surely dead, she could not have lived so far drained of life.

"Never-the-less, Joshua, we must make plans to leave here. It is time to move on." It was a general statement, and I bustled him in to clean himself up and prepare for our merriment while I gave thought to our leaving. It was a fun evening, uneventful, culminating in a delightful performance from the eldest of Mrs. McKendric's daughters, a lass of seventeen with designs on becoming an opera singer. I was pleasantly tired as we returned from the ball. The city was peaceful and quiet, and from my bedroom I could hear the faint sounds of the swollen river a mile or so away. I slipped off to sleep in Joshua's arms, in a dark basement bedroom, a smile still on my face.

The next nights were oddly still, Joshua kept closer to home, killing only when necessary and avoiding the seedy section of town that was his customary hunting ground. We laid plans to leave, heading west into the growing country, but decided to delay our departure until after the already announced party to celebrate our thirteenth anniversary. My slight apprehension over Joshua's near discovery faded and life returned to normal.

That, of course, was when it chose to happen, as we eased our vigilance and Joshua's hunger overcame his caution. When I woke that night, Joshua was, as usual, already gone. I dressed casually for our stroll, a little warmly against the unseasonable chill in the air, and awaited his return, finishing off one bottle of formula and opening another. When I drained that as well, half from hunger, half from boredom, I set about making more, tinkering in the lab for well over an hour. When I came out it was to step onto the porch and sweep my keen eyes up and down the long lane, looking for Joshua.

He was late, alarmingly so, especially after the trouble the month before. Still, I reminded myself harshly, he was a grown man, nearly to his thirteenth year, and capable of taking care of himself.

I forced myself back into the house and busied myself with the plans for the anniversary party. It was almost two hours later that I heard a thud on the front porch, not quite a footstep. I opened the door a little hesitantly, and fell to my knees beside the bloody pile that had been Joshua. His victim's blood was still on his lips, his mouth open in a violent sneer to reveal those devilish fangs. His hands curled around the stake that impaled his body, a small gold cross pendant tangled around one finger. As if mesmerized, I slowly disentangled the dainty chain, pulling it free from his dead hands.

Blood clung to the gold, even as I wiped it on my dress. I'm not sure what brought me out of my shock, but my head snapped up, away from Joshua who was already beginning to resemble the skeleton his body would have been in the grave. I was circled in. A mob had gathered with torches and clubs and other weapons I couldn't see, but could sense. I wiped at the tears in my eyes, angry and more than a little scared. My breath caught in my throat as they came closer. I was paralyzed in a sudden return of fear, those men before me replaced by visions of long dead Hunters on that night so long before.

Old pain remembered, like an icy knife into my soul took my breath from me, robbed me of reason and sent my mind to a dark, forgotten place. The first rock hit my shoulder, sending me sprawling backwards. The second just missed my head by mere inches and the third caught me in the stomach. I scrambled for the door, pulling it frantically shut behind me, turning the key in the lock. My skirt hem caught in the door. As I tried to rip it free, I could hear them coming closer. I pulled loose with a great tear as the first of their torches broke through a window, igniting the drapes. I ran for the back of the house, but more torches greeted me there.

    I was surrounded. My mind raced, unable to think clearly through the fear and adrenaline. My shoulder was bleeding and already badly bruised. There was a deep pain in my stomach that I knew would not heal quickly. I was trapped in a house that by morning would be little more than ashes. I sank to the floor in a pile of skirts and heaved a heavy sigh. At that moment I gave in, gave up at last, and would have willingly died there with Joshua in a fiery, spectacular show, suddenly so weary of it all, of the fight to survive, of a life with no purpose. I felt the fire singing flesh and welcomed the pain, surrendered to it ... but, it was not to be. They did not wish my end to come so easy as that. They were coming now, breaking in the doors, searching the rooms, pulling me to my feet and out into the night. The Change flickered in me, but left quickly, my fury gone. I was calm and defeated as they dragged me out into their midst and pinned me to the ground beneath them. There they staked me down against the hard ground, where I could watch my house and Joshua burn.

I withdrew inside myself, beyond even that place where the terror nibbled at the corners of my heart, past the haunting memories of another night, another burning building. I closed my eyes on the sight and settled my soul into the moment of death. I heard them around me, their fear and hatred tainting their once friendly voices. They spoke of the myriad dead found in the city over the last thirteen years, nearly one a night. They spoke of demons and monsters I had thought long buried in human folklore. They spoke like the fevered Hunters of old, spouting religious dogma and rhetoric as if it might protect them from me.

Then, they turned on me. The fire had nearly consumed the house, and Joshua was gone. Their beating was vicious and cruel, striking at me with sticks and rocks and feet and fists until I bled and could barely remain conscious. Still, nothing stirred within me, nothing until I heard my name, whispered in the far recess of my mind, in a voice dead for more than a century, Rebeka's voice. I saw her face as it had been in death, so beautiful, so peaceful. She called to me, urged me to open my eyes, to live. Then I saw Joshua, as he had been in death, cruel, ugly death. Something small lived in me still; my heart beat loudly in my chest. I opened my eyes.

At least one of these men had somehow known the truth, the truth beyond the harmless mythology of their day, beyond the campfire stories. One of them had known how to kill Joshua. I knew then that this had been no accident. There was a Hunter among them.

I lay still and watched them watching me, trying to determine which of them it might be, or if he was even among them. My body was broken, more so than during my captivity at the hands of the first Hunters, but not nearly what it was after the fall, my heart beat was slow and irregular. For a long time I waited, watched, thought. I listened to Rebeka whispering in my head and I wondered what their plans were for me.

It was less than an hour before dawn before I realized what they meant for me. They scattered into small groups, standing in turns to guard me. They would leave me there to watch the sunrise as I had the burning of my home, to die like an animal, chained to the ground, caught in their trap as my demise approached. The thought terrified me. Visions of my brave and wondrous Jesse as he walked into that final sunrise filled my mind. I found my desire to live in the terror. It took all of my considerable strength of will not to thrash about in my bindings, screaming and hoping to break free.

Instead, I lay there and held myself tightly, praying that I might find the strength Jesse had that fateful morning all those years before, to face that sunrise with stoic bravery. I would get no chance to sink hungry fangs into a soft neck as one of them bent to stake me. They dispersed as the sun came, bringing its painful, lingering death over the distant horizon. Only one young man was left to guard me, so sure were they that within minutes I would be dead.

I felt it first on the soles of my bare feet which faced east into the coming dawn, that old, half familiar pain, the searing of my own flesh. It grew in intensity as the moments stretched outward. Just as I thought I could bear no more of it, it rose up my half exposed legs, touched my hands. I held my breath and tried not to let the pain register as it became stronger, and the smell of undead, unliving flesh filled the early morning air. I bit my tongue against it, held my breath. In my memory I could see that circle of daylight my cell window had let in, the vision of the priest standing in that puddle of light to protect himself from me. I tossed in my chains as the pain increased, and my dark hair scattered across my face, covering my tightly closed eyes. I prayed that I might die before I had to feel the touch of that light I had once lusted for upon my face.

Then I felt it. A shadow crossed the path of the sun. A dark, cooling shadow. A cloud had come to offer me respite. I waited for it to move on and the torture to resume. Lightning flashed, to be followed by a tiny droplet of cold water. I scarcely dared hope, barely breathed, as I opened one eye so slowly, and looked up through my hair at my savior. The thundercloud was huge, filling most of the sky above me, blocking out the killing, rising sun and drenching me with cold, soothing rain. I think I was laughing as I strained once more at the chains, feeling something akin to strength flooding once more as I let the Change take me and the inhuman power of my mother's clan filled me. I pulled at the stakes which held me until they gave way and climbed to my feet to face the young man who now approached me with a wooden stake in hand.

"I will not harm you, little one," I said through my protruding fangs. "Go and tell them I am gone."

"I can't do that, demon," He spat back, swinging his stake in my direction.

"I was afraid of that." I hit him with the chains that still dangled from my wrists, knocking him to his knees. I was on him faster than he could even see, pinning him to the ground beneath me while I searched him for the keys which would free me from the hanging weight of the shackles. It took me a minute to find them, and by the time I did I was beginning to feel the adrenaline fade. I would have to find food soon. I thought briefly about feeding on my prisoner, but decided not to further fuel the fire which had killed Joshua. Instead, I merely chained him to a nearby tree, knowing the others would return soon enough. Indeed, I could already hear the approaching carriages coming to the turn of the drive.

I wasted no more time, simply grabbed the young man's cloak and dashed off into the woods. Thunder shook the ground and lightning streaked the sky. I ran for hours on feet burned and bloodied in the twilight of the storm. I gave no thought to direction or time or distance. I raced to put space between me and my imagined pursuit. Somewhere about an hour before sunset, the cloud cover broke and the sun began to shine through. I found an old, felled tree covered in moss and leaves and slipped beneath it, covering myself completely with the stolen cloak and leaves.

I slept fitfully for several hours, tossed by fevered dreams of Jesse and Joshua and Rebeka, and woke to distant shouts and the sounds of dogs. The pain from my wounds crashed into me as I pulled myself from my hiding place. It almost forced me back to my knees, but somehow I managed to come somewhat upright and begin to move once more. The sounds of pursuit grew close, then backed off again as they lost my trail. I tied the cloak around my shoulders and took off at a sort of run, heading uphill, into the mountains. I was delirious with fever and pain, leaving a trail of bloodied footsteps for them to follow. I ran the entire night, until my wounds and the cold brought me to my knees. A small, cold stream offered some respite for the burns, and for my torn feet, which I then bandaged with pieces I ripped from my ruined dress. I crawled upstream in the water, hoping to throw off the scent the dogs were following, then dug myself a grave. The thought terrified me, to once more consign myself to the earth, but I needed the rest, the chance to recover. I needed the safety only a secure place could afford. So, fighting my own memory, I dug a shallow grave with my bare hands and crawled inside. I struggled to pull the dirt back over me enough to protect myself from the coming sun, but finally succeeded. With the damp earth pulled over me like a blanket, I closed my eyes and slept.

When I woke, I listened for nearly an hour for signs of my Hunters, but there were none. I had no way of knowing how long I slept, how many days and nights had passed since I had buried myself in the earth, or whether or not they had given up pursuit of me. I rose cautiously, pulling myself up from the ground slowly so as not to jar my injuries too much. I trapped a rabbit and fed, but it lay cold and hard in my belly. I need to fully feed, to rest in blessed darkness. Daylight was coming once more. My hunger brought me to another rabbit and several small birds. I move painfully, slowly, limping on feet that gave out on me often.

In a meadow filled with wildflowers I fell to my knees in combined exhaustion and agony. My breathing was ragged and the small amount I had put into my stomach threatened to explode violently from me. I had little hope at that moment besides crawling back into the earth. Then, my eyes fell on the tiny little cottage, nestled back among the trees, its windows lighting up in the wee morning hours. With nowhere else to go, I staggered to the door, and collapsed.

Chapter 17

THE WOMAN who opened the door was perhaps sixty, and instantly maternal, calling her husband to help me inside. They questioned me as they washed and dressed my wounds and fed me a loaf of warm bread, but didn't seem bothered that I didn't answer most of their questions. I was shivering in shock and hurt, barely speaking. After she had seen me eat the better part of the loaf of bread, the good woman wrapped me in a quilt and laid me down in a soft feather bed in a loft room with no windows. I gave up caring about anything, and fell deeply asleep as I imagine daylight was rounding the horizon outside.

Horrifying dreams chased me into the day, nightmarish visions of Hunters and their prey, fires that lit the night skies and Jesse's voice condemning what he had become, what I had always been. Somewhere in the long hours they drifted away and I settled into the ethereal sleep of my mother's people, where the wounds could begin their healing and rest might restore my fear-crazed mind. I woke just after sunset to the aroma of dinner cooking and the sound of humming. I sat up stiffly, taking inventory of myself now that I was at the very least rested. My feet and legs had burned pretty badly, and the mad running had done them little good. My hands had been scorched some too, and my wrists and ankles chaffed from the chains. There was a long gash down my left leg from some shattered glass or whipping tree limb and my face was bruised from the beating. The wound in my shoulder was severe, stiff and crusted over with blood, and my stomach was bruised an ugly shade of black and purple beneath the tear in my dress. The healing had already begun, as I had known it would. The intense need grew within me. I craved that which would speed my recovery. I was well enough. I rose on shaky legs and wrapped the quilt around me. I shuffled to the door and opened it onto a very safe and domestic scene. The woman and her husband were sitting at the table to eat, and beside them a man, a young man whose eyes never left his dish. I must have started at seeing him, for the woman rose and came to me. "Don't be frightened, dear. This is my son, Francis."

She gently steered me to a chair between Francis and her husband. "Sit, I'll fetch you some dinner."

I felt awkward and out of place sitting there, as she put a plate full of a rich looking stew in front of me. "I apologize, for intruding this way," I said after a long time. "And, for not answering your questions this morning. I was frightened, and I had nowhere to go."

"Don't worry yourself, child. Eat your supper. I'll set you a bath after and you can tidy up. Then, if you're up to it, we'll talk."

Sitting there I could smell them, the warm, inviting smell of life. It resonated around me under the more powerful scents of the dinner, of the damp earth outside, of the rain due to fall, of the burning logs in the fire. I wrestled the demon within as I ate, chewing each bite so thoroughly as to have nearly nothing left when I at last swallowed.

I dared not speak, nor look at them for fear I might lose control of it. I felt the Change within, begging to be released, the voice of the hunger whispering in my head as they made pleasant small talk about the day. It would be so easy, it said, so easy. They're old and won't fight. Old blood is thick and rich and filled with so much life. The young man won't even see me coming. Three of them would have me whole in no time. I swallowed it over and over, trying to ignore the words, the thoughts. I closed my eyes so I couldn't see them, but it only made the smell of them stronger. My breathing was becoming ragged ... they would notice soon.

I took a deep breath and opened my eyes. If they had noticed they didn't say a word. I bit harshly into my piece of bread and forced myself into their conversation. The voice in my head subsided, but I could still hear it whispering insidiously. I learned of them that night, all that there was to know was there at that supper table. They loved each other immensely, and the child they had raised here to protect him from the cruelty of the world. They were hard working people, good and kind and generous. It only made me want them more.

Francis never said a word through dinner, and when he had finished eating he left the table without even excusing himself. I watched him walk away, and sighed. The woman took this as some manner of cue, and rose to fill the bath she had promised me. The water was rather cool as I slid into it, feeling some of the tension and ache drift away. When I began to grow chill, I rose, and found a clean sleeping gown awaiting me. I pulled it on, followed by the robe lying across the chair nearest the tub in the little kitchen, and went back out by the fire where the woman and her husband were sitting.

I told them a story of my husband who had been killed, by men who had wanted him to help them rob the bank where he worked. I said that the men who had done it had come after me as well. I even threw in the truth about the fire, to explain the burns. I told them I had barely gotten away and had run through the woods for days before finding them. I let enough of my hunger show to make my face as afraid and desperate as I could. I said I was afraid that if I returned they would finish me off, to keep me quiet. When I finished my tale, they appeared to believe the better part of it, and being the kind folks I could already tell them to be, they invited me to stay on, to rest and recover. I thanked them and sat with them for an hour or so, making small talk and exchanging pleasantries before I excused myself back to the bedroom. I was shaking from head to toe with barely controlled desire. I lay down on the soft bed, but sleep was a long way off now. The hours spent in the company of so much warm blood had me so agitated I wouldn't sleep now until I had tasted it. I needed to feed.

I waited until the old man and woman had retired and the sounds of a house settling in for the night had ceased. I rose from the bed and pulled the robe close around me. The Change was full upon me as I opened the door to the little room and tiptoed through the cottage. Before I knew how I stood at the door of the old couple, looking in on them sleeping curled together. Her long, white hair draped the pillow beside her and over his one shoulder. I know my teeth were bared as I fought myself in that door and had either of them woke, they might have died in fright of what they had let into their home.

It took every ounce of myself to pull me away from them, clenching my hands around my elbows in an iron grip as my feet stumbled through the unfamiliar rooms and out into the night, walking softly on raw and tender feet. There were any number of wild beasts about and I had little trouble finding what I sought. I fell upon a deer first, ripping its neck savagely and gulping its blood greedily. I was insane with it, stalking the shadows for each quivering life I could find. When I was sated and full of life once more, I returned quietly to the small cottage and to my bed. The next weeks were filled with manic hunting and fighting myself. Each night I would rise hungrier than the night before. I would eat with my hosts, and retire once more to my room until they slept, then into the night I would run to feed.

    I kept largely to myself, easy enough to do, upon explaining to my benefactors soon after that first night that my skin and eyes were too sensitive, and sunlight bothered me immensely, the result of a childhood ailment not treated early enough, I had said. Thus, they did not question my long days sleeping in the darkness of my room, or my appearance only after sun down.

I healed, in direct response to the food and the feeding, my body reclaimed itself, the pains eased, the aches dissipated. I saw little of the young man, Francis, and less of the husband, but thought that fair enough in the measure of safety. My nightly visits to the forest kept me alive and healing, and offered me the solace and solitude I needed to come to terms with myself once more.

One night while returning to the cottage from my hunt, I saw Francis, standing barefoot on the stone path, his hand on the rope railing. It was early summer, the night warm, moist with the hint of coming rains. Only the slightest of breezes stirred the heavy air. He was standing with his face turned toward the full moon, his eyes closed. He appeared to me serene, like a man who knows exactly his own place in life, and is perfectly at home within it. I watched for a long moment, then walked in his direction.

"It's a beautiful night, isn't it?" I said softly. He jumped a little, startled at my voice so close, but didn't open his eyes.

"I love nights like this," he said in response, once he had recovered from his shock.

"Hmmm ... me too." I turned to look up at the moon which had held his interest so. "I do my best thinking at night."

"Sometimes, standing here, when I know the moon is full, I can almost imagine that I can see it, all full and bright."

I squinted in his direction, for I hadn't known that he was blind. "Since birth," he said as if he could hear the question. "I've never seen that moon, or the sunrise, or this wonderful mountain we live on." He sighed and it sounded lonely, and yet not.

"Would it help if I told you that I have also never seen the sun rise?" I asked softly, a flash of my only sunrise returning to me as I came to stand beside him, turning my face back to the giant moon above. "This is the only light I know. But, somehow, the moon suits me."

"Yes, me too," he said.

That was the beginning of our friendship, and our nightly ritual. He would always be there, waiting for me on that path when I returned from my walk, and we would stand there and talk until the first rays of dawn were just making themselves felt in the far distant east. I understood then why I had seen so little of him in those early days. Like me he was more comfortable in the dark, and he seldom ventured out of his rooms until I had already left the house to hunt. There was a place, at the end of the path with its rope railing where he would pass the time, listening to water gurgling through a creek. My path seldom brought me near it, preferring the easier way through the meadow.

I healed faster than I imagined, and my appetite eased. I began making short trips down the mountain to a small town north of the city I had fled. The old man was increasingly ill, barely able to tend the small field he planted to sell, and the trip was difficult for him. I started going for supplies, trading the family's crops for things they required. Fortunately for me, the trip was short, and I only had to reach the farm of the old man's brother. He had no problem meeting me in the early hours before dawn, and he brought me the supplies so I didn't have to go into the town itself. I was fearful of mankind, and kept to myself on the road and in town. It was almost irrational, but well understood given my last experience in civilization.

Three trips over two months in the crisp fall air and I brought back the last of the food and other necessities for the winter. I managed to trade a few rabbit pelts and deerskins for enough equipment to begin making my formula again. I set up my lab in a cavern not far from the cabin I now called home, but distant enough not to be easily found. Once I had re-learned the formula, I slowly weaned myself off the taste of fresh blood once more. I took easily to the quiet life there in the hills, the ease of things, the serenity of nature. I seemed to fit smoothly into their lives, taking up chores that once the old couple might have done, but which had fallen into undone. I was like a mostly unseen guest, a ghostly wraith who flitted through the shadows, leaving only neatly piled wood and well-tended gardens in her wake. As winter settled in, I made a formal request to stay out the winter. They were kind enough to offer me the continued use of the loft, in exchange for my continued help.

Early that spring, the old man died, quietly, in his sleep. The old woman seemed to lose her desire for life, and by the time planting season came along, she had passed away as well, leaving their only son into my care. The old woman asked me to stay and look after him, which seemed only fair and fitting after all they had done for me. Besides which, I had grown rather fond of him. We shared a great many things in common, other than our love of the dark. He had a great passion for music, both classical and common, he loved to pass hours by the fire while I read to him, and long walks beneath the moon. Ours was a deep, abiding friendship, not the hot passion of my love for Jesse, or the playful, gaming relationship I had shared with Joshua, but a calm, almost soothing bond.

He was approaching middle age, still a slight man with brown hair just beginning to grow gray at the temples, and long blind eyes that still sparkled when he spoke of poetry or music. He was intelligent and witty, understanding my complexity perhaps better than I myself. We spoke of ancient times, and sometimes I thought he sensed the truth behind my observations. Once or twice I nearly told him, simply blurting it out as he held me in his arms after the gentle lovemaking that was ours. Always something withheld me from it though. He suspected I had secrets, hinting at them without ever actually asking about them, and pulling back away from the intrusion with a small pun and a smile. I even considered bringing him to me, to share this calm, tender love into eternity, but then I remembered Jesse and how he detested what he became. I couldn't have done that to Francis.

We talked at length about family and children. He wanted a daughter he said, and asked me if I had ever thought about having children of my own.

"I have a daughter, of sorts," I said in response, thinking of Moira for the first time in years.

"What does that mean?" he asked.

"Hmmm, well, she's not really my child, but I found her when she was young and taught her, raised her to be who she is."

"Do you love her?"

"More than I thought possible. She is the closest thing I will ever have to a child of my own."

"Where is she?" he asked, sensing perhaps the vague melancholy that had settled over me.

"Oh, I'm not sure. She's fully grown, living a life of her own. I haven't seen her in a long, long time." I laughed and ran my fingers through his hair. "What does it matter?"

"I would like to have known her. She must be wonderful." He sat up and reached for his glass of wine. "There are a great many things about you that I would like to know better." The look on his face was distant, as if he were attempting to picture me, or some aspect of my life he had imagined.

"I'm sure there are," I said playfully, getting up to take our empty dinner plates into the kitchen from the sitting room where we had dined on the floor by the fire.

"Still going to pretend it's some big mystery, my dear? Shall I guess at them?"

"Please don't. I'm not sure I want to know what grand tales you've created in that mind of yours," I responded upon returning to the room. "I would much rather forget the history of it and move on to now."

"Oh, afraid I might have figured you out?"

"No, afraid you might paint my life more interesting than it actually is and then I would get depressed and have to go out and jump off the cliff." As I said it, a memory of my one particular journey off a cliff flitted past. It was almost as if he had somehow shared the thought.

"Ouch, that hurts," he said softly.

"You have no idea."

I took a deep breath to shake the memory and kissed him. "Come on, let's walk."

And, so we were, when I began to hear the whispers of the others. It had been many years since I had marked the passing of any of my kin, but in the space of only several months, I had counted six passing by, and two who had stayed long enough to investigate what dark soul hid away in these hills. I dreaded the moment that was inevitable, and I fretted about poor Francis and what to tell him, how to warn him … or if I shouldn't simply leave before they arrived. We had talked about moving him down to his uncle's farm, but he was dead set against the idea, preferring the solitude his parents had brought him up the mountain for.

The choice was taken quite out of my hands, however. It was late into the summer, nearly to the fall. Francis and I were out for our nightly stroll, hand in hand along the cold creek. It had been a mild summer, and the air was cold, but not frigid enough to chase us indoors. The forest was quiet around us, too quiet. Nothing stirred, not even a breeze to ruffle the trees. My stomach tightened as we neared the cottage and I sniffed the air, trying to place the uneasy feeling in my soul. When the odor finally reached me, the distinct smell of an old one, I tried not to panic, but Francis could sense my sudden fear.

"What is it?" he asked.

I was looking around frantically, but couldn't see him. I knew he was there, and watching us. "Francis, listen to me. We're only about a hundred feet from the house. You're pointing straight at it. I want you to go as fast as you can and lock yourself in."

"Why? What's wrong?"

"I'll explain it later. Can you make it?"

"Yes, I think so."

"Good, go." I gave him a little push to get him going, following just two steps behind, trying to watch all around the exposed walk at once. I could almost feel our unwelcome visitor circling us, barely heard him as he made his rush. I pushed Francis to the ground and told him to stay down. The other's hands were already around my shoulder, pulling me backward. I let the Change come over me, turning an angry face to my attacker.

"I have hunted for you for a long time, Sister." he said, baring his teeth. "You who kill your own people." I kicked hard and swiped his feet out from under him, falling on top of him as he went down. We grappled for several long moments, then I raked my nails across his face, drawing long, bloody welts down his cheek. He screamed in rage and tossed me aside. I hit a tree and felt blood on the back of my head. He rose and came toward me, wiping at the scratches. "I am the last of Crenoral's clan. I have come to claim vengeance, and hold you accountable for their deaths."

I used the tree behind me for balance as I pulled myself to my feet. "Crenoral is dead, and so are his children. You are but a remnant of what they once were. Leave here now, and I will not kill you as well." I did not know him, but I had been away from the clan for so long before Jesse and I decimated it, there was no way of knowing how many had joined them in my absence.

"That is big talk for one in your position. Come, let me show you death."

He was strong, far stronger than I, and I knew only moments later that I would more than likely not survive this fight, but that I would take him with me, to protect poor Francis. I could feel the wound at the base of my skull draining slowly, seeping precious blood into my hair and down my neck. His teeth nicked a shoulder as I pulled myself free of him and a long line of blood sprang up there as well. I hissed in anger and pain and tried to direct some of that emotion into my draining physical reserves. I scored another blow across his face, making a matching wound to the first. I was tiring rapidly.

He fell on me, using his superior strength to great advantage, working me down to my knees, then ever so slowly, down, until I felt the hard, cold ground against my bruised shoulders. I was pinned, his knee on my neck as he raised my scarred wrist to his lips and bit. I bucked beneath him, but he held fast, drinking away my life as I had to countless victims. I fought against him until I could no more, and when he felt my resistance die, he let go of me, leaving me alive to witness what he would do with Francis.

Francis was sitting still where I had left him, his eyes wild as he tried to hear what was happening. He called my name repeatedly, but I was too weak to respond. I watched the other circle around him, closer and closer, taunting the blind man, and finally sinking to his knees behind him, drawing him closer, and bending to his neck. His eyes closed as the taste filled him, the exquisite taste of goodness and beauty. I had long imagined what ecstasy must be there in Franciss' blood, had craved it, and held to the desire for him that was almost more pleasurable than the deed might have been.

I closed my eyes, imagining the taste. There was a tiny movement inside of me when Francis whispered my name once more. My eyes fluttered open and looked upon him. The sluggish beating of my heart seemed to echo in the pit of my stomach. The other's eyes were still closed, savoring the sweetness that was Francis. I found myself crawling in painful slowness toward them, pulling strength from within, the strength Jesse must have possessed as he walked out of that tomb. I pulled myself onto my knees and fell on him, driving my teeth into his neck as he pulled away from Francis with surprise. I locked my jaws and dug in, drinking back all that he had stolen from me, and all that was Francis, all that remained. I drank quickly, harshly, leaving nothing but a jagged wound when I at last dropped him, fully satisfied and strong once more.

Francis was dead, and there was little left but to mourn his passing. I buried him beside his mother and father, and left the ashes of my ancient enemy to the winds. It was with more than a little sadness that I left that little cottage and the brief contentment I had found there. I could smell the others in the air, perhaps drawn by the scent of death, perhaps searching for me as the other had been. I did not care to be there to find out. Once more, I gathered my belongings and fled my home.

The world below our mountain had grown, and the young country was building a political turmoil. Friends and families argued vague points of political ambition and freedoms. There was an aroma on the air of impending war, of fear and ultimately, of death. I did not like the smell, or the contagious atmosphere that bred it. I had last heard rumors of such things from the farmer, but had chalked them up to gossip, the human need to speculate the worst of things before analyzing the truth of them. Now, I as I traveled off the mountain, I could see I had misjudged the situation. Already armies were being gathered and the sides had been drawn. War was inevitable, though still a way off.

The charge in the air set me on edge and left me too close to uncontrolled for my tastes. I had no wish to get caught up in such a terrible conflict as this was to be, brother against brother over the trivial political differences and great sweeping judgments of humanity. I wandered westward, away from the divisions of the young country, into the wilderness that was already beginning to grow more civilized. I had loved the wild, open expanses when I had walked and rode them with Lianna. I hoped to enjoy them again.

Perhaps two years I wandered alone and unmarred. I slept in caves and caverns and other dark places, and I strolled unhurried beneath the stars. I carried little with me, save a small amount of cash, and a change of clothes, sometimes not even that much. I found it more difficult to find the supplies needed for the formula while wandering that way, and as if in response to that, I felt my hunger, my need for sustenance increasing. Whether it was the physical activity, or the effects of the fresh, nighttime air, I found it needful to supplement my diet with an occasional animal, very often roasting the meat after draining it, and eating voraciously yet again.

I indulged myself while in the wilds, and yet constrained myself most effectively while in the company of humanity. I would feed well as I approached a populated area, to take the edge off of the temptation, and avoid private meetings for the first day or two. Then, it was as if I had been among them for years. I would trade a small gem or ancient jewel for what money I needed, spend a few days in whatever town I happened to find myself in, then wander off once more.

It was a calm, carefree moment in my long existence, when I dealt best with who and what I was. I was then, perhaps only then, at peace with the monster and the woman inside of me, giving both their place in the night. My thoughts didn't wander to my past loves, losses, or pain. I did not think of my long gone Jesse or Rebeka, Joshua, or even Francis. Moira and Leonard were far from me, as were those other children I had abandoned into the night. There was only me and the stars, in the wild country as it was meant to be.

Chapter 18

I was wandering through San Francisco in the far west, considering a return to my homeland, or perhaps a visit to China or London, when I caught sight of my reflection in a store window. I stopped, staring in amazement. I had not noticed anything before that moment, but standing there, gazing at my profile, I imagined that I saw a gentle, slight bulge in my belly where there had been none before. My hand slipped there to caress it, touch it, my eyes glued to my reflection. No, I chided myself for my imagination, for even thinking that which I had been thinking. I had been indulging my appetite far too much. I made a mental note to try to control myself more often.

Weight had never been a problem for me, except perhaps in the regard of not weighing enough, of appearing emaciated, a thing all those of the night are accustomed to. One of my kind must feed exceedingly well to exhibit anything that might appear as obesity. I reasoned that I had been feeding far too well.

The next evening as I rose from my slumber, I reached instinctively for the bottle of formula by my bed and I drained it. It felt strange, tasted dry and bland. Perhaps I had mixed it a trifle off. I rose from my bed, and almost before my feet had touched the floor, I felt the first wave of nausea, followed quickly by a second, and a third. I found myself retching violently on the floor, coughing as I choked up every drop I had swallowed. It left a curious puddle of red, the sight of which only served to sicken me further. I climbed to my feet rather shakily and moved away from the slowly spreading liquid. I felt rather foolish, but somehow, I simply didn't want it to touch me.

I was dizzy then, and weak, confused. Never before had I felt this way, never before had I known illness, except that caused by my conscience or poison. I dressed slowly, cautiously, lest the nausea return, and left my small dark apartment. In the fading light of twilight, I made my way to my favorite local restaurant and ordered myself some dinner, nothing heavy; some soup, my favorite wine, cheese, and bread. The queasy feelings began to subside. I thought about the evening, and decided that the formula must have gone bad through the night ... and, I needed new equipment. Mine was so old, I could have used my lab for a museum exhibit. I convinced myself of it, and swore I would buy new equipment that very evening.

I ate slowly, picking around anything that set off the nausea again. There was still nearly a plateful when I rose, tossed some money on the table and left to seek out a store to purchase what I would need. Again, I saw myself as I passed the rows of picture windows, and again, I found my hand cupping itself to the small bulge just above my pelvic area. There was a vague, distant smile on my face I didn't recognize as my own.

In a store for general merchandise, I spent an hour looking through a catalogue of medical supplies, carefully picking out the new items I would need. I ordered them, paid the man in cash, including a little extra for his time and set out again. I made for home, my weakness and the nausea driving me to rest. I was nearly to the street where my apartment was, above a barbershop, when, out of the corner of my eye, I saw a young couple, obviously just returning from some trip, a baby asleep in her arms. They drew me. Something about them called out to me and before I knew what I was doing, I was crossing the street to them. My eyes were locked on the face of that sleeping child. I could smell the sweetness of her, could taste the love between the man and the woman and the child, could hear their thoughts about and to each other. As I stepped off the street, an arm's length away from them, the man dropped two bags he was trying to get down off the wagon.

Instinctively I bent to help them, retrieving one and standing, suddenly face to face with the woman. "Thank you," she said, so polite, so ... human. The man took the bag with a little bow. Her eyes stole to my belly and she smiled. "But, you shouldn't be lifting in your condition."

My hand stole back, my breath left me. I must have looked confused. She smiled again. "It does take some getting used to, not being able to do so many things, but it's worth it in the end."

The child shifted, opened her beautiful blue eyes. I tried to cover my shock, my fear ... my sudden elation. My lungs exploded and my stomach twisted as it dawned within me. I locked onto that child, as if her face would hold me to the earth at that moment. "What a beautiful child," I said, smiling myself.

"My pride and joy," she responded, holding her up where I could see her better. "Would you like to hold her?"

I nodded. Suddenly it was all I wanted to do, to hold her tiny body, to feel her heart moving in that rapid rhythm of a child full of life. She handed her to me and I brought her to my chest, feeling my heart increase its rhythm to match hers. "Her name is Joy," her mother said.

I was insane. I heard my mind whispering it. She looked at me with wide, innocent eyes and I felt something move inside of me. I felt myself flush with some unnamed, unrecognized emotion. It was foreign and embarrassing and what little bit of blood remained in me rose to my pale cheeks.

Joy. She was that. I cradled her against me and closed my eyes. She was so warm and soft. My heartbeat entangled around hers and I felt a connection, something vital linking this mortal child and myself.

Eventually, I sensed a nervousness growing in the mother and father and managed, somehow, to pull myself away, to hand Joy back to her mother and smile softly, almost ... maternally. "She is most wonderful." I said, my ancient accent creeping oddly into my voice. "Please, allow me to gift you and your child." I fished into my purse, digging for something I kept there for emergencies: a small sapphire, one of the remaining gems from the Family vaults, the size of my small fingernail. It seemed the absolute color of the baby's eyes. I handed it to her. I knew she wouldn't take it immediately. "Please, no arguments. It is old, and I have so many more. Take it, keep it for her. One day, when she is of an age, give it to her and tell her of how she touched my heart."

The woman had tears in her eyes as her hand closed around my gift. I discovered I did also. I touched that tiny cheek one more time and hurried away, not looking back, lest I be drawn further into their lives. I knew that one gem was worth perhaps more than that family would see in a lifetime, a gift without measure. It had meant little to me, but now I knew it would mean so much more.

I hurried home, trying desperately not to think, not to acknowledge what had begun on that night, what I had discovered in those few short hours. I was filled with apprehension, and unbelievable delight. I had not thought it possible ... all these years, and a handful of relationships ... no, not possible at all. Of course, neither had I believed myself capable of creating the monster, until Moira. Still, it had been two years since Francis's death, and another fifteen since Joshua. It couldn't be. I was losing my mind. My sanity was finally gone, torn away by the long years in the night and the deaths of so many I had held so dear.

I stood before my mirror and touched my belly. It seemed hard, round. There was simply no denying the change in my weight, in my body. I stripped out of my clothes and returned to the mirror naked. My pale flesh fairly gleamed in the firelight, my black hair contrasting sharply, making my skin all the more pale. I had not truly looked at myself in many years.

I was not one concerned with appearance as much as my mortal sisters. Occasionally I was concerned about the odd white coloring of my skin, enough to attempt to shade it with powders and such cosmetics as the world had to offer at a given time. My hair I allowed to grow long and straight, cutting it only when it became unmanageable. It was black, dark as midnight and filled with the shine of the stars. My face is long and narrow, my dark eyes set wide apart. That night they shined brightly back at me from the face of the mirror.

I let my gaze wander to the slim, but deceptively strong shoulders and arms, the smallish, but pert and still very young looking breasts, down the soft skin to where that little pouch began. My hands caressed it repeatedly, as if trying somehow to feel what lay beneath the surface, to know it completely by a touch. I was still there, staring into that mirrored reflection of the truth as the distant sun began its rise. Reluctantly, I pulled a nightgown over my head and set about preparing to retire for the day.

I may have lain quietly in my black draped queen size bed, but I doubt I closed my eyes all day, except to savor the feeling growing within me, the delicious, unbelievable clarity and joy that welled up each time I let my mind wander to the prospect. Eventually, near on to nightfall, I began to think about the years ahead of me. A child ... the long pregnancy, the most-assuredly difficult delivery. I tried to remember everything my mother may have ever said to me regarding my own birthing. There was precious little to remember. I determined at that moment that this child would have the best childhood I could give it, the most carefree and loving home, the best teachers and books. I wanted to instill the still unborn creature with a love of life and discipline, a moral obligation to the world around us. This, at long last, would be my reparation. A child, grown of my years of wisdom and raised in absolute love and tolerance to help the world to reach a place of lasting peace.

I had no idea what manner of child this might be, but I had hopes that it would bear all the human traits of its father and myself, with little or no appearance of the other that I was. I set about making plans for the arrival, though I hadn't any knowledge of how long a wait I might have, or how many years it would take to bring this to fruition. I consolidated bank accounts, drew up plans and sent them on to an agent of mine in London. He would arrange what I asked for, while I journeyed to meet him. I set about my travel arrangements, a private carriage east and north, to the port city called New York where I would board a ship bound for France. From there I would journey by hired coach, several weeks to a place not far from that of my birth, half way up a mountainside where caves hid my personal treasures from the world.

I had need also of a personal servant, a maid, preferably a midwife of strong personal will, who would not frighten easily at the truth of what I was. I began the search for her immediately, wanting her with me as I underwent this journey. I found my way to various doctors, midwives and mothers, asking discreet questions in an attempt to discern the time of the arrival. I determined that I was close onto what humans would consider the fourth month of gestation, Four months, in two years' time. That would give me two and a half years, give or take a month or two.

I was drawn in the early evenings in those first months to little Joy. I could hear her cries and laughter from across town and would inevitably find myself outside her window. The mother and father, so in love with each other and their precious gift, they had no notice of me, or the potential for danger I represented. Not that I wanted to hurt them, but I wanted. Deeply I felt the resonance of her tiny voice, sensed something in her I never had before. Her blue eyes knew me, knew what I was. Her heart sensed my presence and reached out to me. I would hover outside her nursery and she would look at me with eyes somehow filled with the knowledge of me. I ached inside to look upon her.

It was insanity, I should have been leaving that town, but instead I lingered, pausing to bestow gifts upon this stranger's child. I found a lawyer with a reputable firm and set about preparing a trust for the child, a fund to educate her in the finest schools. I contacted the man's employer, and persuaded him to promote the man, by providing a large sum to pay the balance of his salary. I then produced a small inheritance for the woman, some jewelry and money, to be delivered to her as if from some distant and unknown relative. I gave instruction to the lawyer as to how I could be reached once I had left for Europe, and that I was to be notified if anything were to happen to any of them.

That done, I chanced to visit them once more. It was early evening, the sun barely down when I knocked at their door. I was admitted easily enough, for such a gift as I had given on the street that day is not difficult to remember. I spoke with them for quite some time, playing with Joy until she fell asleep at my breast.

"I cannot begin to make you understand what your daughter has done to me," I said, the lilt of my accent adding a foreign touch to my words. "I will be leaving here soon, to birth my child in the lands of my birth. I wonder if I might occasionally write to you, and to Joy? I want to know how she fares, where her life takes her. Perhaps even one day she can meet my wee one." Her tiny heart beat tangled around mine even in her sleep, so soft and gentle, hypnotic. They had no way of knowing the benefits my affection would bring, for they would be told nothing of it until I was gone. They agreed of course, already feeling indebted to my kindness. I handed Joy back to her mother and rose to leave. "Thank you for indulging me. It is not often in a lifetime one finds such remarkable beauty of body and spirit. Teach her well and the world will bow to her command."

That accomplished, I turned myself more seriously to finding the servant I would require in the coming years and to the caring for my physical needs, which I found changing from day to day. I switched my diet to consist almost entirely of human foods, cutting back even my formula to only those moments when the hunger got the better of me. Perhaps I was delusional, or merely foolish, but some part of me believed that if I denied myself my darker nature while carrying this child, it might never have need of that perverse sustenance we survive upon.

Nearly three months after my discovery of my impending motherhood, I found the perfect woman to join me on my journey. She was a young

Chinese woman, orphaned at a young age and raised by a midwife. Her name was Lu Sin. She was quiet, intelligent and easily convinced by the promise of travel and good pay to join me. I bought us a closed coach, fully darkened within by heavy drapes to guard the smallest cracks, and a driver for it. I would use the long travel from the west coast to the east to explain myself to my young companion, to instruct her in all the things she need know about me.

To my surprise, she took all I had to say without a word, only a knowing acceptance in her dark eyes, and a nod or two as things I said related to similar myths in her ancient heritage. She had a few questions, mostly having to do with my moral choices and how I had arrived at them.

"How long then, has it been since you last tasted human blood?" she asked, her voice soft, her dark eyes squarely on my face.

"Let me think a moment. Hmmm ... more than a hundred years, unless you wish to count the Vampyre I killed. He had fed on a human moments before I took his life."

"And you survive on human food?"

"Yes, I can. However, the hunger often runs to blood. I have a formula that I make, a mixture of compounds that is and is not blood. My body is mostly fooled."

"What of the child? Her father?"

"He is dead. Gone since before I had known of her."

"Will she be human?"

"I hope so. Her father was, I am half, with any luck she will inherit that and little of the other."

"Luck has little to do with it, my friend. It will depend on you, on what happens between now and the birthing, and after as she is raised. We will do what can be done. She will never have need to know her darker side."

I had chosen well. We became quiet friends in those first months, as we made the long, grueling journey that I did not remember being so difficult the first time. It did not help that war had begun and we were forced to keep well to the north to avoid the battle lines. The child within me grew incessantly, I could almost feel it expand some days. Others it sat silent and scarcely moving within. By the time we arrived in New York, the little bulge that I had first noticed had become more apparent, and I found it necessary to loosen the waist of my dresses.

We were two days early for our ship's departure aboard an Inman line vessel, so we arranged to spend them in a hotel not far from the piers. I sold the coach and paid the driver and we waited. Already, Lu Sin had grown maternal in her duties, hurrying me off to the privacy of the bedroom when daylight had only begun to think about arriving, and greeting me at nightfall with more food than three pregnant women could eat. We were at long last given permission to board, and we immediately secured our new lodgings with locks I had brought to guard against the daytime entry of any well-meaning passengers or crew. I had already decided we should keep primarily to ourselves this voyage, and Lu Sin alone would interact with the other mortals aboard. I had brought a meager lab set up and supplies, for those moments of weakness, and found her an eager study. A week out of New York, she was making my formula for me.

She learned quickly what mortal foods I could and could not manage, and how to tell by my coloring when the hunger was raging and I needed to feed it, whether I wanted to or not. She fit in so well there beside me that I began to wonder what I ever did before she found her way there. Half way to our destination, the seas turned ugly, storms tossing us about and creating fear among once carefree passengers. Lu Sin seemed the only center of calm among them, passing quietly through their ranks to assure them that we were in good hands and that the high winds would only bring us to our destination sooner than expected.

She was, somehow, correct. We arrived in Liverpool a full week before our scheduled arrival, slipping off the boat in the darkness almost before she had fully docked. The child did not enjoy the watery excursion, roiling riotously within throughout the trip. That morning, as I drifted to sleep in a comfortable room, it quieted for the first time. I woke several hours later. Lu Sin slept nearby, her soft, scarcely audible breathing somehow reassuring to me. I stretched beneath the luxurious linens, feeling my growing stomach against the cloth, and imagining I could feel tiny hands stretching up to feel it too. I listened to my heart beating, to my lungs slowly giving and taking air, then ... oh, so tender, so tiny ... the other within ... beating in echo to mine ... not quite in rhythm. I closed my eyes and tried to picture that small, little body, curled up inside of mine. I almost imagined I could feel her respond. I wanted to hold her then, to have this long pregnancy ended and be holding my child in my arms. I drifted back to sleep with a picture of her in my mind.

I woke once more near sunset and rose to bathe before Lu Sin woke. I wanted to be off to Paris by the following sunset, and that meant we had arrangements to make. Once dressed, Lu Sin and I walked to the offices of a lawyer who was to receive my mail and other necessities from my London agent. The word had come that my new home was fully prepared for me, and that he would meet me in the small town some two days' drive from the villa. A smaller ship would take us from Liverpool south to Paris, where we would arrange overland passage. We paused for a late supper before arranging for the carriage to take us there. Then, wrapped entirely in heavy black clothing, I braved the setting sun the following day to be underway.

The late summer weather was alternately balmy and threatening, the night sky dominated by billowing black clouds and the strong scent of the sea. I found myself restless as we sailed, stopping in various ports to unload goods or passengers. By the time we reached Paris I was irritable and anxious. I was at this point quite obviously pregnant and forced to endure the cooing and touching of the female passengers with a grace I did not feel. Lu Sin was a quiet peace beside me, but it did little to affect my mood.

I had determined that the pregnancy was developing faster than my earlier prediction, though I couldn't be certain by how much. I made mention of this to Lu Sin on the evening before our arrival in Paris and after examining my growing belly she nodded. "Perhaps it is the lack of blood in your diet," she said, as she finished corking a bottle of formula. "You have partaken of little of the formula, and no blood. Perhaps this has affected the timing."

It sounded reasonable. I was beyond caring though as I loosened my skirt yet again and made ready to join the other passengers for dinner. I only knew that I wanted off this damned boat and away from the people on it. The next day, Lu Sin bundled me in black, careful to protect my face with a dark veil she draped from a hat, and we braved the late afternoon, though the sun was scarce to be seen through the clouds, to find a suitable hotel for the night. I wanted to be off the next morning, but after Lu Sin had visited with the agency I learned that we had to wait a few days. Normally, a sojourn in Paris would have brought a spring to my step and a desire to visit the operas and theaters. As I sat in my rooms eating food that tasted completely retched to me, I felt none of it. I was tired in a way I had never felt, worn through the skin. My heart beat was slow, deep inside me as if isolated. My back ached and my hunger was no longer appeased by those things I would allow myself to partake in.

Two days after reaching Paris, six months after discovering I was with child, I was once more bundled up and scurried off in the early morning light, this time into a private carriage for the long overland journey to the mountains that had been my first home. It had been a long time since I had seen them last and I longed for them. I longed for home.

I had reached a rather uncomfortable stage in my long pregnancy, and it was stuffy and warm in the carriage, even long after the sun went down. Lu Sin did all she could to put me at ease, but my body was at war with the growing child. My stomach seemed stretched beyond its capacity, my back ached and I had to pause our journey frequently to relieve myself and to eat. The roads were old and rutted and bumpy beyond belief, no help to me at all. The second night out of Paris I was praying to whichever god still fancied me that it all be over soon.

The nights stretched into weeks, the weeks nearly to a month, bad weather forcing us to pause in a quaint little town only four nights out. By the time we reached the village where we were to meet my agent, I was ill tempered, ravenous, and weary of it all. My words were not kind when I was told we would be delaying what remained of the trip until the following night due to the increasing inclement weather. I ranted about the rash of rain and the moonless nights, raved about the beautiful nights I had left behind me. Even Lu Sin kept her distance from me as dawn broke and my arguments against nature became moot. I sank into the softness of the inn's bed, wrapping my aching body in fresh smelling linens and soft, warm blankets which took the edge of chill from the air.

I woke early, with the impending feeling of … something … I couldn't place. I waited anxiously as Lu Sin and Gregory, my agent, loaded our things. I climbed clumsily into the carriage for what I prayed would be the last time. The double team of horses pulled and strained in the deep mud, and going was slow, but at long last, near dawn of the second night, the carriage came to a halt.

Gregory helped me down and I, ill-tempered and all, laid eyes upon what would be my home for the next century. Exactly as I had requested, the perfect image of what my mind only could see, the cottage was small, but adequate for three or four, and built up to the side of the mountain, hiding the caves I knew to be there. The windows glowed with light and with my dark eyes I could see the gardens surrounding it, wood stacked neatly near the door. I held my breath and held Lu Sin by the arm as I stepped toward it.

Inside, the smell of earth and wood combined with the soft glow of fire and candlelight to offer up a homey feeling that settled deep inside of me almost in a moment. The child felt it too, rolling to one side within and resting there. The kitchen was filled with a giant cast iron stove and a table of solid oak. The cupboards were well provisioned; enough to not need a trip to town for several weeks. Two steps down from the kitchen was a massive common room, carpeted in plush forest green and furnished with hand carved pieces made comfortable with large pillows. Down the hall we entered the mountain itself, where the bedrooms had been built from the caves that had existed there for centuries.

The rooms were spacious and amply furnished. The bulk of our belongings had arrived earlier and were already put in appropriate enough places. The nursery was between Lu Sin's room and my own, and was filled with clothes to cover a hundred children. Of all the rooms in the cottage, mine was perhaps the most severe, the dark wood of the furniture shining dully in the light of the fire. Justine's painting of Crenoral and his brothers hung there, to remind me of my past, of my own childhood, and all that I wanted different for my child. The bed was stately, like that of a queen, with four hand carved posters and canopy that supported black velvet drapes. Golden candlesticks at the four corners of the room held black tapers that would illuminate it as though it were daylight. Personal things that had once adorned my room in Crenoral's mansion and had spirited away before my escape filled the chamber, making it more of a homecoming than I had anticipated. I sensed Dovan had been there, spotting things that he had given me in another cavern bedroom years before. His own cave was further up that same mountain, and once the child was born I had plans to visit.

With little preamble, I shed my outer garments and crawled into the bed, leaving Lu Sin to deal with the agent and the business of setting up our new home. I was exhausted, more so than I imagined, and fell deeply asleep almost instantly. My next true conscious thought was one of hunger, not the roaring need for blood, but the more human craving for food that had become a rather constant companion of late. My stomach growled and I felt an echo in the child within. It was enough to bring me from my bed to my feet. I made for the door, but paused as I passed the ancient mirror. The dress I had worn for too many days to count, was dirty and dusty, like my hair which had fallen from its braid. My hands cupped around my enlarged belly, the sensitive fingers almost feeling the baby which slept somewhere beneath them.

As my eyes rose to the reflection of my face, I smiled, a soft, maternal smile that would become a regular part of my countenance in the coming months. I liked what I saw. I liked how I felt, as if I were now a part of something beyond my own existence. I opened the door to my room and padded softly down the carpeted hallway. I could smell bacon cooking, and warm bread. I hastened my pace, the hunger that had woke me coming to the forefront. I didn't even check to see if the sun had gone down, I was so eager for the food. Luckily, it was dark, and Lu Sin stood at the stove cooking a breakfast fit for a queen.

"Come, eat," she said, her voice musical. "You must be half-starved."

I sat at the table and let her serve me. She had an eerie way of knowing exactly what I would want. "You've been asleep for days." She sat lightly opposite me, her own plate more empty than full. "I notice the child has shifted again. We shouldn't have long to wait."

It had been a year and a month since I had stood on that dusty street in San Francisco and felt that thrill inside me. By my revised reckoning our wait was to be another two months or three even, but admittedly, I knew nothing of how this was to work, of what to expect. We took what time there would be to arrange the comfort of our lives, the ease of which still amazes me. Every now and then I can see the two of us by the fire, reading quietly, or stitching some piece of needlework. If I close my eyes I can smell the soft, exotic scent of her. She was the calm spot at my side when I thought the wait alone might make me mad. Two months passed. Lu Sin made two trips down the mountain for supplies while I puttered around with my books and the baby things.

Chapter 19

As with all great events of my life, I should have been prepared for the coming of my child, should have seen and understood the precursors that heralded it days in advance. I was so preoccupied with the material preparations, that I neglected the first inklings of it, the first tightening of muscles. I had told Lu Sin to expect strange things from me during the delivery, but hadn't had the time or inclination to actually display myself with the Change upon me to give my warnings focus. I had the nursery as I wanted it, and the rest of the house was in order. I, however, was not.

The contractions became undeniable, the pain unmistakable. There would be a birthing. Lu Sin was due home that night, having gone to town several days before for supplies. She had not wanted to go, but I had insisted. Now, I wished she were here with me as the contractions woke me somewhere near to noon. I paced my room, through the worst of each pain, and rested when it was gone. This was only the beginning. I knew from the stories Lu Sin and others had told me that I was in for a bumpy ride.

As they began to come closer together, I gathered the things Lu Sin had said we would need. It was busy work, meant to keep my mind off the coming events, but it did not. If anything, it seemed to amplify each round of clenching and unclenching, nearly dropping me to my knees several times. I wondered as I crawled into my bed if I could indeed do this thing which mortal women take for granted.

The pains grew in intensity and I questioned my own sanity in wanting this child as much as I had come to. The room was as prepared as I could make it on my own. I tried to concentrate on anything except the pain, but it was overwhelming. I lay on the bed and waited, feeling my body preparing to tear in two. I am sure I talked to myself as the time passed, cursing any man I had ever known.

I tried to hear the child within me, but the noise of my own body was too overwhelming. My breath came in long, ragged gasps, my heart beat wildly out of control. The skin surrounding the baby seemed alive, burning, twitching. I shook with each contraction, fighting off the Change, which came in response to the pain. Hours went by and it continued, weakening me in ways I had been unprepared for. I imagined dark must have come outside and absolute fear that Lu Sin would not return in time overtook me. I was sure I wouldn't be able to do this thing without her. I screamed her name as if that would bring her to me, all the while clutching madly at the bed sheets with each pain.

I tried to calm my insanity, to rationalize my thoughts. There was no reason I couldn't do this, I told myself. Women all over the world do it every day. If I was capable of conceiving this child, I was capable of delivering it. I turned my inner battle to the physical act, abandoning all efforts to keep the Change from taking me. I roared with the pain and committed myself to the act of the birthing. I felt the child respond, grasping its own life as I had mine. The hard pains came, urging me to push against them, and there instinct took the place of reason.

Distantly I heard the sound of Lu Sin's horse, the door opening, her footsteps, but they were only side notes to my thinking. I was relieved when she at last burst through the door of my room, taking stock of the entire situation in a heartbeat and joining in quickly. She took her place at the end of the bed, spreading my legs open as if I were a wishbone after the family feast. My insides were screaming to be released and the child had begun its final arrival. Her voice was soothing, but I don't remember a single word she said. I saw her face pale as she looked upon my Changed face, but she turned herself immediately back to the task at hand, and the child's head, which she then held in her hand.

My screams shook the rock walls of the cavern from which the bedroom had been made, echoing into the night. Never in all my days had I felt such a thing, as though she were tearing her way out of me. Then, quite unexpectedly, it was over. The child was born, held in Lu Sin's arms.

I lay there upon the bed, gasping for air and attempting to calm my heart, all the while straining to get a glimpse of her. I heard the sharp slap of flesh against flesh then the sound of a baby's first cry. It all left me then, the doubt and uncertainty, the fear of inadequacy, the unequaled pain. Lu Sin brought her to me, cleaning the blood and muck of birthing from her tiny body.

"Your daughter," she said as she handed her to me.

"My daughter," I echoed needlessly. I looked down at her for the first time and my breath caught in my throat. Dark brown hair covered her head. Her wrinkled up skin was all red and pink and warm. I had no words for her or for Lu Sin. I held her to me and let the tears come, streaming down my sweat stained and still Changed face. I was exhausted, hungry and taken by the touch of her tiny little hand. I might have sat there for hours, unmoving, but for Lu Sin. Suddenly she was at my side, a bottle of formula in her hands.

"You should feed." She uncorked the bottle and handed it to me. "And so should the babe." I drank deeply, welcoming the feeling of it filling me. With

Lu Sin's assistance, I managed to arrange myself in such a way as to give the child my breast while I took my sustenance as well. I watched as she found her way to it, one little fist balled up to bat the air as she sucked. It was an odd thing to me, a feeling not all together unlike that of one of my Brethren feeding from me, but so much different as well. I watched in amazement.

I was vaguely aware of Lu Sin cleaning up the room, removing the bloodied sheets. The child fell asleep at my breast and the very sight of her so contentedly asleep bewitched my own eyes. My heartbeat had at last returned to normal. The Change was fading. I felt Lu Sin lift my daughter from my arms and smooth a blanket over me, then I slept.

I woke to a quiet house, only the light of the fire lit up my room. I sat up, suddenly remembering the agony I had been through only recently as the aches made themselves known. My feet held me however and I moved only somewhat slowly out into the hall. A fire burned in the nursery, low and dim. My eyes made out the form of Lu Sin asleep in the chair. I moved in closer, to the crib where the infant slept.

I found myself smiling foolishly to myself in the dark as I watched her, completely enamored of this thing I had somehow done. It had been inconceivable to me at one time, that this could ever be true. It seemed impossible at that moment to imagine my life before she had come to be a part of it.

"She is beautiful," a voice said in the dark behind me. It was not Lu Sin's voice.

I spun around, instantly defensive. Dovan divorced himself from the shadows by the door. "I heard your pain, and assumed she must have come. I couldn't stay away."

I smiled and reached a hand out to him. He came to me and we stood together staring down at her. "Have you named her?" he asked gently.

"Francis , for her father. Dovana, for her great-grandfather." I closed my eyes and savored the feeling of home and comfort in that room. Dovan's presence filled it with a sense of strength.

"And her family name?"

"Stuart, for Francis's family. Francis Dovana Stuart, my daughter."

"I have brought you a gift." He took my hand and drew me out of the nursery and out into the living room where he had already lit several candles. We sat on the sofa and he handed me a small box. I held it for a long moment before opening it. Inside was a silver ring, ancient and highly polished. I held my breath as I lifted it from its satin bed. "It was your grandmother's. I gave it to her on the night our first child was born. She had always intended for her daughter to receive it, but we had only sons. When she died she wanted it to be given to her first granddaughter on the day when she gave birth."

"Thank you." I slipped it onto my right ring finger. It was like it had been made for me. "I don't know what to say."

"You don't have to say anything. It belongs there." He smiled a surprisingly human smile, filled with warmth and love. "You have made me exceedingly proud, Amara. You have been the one piece of humanity in my existence. I have watched you grow into a wonderful, courageous woman. You cannot know what that means to me."

"I think I shall find out," I said, my thoughts sweeping back down the hall to my child. A part of me already understood him, a part of me wanted to throw myself into his arms and weep with joy. I restrained myself.

I could hear the sounds of Lu Sin waking, checking on the still sleeping infant, then moving toward us. "Ah, Lu Sin, come here. I would like you to meet someone."

She stretched and yawned as she padded toward us in soft slippers. "Lu Sin, this is Dovan, my grandfather. Dovan, my friend, Lu Sin."

Dovan inclined his head in perfect time to Lu Sin. He seemed cautious, but accepting of her presence. "It is a pleasure to make the acquaintance of the one who helped to bring my great-granddaughter into the world. Please sit down, join us."

She sat slowly, cautious as well. She had heard me mention his name, had seen his picture in my bedroom. She knew what he was. If she was afraid, she held it in check well, deferring to my wishes. It was something of a defining moment in our relationship, an expression of her trust that no harm would come to her in my home.

We spoke a while, then I heard Francis beginning to wake. I stood and Dovan followed. "She'll be hungry, Child. Take good care of her."

"I will Dovan. Will I see you again?"

"I think you will. Perhaps when I return I'll bring Justine with me."

"I would like that." He kissed my cheek and was gone. I yawned and went to Francis. Her little face had just begun to wrinkle up as she started to cry. I picked her up and cradled her in my arms, cooing to her as I settled into the chair. I suckled her to my breast and found myself humming to her some ancient lullaby from some by-gone era that I barely remembered, but couldn't tell from where. Certainly my mother never sang to me, she had never been that maternal.

"You should see yourself," Lu Sin said from the doorway. "I'll bet you've never looked more human, more normal."

I snickered. "No, I'll bet I looked fairly human laying at the bottom of that ravine up the mountain, human and dead."

"You look like a mother," she said.

A mother. I, somehow in my twisted existence, I had become a mother. My thoughts drifted to my last experience with motherhood, with raising other women's children and to Moira. I wondered if she had somehow heard, as Dovan had ... if she would come. I suddenly wanted to see her.

Francis was asleep at my breast and I was suddenly taken with exhaustion. I lay her in the cradle and wearily found my way back to my bed. I was asleep before I was fully ensconced. The next days would be spent achieving some manner of a normal routine, with the child in our lives dictating sleeping and eating hours and rearranging everything.

It was awkward at first, spending all my time with an infant, my infant. For the first time in my life I had no urges toward a human life, except to keep and protect it. Even my closest mortal friends had always held some desire, some craving for me. I had fought myself for so long, I didn't know how to react to this. My need for the formula diminished and my appetite for mortal food increased. I could sit alone in a room and feel ... something other than hatred or anguish or self-loathing ... something more than physical desire of one kind or another. It was several days before it dawned on me what it was. I loved.

I would find myself sitting beside the cradle, looking at my child as she slept. I saw with eyes that wondered at every movement of her, every breath she took. I marveled as she drank from my breast, taking her life from me in a way very unlike anyone else ever had. Her tiny fingers and toes held a fascination beyond even the curiosity of her birth. I could completely forget myself when alone with her, so intent upon her being, so in love with her I could simply forget to breathe.

She seemed blessedly unburdened with the curse of my own existence, though her face paled far more than normal after the rush of the birthing was done. There were no lethal fangs in her mouth, no biting instinct when she fed. Her dark brown hair was so soft to touch, so perfect. She was more mortal than even I had hoped. I could sense the other in her, but only as a distant genetic reminder, an instinct, a Family sense. She would likely develop some of the gifts as she grew older, but for the time, she was not unlike any other infant in the world.

It was well into the night, several months after the birth, I sat outside our home in the light of a half moon, cradling Francis in my arms and savoring the soft night air. I felt them come, and shifted a little, my eyes scanning the trees. Moira appeared first, slipping from the line of trees nearest the garden and gliding my way, her smile gentle.

"Hello, Mother," she said as she neared me. I felt the baby jump, startled by the voice, or the feeling of her presence.

"Moira." I reached out my free hand to draw her close to me. "I have missed you." My smile was genuine as Leonard also came into view. "I have missed you both."

"We heard the news, and thought to come see for ourselves," Leonard said, sweeping off his hat.

"A child," Moira said, barely more than breathing the word. Her nimble fingers brushed Francis's face and she smiled again. "How?"

I smiled myself. "The same way a mortal might accomplish it, I imagine," I replied. It felt good having them near me again. "How did you hear?" I asked, thinking perhaps Dovan had sought them out.

Leonard shifted nervously. "You are the talk of many of our kind, Mother. They speak of you in whispers, the one who kills her own kind and gives birth to human children."

Moira took his hand. "They are afraid of you."

"People are always afraid of things that they do not understand," Lu Sin said from the doorway. "Your kind can not fathom your humanity, as Mortals cannot fathom your other half."

"And so she stands alone," Moira said in that sad way of hers.

A quiet settled over us, a tad melancholy. Francis stirred in my arms and I stood. "Enough of this talk. My Moira has come to see me. Lu Sin, please take the child inside, I should like to spend some time with Moira and Leonard."

I handed off the bundled up form of Francis, then slipped an arm through Moira's. "Tell me all about you." I invited as we set off to walk in the woods. They told me of the places they had visited, and the various people they had seen. Some part of me longed to return to that kind of life, wandering from place to place, but my heart beat in my daughter's chest. For me, that time had passed. They spoke at length of traveling to America, and I told them of my time there. Near to dawn, we withdrew into my home, to sleep away the daylight hours. I had not realized how much I had missed them, my first children, and the way they were with one another. None of it had changed. Moira still seemed more alive, more real when Leonard was near. Leonard was still entirely focused on Moira and the rest of the world disappeared when he held her in his arms.

Three nights after their arrival, I watched them slip off into the trees, Francis asleep on my shoulder, Lu Sin beside me. It hurt me to see them go. There had been a feeling of completion with them there, as if I had come full circle.

The nights stretched outward, beyond my even taking notice of them, weeks and months whirled past. She grew slowly, though not nearly as slowly as my own torturous climb from infancy. In her first year she seemed to develop almost as a human infant would, a little slower in physical growth, but she made up for it in intellect and a knack for learning. She took her first steps when she was not quite three, while I sat on the floor of the cabin and watched in gleeful motherhood. She was my pride and my joy, my greatest achievement.

In my joy of her I lost sight of the grand promises I had made to myself. I had seen her as my gift to the world before I had ever held her in my arms, but she was so much more. Her eyes sparkled with a light that spoke of her father, and her curious nature reminded me of myself as a child.

I was afraid to test her to the daylight, though Lu Sin and I debated the issue greatly. Lu Sin believed her nearly human skin would withstand daylight, though a certain sensitivity to it would remain. I however was terrified of the thought of letting her take my vulnerable child into the sun. I forbid it.

It was the first of our disagreements, Lu Sin and I. Most often she was right, but I was too stubborn to admit it. My paranoia made me guard Francis jealously against anything that had a remote chance to harm her, Lu Sin saw things more levelly and knew that my over-protective nature would one day be a detriment to us all. Still, I always insisted, always won. I was content with everything around me, even the bickering and sometimes strained relationship that Lu Sin and I had come to share. When first I had met her she had been a quiet woman, not given to strong statements of opinion or disagreements. It seemed as time passed that she contradicted most of my decisions, and her opinions were strong and stated loudly.

It wasn't until Francis was nearly five that I finally agreed to the first testing, watching from the shadows as Lu Sin held her hand and coaxed her out into the twilight just before dark. The skies were orange and I had visions of that tender skin blistering beneath even this distant sun, weakened by its descent. I held my breath, as my precious child looked around her, wide-eyed and amazed. The setting sun cast a ruddy appearance to the house that seemed to fascinate her. Her eyes squinted as she sought out the source of light. It was all I could do to contain myself for the ten minutes they were outside before the reticent sun slunk away behind the trees.

I pulled her to me as they came back inside, running my hands over her exposed arms and face, looking for marks that the sunlight had damaged her. She was unharmed, though the brightness of the light had brought tears to her sensitive eyes. "Did you see, Mama?" she asked, her eyes widening. "The skies were bright."

"Yes, Francis, Mama saw," I said, hugging her. Lu Sin smiled briefly, then set about making breakfast.

Once we were done eating, and Francis had gone off to play, Lu Sin and I sat at the table together, our collected teaching materials between us. We had been working on our plans for Francis's education, and the problems with bringing a tutor into our lives, further aggravated by our odd living schedule. We now knew that Francis could live her life in daylight, which eased part of the difficulty. I wanted to give her the best of everything, and that meant teachers who possessed greater knowledge than Lu Sin and I together.

"We can still get through the next few years," Lu Sin said, sorting through a stack of readers she had brought with her from San Francisco. "But, we should begin looking for tutors before much more time has passed. It will take months to get the advertisements out, and responses to them."

I nodded, absently fingering the stationary on which we had begun listing the subjects we wanted Francis to learn. It was an ambitious list, including the basics of reading and writing, mathematics and rudimentary science, botany, astronomy, art, music, history, as well as her own special heritage. I knew the time had come to begin formal lessons, structured times for each task. I sighed and looked at Lu Sin, who seemed tired and pale. "Are you well?" I asked, vaguely concerned.

She smiled. "You are perceptive. I didn't sleep well. Something I ate disagreed with me."

I smiled too, my own mind twisting that thought into a memory of a time when something I ate had disagreed with me before he died. She must have seen an echo of it and she laughed faintly. "You know what I meant," she said.

"I am going to walk a bit," I said after a long silence.

I was restless, the anxiety of the early evening still burning inside of me. I walked a long time, not really paying attention to where my footsteps took me, except to keep the house within a distance to reach before sunrise. My stomach rumbled and an echo of that other hunger followed. A part of me longed to follow after Moira and Leonard, who must surely be somewhere in America, enjoying the growing culture around them. I missed culture, operas, quiet dinners among the denizens of a bustling city.

Yet, a part of me too was content, happy. The image of Francis asleep in her bed warmed me as I paused beside a cold stream. She was an amazement to me, still. I sighed and it seemed to echo around me.

Squatting beside the stream, I let my hands play in the icy water for a moment, retrieving a shiny, smooth stone that Francis would giggle excitedly over. I dried it on my skirt and went to put it in the pocket of my dress. My hand brushed something in the pocket and in curiosity I pulled it out, angling it to the slip of moonlight that filtered through the trees.

It was a letter, the last that Lu Sin had brought up from town the week before. I had forgotten about it. It was from the parents of the beautiful child in San Francisco, warm news of her excellence in school, her adoration for her new studies, and news of their small family.

I had maintained a correspondence with Joy and her parents, gifting her with trinkets and invitations to visit. There was some connection there, even across the miles that separated us. The parents wrote, telling me about the mysterious benefactor who had left a small fortune to them, of the promotion he had received, and all the news of the child who had so enchanted me. I used those letters as a guide of sorts of what to expect from my own child, though I took into account the difference in their developmental patterns.

I longed for her still, with five years and half a world between us. I could still see her eyes staring up into mine as if they knew everything. Perhaps it was this longing, more than anything that had brought the restlessness. I hungered for the first time in years. Replacing the letter, I made for home, covering ground quickly. I found Lu Sin tucking Francis into bed, already nearly asleep. I kissed Francis goodnight, then withdrew to my room, to sip off a bottle of formula and re-read the letter.

I drifted to sleep thinking of Joy, and my dreams brought images of an older Joy, blonde curls and blue eyes, playing with Francis in the night. The next morning, we started our lessons, setting times for reading lessons and simple math. We also agreed to a new schedule, in which Lu Sin would rise several hours before sunset, wake and feed Francis, then take her out into the sun to learn of things which can only be seen in daylight.

Francis proved to be a quick study, nimble with numbers and with a desire to read that surpassed anything I had ever felt, even when my hunger for knowledge had driven me. Within the first year, we ran out of material for her, and she surprised us by moving onto the readers for older students. Our advertisements went out, seeking a tutor accustomed to hard living and few amenities, who spoke English and Latin at a minimum. It took quite some time to receive responses, and most were rather demanding. Finding a suitable tutor was going to be a difficult task.

More than a year after beginning to look, a letter arrived which showed much promise. It was a young teacher from London, who was seeking travel and work. She was single, with no children, well-schooled and offered good recommendations from two previous employers, both of whom had employed her in a private manner similar to ours. She offered us four years, after which we could re-negotiate, and her only desire for salary was room and board and a small stipend for personal items.

By the time she would arrive, Francis would be nearly seven. Lu Sin made another trip into town to post our acceptance letter, as well as to pick up the things we would need to prepare a room for the new person. We had several unused rooms, though they were all filled with cast off items of furniture and clothing. For the next months we sewed curtains and bed linens, moved boxes and furniture and made ready for the arrival of the teacher.

She arrived by coach a month before Francis's birthday, and Lu Sin escorted her up the mountain to our home, arriving with the setting of the sun. She was a small woman, barely five feet tall, with a mousy face, creamy cheeks and small, dark eyes. She smelled of lavender as she stepped down out of the carriage and introduced herself to Francis, who clung tightly to my hand.

"It is my pleasure to make your acquaintance, Miss Francis. I am Miss Willemenia Brockard. You may call me Miss Willy." Her voice was slightly nasal, with a lilting accent that was more courtly than Cockney.

Francis put her arms around my leg and held me close. I could feel her heart racing against me. "Welcome to our home, Miss Brockard. I am Amara."

She inclined her head, then looked around her. "It is lovely here. Thank you for having me."

I smiled and offered to show her inside, with Francis still clinging to me as if I might disappear. Lu Sin set about preparing a meal, while I took Willemenia to her room, showed her around the small house and went over the schedules and ground rules. She seemed surprised by our odd schedules, but accepting of them.

As we ate, I watched her, trying to place the odd sensation that had come upon me. Nothing about her aroused me, to hunger or to hate, affection or desire. She was blank, unknown. I could not sense her thoughts or her emotions, I could not feel her heartbeat. She felt my eyes and looked up. Embarrassed, I looked away.

After dinner, Lu Sin reviewed our course of training with our new tutor, while I played with Francis. "I am impressed," she said after a long while. "You ladies hardly need me at all." She smiled, and her eyes pinned me. "I shall only make a few small changes. We can begin tomorrow."

She stood and nodded, her brown hair bobbing in time to the movement. After she had left the room, Lu Sin came to sit with us. "She's an odd one, isn't she?"

I looked up at her. "It isn't just me then?" Lu Sin shook her head. "Well, she's nice enough, and seems capable. And it isn't as if we are the image of normal," I said, still trying to place what her oddity was.

"Shall we go see if we can catch some fish for dinner?" Lu Sin asked Francis, who was up and half way to the door before she had finished. I watched them go and sat back against the wall.

Chapter 20

A DJUSTING TO having Miss Willy with us was a little awkward, in no small way due to the oddities I couldn't place about her. Francis took quite some time to warm up to her, her dark eyes tracing her movements whenever they shared a room. I had a measure of concern, though Lu Sin assured me that it was Francis's lack of experience with others, and nothing untoward with the teacher.

I left her pretty much to herself her first week with us, giving her a chance to settle in and become accustomed to the soft working rhythm of the house. I watched her though, my senses all keyed in her direction. She could move through the shadows nearly as quietly as I, and seemed to always know where each of us were, whether she could see us or not.

Francis and Lu Sin were out getting the carriage ready for a trip to town for supplies, nearly a month after the arrival of Miss Willy. She sat at the kitchen table, going over some of the work Francis had completed the day before. The scent of her lavender perfume wafted my way and brought my eyes to her. I was surprised to find her looking at me.

"You wish to know more about me," she said with confidence. "I am a very private person. I sense there is something about me that makes you uneasy. Let me set you at ease. I shall not cause harm to any in this house, nor allow for harm to come to it. My secrets are mine to keep, as yours are to you."

Her eyes were dark, the pupils dilated. I could read nothing in them but her sincerity. I felt no danger, just the vague unease of not being able to know her in the way I had come to know everyone in my life. I nodded slowly, and she turned back to her work.

For my part, I chose to go outside and help Lu Sin, sending Francis back inside to begin her lessons. Under Miss Willy's tutelage, Francis learned quickly. The new tutor was far more patient with the myriad questions Francis always had than either Lu Sin or I had ever been.

There were orders for new books in just a few months, and a growing understanding of a new need for our tiny family. The money was beginning to run short. I had seldom had to think about it in my life, having first simply taken from my victims, later from my family. There was still some in the bank in town, and a few remaining pieces of jewelry that could be sold, but the time was coming when we would need to find another source of income. It was a concept foreign to me.

I took to hunting in the night, bringing home meat to compliment the vegetables Lu Sin planted in our gardens. We wanted to spare no expense on the education we gave Francis, but that would mean sparing expenses elsewhere. It was while I was hunting one crisp autumn evening that I heard Dovan's voice whispering through the trees, drawing me further up the mountain to where he waited for me in a clearing under the waning moon.

It had been some time since I had seen him. He looked pale, but happy, his smile wide as I came around a large oak into the clearing. He opened his arms and I let him wrap me in a hug that had become our customary greeting. The dust of his most recent travels paled the black of his clothing and painted his face a shade darker than its norm. "It is good to see you again, Dovan."

"And you, my dear. We were on our way home when I sensed you about. I sent Justine on ahead." He felt solid, secure beside me. I liked the feeling after so long in the company of Willy's nebulous presence. "How fares my great-granddaughter?"

I smiled. He had been the doting grandfather since Francis was born. "She is quite well. She has a new tutor."

We were walking toward the edge of the clearing and he paused, his eyes narrowing as he read me. "You don't care for her."

I shook my head. "She is capable, and good with Francis. She is just ... odd."

He chuckled. "All of mankind seems odd to me, Amara."

I could see his point. "True enough. It just unsettles me." We resumed walking, following some unseen path into the trees. We were quiet for a time before we spoke of his recent travels, to Paris and Madrid, and the things he had seen. He had brought gifts for Francis and promised to bring them down the mountain in a few days. We parted ways, with several hours till dawn and I turned for home.

As I came into view of our cottage I paused, leaning against a tree and watching as I used to watch humans in my childhood. Lu Sin was reading beside the fire. Francis sat at the kitchen table, her head bent over some task, her dark hair cascading to hide her face. Willy was beside Francis, her chin resting on her hand, staring off out the front window. I found myself wondering what she was thinking or feeling. I could sense no malice, no joy, no contentment from her. I had never heard her raise her voice or seen her cry, or laugh. How odd it must be to live a life with no emotion. I wondered if that was the strangeness that distanced her from me.

Lu Sin must have felt my eyes upon her, for her head raised and she looked around, eventually looking out the window in my direction. She seemed pale again, though I supposed that could be the lack of sunlight, or lack of sleep. I marveled at how much affection I felt for her, and how little I actually knew about her.

With a sigh, I headed toward the door, breathing in the warm scent of burning wood, mingled with the remains of the stew Lu Sin had made for dinner. I smiled at Francis as she looked up expectantly. Willy excused herself and went off to bed. I felt at home, content. I was happy with my life.

Thus it continued for a time. Francis grew, time passed, and I watched. Lu Sin began making trips to town more frequently, occasionally taking Willy with her. She assured me always when she returned that there was yet enough money left. Then came the news of tragedy. Lu Sin returned from town, with a letter from America. There had been some sort of accident; Joy's parents were dead. The child was alone in the world.

The parents, having no relatives, had left instructions that were anything to happen to them,

Joy should be sent to live with me, knowing I would care for her. She was to arrive two nights before Francis's eleventh birthday. I contemplated leaving Francis home with Willy, but she begged to be allowed to come along. She had never been to town, had never met anyone who hadn't come to the cottage. I knew it was time she started to know the world, so I dressed her in her best dress and we set off down the hill to meet the stage in town. Lu Sin drove the carriage, while Francis and I remained safely hidden in the darkened interior. Francis was wide-eyed, for never had she been away from the house like this before. She had seen Lu Sin go into town in the carriage, but had never ridden in it. She jumped with every bump in the road, clutching my arm for comfort, but not wanting to express her fear.

"Mama, who are we going to meet?" she asked, as if to distract herself from her fear.

I pulled her up into my lap and thought about how to answer her. She had grown so much, and physically resembled a child of eight or nine. Mentally however, she was well beyond her eleven years. "Well, many years ago, before you were born, I met a lady who had a child. The child was a little girl named Joy. She is coming to visit us."

That seemed to content her for the moment and she returned to looking out the windows, which had me somewhat nervous. It wasn't quite dawn yet, but being away from the comfort of my stone walls, I worried about the amount of shelter the small carriage could provide. As her normal bedtime neared, she curled up beside me on the padded seat and fell soundly asleep. I was asleep soon myself. When I woke that evening, Lu Sin had stopped the carriage for rest and was asleep on the opposite bench. I stretched and yawned. I had forgotten what a long trip this could be.

I let them sleep, and after making sure the sun was down, I climbed into the driver's seat. Six hours later we pulled into town. Joy wasn't due to arrive until 10am that morning, so I parked the carriage just outside of town and coaxed Francis from its dark confines. Her little eyes grew big with excitement and apprehension as they wandered the foreign sights. Lu Sin joined us as we walked around the buildings furthest from town, a blacksmith and a livery and the brothel's staff's sleeping quarters. Francis clung tightly to our hands, and yet ran to every new sight to explore. "What is it, Mama?" she would ask of everything, and then not wait for an answer as she hurried on to the next thing.

Lu Sin smiled a lot in those early morning hours, and I suppose now that I think about it that I did too. She was a wonder to me, as much as the foreign air of town was to her. However, it couldn't last as long as I would have liked, for dawn approached. Probably earlier than was necessary, I was carrying her back to the carriage to wait out the final hours in the cool darkness. She was asleep quickly, worn out by the thrill of the entire trip.

I held her in my arms, not quite as easily as I had once, her long form draping from my shoulder to below my knees. I was struck with how much she had grown in the last year, suddenly, as if I hadn't seen it in her as the days passed. "I love you," I whispered into her hair as we settled to a seat on the cushioned bench.

Lu Sin smiled. "And I'll bet you never anticipated how much you would, did you?"

"No, I could never have thought that I was capable. Not that I have never loved ... it was just ... different."

She nodded. She was quiet then, unusually so. It occurred to me then that there was something more wrong than the normal disagreements. We had argued over my bringing Joy into our lives. She hadn't thought it wise, given the precarious situations of our lives. I, as usual, had insisted. But it was more now, I could see that.

"What are you keeping from me, Lu Sin?"

"As if I could keep anything from you."

"Not for long, anyway. What is it?"

"I have a hard favor to ask of you."

I squinted at her, as if that would project my thoughts beyond the protective wall she had around her. "Ask me anything, you know that."

"I'm not sure you'll say that once I've asked." She was genuinely uncomfortable, her hands folded in her lap, hunched forward as if to make herself as small as possible. "I am not well," she said it softly, hushed, but it cut through to my heart. "Indeed, I have little more than a year or two left of my life, if the doctor is to be believed."

The breath left me, and I stared at her for a long moment of silence, trying to see it in her, trying to figure how I had missed its coming. "I have kept it hidden a long time," she said, as if in response to the unspoken thought. "I did not wish to worry you."

"What is it?" I asked in a whisper, wanting to reach out to her, but prevented by Francis's body in my lap.

"They do not seem to know. It is eating away at me from the inside, and there is nothing they can do."

"We will send for another doctor."

"I have seen two already. That is not the favor I would have of you."

I held my breath and waited, anticipating everything, everything except what she ultimately asked me for.

"Bring me to you," she said, looking me in the eye so there could be no denying what she meant.

I recoiled, physically leaning away from her. "No," I said instinctively, reactively. I couldn't think beyond it, about it. There was only "No" in my mind at that moment. I was frozen by the request.

In all of our years together it was the first time she had spoken of such things, or asked anything of me. It was the first selfish thing I had ever heard her say. I could see in her eyes that she had convinced herself of it, and would stubbornly refuse any logic I offered to dissuade her. I shook my head, trying to fathom what she was asking. "You have no idea what you will become. You will not be like me, you will be like Dovan, like the others. You will require human blood to live."

"I know the price. I have thought about this a long time, contemplated everything. It is what I want."

"Lu Sin, there must be something else, anything else we can do. This—this can't be the only solution."

"Maybe not, but it is the solution I have chosen."

"No. I could not do it; I haven't got the strength to go through it all over again."

"Do you want to watch me die?" she asked, a hint of acid in her tone.

I cringed, closing my eyes against the sight of her, trying not to picture her face taken with the Change upon it. She was older than those I had last changed, and she was asking where they had not ... but I could not help but think of Rene and Racelle and the others ... of the terrible day I made monsters out of children. I shuddered. "No, I do not want to see you die. You are a very dear friend; without you I could not have made it through these last years. I love you. That is why I say no."

"Are you afraid that I will turn out like the one who kills your children, this Hunter who terrifies you?"

Visions of my lost enemy filled me, but I shook my head. "You are nothing like him. It doesn't work like that. It doesn't change your most basic person ... it changes your body. The soul usually follows the body, or the body doesn't last long. The need and the hunger and the killing is what changes them, not the act of creation alone. You are strong, and would probably be a very restrained, very decent vampire...if there is such a thing."

"And yet you refuse me."

I nodded. "Yes, I'm afraid I do. At least for now."

It was silent in the carriage then, cold and quiet and it hurt me to see her withdraw into herself.

When the time came, she exited the carriage and waited for the arrival of the agent who was escorting Joy. I knew how it must seem to her, but I was convinced of the morality of my decision. I would do anything I could to keep her alive, hold back nothing in her treatment, but I simply could not do as she asked.

Then, Joy was there, gently opening the carriage and climbing in carefully. She was a remarkable young woman, I could see it in her every movement, even before she opened her mouth to speak. White-blonde curls framed her angelic, prepubescent face, those sapphire eyes that had so enchanted me sparkled with excitement, fear ... who knew what else. She closed the door behind her and I heard Lu Sin climb into the driver's seat. The cold silence radiated to me even from there. I returned my attention to Joy. "I am Amara," I said. "Welcome, Joy. I have anticipated this day for a long time."

"I thank you for your kindness, ma'am. I have no family left to me. Your invitation is most kind."

Kindness hadn't been my reason all those years ago. Selfishness might have been. I had wanted her desperately then, and a quick check of my self-control revealed that I still did. "You are most welcome among my family. I apologize for Francis, she has been up long past her bedtime and as excited as she was to meet you, she couldn't stay awake. There will be time enough later for introductions."

We spoke then of her long journey, of her parents. I was taken wholly in, just as I had been when I had held her in my arms as a baby. She was intelligent, and well-schooled. She smiled frequently, which made my heart palpitate with desire and caused me to inhale sharply from time to time. By the time Lu Sin stopped for the night to rest, I was nearly undone. I left Joy sleeping, and Francis in Lu Sin's care, then disappeared into the night to try to put myself back together. When I returned, Francis played on the ground outside the carriage and the others slept inside. I called Francis up into the driver's seat and started us off again. It was better to get back to the comfort of our home where my control didn't unravel so easily.

When at last we arrived there, Joy seemed tired by her ordeal. Lu Sin had withdrawn further from me. Francis alone seemed untouched by the journey. As excited as she had been when we had left, she took Joy by the hand and led her to the rooms we had prepared and introduced her to Miss Willy. I fell into bed as morning approached. The air in the house seemed newly strained, burdened with a new presence, and the fading of an old one. I reached out a thought to Lu Sin, but she had completely hidden herself away from me. It hurt me that she didn't see my point of view, hadn't even tried, but I knew it was the fear of dying and not any genuine hatred of me. That helped a little. I listened to the sounds of Joy and Francis getting ready for bed and drifted off to sleep.

Chapter 21

Those first days were strained and difficult. The pleasure of Joy's company was contradicted by the tense pain of Lu Sin's illness and anger. I was torn between them, between the return of the intense longing that had accompanied Joy's presence since that first moment when I saw her in her mother's arms and the desire to comfort and console my friend and companion. Joy was forced to accept her new surroundings, her new place in the world, and our darkened schedule. She hadn't yet recovered from the shock of her parent's passing, a fact I discovered only nights after her arrival when I heard her sobbing quietly into her pillow. In that moment I knew my downfall, my error in judgment in bringing her to that place of solitude. I had come to terms with the old desire I bore for Lu Sin, the craving for the exotic mix of old and new within her. I had grown complacent with Willy, despite my unease with her. I had nearly forgotten what it was like to be around any other humans.

At first I could do little more than watch from the relative safety of the doorway, but her pain was so tangible, filling the small room though her tears were nearly silent. Then, I broke. Something inside me collapsed and I went to her, wrapping myself around her small frame, holding that fragile existence so close to me that her presence filled me. Her tears became my own, her heartbeat swallowing mine. I was as close to the end of myself as I may have ever come. My soul echoed her sobbing. My breath came raggedly as my control unraveled and I ached inside for wanting her. Then, she turned her tear-stained face to me, and those incredible blue eyes starred into mine for so long I thought she must surely see me the way she did once before. She blinked and it passed and she was just a frightened, lonely child.

"I miss them so," she said in a small, small voice.

"I know you do, Child. I know." I took a deep, unsteady breath and kissed her cheek. "Get some rest. I know this hasn't been easy for you."

I tucked her back into bed, kissing her forehead and feeling the Change just beneath the surface, waiting, wanting. "I'll be out in the kitchen if you need me."

She nodded and I nearly flew from the room. My senses had been heightened by the whole episode. I could feel Lu Sin's illness rising up from her silent bedroom and I wondered why I hadn't sensed it before. I knew Francis was up and about her studies with Willy, the forest outside our small home was crawling with warm-blooded animals. For the first time in years I did not go to the lab, I let myself out the front door and took to the night. I fed well that night, roaring my self-loathing into the skies as I drank.

I was only slightly sated when I returned. Lu Sin scowled at me, as if she somehow knew where I had been, what I had done. Joy and Francis were at play on the floor. I settled in to read from some ancient text. My eyes would flash between them, my friend and my surrogate child. I forced myself to remain calm, to stay seated in my chair with my book and my flickering flame. I forced myself to ignore them, to not notice the scent of them haunting me. Willy joined us after a time, and we gathered to discuss the progress Francis had recently made and the addition of Joy's needs in our curriculum. When it came time, at last, to send the children off to bed, I nearly burst from my chair. Francis whined that she wanted another hour to share with her new found friend, but rather harshly I denied it and sent them both to wash up and change into their night clothes.

Dawn was still two hours off, but I tucked them both tightly in and returned to the kitchen where Lu Sin sat contemplating a cup of tea.

"You had become complacent," she said in way of observation as I sat beside her. "You were not expecting this reaction."

"No." I couldn't argue. It had been years since I had allowed myself any company but herself or Francis and then Willy. "No, I had no idea it would be this ... difficult."

"I did." She didn't look up, just sipped at her tea. "I knew where this would lead many, many years ago. You do not listen when I speak of such things, as if I would not understand."

"Do you? Do you think you could understand?"

I glanced aside at Willy who was cleaning up her books. She looked back at me, a measured glance, as if weighing me against some standard I knew nothing about. Once her belongings were gathered, she nodded and retired from the room.

After a long silent moment Lu Sin looked up, her dark eyes meeting mine squarely. "You desire her, crave her ... the same as I do you. Do you think I could not understand merely because I am mortal?"

"It is ... nothing you can fathom now."

"But I could, if only you would give me the one thing I have ever asked for." She finished her tea. "I will be gone from your life before too long, but until then I am here. I will see to it that you feel every minute of my suffering, taste every ounce of my fear. In the end, you will bring me to you, or cry as I die in your arms."

She left me then, with the empty teacup, my aching cravings and the approaching dawn. It was the first of many days when I would get little sleep.

It would take a few weeks for us to adjust. Joy did it gracefully, filling spaces I hadn't noticed before in our routine. As she moved into place, it seemed Lu Sin stepped away, mentally if not physically. Joy and Francis became fast friends, melding into a sisterhood that might not have occurred had they actually been blood relation. They rose together in the early afternoon to study their lessons and played in the evenings. Francis bloomed in the friendship and I watched Joy relinquish her pain a little more with each passing day. It seemed as if I alone was stagnant, unmoving as the world and my existence shifted around me and all I could do was hold on to keep from getting knocked aside.

Joy had become a delightful young woman, and her parents had used their gifts well enough to her benefit. If I closed my eyes I could still see her, as she was in that nursery where I would watch her sleep. I wondered if she could still see through to my soul the way she had then, if she knew what I was and accepted it unquestioningly. I watched her as though she were an angel come to visit earth, those blue eyes hypnotizing, enticing. I was smitten with her. I would watch her with Francis and feel the desires that had brought me to her first. I sometimes cried into my pillow with emotions that had left me with the coming of my daughter. Through all of it she remained bright and beautiful, and blissfully unaware of my desire.

Lu Sin, however, was very well aware, watching me as I did Joy. Her anger was cold, her resentment of my immortality and Joy's youth resounded silently around her. I do not know how, but she made good on her promise, haunting my dreams with her coughs and shallow breathing. Her ever-weakening voice echoed in my head. I knew without seeing her how much she hurt and where. For a long time, I held myself from her company, afraid that I might cave completely if left alone in her presence for long. Eventually, I turned myself to her, and began the work to mend the wound I had created. Now that I had been made aware, I could see the signs of the sickness in her body, the weakness that was taking the place of her constant strength. I saw the graying pallor of her skin, the touch of age in her smile. She withdrew from my every gesture of comfort or aide, yet she remained, a constant shadow in the rooms infused with the sunlight of Joy and Francis at play.

There were times when her anger at my continued refusal of her request was enough to make me doubt myself, to question my right to refuse. She had, after all, done more for me without asking anything in return. I was, truthfully, being selfish, and self-righteous. I can see that now. I tried to make her understand, but that only seemed to make it worse between us. Eventually I abandoned the effort and settled for taking care of her physically.

Doctors came and went as I searched for one who could offer some hope, some shred of cure. More than ten made that long trip up the mountain, and they all left with the same response ... a year, two at most. Nearly a year passed from the time Joy came until the last of the doctors left. I sank into my chair at the kitchen table, weary and frustrated.

"Your friend is very ill," Willy said, watching me from the doorway.

I looked up and nodded. "She is ... and there is nothing to be done."

She sat next to me, her soft brown hair a cascade over her nightdress. "In my family there is a tale of an ancestor spirit who comes, when all other hope has fled. He transforms the ill, the dying, and they live again."

Her hand touched mine and I looked up, suddenly seeing something in her face I hadn't before. My hand raised to touch her face before I realized what I was doing and pulled it back. "You remind me of someone," I said distractedly, my eyes tracking a movement outside the window. "Dovan."

The skies had only been dark a short while, so his presence surprised me. He opened the door with a smile, which dimmed only slightly when he spotted the tutor. "Am I intruding?"

I smiled. "Never, please come in."

"I brought something for Lu Sin." He held up a canvas bag. "From Justine, for the cough."

I got up to take it, brushing his hand in thanks. "She will be grateful." I followed his eyes to Willy, who stood slowly, her eyes wide. "Oh, Dovan, this is Miss Willemenia Brockard, the girls' tutor. Miss Willy, this is my grandfather." I said it without thinking. He looked no older than I, but she only nodded.

The two of them regarded each other for a long moment before she finally moved. "I have seen you before," she said simply, though her expression told me that she didn't mean on one of his other visits, which usually happened long after she had gone to bed.

"Have you?" His voice was pleasant, but guarded.

"I was very small, and my father was very ill. Mother told me I imagined you."

"Perhaps you did." Dovan smiled.

"Perhaps." She looked to me with wide eyes, then shook her head. "I should be in bed. Goodnight."

She left the room in a flutter, leaving Dovan and I alone. "What was that about?" I asked as I took the herbal remedy he had brought from the bag.

"She ... is kin," he said almost incredulously.

Kin. I couldn't begin to count the generations that separated us or fathom the odds of having invited someone of Dovan's bloodline into my life. "Kin?"

"Brockard ... is one of the family names I can still trace, a direct line back to Gregor's children."

"And her father?"

"A disease of the lungs. I offered him an ending of the pain, death, quiet and peaceful with his family, or life away from them. He chose to die."

Dovan looked profoundly sad. I sat at the table. "You would have changed him?" I could feel Lu Sin, suddenly awake and hovering just outside my awareness.

"Yes, he was so like your father. I couldn't stand to see him in that pain."

We were silent a moment, letting his words lie there on the table between us. "It explains much," I said finally. I had never craved Francis and Willy felt much the same. Indeed, even my affection for Dovan held no darker motives or desires. They were my blood. Kin.

"And what of Lu Sin?" he asked.

I sighed. So pointed the question, so uncertain the answer. "She wishes ... she's asked me to make her one of us."

"Will you?"

"I—I've said no. You'll notice I have little success in mothering the monster."

"Moira is not a disaster."

"No." I had to concede that point. "She is most remarkable." I looked away. There was a part of me that wanted it, to hold Lu Sin to me forever. "Would I not be a hypocrite, to give up killing to salve my conscience only to unleash another killer?"

We were quiet again for a time after that. When Lu Sin's coughing called me, he said his goodbyes, promising more medicine on his next visit. I brewed the tea Justine had sent and went in to sooth my friend's cough. When she at last had breath to speak, she seemed concerned. "Dovan was here."

I nodded and tucked the blankets around her. "He was. He brought the tea."

"His visit troubled you."

I sighed and sat beside her. "He has a way of asking difficult questions."

She nodded. "He is a very interesting man."

"You should rest."

"I am not tired. Would you read to me?"

I conceded and retrieved a volume of poetry I had read from when last she had asked. I settled into the soft pillows of the chair beside her bed and opened the book. Lu Sin sipped her tea and closed her eyes, drifting on the sound of the words. I read until she had fallen asleep, before retiring to my own bed, where I lay in the long daylight hours without sleeping, listening to the sounds of my home, the beating of four hearts.

Joy easily filled in the places in our lives that Lu Sin once filled, taking over the chores Lu Sin could no longer perform and spending time with Francis that I had never realized Francis needed. Francis had only ever had Lu Sin and myself as companions. I began to realize how cruel that had been for her as I watched her with Joy. It made me smile the way Francis would light up as Joy told her stories of her life before coming to our little cabin. Francis had only been to town on the day Joy came, while Joy had lived in great cities and attended schools with other children.

I had been selfish, hiding us away as I had. I owed my daughter more. Admitting that made me reconsider Lu Sin. My selfishness had cost her too.

I tried to compensate by spending more of my time with my dying friend. I wanted her to understand that I truly did love her, and I was finding it increasingly hard to be around Joy. The long neglected controls that had governed so much of my existence before had nearly disappeared completely and it was all I could do not to go to her in the early hours of evening and bring her to me. Instead, I spent those hours with Lu Sin, fighting the urge there as well, but it was not so vehement a battle. There it was a battle of logic against sympathy, not passion.

However, to sit there beside her was a difficult thing for me to do. Never before had I been faced with so certain an ending, so long in advance of the actual event. Never before had I felt so helpless, so inadequate. In all my life there had been action, a thing to do to prevent or to accomplish an ending. Now, I was forced to simply wait and watch. She grew smaller as time went on, dropping several pounds a month as her appetite faded. Her sparkling eyes lost some of their gleam, and the fire was gone from her voice. The symptoms which I had failed to notice before became more evident, the pain undeniable. A cough so deep as to seem to come from somewhere outside herself racked her body. Her eyes grew sunken and darkened with the struggle to breathe. Her heartbeat slowed. I could hardly stand to be there, and yet I could have been nowhere else.

"Is this how your whole life has been, constantly replacing the dying with the new?" she asked one night as I sat beside her bed.

"No, actually ... I have never seen death like this before. Always to me it comes quickly, harshly. Never is it expected, anticipated. This is new to me too," I said softly, my eyes on her pale hand.

"She will become what I can never be," she said. "Her you will bring to you, if you don't kill her first."

"No, Lu Sin, please. I decided long ago that I would never do that again." I held myself still beside her, hoping to contain the truth within myself, that she might not see it. My voice was scarcely a whisper, the words escaping despite my fear to speak.

"You told me once that you had wanted her when she was still an infant. Do you deny that the desire has only grown stronger now that she is grown?"

"No, I won't deny it. Nor will I lie and say that I have never desired you as well. Even now there is some measure of it in me, some craving to know you in ways only a killer can know."

There was silence for a while then, before the coughing spell shook her increasingly frail frame. When it subsided she smiled weakly. "I know why you deny me, my friend. I know, and I forgive you. I hope that before it is over you will change your mind, but if I die first, I wanted you to know."

I stayed with her until she slept, then rose, surprised to find Joy in the doorway. "She hasn't long, you know," she said softly. "Another week, maybe a month."

Her blue eyes were dark and glazed over, as if she wasn't truly seeing the room or anything in it. "Will you save her?" she asked breathlessly as her eyes snapped back to me.

I wondered if she knew what that meant, but it was clear that she accepted unequivocally that I was able to save her. "I cannot. She knows that."

"Does she?" She sighed, heavier than a child of her small years should have been able. I touched her arm, feeling my soul fill with her, as it had when I had held her in my arms. I closed my eyes and echoed the sigh. I let myself melt a little, let her arms fold around me. It seemed as though I had felt that touch before. My head was swimming with images, my heart pounding with suddenly remembered desires. The touch of her skin on mine was like an iron hot from the fire, awakening me. The smell of her overpowered the odor of dying in the room, overwhelmed my senses. I could feel the life moving through her with every beat of that tender heart and I craved the taste of it. I was trembling when I at last pulled away, trembling with the effort to restrain the sudden swarming of need within me. I left her there in the hall and fled out into the night.

It was nearly dawn before I returned, quietly sliding off to my room without even checking on the children or Lu Sin. I was afraid of myself. I had hunted while I wandered the night, but found myself unwilling to feed. The animals that I could have easily were not what my soul craved.

I crawled into my bed fully dressed and aching. I could smell them both as though they were in the room with me. Lu Sin's dying body cried out for release, the stench of impending death drawing and repelling me at the same time. Joy's rapid, youthful heartbeat danced around it, dizzying as her warm, living scent beckoned. I bit my own lip, feeling the Change come, unable to prevent it. I tasted blood as the sharp fangs fell into place.

I covered my head and closed my eyes, but visions of them filled my head, Joy innocent and laughing, Lu Sin pleading for mercy from her pale face. I rose from the bed and began pacing my room in an agitated pace, my hands balled tightly at my sides as I fought my inner demon. Lu Sin's coughing had grown worse. I longed for her, to be with her, comfort her … hold her while I at long last tasted of her. I had always wanted her, as I did all of humanity that I let get close enough. The more I knew of her, the worse the wanting had become. Now it mixed with my desire to offer her mercy, to ease her passing.

I was rationalizing. I drew a deep, tight breath and released it slowly. I found myself at the bedroom door. One step beyond that door and my control would disappear completely. I knew it beyond a doubt. I forced myself from the door to perch precariously on the edge of the bed. I reached for the bottle on my nightstand, but I had drained it that evening upon rising. I threw it against the wall in a rage. I would have to make more to get through this day. It might be the only thing that would save my friends. I flew from the room to the lab and into the work. The Change refused to leave me as I pounded through the familiar routine. In three-quarters of an hour I had a nearly full bottle and drank deeply.

I spit it out almost immediately, the red-pink, thick fluid still warm and absolutely retched in my current state of mind. I paced then around the lab, breaking beakers and flasks older than my daughter in my anger at my inability to control myself. I heard Lu Sin moving about, the noise had wakened her. I didn't want her to see me, I was ashamed of myself, and I knew she would hate me to see me this way and unable to bring her to me as she wanted. I listened for a long time, until the noises had subsided, then let myself back out into the hall.

Four heartbeats twisted around one another in the languid rhythms of sleep. Two of them seemed to echo one another, playing tag with my attention. I was breathless as I found myself at Joy's door, watching as she slept. Her angelic face was peaceful, so unaware of the monster that stood to prey on her.

I don't remember entering that room, or sitting on that bed. I cannot recall bending to her tender neck or opening my fanged mouth to that insistently beating vein. But, I do know the exact moment when the divinity of her taste first touched me. A moment I tasted, lingering on that first touch ... the warmth, the fresh, sweet ecstasy of it. A fire raced within me, igniting my mind and heart and soul. In that one taste, I became aware.

Joy ... this child, had a soul as old as mine, handed down for centuries past in search of the one who had saved it from destruction. I saw from a child's eyes as a demon with the body of a girl left it abandoned beside two dead bodies. I saw a celebrated lifetime as a holy woman who had performed miracles as a child. I saw a hundred lifetimes come and go. I saw Adroushan, I saw Rebeka. This ... child, and that, and all of them in between. All with the same blonde hair, the same sapphire eyes ... all looking somehow for me.

I pulled back, her blood still on my lips. I wiped at the wound I had made and backed away from her. Tears stung my eyes and rolled over my cheeks. I hated myself, and whatever had brought this soul back to me. I was mad with need and incensed with her blood. My body screamed for more.

Before I had become fully aware of myself I was beside Lu Sin's bed. The sound of her filled the room, the scent of her decaying flesh rose to me and competed with the fresh perfume of Joy that still clung to me. Her eyes alone betrayed the fear that suddenly rose in her. I was the picture of death come to take the remainder of her life from her. I fell on her before either of us could speak to deter me from it. I tore into her tender, graceful neck and drank deeply. The blood was thicker than that of the child's, richer ... darker. It was hot with the fever. It tasted of the illness which worked to claim her life. But, I wasn't going to let it have her. In my delusional state, she was mine and in that moment of complete irrationality I took the disease into myself, for it would have to conquer me before I would let it take her.

It was over in minutes. I knelt beside her, the Change subsiding, the fire diminished. My tears soaked the dress I still wore. There was blood on it as well. It was over. The dying was done for that day. "Forgive me," I said softly as I rose to leave the room.

"There is nothing to forgive," she said.

I did not sleep the rest of the day, but I lay in my bed, dressed and unable to move. I had done that which I had sworn not to, I had taken yet another life. Things would be forever different in our home. When I arose it was early, still an hour or more before dark. I went first to Willemenia's room, where she was preparing a lesson. "I cannot explain, but there is a chance you will no longer be safe here. You should gather your belongings and go to town. I will forward your final pay and a letter of recommendation."

Her dark eyes regarded me for a long moment. "Is it your friend?"

I nodded, stepping back to give her space to rise from the chair. "Yes."

"Has he come for her?"

I somehow knew she meant Dovan. "No, I did it myself."

"What of the children?"

I didn't want to think about that. "I will care for them." She stood and began packing her belongings. "I am glad to have met you, Willemenia. I am sorry we couldn't have known one another better." I left her then, trusting that she would be gone shortly. I gathered the children then and set off into the night. I did not want to be there when Lu Sin woke and discovered what it was she had asked to become. We walked half the night, wandering and playing in the wild fields and meadows. If Joy knew anything of the night before she said nothing. The wound on her neck was small, and healing already. They spoke nothing of Lu Sin, for which I was grateful. For a moment there was just the three of us at play.

Eventually, when we had gone too far to return before daylight, I made the decision that we would stop in to visit Dovan. We arrived in the early hours of the morning when he and Justine were just settling in to sleep. They welcomed us eagerly, putting the yawning children to bed in my former room, and sitting casually with me near a drowsy fire.

"So, your young friend is dead?" he asked in that casual, yet piercing way of his.

"In a manner of speaking," I replied, my eyes locked unseeing on the tiny blaze.

He didn't say anything, just took Justine's hand. For a long time we sat there, the three of us, silently watching the dimming flame. Then they rose and retired to their room. I sat in that cavern, watching the shifting patterns of light at the entrance as daylight came to the mountain. I had a passing thought of Lu Sin, and then I too rose. I walked to the small pool of daylight, squinting into the brightness. My mind was absent of anything. There was only this empty, hollow feeling inside of me, with no real emotion or desire or thought. I was suddenly exhausted, alone.

I stood there a long, long time, just inside the morning glare. I don't know why or what eventually propelled me to leave the light and crawl into bed with the children, but I did. I fell quickly into the deep, undisturbed sleep of my mother's people, letting it drain the fatigue from me. When I woke it was quiet around me. The children were gone. I rose and stretched. It felt strange to be there in that room again, and yet perfectly comfortable. I could smell something cooking in the common room, and with the rumbling of my stomach, set out to find it.

Dovan was there, alone. He was roasting some type of meat over a low fire, and very obviously waiting for me. I sat beside him. It was quiet for a long time. "They are lovely children. Francis seems to have blossomed since I saw her last."

"Thank you, Dovan. She is my pride."

"Joy is ... dangerous. She seems to know things which she is too young to know."

I nodded. "Indeed. She will be a great woman one day."

"If she lives that long." He rubbed his neck with his free hand to indicate he had seen the bite marks.

"A moment of weakness," I said, dropping my gaze.

"The same moment in which you went to your friend?"

"The same." I wanted to cry, to feel him fold his arms around me and tell me that it was going to be all right.

"I've been down to see her. She's is well enough, considering she has only animals to feed on. That is hard on a young one."

"I warned her of it. She wanted it anyway. I never meant this."

"And the tutor?"

"I sent her away."

The sounds of the children returning ended the conversation, but I knew it was only the beginning. I would have to return to Lu Sin, I would have to begin her new life. I wanted to crawl into the ground instead. It was a quiet meal, with Justine entertaining Francis and Joy while I sulked. When it was done I thanked Dovan for his hospitality and led my family back down the mountain. We would make it just before sunrise if we hurried.

Chapter 22

L U SIN was quiet. I could feel her hunger, her fear before we had even reached the cottage. Joy could sense it too I think. Her face was pale and drawn with more than weariness as we approached. I was slightly apprehensive, for now Lu Sin would understand the desires I had barely in check ... now she too would have to fight herself to keep Joy alive. More than that, she had no familial connection to Francis, so I had to consider the danger there as well. I took a deep breath and led the children inside. Lu Sin was in her room, waiting perhaps for my return. I sent the children off to bed quickly and knocked at her door.

She sat wrapped in a quilt, looking more robust and lively than she had in a year or more. Her eyes were bright, even in the dark of the room, and they spoke of the illumination inside of her with the quickening of her new life. "Are you well?" I asked as I sat on the bed across from her chair.

"Well enough. And you?"

I inclined my head in a motion of acceptance. "I will survive this." It was strange to me, the absolute lack of emotion I felt at that moment. This was a child of mine, as was Moira and Racelle and the others, and yet there was nothing of a guardianship feeling to it, nothing but the absence of anything. I hung my head as I considered it.

Her cold hand touched my knee. "I asked, and you gave what I asked for. Do not blame yourself for what I have become."

"Do you blame me?"

She was quiet and when I looked up she seemed to be listening to something I didn't hear. "It was as it was meant to be. I was brought to you, exactly for this. I could blame you no more than I blame the mother who birthed me." Her voice had the ring of antiquity in it, her accent suddenly thick and untouched by her years among the English speaking.

So she said to me whenever I took pause to ask her, and yet the very air in that cabin changed.

It was either charged with the electricity of the youth or our desire of it, or stale and unmoving. There was nothing in the middle anymore. Every night Lu Sin was gone longer and longer, journeying further and further from our home in search of satisfying meals. Sooner or later the need would lead her away from us entirely.

She was much as I had pictured she would be, a solitary and simple vampire, who saw her needs as natural and to be dealt with efficiently, as humanity does its meals. She slowly dropped all pretenses at prettying herself, beyond the combing of that long, straight black mane. Her clothes were simple, black and long, the better to shield her from the rising of the sun should she be caught out late. She withdrew into her room for weeks on end, pouring herself over the immense library of ancient texts which she had previously shown no interest in. Her comings and goings were nearly silent and unnoticed by us, she was simply there and gone.

Joy's gifts, handed down through centuries were honed in those months, and she would look up from some game with Francis and her eyes betrayed the knowledge her mind held. She knew Lu Sin's frenzied feeding. She felt the waves of desire that often brought me within inches of her young heart. Francis occasionally caught glimpses of it, her own gifts, those my own unnatural creation had given to her, lending her the vision to see into her friend's mind. It was a time of learning, a time when none of us could truly trust the others, save for young Francis. The world revolved around her and her growth. It was as if we had all assembled in that place to offer her what knowledge we each had.

The rest went on around her, and other than those moments when she touched Joy's mind, she was unaware. I lay awake many mornings, listening to Joy and Francis settling into bed, listening to Lu Sin's returning or absence ... or pacing in her room. I stood at the bedroom door where my foster child slept and watched, seeming as if I could see her physically growing, maturing. I ached inside, but the desires had dimmed somewhat with the making of Lu Sin, as had the other emotions in my life.

We rarely spoke of anything, Lu Sin and I communicated with looks and gestures and the silent phrases of the blood we now shared. Francis was completely caught up in her friendship with Joy, and the words between them were likewise few. Their silent conversations floated around me, mine for the asking, but I refrained.

A year passed, two, in this way. I missed the way it had been, the laughter and precious moments we had shared before Joy had joined us. I didn't resent her coming, but I knew now, as Lu Sin had before that it was not the right thing to have done, for her or for us. Francis was to be thirteen; Joy had matured into a beautiful young woman, nearly sixteen years old. We planned to celebrate with a party, gifts, and cake. I had even journeyed into town myself, braving the bright spring sun to purchase gifts for my girls.

On the designated night, Lu Sin was gone on her hunt for a short time, returning with a spring in her step and a true smile on her face for the first time in many, many months. We sang songs from our childhoods for the children, and they sang songs Joy had learned in school. We ate white cake with white frosting and a pudding Joy had taught me to make. It was a scene filled with family love, the last I was to remember from that time.

It came time for the gifts. For Francis I had purchased a beautiful china doll, complete with a matching dress for her to wear. To Joy I gave a hand-painted horse sculpture. It had reminded me of her when I saw it in the store window. Somewhere in her past there was a great love of horses she had yet to find in this life. Lu Sin rose then, and brought in her gifts, two pure black Labrador puppies. The girls squealed with delight, each reaching into the box to pull out one of the dogs and hug it tightly to them.

"They are beautiful, are they not?" she asked me as we watched the two girls playing.

"Indeed. It is a most thoughtful gift. Thank you, my friend."

"I have brought a gift for you as well," she lifted a small package onto the table. I looked at it for a long time before I moved to accept it.

"There was no need–"

"Yes, there was."

I inclined my head and opened it. Inside there was a small book, with leather binding and blank pages and the word "Journal" written in gold on the front cover. Beside it was a quill pen of the kind I had used when I was younger, and a small vial of black ink. Beneath it all the surface of a mirror shined up at me. I slowly pulled the mirror up and held it up to the flickering light of the nearby candles. It was a beautiful piece of work, done all in silver with tiny flecks of gemstones highlighting the delicate design. The smooth surface of the mirror was nearly hypnotic as I peered in at my reflection. I was somewhat shocked at what I saw there, the gray that had come to highlight the hair at my crown and temples, the tiny imperfections in my once flawless skin. My eyes alone remained untouched by my years in the solitary wilderness. They sparkled as Lu Sin's did.

"I would like for you to write for me," she said quietly. "I have enjoyed what little I have read of your words, and your life is so full of history. I pray you take this as an invitation to share it with the world."

"And the mirror?" I asked, my eyes dancing to where the puppies were playfully tugging at the children.

"To remind you of how you are ... of how strong and wonderful you are. Every now and then it doesn't hurt to admit to yourself, Amara."

It was the first time she had used my name so casually. It felt ... comfortable. I suddenly realized she was leaving, and a sharp pain stabbed at me. I wanted her to stay, I was afraid of myself without her. She touched my arm and the old desires came floating back into my mind. A vague memory of the night Francis had been born and Lu Sin's comforting ways and touches filled me. If she sensed it, she remained silent.

"Come, hunt with me," she said finally, when the silence had grown too long.

It was the first time she had ever offered, perhaps because she had known I would always refuse her. Until that moment. I rose from my place and slipped into my shoes. "Girls, behave yourselves. Lu Sin and I are going out for a walk."

We went into the woods which had begun encroaching on our little house. I made a mental note to get someone to cut back the young trees. The night was still, and somewhat chilly, the last vestiges of a cruel winter blowing through the thick trees. There was precious little wildlife about, and Lu Sin didn't seem particularly interested with any of it. We walked, arm in arm through the familiar territory like two friends who knew that at the end of their walk would be something to change them forever.

Nearly an hour from the cabin, she took her arm from mine and turned to face me. "I want you to know how much these last years have meant to me," she said. "I might have died alone and poor in the streets of some cold city, but you came for me, took me away from the ugliness of my life, brought me to this beautiful place. You gave me a purpose, and desires. I should have been a better friend for it." She took both my hands and held them between us. "Never blame yourself for this. I knew the moment I laid eyes on you that you had come to save me. I knew what you were then, and waited for the moment to arrive when you would make me like you."

I think I felt tears welling up inside me as she spoke, knowing this would be goodbye forever. "Don't leave, Lu Sin. I need you here."

She smiled a sad little smile. "No you don't, you never did. You let yourself be convinced that you need people, but you are so strong, so self-willed. There will never be anyone you need more than yourself. You will survive."

The words of Crenoral floated to me on a night breeze, echoing in my head as if to taunt me. "Your will to live is too strong," he had said on the night he died.

"You have taught me a great deal, my friend. I shall never forget you for that." I squeezed her hand lightly.

She kissed my cheek then, and let me go. I closed my eyes and waited, not wanting to watch her walk away. When I knew she had gone I turned and headed for the house. It was quiet when I returned, the exhausted puppies piled in a heap of black fur on the living room rug while Francis and Joy studied their lessons by the fire. I set about cleaning up after our party, putting dirty dishes in the basin to be washed and gathering the crinkled colored paper of the wrappings to be used another time.

There was an emptiness in the air, a hollow feeling I couldn't seem to shake, even as I tucked Francis into bed, a tiny kiss on her forehead. "Is Lu Sin ever coming home?" she asked, her dark eyes half closed.

"No, Francis, my love. Lu Sin has moved onto another place. We will likely never see her again."

"She is my friend." Francis had a way of saying things simply.

"I know. She is my friend as well. We will wish all good things her way."

I left her nearly asleep to check on Joy. It was more out of habit than necessity, after all she was no longer a child. She was sitting at her vanity, combing out the long blonde tresses I so adored. Her cotton nightgown glowed in the soft light. I smiled. She did too.

"Sleep well," I said.

I withdrew then to my room, taking my gifts with me. I lay across the bed with the mirror, exploring a face I hadn't really seen in years. The tiny wrinkles that kissed my eyes and mouth were as foreign to me as the gray in my hair. How long had it been, I asked myself? How long? I heard the creak of a board and looked up to find Joy in the doorway. "Might I come in?"

"Of course, Child." I sat up, beckoning her closer. I set aside the mirror. "What is it?"

"I don't know. I felt like you needed something."

I smiled and took her hand. "I am told that I need nothing," I said, glancing at the journal. "Did you have fun tonight?"

"Yes, thank you. My parents never really thought much about birthdays." She tossed her blonde curls over one shoulder and I could see that she was wearing the sapphire I had given her all those years before. "I think about them sometimes, and everything they did for me. Is it wrong to think of them as strangers?" There was an air about her of the lost, struggling to put into words what her heart and soul were whispering to her. Perhaps it was time she came to know herself.

I shook my head. "No, they were good people, but you were already looking for someone else when they brought you into this world. You are older than they, merely staying with them while your body matured. Even had they lived a while longer, you might have eventually come to feel that way."

Her eyes grew distant, and I sensed she was tapping into that other person, that ancient soul. "I was looking for you," she said. "I've looked for you over and over."

I drew her to me, laying her head to rest on my shoulder. "Aye, you have. Once before you found me, but I was unable to save you."

"I was like you, and I was...." She sat up, her face pale and her eyes big. I could see in their depths a shiver of shared memory, of a horror that shook us both.

I closed my mind to it, shutting off the darkest chapter in my life and shushing her stammered phrases that sought to describe it. "It's long past now, love, long gone into the history of time. Let us not speak of it again." I held her for a long moment, until I felt her control tighten on her new-found memory, then she sat up.

"When you first knew me, when I was still a baby ... I knew then, didn't I?" she asked, and in her face was the awe and wonderment of a woman discovering herself.

"Yes, I believe you did. That is probably what drew me to you then."

"And now?"

I yawned, suddenly weary of the whole night's events. "That is up to you, Joy. In the next weeks and months, you will likely begin to remember more about us, about your past. It will be up to you to decide what to do then. For now, I suggest a good sleep and some time to adjust to the changes in our lives."

She smiled then, and the oddity of her expression vanished, she was once again a young girl on the verge of womanhood, beautiful and awkward and so divine. She kissed my cheek and left the room. My heart was pounding fiercely. It came upon me so quickly that I was glad she had left me alone. I hadn't been prepared for the ferocity of it, the smell of her fresh, young blood and the sight of her smile overwhelmed me. I turned myself back to the mirror, staring into the Changed face, wondering what manner of man would invite this demon into its life.

Slowly, the Change left me and I sat staring in at the face of a woman who seemed to age before my eyes. It was as if my myriad years attacked me and painted my hair with gray as I sat there. I put the mirror down and picked up the journal. It smelled clean, of new leather and well pressed paper. I opened it slowly, staring at the blank ivory page for a long time before my hand reached for the quill and ink. I had no idea where to start, what to say. So much history, so many gory details. I held the pen and waited. I had often written pieces of myself, chapters of remembrances I cared to save. Tidbits of forever. Now, Lu Sin had asked for the whole.

The words began themselves, spinning onto the page in a rush. I wrote for hours, beginning at the beginning of time, spilling my soul and memory out in a spreading display of black ink. There were times I felt out of breath, taken in by my own story, and times when I felt as cold and distant as the Others I wrote about. Before I was aware of the passing of time, the sun was setting and I could hear the girls rising. I set aside my pen and journal and rose.

The puppies were named Princess and Prince respectively, although which one belonged to whom was up in the air. If Joy remembered any of our conversation, she said nothing, simply setting about her chores, as did Francis. So much had changed in the last twenty-four hours, so little appeared different. I smiled as Francis played with the puppies, as I watched Joy making breakfast. It was comfortable, and yet chaffing, restricting. My mind flashed from that moment to the times I had been writing about, when my own self-control had not yet exerted itself and my life had been filled with the darkness of the demon, the freedom of the night.

So would many of the next nights be, the changes subtly influencing our small lives, slowly marking the next turn. Time moved on, and Francis followed Joy's example, maturing into a beautiful young woman before my very eyes. She was the dark shadow of Joy's light, the perfect balance between them. Those gifts of my unnatural creation made themselves manifest, lending her an air of mystery, distraction. In her eyes I saw what I was to her, what I had somehow become. She knew the dark side of me, but somehow I was more than that. Her love for me dressed me as a good woman, a mother, giving, strong, able to protect her from anything the night could create.

In my mirror, I aged. Slowly to be sure, but the signs of encroaching age were unavoidable. How long had it been since I had last tasted death? How long since warm, fresh blood had crossed my lips unhindered? I wondered if that was the cause of my decay, if without it I was as my mortal brethren, running from time as if from the day. I looked up from my usual place, in my chair, beside the fire. Francis was at the table, an ancient book in her hands. Joy sat near me, knitting something.

I didn't see the children in them anymore. Suddenly in that moment they were women, full grown and wise beyond their collective years. As if sensing the direction of my thoughts, Joy looked up. That forbidden knowledge looked back at me. Her blue eyes sparkled with what could only be described as love. It was the same look I often saw in my daughter's eyes for me. It quickened the beating of my heart, stirred the never quite extinguished coals of desire. I looked away.

Francis had felt it ... I could feel her eyes on me. I rose and went to join her. "What are you reading, darling?"

"History," she replied simply. Hers was not the gift of many words. "Are you all right, Mother?"

I nodded wearily and sat beside her at the old, hand carved table. "Yes, Francis, I'm fine. A little tired perhaps." I felt old sitting there beside her, old and out of place. More than twenty years had passed since I had first come to that place, heavy with the burden of my child. Nothing seemed to have moved in that time, all the furnishings, all the décor. Only the people in it moved. Princess raised her head from the floor to look at me, as if to add herself to my appraisal. Prince made some noise in his sleep and ignored me.

I patted Francis's hand reassuringly, and left the room. In the privacy of my bedchamber, I relaxed. It was my private sanctuary, where even my greatest self-torments left me alone. I turned to writing, as I often did when feeling my own age. It was as if I could reclaim that youth as I wrote it down.

The restless spirit wouldn't leave me, as if something were coming, something near, but not yet visible. I tossed and turned and rose from my bed. I paced the room, drinking down formula. I found myself outside, in the early hours of the morning, looking into the slowly lightening sky. Idly I wondered if I could sit there as dawn came. I knew I never would. I sighed repeatedly, longing for something I dared not name.

She came to me, perhaps feeling whatever it was that had called me out there, maybe just knowing I needed her. I felt her approach, deep inside of me I could feel every movement as she came. My heartbeat matched hers, as it always did when she was close to me, my breathing was rapid, shallow. I could smell her, and I craved to taste her. My tongue remembered it, that one moment of weakness when I had tasted the divinity of her ... remembered it and wanted more.

It would be different now, slightly aged, richer than it had been, but still so sweet a taste ... so delicious. I closed my eyes as she sat beside me on the small bench. "What keeps you up so late, Mother?" she asked.

I caught my breath as I felt her hand touch the side of my face. Her touch was soft, sensual. Her concern for me was likely to be my final undoing. She couldn't know what her presence beside me did to me. Perhaps she did, and her aim was to torment me out of this sulking melancholy that had taken me when Lu Sin had left. I wouldn't look at her. "I couldn't sleep, Joy. It is nothing."

"You are so restless. Shall I rub your back for you?" Her hands slipped up to my shoulders, her strong fingers kneading at the tense muscles. I closed my eyes and took a deep, harsh breath. It was nearly impossible to sit still as her hands touched me, trailing fire across my back as she rubbed. She couldn't see it in me, so intent in her task, but it boiled, breaking the surface and changing me.

I didn't move. She couldn't see this face, she couldn't know. I couldn't look upon her and not fall to feeding. I kept my face down, covered by the cascade of hair. I bit my lip to keep from jumping from the bench. Still, she continued. "Stop!" I said breathlessly, pulling forward just a bit. "Go inside, Joy. Go to bed. I will be in shortly."

She must have heard the harshness in my voice, the fear, the self-loathing. She had to leave me, I could contain myself no longer. She stepped away, but did not do as I asked. For a heartbeat we simply sat in perfect stillness, then she was at my feet, looking up into my Changed face, her blue eyes wide with love and fear. "No," she said. "No, this time I will not make it easy for you. I am here. You will have to face me."

"No." I pulled back from her, turning my face to the sky. "No, go away from me. I cannot fight this."

She didn't move, just sat there on her knees before me, holding my hands and rooting me to my spot. My body trembled; my soul wavered between accepting what I was and continuing to rebel against myself. "Joy, I beg of you, go inside."

"No." She reached a hand up to touch my cheek. I could hear the rush of blood at her wrist, nearly taste it as it paused so close to my mouth. The smell was overpowering. I kissed her palm and moaned with the exertion it took to pull away. "You have desired me since the dawn of time, Mother, since that day when you left me on the side of a dirt road. Here I am."

"I spared you then. I would do the same now."

"Maybe it isn't your choice. Maybe you were meant to take my life centuries ago. Perhaps that is why I have sought you out over and over."

"Joy, please." My head was swimming with images, of that girl so long ago, of Rebeka, mine for so short a time. "I could never forgive myself."

"I forgive you already." She rose up on her knees, her eyes seeking out mine. Her throat lay there before me, unprotected, beating with life. "Come. If you truly cannot resist me, come and taste."

I came undone, falling to my knees in the dewy grass and pulling her into my tight embrace. My mouth quivered as it neared her milky flesh, and my heartbeat wrapped around hers. She shivered as my teeth penetrated the skin, as the first taste of her danced onto my tongue. Then she was still. The warmth of life flooded me, erasing an ancient chill I hadn't recognized before. I drank deeply, pulling the exquisiteness of her into me. As always, with the blood came her memories, her life. As that time before when I had held her in my arms and drank from her, I saw the flashing images of her myriad lives. I saw the child who had haunted my nights, the woman who healed the sick in Nepal. I saw my poor, doomed Adroushan. I saw my Rebeka as a child, maturing into the half-woman, half-girl I had known. I saw her die. Through her eyes, I saw the Hunter.

I pulled away, blood smearing my face and staining my nightgown. She lay on the grass, stunned, dazed by the loss of blood. I looked up and around me, half expecting the Hunter to be there with us. He was not. It was only the two of us. The Change slipped away from me and I leaned over Joy. She would live. Her blood coursed through me, erasing the weariness and fatigue that had plagued me. I was hot, feeling the returning strength and embarrassment, anger at my lack of control, at her temptation. I scooped her up and carried her into her bedroom. I lay her out on her bed, covering her lovingly. I never looked back, fleeing out into the waning night as if there were demons chasing me. Perhaps there were.

Chapter 23

THE NIGHT was nearly over, I could sense daylight hanging just behind the nearest peak. I ran without thinking, without caring where I was going, as long as it was away from myself. In a shallow cave barely able to contain me I spent the day, shivering in cold and fear and hunger. It was worse for having tasted of her, for knowing all that she was. Only the image of the Hunter, Daniel was what Dovan had called him, had spared Joy. The sight of him had jarred me enough to cool the hunger a little, startled me into remembering myself.

The day passed, and the next night followed. Still, I remained in the cave, unmoving, unresponsive. I was lost somewhere inside myself, buried deeply in my own dark soul. I longed for the cool, soothing presence of Moira ... or the damning, seething presence of Jesse ... anything but this solitary battle I was enduring. Everything within me wanted to return to that cabin, claim what had been offered up to me, bring that soul of beauty and light to my bosom forever.

As I drifted in and out of sleep I dreamed of Francis, searching the night frantically for me. Joy wouldn't tell her what had happened, only that I had gone away, and would return when I was ready. I wished I could tell her the truth, that I had told her the truth about me, about herself. It had been too ugly a topic for our artificial Eden, and I had avoided the confirmation of her visions.

Three nights after I left them, I managed to leave the cave, hunting viciously, but barely feeding. The deer and other wildlife of the area simply did not appeal to me. I worked my way down the mountain, taking enough food to survive, but leaving the hunger burning deep inside of me. It would have to be appeased, but for the moment I reveled in it. I closed my mind to rational thought, becoming very much like the animals I hunted, very much like the creature Crenoral had once been. I lost myself in it, distancing myself from the poised, elegant woman I had often claimed to be. I reverted to the person I was when Crenoral first took me out into the night.

When I reached the base of the mountain, who knows how many days or weeks later, I haunted the populated areas, the hunger in me raging, craving. I prowled the night around the village, hanging just out of sight, passing unheard on the streets. I did not feed, but I could have. I could have had that whole village. I listened, I watched. The world had become a different place in those years, modern advances had begun to change even the lives of that remote town. I was a stranger looking in on a society I had once known, overrun by progress, left behind for dead. That thought made me smile, for surely I was as close to dead as any living creature could come.

The telegraph machines I had known had been replaced by a new wonder that sent words and voice over miles and miles, emulating the ability my brethren shared. The town actually had two of them, one in the general store and one in the home of the town's richest socialite. If I stood still outside that house, I could almost hear the voices screaming silently through the air around me.

The library was filled with books that discussed religion and philosophy, and things like evolution. I found treatises on witchcraft and vampirism, most of which was mere superstition and conjecture. I heard tales of vast modern plagues that had swept the countryside and decimated whole towns. I read accounts of experiments with the sick and dying, or the dead. Medical science had made great strides into understanding the human body, but not the human soul. There was considerable conversation in the newspapers and in the homes of townsfolk regarding the ability of science to create life outside of a mother's womb.

I drank it in, all of it, as if it were blood to warm me. I absorbed the new views and arguments, filled myself with knowledge. All the while I fed on animals in the forest, enough to survive at least. I hovered just outside of the awareness of that town, feeding my lust for knowledge, my love of words. Slowly I was returning to myself, recovering from the wounds of my own actions. The demon within was withdrawing.

Eventually, I knew I would have to return, to face what I had done, what I had become. That didn't make it easier to do. When at last I was ready, I began the long journey with no more than I had left them with. Clad simply in a black dress stolen from a clothesline I went. The night air was chill with the approach of winter. The wild flowers were dying. The abundant animal life of those mountains was sparse, and those to be found were wily, harder to catch than their milder relatives.

I found my way back there as if I had only left that cabin days before. I stood in the moonlight looking at it for a long, long time. No lights lit the windows, no sound stirred the breeze. There was no fire sending lazy smoke curling out of the chimney. There was only the silence of an empty place. They were gone. I let myself in, an easy thing since they had left the door unlocked. It looked as it did the night I left, quiet, peaceful. A home where children had been raised and life had been simple. A layer of dust covered the furnishings, telling me that their absence was not recent. On the table there was a piece of paper.

"My dearest Mother." It read, in Francis's handwriting. "We are leaving tonight, not knowing how long you will be gone. Joy and I must move on to the places we were meant to be. I know that you will understand this. I wish you were here for me to kiss goodbye, but my words will have to do. Should you wish to find us, you should begin your search in London, where we plan to begin our new lives. I have no doubts that you will be quite capable if you desire it. Until that day, remember that we both love you, beyond even your ability to comprehend. Good-bye, Francis."

I dropped the page to the table, scarcely fathoming the words. Gone, both of them, gone. I wandered through the house, half-expecting Prince or Princess to come charging around the corners, or bounding in through the back door. Only those things which had been personal to either of the girls were missing, everything else was exactly where it had been. I sat on Joy's bed numbly, trying to smell the essence she always carried with her. Even that was gone. As I rose from the bed, my eyes caught on the mirror of her vanity. A wraith in black stared back at me.

My skin was so white as to be translucent, reflecting the light of the moon outside her window in the eeriest way. My body was so thin as to appear painful, though the only pain I felt was in my heart. Most astonishing was the gray covering the once raven tresses on my head. I moved toward the mirror slowly, as if I expected the vision to disappear. One hand trembled as I raised it to touch the surface. The hair was long, touching nearly to the floor, and matted with leaves and dirt, tangled in knots around itself. The dress I wore was torn in places, smudged with dirt. I looked like I had crawled out of my grave again.

For a long time, I stood staring into that reflection. Then, in a moment of absolute clarity, I became myself again. The solitary, self-sufficient survivor re-emerged from within. I drew water from the well and heated it, filling a bath. I sank into the steamy waters, submerging myself and feeling the grime of my animal nature washing away. I toweled dry and wrapped myself in a robe. Sitting at Joy's vanity, I brushed out the long, long tresses, and cut them to shoulder length. The gray in them still amazed me, enough that I took a small bunch of it, tied it in a ribbon and tucked it in a drawer of remembrances I had kept throughout my life.

That done, I turned to my lab. My equipment was whole, save for a few pieces broken by who knew what. I cleaned it, scrubbing at the dust and grime until it sparkled. Then I set about making formula. It took several tries to find the rhythm again, but it came back to me. When I had filled several bottles, I withdrew to my room. There I cleaned as well, shaking out the linens, dusting the cabinets and dresser. Then, as dawn approached, I slid into the comfort of my bed and fell instantly into sleep.

It was, perhaps, the first time in those months that I had actually slept deeply. It was amazingly comforting, waking just before sunset to stretch and relax in the familiar surroundings. When I finally rose, several hours later, to drain the last of the formula I had made the night before, I began the cleaning of the rest of the house, returning it to the pristine order which Lu Sin had always demanded. I hunted, bringing back a rabbit to cook into stew. The garden had grown wild, but there were a few vegetables worth using. I dug up some carrots and radishes, found some beans that had not fallen from their bushes yet, even a few berries that had not yet rotted. It was the first meal I had eaten in months, and it was exquisite. I savored every bite, finishing off the entire stew and chasing it down with an entire bottle of formula.

Two weeks after my arrival, I left the small house to journey up the mountain to visit Dovan. I knew that he would know where my children had gone, and though I was not yet ready to seek them out, I did desire to know their whereabouts and whether or not they were well. The mountain was strangely quiet, and cold. Winter was settling rapidly. I called out as I neared the cavern Dovan called home, listening for some sign that he was around. There was no answer. The cave was empty, all but the room where I had lain and healed. Dovan and Justine were gone. I was alone.

On the bed in that cavern room was another note and a small leather bag. I hefted the bag and found it filled with gold coins and random bits of jewelry. With a breath, I lifted the note.

"This should see you to London, when you are ready to go. I will keep an eye on them until then. Dovan."

I was stunned, standing dumbfounded in the cave entrance as dawn approached. They had left me. Then, I remembered that it had been myself who had left first. I couldn't expect them to wait for me. I couldn't expect my life to continue the way it had been. It had been the complacency of that life that had driven me over the edge. It had been the nearness of those that I loved which had tempted me to the vilest of acts. Now, they were all safely away from me. It was as it should be. I waited in the darkness for the day to end, then returned to my home.

All told, the time spent in the solitude of the mountain after my Francis and Joy had left me, was miniscule compared to the rest of my life. I swiftly grew bored, and lonely. Although, I still was not ready to return myself to their lives, I hungered to know where they were, and what they had accomplished. So it was, in the early spring when snow still dotted the mountainside, I packed a small bag of equipment and clothing and set off down the mountain.

In the village there, I procured a horse and without pause, left for London. It was there that my Francis had said they would go. It was there, then, that I would begin. The trip was largely uneventful, save for it being the first time I had truly passed through civilization since Francis's birth. I moved swiftly, stopping only when I encountered something unfamiliar, new. As I neared Paris, that became more and more frequent. The telephones that had been so new upon my last knowledge of man's advances were prevalent, filling the night air with the sounds of voices. Electric lights were ever so slowly taking the place of gas lamps and candles.

It was a new world, filled with strange and frightening things. The closer I came to the great city, the more I feared my arrival there. I felt entirely backward and unprepared, an unfamiliar thing to be sure. I was accustomed to a certain confidence in myself, a knack for getting along in the world. Paris should have felt as comfortable to me as that mountain cabin I had so recently abandoned.

To be truthful, it had been close to thirty years since I had last been in Paris, thirty years had never seemed so long a time. On my first night in Paris, I found my way to the law firm who had represented me in the past, and upon securing a room for myself at the nearest hotel, set about the waiting for daylight. Bundled tightly in the blackest of fabrics, I hired a coach and arrived at the front steps of the firm in the late afternoon of the next day.

I presented myself there as my own daughter, as I had often enough in the past. A letter in my own hand gave me access to those things I had kept in their keeping, including the prestige of nobility, credit and all the privilege of my former station in life. It was an easy thing then to arrange for clothing and other necessities, while seeing to the matters of my trip. I explained to the young man who so resembled that other lawyer from years before, that my accommodations must be absolutely discreet, and without fear of prying eyes or stray bits of daylight. In this it was more difficult than it had been in the past, convincing a modern man of a mysterious affliction which precluded sunlight, but at the rates he would be paid, it was eventually done.

I left him then and made straight for the hotel. Safely within the confines of my room, I set about my own preparations, drinking down a bottle and a half of formula while I awaited the arrival of my purchases and word of the travel arrangements. Nearly an hour passed before the first of the clothing arrived, along with some jewelry, and other accessories. I must admit to enjoying it rather much to don such finery after so long in rags and antiques. I fitted myself into a beautiful gown of purple and white, which the seamstress assured me was the utmost in fashion for the day. I swept up my gray and black hair beneath a matching hat, touched my pale, pale skin with a bit of cosmetic powder, darkening it ever so slightly, and set out to visit the city.

I moved somewhere between invisible and detached that night, floating through the city of lights with eyes as big as a child's, exploring the wondrous, unfathomable delights gathered there.

I found myself outside an opera house, listening in amazement at the glorious sounds emanating from within. Electric lights lit the billboard there, proclaiming for all to see what stars performed. I didn't know the names, but the voices were simply divine. I walked miles and miles in the darkness, long after the city had settled to its quietest, peering in at windows of shops and diners and boutiques. I heard the whispers of my own kind for the first time in years ... vaguely, distant, but somehow comforting. I scanned them for signs of my children, but they were voices I didn't know. I pulled back into myself and contemplated the beauty of that night. The sky was filled with the brilliance of a million stars, the air was fresh and scented with life. I felt warm, sedate ... at ease with myself. I wandered slowly back to my hotel, letting myself inside as dawn's first light broke the distant horizon.

The next nights were much the same, as I acclimated myself to the world again. I found my way to the library, and spent many of those nights reading. So much had taken place in my absence from the world, so much just since my time in that small village where I had last read of the advances of mankind. In the land across the sea, where I had known and loved Joshua and Francis, scientific advances were being made, and great men were heralded for their achievements. A creation being called a horseless carriage was touted as the next step in travel. With a motor in place of horses, this wheeled wonder could travel at speeds of up to fifteen miles per hour. There were rumors of men trying to fly like birds. Radio transmitters were being used to broadcast music and news across great distances.

My mind swam with it all; the amount of knowledge that had accumulated amazed me. On my fifth night in Paris, word came from my agent that he had booked my passage on a steamer bound for England. It would leave in three weeks. There was some apprehension as I gathered my new belongings and climbed into the rented carriage for the journey. I did not know what I might find in London, or if Francis and Joy remained there still. Even yet, if they resided happily there, what right had I to return to their lives? I, who had not long before nearly destroyed us all.

I stayed fairly much to myself aboard that ship, secreted away in a room in the very bowels of the ship, sipping cautiously on formula that seemed all together flat and pale. Thankfully it was a short journey, one with very little to remark on. The sailors left me be and the captain himself knocked on my door in the early hours of the evening to let me know we had safely arrived.

It had been so long since my last moments in London ... so long and yet it was like no time had passed at all. The filthy streets seemed unchanged as I passed through them in my coach. The same taverns and hotels, the same cold air ... only the faces on the people had changed. In my mind I imagined I saw them, my first children. She smiled at me in her sad way, and he tipped his hat as I passed. I shook off the feeling as we neared our destination, a town house I had owned for more than a century. It had been leased out over the years, and its last tenants had left it only months before. That money had been kept in a forgotten account, money that would certainly see me through the next years. My lawyer in Paris had arranged to have it cleaned and furnished for my arrival.

I dismissed the gathered staff as soon as my luggage had been brought in from the street, explaining that I was far too exhausted from my trip for the proper introductions. Then, with the night still young and a chill settling into my bones, I unloaded my lab equipment myself, setting up in the dreary and damp basement. Once my physical needs had been met, I wrote out instructions for my new servants, explaining to them in sketchy details what I would require of them. It was enough, at first, to simply demand the privacy of a proper lady, and to state that I would nearly never be about in daylight. I hoped they would decide me eccentric, and leave me to it.

Chapter 24

I DIDN'T sleep well that day, my mind filled with visions of past terrors, haunting me even after I rose for the evening. I was uneasy to say the least. The night air tasted of death. It roused me, wakening a fire within. When I closed my eyes I tasted Joy ... saw her as she offered her neck. Flashes of Rebeka and the other child I had once spared mixed with it, and I repeatedly drank from my bottle, only to spit it out in distaste. I roamed the house, hearing each shallow breath of each of the people who slept within its walls. Their hearts beat softly against me, beckoning and repelling. Near to midnight I took to the streets, clad simply in black. I was breathless with anticipation of ... something I couldn't name. I wanted.

Twice I pulled myself away from killing, though neither man deserved the release. Twice I berated myself for the desires ... for what I was. On the mountain I had been nearly contained, surviving casually on the formula and food. Since leaving that place, I had not tasted mortal food, and on that night formula was as water. I craved sustenance ... I craved the thick taste ... the warm splash as it first touches the tongue. I was weak with it, and exhilarated by it, compelled to the darkest corners of a dark city where death was a regular occurrence. It was there, in the shadows of my own soul that I came to myself. I passed a darkened window and beheld it ... the reflection of a ghost.

The ages had come to rest in my eyes; images of my former selves resided there. My pale skin glowed in the light of a full moon and the Change had come upon me unaware. The black silk of the gown blended with my hair, making the silver streaks that much more prominent. I appeared, even to myself, a frail woman of declining years, whose dark secrets would no longer be kept. I stood there near onto an hour, examining the stranger I barely recognized, wondering how old I had come to be. It was as if I stared into my mother's eyes ... not the vacant expression of her addiction to the blood, but the passionate woman underneath. She would not be denied. Then, in a flicker of the nearby light, the Change faded ... and with it my strength.

The walk home was long and by the time I reached the door, I was tired beyond all measure. I decided I needed someone with me ... someone to balance me. I longed for Francis and her unerring ways of making me right. I did not even pretend to retire, only sent a young boy to fetch me a lawyer. When the man arrived, a stale smelling fellow in his mid-fifties, I explained to him that I was searching for my daughter who had last been known to be heading in this direction. I was certain that Francis would expect me to follow, and leave clues as to her whereabouts. I described both her and Joy to the man, and explained the rather large sums available to the one to find her. He left shortly, assuring me that he would use all of his resources to do exactly as I asked.

I found it difficult to sleep, and dangerous to be awake. I felt weak ... old. For the better part of the day and most of the following night, I paced in the confines of my room. When at last I slept, it was in fitful spurts, haunted by nightmares filled with blood and death. It was short, and I rose near to dawn feeling hardly rested. Mrs. Pliece, an elderly, maternal sort who was in charge of the household servants came to offer me breakfast, but I dismissed her immediately, claiming a sour stomach. She withdrew courteously enough, but I could sense that she would return.

I drank down several bottles of formula and disappeared into the basement lab to refill them. When the sun had only begun to turn toward setting, I wrapped myself and took to the streets, prowling. I searched each passing face for something familiar, scoured the shops for what it was I craved. I listened to the night, hearing the voices that echoed unheard by mortal man. As darkness fled, I returned home, tired and hungry. Mrs. Pliece met me at the door and escorted me into the kitchen where she had already prepared a small meal. The tea was hot, steaming. It seemed to comfort something inside me, soothe a part of the animal. She spoke softly, of nothing in particular, but her voice was simple, lightly touched with the courtly tongue of the city. The eggs and meat were tasty, the bread soft and still warm from the oven. I suddenly discovered I was famished and began to devour the food. "That's better," she said, bustling about me. "A good meal will do wonders for you. It's time we put some meat on those bones." She smiled and I found myself smiling back. It was nice to be cared for again.

When I had finished the food she had set before me, she prepared a hot bath, lightly scented with lavender. It reminded me of Willemenia, and I wondered idly what had become of her. She washed my hair, wrapped me in a warm robe, and tucked me into the comfort of my bed. I drifted to sleep, still hearing her voice singing softly somewhere in the room. Each night after that I would rise and venture out into the streets, searching for my lost family, wandering through vaguely familiar streets with no real pattern, no plan beyond finding them. I would return home, each night more exhausted, each night finding the soothing presence of Mrs. Pliece waiting for me at the door. The rest of the house seemed invisible, providing their services without leaving a mark. Only she appeared to me, caring for me as one would their own elderly mother.

Through it all, I aged. I could see it, visibly marking the advancing signs of my years as they etched themselves upon my face. The reports came from the lawyer I had retained, word of his search, of the path of my daughter and Joy. They had indeed come to London, and there had made their home for several months before they had journeyed north. They had lived in a small town for a time, teaching at a school there. Several times the trail grew cold, and it would be months before I would hear from him again. Still, I searched closer to home, somehow believing I would find them there, in that dark city where so many secrets were so easily hidden.

I settled into a manner of existence, finding an uneasy rhythm in the house that never fully felt as my own. The place seemed more to belong to Mrs. Pliece and the small army of servants she commanded, and I was merely a visitor there. A year passed in that way. A year of quasi existence in which I became a doddering old woman who searched the night for her lost children. I dreamed as I slept of times past, of happy days with Jesse, with Rebeka, with Lu Sin and the girls. I woke often speaking their names. At night, when I wasn't searching the city I was writing, pouring my life into the journals that had become my life's last passion. I had determined to put it all down, the pain and joy, the multitude of sins. It went beyond the writing I had done in the past. It became a test of my ability to remember, to admit.

It was winter when it occurred, the event that would shake me out of my complacency. We were closing in on the turn of a century. I ventured out into London, wrapped in a black cloak that swept the damp cobblestone streets, with a knit scarf to protect my frail, translucent skin from the cold night air. It was early in the evening, scarcely after dark. My boots echoed around me, the sound spurring my steps further away from the familiar streets I had been hunting.

There was a scent on the cold breeze. It was familiar, and yet vague. I followed it almost without knowing it. I felt the weight of each of my years on my shoulders as I passed the dismal alleys filled with the stench of rotting food and human waste. The wraith-like image that glimpsed at me from dirty windows seemed like someone else, the image of a woman long past her years. The streets were nearly empty, and the few souls out were scurrying homeward. I watched them, scanning their faces as I had hundreds of them in the last year.

Then, in the dim light of a nearby gaslight I saw it, sensed it. She was hurrying, her eyes down, her head covered by a cloak pulled tightly around her. She didn't see me. I stopped, my eyes caught upon her, locked on the half-familiar face. She had aged some, the nearly three years between that night when I had last held her in my arms and that moment when I beheld her again taking their toll on her young features. I could tell from that one moment that she was no longer the innocent adolescent on the verge of becoming a woman. Her face tilted as she reached the streetlight and it was like looking back in time to the night I had first seen Rebeka.

Still, she didn't spot me, and I was frozen for the moment. She turned a corner and I was freed, scurrying after her. I saw her enter a building, watched as she moved past lighted windows to greet a small child. As I moved closer I could hear laughter, soft conversation. Then I saw Francis. She came from the kitchen, carrying a steaming pot of something. I stood outside that window and watched as they ate, as they spoke of the day, as they retired for the evening.

I returned there the next night, and the night after that. I watched their lives, something within settled simply to see them, to feel them nearby. I hovered outside of their existence, feeling my body age with each passing night. I learned what I could about them, sent word to the lawyer I had retained to find them and set him about the trail.

I learned that Francis would give birth in only a few weeks. Her husband was a teacher, a professor of history with a young daughter of his own whose mother had died in childbirth. They had returned to London when he had accepted the position at the college. Joy was working as a nurse at a nearby hospital, a job she was well suited for.

There were moments when I would have sworn they had felt my presence, the turn of a head, the touch of an eye, but not once was it acknowledged. I kept my distance, but constantly shadowed the small family. I slept deeply in the day, beyond dreams and visions. I rose shortly before sunset, to Mrs. Pliece's care. She would bathe me, comb out the long, gray locks of hair and feed me before I took to the streets. I would carry only a bottle of formula and a few coins in my sack as I haunted the night. I would follow them, stand outside their windows waiting to catch a glimpse of them. They were still night creatures, staying awake long after the streets around them had gone quiet. They spoke softly, read quietly, and retired to their beds wordlessly.

I was there the night the baby came, letting myself into that apartment, slipping in with the soft breeze to hover in the shadows and gaze at them. Francis slept soundly, her light snore resonating around the room, into my soul. The babe slept at her breast, a beautiful daughter... my own granddaughter. I found myself smiling at her. I could sense her strength, her fierce independence.

The husband slept in the chair beside the bed. He was a handsome man, if I were to judge. His hair was a rich brown, full and thick. An equally full mustache hid his upper lip. I sighed silently and drifted into Joy's room.

Joy's sleep was not as deep, she tossed lightly in the grip of some dream. Her scent filled the room, awakening the same emotions that had roused me to nearly take her once before. I inhaled sharply. My heartbeat quickened at the scent. I knelt beside her, near one hand that had fallen outside the coverings. It shined palely, glistening with the vibrant life that called to me. I hovered there, my eyes closed as I centered myself on her once more. I didn't leave there until daylight had already begun to creep in at the windows.

The next night was the same, and for many weeks after that. I was sedated just to be near them, soothed by the scent of them. I began to recapture something of normality, visiting the high society places in town, eating at some of the finest restaurants, attending charity events. Near dawn I would always stop there, at that little apartment. I would steal inside and sit with them as daylight came. Then, I would return to my home, drink from my formula and sleep.

It was the daughter who caught me at it first. I stood by the cradle, watching the infant sleep. I felt her waking, but not quickly enough to hide. Her eyes opened wide as she saw me, but she didn't call out. I held up my hands. "Don't be frightened child. I only came to see the babe," I said.

"Maybe you should have knocked on the door." The sound seared into me, that voice. I caught my breath and looked up.

"Joy." I stepped closer. "I'm sorry. I hadn't thought to intrude."

She shook her head, golden tresses cascading around her face so that I couldn't see her. I worried that she was angry, that she would send me away. I waited breathlessly for her to speak again. It seemed a lifetime would pass.

"Mother ... Amara." She stepped closer, her hands on the child's shoulders. "This is Anna, Bryant's daughter. Anna, this is Amara, Francis's mother."

Those big green eyes blinked and the girl curtsied deeply. "Pleasure, ma'am."

Joy smiled and I melted. "Now, get back to bed before you wake the house." When she was once more tucked under her blankets, Joy came to stand beside me, looking down at the sleeping infant. "And this is Amanda, your granddaughter."

"She's beautiful," I whispered. Joy's hand settled on mine and I inhaled deeply. "Tell me, is he a good man?"

Joy looked at me and nodded. "Yes, very. You would like him."

"And you? Have you met no one since leaving our little home?"

She sighed and rested her head on my shoulder. "There is no one for me but you, Mother. I had hoped you would have learned that by now."

I stroked her hair and felt myself fill with her presence. "I do, I only asked...." What? To reassure myself? I sighed and she looked up at me.

"We should wake Francis."

I stiffened. "There is little time 'til sunrise now."

She hooked her arm through mine. "There is a place here where you will be safe enough. You're not running out on us again."

She drew me through the small home, stopping me outside the bedroom door where Francis and her husband slept. "Wait here." She slipped inside and a few minutes later the door creaked open and Francis was there, looking at me with tears in her eyes. I was crying too as she came and wrapped her arms around me. She was soft and warm and I was comforted. I shook as she released me. Tears rolled down my cheeks and I reached out to hold them both at once, laughing and kissing their hair as though twenty years had passed, rather than just three.

"My beautiful girls," I said when I finally found my voice. "Look at you." I smoothed Francis's hair out of her eyes. "All grown up."

The smile on my daughter's face was bright. "I missed you, Mother." She drew me to the kitchen table and we sat. We were still there, the three of us as dawn ate away the dark and I was forced from the room. We withdrew then into Joy's room, which had no windows. I spent the day with them, held my granddaughter, met my son-in-law, caught up on the details of their lives. By nightfall it was nearly as if we had never been apart.

I took my leave of them in the evening, returning to my home and submitting to Mrs. Pliece's ministrations and scolding for worrying her. I was content. I could smell Joy on my clothes, my daughter forgave me, and she had a beautiful family.

The next months were a whirlwind of visits and getting to know them all over again. My passion returned to me, the hunger that I hadn't fed in years gnawed at me. I hadn't tasted human blood since that night I had last tasted Joy. I found I craved it enough to hunt the dark London streets. I killed twice in the first three months after they had found me out. Both men were killers, and both had provided me a pleasure I hadn't expected, along with the strength and warmth of the feeding.

Chapter 25

I GREW complacent again, dwelling in some dream state that I believed I could control. Of course, my own life should have taught me better. It was in the early spring. London was wet and cold. I was on my way to the theatre, the carriage moving through the muffled streets slowly, weaving around the pedestrian traffic. I was tired, resting my head against the velvet padding. The age of my body had become increasingly difficult for me. The carriage clattered to a halt, waiting for some blockage in the road ahead to clear. Out of the corner of my eye, in the swirling crowd, I spotted him.

It was quick, the momentary glimpse I might have dismissed had it been any other face. It was pale, scant. It reflected years of hunger and internal suffering. If he saw me as well, it didn't show. He disappeared into the mix of human faces. I sat up, moved closer to the window. I searched, but he was gone. The carriage began to move, slowly pulling away from where he had been. The world outside my window seemed to move in slow motion, the people barely breathing.

Then, among them, her face lightly covered with a scarf, was Joy. A single blonde curl escaped the scarf to gently move across her face as she walked. She smiled at a young girl as she passed, her eyes skimmed the crowd. They danced across the carriage, but didn't really see me. Then, he was there again, passing by her, his eyes caught on her face. I could sense the quickening that took place within him, smell the Change boiling within. She slowed her steps, glancing behind her toward him without seeing him. He blended into the crowd, but I knew he had marked her, he felt that which drew me to her.

I called out for the driver to stop the carriage and had opened the door to step out almost before he had. I had lost sight of her in the crowd, but my eyes picked him out, marked the ragged coat he held tightly around him. I sent the driver home and began to follow him, knowing he was following her. My heart was pounding.

We made several turns, crossed several streets. We were approaching the apartment where Joy and Francis and their family lived. The streets had begun to empty out. I spotted Joy ahead of us, then there was another. He was younger, less hungry, but he was definitely one of us. He detached himself from the shadows and stepped toward Joy. I felt a rage fill me, swelling up from somewhere forgotten. My pace quickened.

The Hunter must have sensed me then, for he slowed his pace and half turned. The Change had come upon him, and the smile on his face sickened me. He gave up his pretense to humanity and raced forward, his entire being intent upon Joy, upon beating me to her. She noticed them then, the two of them coming toward her. She recognized what they were, her face paled somewhat. Her eyes searched for escape, at last turning to the open spaces of the small park nearby. She ran, the two of them right behind her. I followed, feeling the Change roar to life within.

She tripped, rolled through the grass and they sprang. Daniel, the Hunter, flew at her, grabbing at her hair as she rolled away. They came up together and the younger one moved in, but felt my hand on his neck before he could reach them. I pulled him to me, my face twisted in rage as I snapped my jaws over the thick vein in his neck, drinking in enough to drop him incapacitated to the ground and move on. The Hunter had Joy, her neck bent to his pleasure. His teeth scraped her skin. She was calm, her eyes rising to meet mine. She trusted me to save her.

I met her eyes, tried to make her feel me the way Rebeka once had. "Hello, Daniel," I said lowly, moving closer to them.

He laughed, his lunacy making the sound hollow and dismal. "Hello, Mother," he snarled, Joy's blood staining his teeth. "This is ironic don't you think?" he asked. He had tasted enough of her to know her, to know the truth. "We've been here before haven't we, Mother?"

"Only this time, Daniel, I will kill you," I said it without emotion, with nothing more than honest conviction. I knew what I had begun all those years before would end on this night, in this park.

He smiled, and bent back to her neck. She groaned a little as he drank, but her eyes never left mine. "I won't let you have her this time, Hunter," I snarled and dove at them. My arms wrapped around Joy's waist and the three of us crashed to the ground. The impact forced him to release her and she and I rolled away.

He was already up and after us by the time I managed to pull free of her. I stood, putting myself between her and him, leaving her to sit somewhat dazed and bleeding in the wet grass. "She tastes so good, Mother. I understand now why you created me, how much it hurt when I took her before." He came closer, her blood staining his face. "Can you remember it? How it was to find her there, dead … with that stake through her heart?"

"I remember how you tasted when I made you, Hunter," I said in return, rolling my neck to loosen it as the blood from the first of them began to work within me. "I remember the horror on your face as you realized what I had done." I smiled fiercely. "I remember watching you kill for the first time. Do you, Hunter? Do you remember the first one? That day in the church? She was young, innocent, sweet." His eyes fluttered and I could tell he was tasting her again. I moved swiftly then, charging forward, my nails scratching across his face. I dropped him to the ground, landing on top of him. I didn't want to taste him again ... I couldn't risk bringing his sickness inside of me again.

Instead I began to pummel him with my fists, kneeling astride his chest as I unleashed a lifetime of pent up rage upon his face, pounding until my hands turned red with his blood. I felt his consciousness go and still I beat on him. It wasn't until I heard Joy's low moan that I stopped. I turned to find her. She lay in a shallow puddle of blood, the grass around her slick with it. I left him then and went to her, gathering her up into my lap, smoothing her hair with my bloodied hands. She had lost a great deal of blood, perhaps too much.

Her eyes opened. No words passed between us, nothing needed to be said. Everyone she had ever been rested there for me to read. Every thought was open to me. The wound in her neck had slowed its bleeding, but it had done its work, leaving her at the edge of life. I saw Rebeka as I had found her, Rebeka as she had been with me. I knew what must occur, what had been meant to be for a thousand lifetimes. I saw it echo in her eyes, the shadows of those lives. Wordlessly I bent closer, and I could smell her, taste her. My tongue touched the wound softly, licking at the slightly cooling blood. It was thick, and the familiar flavor sent shivers through my soul. My mouth opened almost without thought and closed over the wound, drawing her essence inside of me. That first mouthful I held momentarily, savoring it before swallowing. I drank quickly then, knowing the precious moments were passing, taking her further and further from me. There was so little left, so little to work with. I pulled her life from her, as I had craved doing so many times in the past. Then I began the harder part, forcing myself back into her, pushing my will inside of her. There was so little, my strength was not what it had been when I was younger. As I drank and gave back to her I enveloped her, our minds and souls enmeshed within each other, protective and possessive.

My eyes were closed, savoring the moment. I felt it begin within her. I clung to her, my lips closed over the wound, even as it healed. I held her, cradled her in my arms. She shook with it, and settled silently into it. Slowly, she stirred, lifting her head from my arms. Her scream split the night and I bolted, just as the Hunter's hands closed around my neck and sent me reeling backwards. My breath left me as his bloody face hovered over me. My vision swam, his grip was strong around my throat. He howled into the night sky, and I struggled to pry his hands free. His blood dripped over my face, painting my skin with it. I pushed at him, and still he squeezed my life from me.

Then, he moved, upward. His hands pulled me with him, not quite loosening from my throat as his head snapped backwards. Then I saw her, Joy, her face changed, her mouth turned slightly in a wry smile, sharp white teeth gleaming. Her arm snapped down and I heard the bones in his wrist crack. He let go of me and I fell back to the ground. She pulled him clear of me, tossing him into the nearest tree as if he were a doll. I climbed to my feet and joined her, stalking him between us. He seemed dazed, shaking his head as if to clear it of some thought. He had not fed in some time, and it showed on him. I sensed victory, at long last complete vengeance for my Rebeka. I snatched up a broken branch from the ground, and Joy followed suit. We circled him, taunting him.

Joy closed in first, and in her face I saw the familiar killer that had been Rebeka. There would be no mercy, no pleas for it. The circle had come full upon them. Even he recognized it, his eyes rising to meet hers. She held the broken stick as though it were a sword, and pressed it slowly into him. His eyes locked onto her face, his arms raised to his side as if welcoming the release she offered. My heart froze, recognizing the look ... the expression so like the one Jesse wore as he walked out into the morning light. In the blink of an eye, it was done, the wood buried deeply into the cavity where once a human heart had beat, a human heart I had taken away. He fell to pieces, scattering into dust that washed away in the new rain. I held out my arms to her and she came. We were together, as it had been meant to be. I could read her mind as easily as if she were speaking to me, and mine was just as open to her. We held each other in the late night rain, clinging to each other and letting the rain wash away the bloody evidence of our acts.

When at last we released each other it was to begin the long walk back to the townhouse, arm in arm. Mrs. Pliece met us at the door, wrapping us both in warm blankets and hurrying us inside. Joy was hungered, and yet remarkably in control, the soft, beautiful serenity on her face belying the fierce appetite I could feel. I smiled and held her hand, as the servants bustled about, making us warm and comfortable.

That night I slept with her in my arms, feeling my entire body on fire with the nearness of her, with the wash of her blood working within me. I clung to her, feeling her skin cool, her heart silent, her breathing become more and more shallow. When she rose at sunset she left an empty place beside me. I knew she had gone out to feed and I welcomed the hot exchange that would follow. I rose, but could not bring myself to leave the bedroom. I did not wish to be seen by my servants.

I rang for Mrs. Pliece and asked that she draw a hot bath.

As I sat at my vanity and brushed out the gray hair with a silver brush that had been mine for more years than I could remember, I could taste Joy's sweetness in my mouth. In the mirror I saw a reflection of a woman I had forgotten I had been, a woman not so content with herself, a woman filled with passions that ignited at the touch of another of her kind. However, the hands that held that brush were no longer young, no longer possessed the passion they had once. They shook if I held them out for too long. The wrinkles that had become so familiar in the last years seemed suddenly out of place, as if they belonged to another. I looked again and I was taken with the Change, melting away the years some, transforming the image into something I wasn't quite ready to become again.

I sank into the tub of steaming waters, letting the heat fill me and pull out some of the aches from the previous night's activity. I was still there when she came to me, her pale skin flush with her dinner, her heart calling my name as she sank beside the tub and offered to me her wrist. I drank then, slowly, savoring each drop of the mortal killer she had found in the cold streets of London, flavored slightly with the remains of her own chemistry. I raised my wrist to her lips and we fed, sharing each other more completely than any lovers could.

When we had done, she washed my hair, pampering me as she might have had I been her mortal mother. We spent most of the night speaking silently of the years we had been apart, of our need to be together. As dawn approached we spoke of Francis. She would need to be told something. Joy was as much a part of her life as she had been of mine. The child relied upon her as well. We toyed with the idea of telling her the truth, but I wasn't sure how to finally tell her what I was, what I had made Joy into.

I discarded the idea then, and chose instead some peculiar lies to send Joy and I off into the life we had been destined to share. We worked out the details, first Joy came to stay with me, to care for me. Francis and the children visited and we spoke of travel. There was so much to see. I think she may have suspected, her connection to Joy giving her glimpses of the change in her friend. She spoke of Lu Sin one late evening when the three of us had finished the dinner dishes and were relaxing. I saw the look on Joy's face and smiled. "I have missed her as well," I said softly into the space left after her words.

I set about the matter of arranging a trust after that night, much as I once had for Joy. There would be money for food and education for the children, all that was left of the gift Dovan had given me, the house and servants. We would have no need of such things once we left London. Joy would journey out in the early evening, many nights coming home without having fed. On those nights she watched over Francis. On other nights she would walk the damp streets as a shadow, guided by some unknown hand to those to whom death was welcome. Always she tasted of sadness, and relief ... the joy of release from life's pain.

Three weeks after it began, I followed her out into the night. Arm in arm we strolled through the town, which suddenly looked so much different to me. She was so vibrant, so ... alive beside me. I felt young again, as I had when I had hunted beside my brothers and sisters, as I had under Crenoral's hand. We watched a play, talked quietly with each other about the silent symbolism and macabre sets. She pouted when I suggested we call it an evening. I nearly called her Rebeka.

It was that night, upon our return, as she brushed out my hair that it was first noticeable. Even so, it was so small, so minute, that I brushed it off. The tiny lines around my eyes seemed ... less. As if something had come along to fill them. My green eyes sparkled darkly by the lamp light, as they had long ago. My hair seemed less gray in her hands.

The next night, after feeding and a long walk, I thought I saw it again. It was several nights before I began to realize the implications. Each night a piece of the age I had carried since losing Joy and Francis was washing away. As I fed, and filled my life with her, it returned to me that which I had been. I knew we needed to escalate our plans before the changes became obvious.

I went to Francis in the early hours of the night, held her in my arms. We spoke a long time before she looked at me, forbidden knowledge shining in her eyes. "I am glad you are taking Joy with you. I have not seen her so happy since she was last with you." Her smile was sad.

I sighed, holding her closer. "We will return."

"I know. You have to. Your granddaughter will need you."

I smiled at the thought, suddenly realizing the one thing that had been missing from this time with my family. "Has Dovan seen her?"

"I have not seen him since the night before the wedding," Francis said. "Justine said that she wished to see America."

I nodded and held her close. "I am leaving you the townhouse. Mrs. Pliece is expecting you. The servants are paid through the end of the year."

I could feel her smile, even though I couldn't see it in the dark. "Will you stay long enough for Amanda's birthday?"

"Yes, Joy and I plan to leave a few days after."

"Good." She settled back against me, her head on my shoulder. I listened to the sound of her heartbeat, so soft and nearly hypnotic. Beyond it I could feel the deeper sound of her husband's heart, and the more rapid ones of the two girls.

I stayed until dawn was only an hour away and Francis was sleeping in my arms. The next nights I spent there with my daughter as Joy hunted. On the night of my granddaughter's first birthday, we gathered there in that apartment to celebrate and say our farewells.

Then, carrying only a small pack apiece, Joy and I set off on our life together. We left London and journeyed into the highlands, across Ireland, and Scotland. Anywhere we might find a soul in need of easing, we went. We ministered to them, taking medicines and when all else had failed and there was no further help, Joy would ease them into the next life.

As slowly as it had come, the gray hair faded, replaced by the shiny veneer of my natural black. We lived simply, and often I fed on little more than bread and water, perhaps a small piece of fruit gathered on our journeys. When Joy fed, she would share herself with me, as Rebeka had before her. By day we bedded in each other's arms, wrapped in dark blankets and memories of lifetimes together and apart. We cared little for where we went, or how we traveled. The nights we lived, as only those who have first tasted death can. From the last ruddy ray of the setting sun until the first pale hints of dawn we were ... living as brightly and boldly as we were able.

Joy's gifts, always powerful, always just beneath the mortal surface, blossomed in the night. Her eyes glowed with the knowledge of all she had ever been, and all that lay now at her feet. Her soul saw deep into the shrouded mysteries, bringing back thoughts and ideas that could heal, touch and divide. It was as if all of her many incarnations had led her to this exact thing, this time and place ... this person she was becoming.

I followed her, ensnared by her soft voice and gentle touch, bewitched by her caring eyes and powerful presence. All around us the world was changing. The silent nights of my remembrance, the quiet hours passed in the dark, were gone and in their place came nights filled with life and light and noise. It would make it easier for those of us who made their way by dark. Joy embraced the newness of it all with all the passion and soul she possessed. She made it possible for me to ease myself out of my past, to put away the fears and fetters of my long life and step tentatively toward the future.

The advances of mankind continually amazed me, as we passed through towns and cities. The inventions that little more than fifty years before had been nothing but science fiction now filled up the homes of average people. The horseless carriage had given way to automobiles and trucks. Electric lamps filled the night with light as golden and magnificent as the sunrise.

We let our travels bring us back to London often. Francis and Bryant had a son three years after Amanda and named him Jesse. He had my dark hair and his father's long legs and his mother's knack for seeing in the dark and knowing when I was near. Francis was a better mother than I could ever have been, and her children glowed with their humanity. I was very proud.

At long last, who knows how many years after we had begun, we came to the place of her birth, across the great ocean to the place where her fate had put her into my hands. The streets of San Francisco were crowded as we walked through them hand in hand and I told her the story of the moment when I had first held her.

She knew the tale, of course, as she knew everything there was to know about me, but loved to hear me tell it. Many of the landmarks I had known then were gone, but by some odd twist of fate, the small, back room apartment I had leased then was still there, and empty. It looked much the same as it had when I had awoken that morning, the day I had first come to realize that Francis was on her way. We passed the day there, speaking of her parents and her life here in this city. It seemed ages ago, though it could only have been forty-five years or so.

As dark fell, she wanted to visit the graves where her parents lay. I walked with her, silently, withdrawn within myself to offer her what privacy I could. So much had changed for her, I wondered what she would say to them now. At the gate to the graveyard, I slipped my hand from hers and, with a kiss on my cheek to thank me, she glided away into the shadows. I turned and walked toward the grandiose church, remembering a time when it had been little more than a timber shack with a wooden cross atop it.

Chapter 26

I STOOD on the sidewalk of the quiet street, gazing about me contentedly, distractedly, a part of my attention attached to Joy, the rest simply being there, waiting. At first I didn't recognize her, though that seems impossible to me now. I had not heard from her or about her in so many years, not since Francis had been born. I hadn't thought much of her since Joy had come to be with me, but there she stood, a vision of haunting beauty.

She looked nearly as lost as she had when I had first known her, looking as if she might cry at any moment, or run away into the night. She stood upon the steps of the church, unable to go inside. The full moon cast a hazy glow over her, tinted her pale skin ever so slightly to make her look almost human. I stood nearly a block away, watching, and waiting for her to notice me. She turned, slowly, her eyes lifting to meet mine. We were alone on the street and I smiled a half smile as I started toward her. She glided gracefully down the steps to the street, but her smile was sad. "Hello, Moira," I said softly. It seemed I always spoke to her that way.

"It has been a long time," she said, her voice full and rich, sensual.

I had forgotten how it felt to be with her, this creature who had been human when I first found her, human and lost, not far from death, the first of my children. "Are you all right?" I asked her, wanting to comfort the tears I could see in her eyes as she shook her head.

"They've taken Leonard," she said, her voice shaking and soft.

"Where?" I asked, putting a hand on her arm to steady her. It awakened the maternal instinct in me, the side that rose up to protect and avenge.

"In there. They came just before sunset. I was already awake, and I had gone downstairs to work. I came up when I heard the commotion, but they had already dragged him out. As soon as the sun was down, I followed. They came here." We both turned to look at the church and I could feel her pain.

I was so in tune with her that I found tears in my eyes, and a rage swelling within my heart. It was as if this time spent with Joy had unplugged all the last blockages to my humanity and I was free to love and fear and cry. I stepped toward the church, but Moira's hand on my arm held me. She was bound by what she was, and could not step foot inside that hallowed hall. I calmed her as best I could and handed her my bag. I was traveling lightly and would have little need of anything in it inside the church. I beckoned Joy with a light thought and waited for her to emerge from the graveyard. "This is Joy, she is my friend and confidant. Go with her. I will go in for Leonard."

Joy instantly knew Moira from my thoughts, and gathered her like a wounded bird into her arms. "Come, Moira, let us find a quiet place to wait. All will be well." She cooed and persuaded Moira as I ran up the steps to the doors of the church. They were, of course, locked. True hunters wouldn't want anyone to see them at work. I circled the building, trying to hear beyond the cold stone walls. I found an open window at last, in a back office. I crawled through and slipped through the deserted halls.

Leonard was too proud to cry out, even if he were to think anyone would come for him. I listened instead for the sound of men's voices, for the racing heartbeats and harsh breathing. My senses were heightened by my excitement and fear for the life of the man who had been like a son-in-law to me. I sniffed the stale air as I slid through the shadows beneath stained glass windows and sidled slowly into the sanctuary.

Crouched there behind the last pew, I peered into the darkened sanctuary, and there I found them. For the briefest of moments it swept over me, the vision of a time past, and I felt my heart palpitate as Rebeka's face flashed in my mind. I blinked, and some part of me reached out to Joy. Her mind brushed against me like the familiar touch of a lover, and my thoughts cleared. There were three of them, modern images of a demon worse than that which they sought to kill. Pale images, I saw as I moved a little closer, for they seemed to have lost some of the truths about our kind once so preciously guarded by theirs. Two of them wore strings of garlic around their necks, along with their crosses. The stench of their fear and anger mingled with sweat and blood, raising the level of rage within me.

Leonard was tied across the altar, the ropes stained with his blood where they cut into him. A crucifix lay across his chest, and smoke was beginning to rise from it as his skin reacted. His feet were burned from where they had found the sunlight and his long hair lay across his face. His hands were clenched into fists at his sides, pounding uselessly against the cold marble slab of the altar. There was a low growl coming from him that I knew would have been a roar of rage anywhere else. It filled the air … or perhaps just my ears, for the others seemed not to notice.

I called to him silently, pressing my presence close enough and strong enough that the tone of the growl shifted. He was too weak to respond in kind, but it was enough that he knew I was there and would do what I could to help him. The men seemed oblivious to all but the task at hand, and I let the Change come over me as I glided closer. Almost silently I moved in the flickering candlelight, closer and closer to them. The first of them died with a broken neck before the others even knew I was there.

The noise of my anger filled the cavernous room, echoing off the hand-polished timbers. The Hunter closest to Leonard raised a wooden stake in preparation for the kill, leaving the third to confront me and keep me at bay long enough to finish their sacrifice. I had other plans however, and paid little heed to the one now charging at me, another stake in hand. Instead, I dove at Leonard, landing atop him and biting into my own wrist. I pressed the bleeding wound to his lips and reached out for the Hunter with my other hand.

I caught him by the collar and pulled him close, snarling in his face as I bent him so that I could reach his neck. He smelled of his fear, his self-righteousness. His eyes went wide as he realized his error. I didn't give him time to regret it, biting harsh and deep, drinking quickly to replenish that which I was feeding Leonard. The blood was hot and fiery, slipping in and out of me with scarcely a thought. The third Hunter grabbed me by the hair and tried to pull me off backwards. I pulled my wrist from Leonard and snatched the stake from the lifeless hands of the first Hunter, scratching it across the face of the attacker.

I dropped the all but dead Hunter and flung myself off of Leonard at the last of them. He paled and backed away, down the steps, holding a tiny silver crucifix between us. It gave Leonard pause, but I merely tossed my cloak to him and told him to cover his eyes. Then, my whole attention was on the little Hunter. He was frightened, all of his conviction and bravado gone in the face of a monster he had been unprepared to face. He began running down the aisle, but he was no match for the speed of my mother's people. He died before he could reach the doors, falling limply to the scarlet carpeting at my feet.

I returned then for Leonard, who had gone to squat beside the remaining Hunter. He was still alive, but only barely so. I reached down to snap his neck, to finish this night, but Leonard stopped me and shook his head. I could read his intent and backed away. I couldn't have approved, but neither could I deny him the right to his own manner of vengeance. "Think carefully, Leonard, for this decision will surely haunt you," was all I said in way of warning. Then I scooped up the limp body and carried him out into the predawn silence, Leonard following. Just off holy ground, I laid him in the grass and watched as Leonard hovered over him, then leaned in.

Had I not done the same once, taking my revenge in the most horrific way I could see? For many, many years it haunted me, the Hunter returning time and again to mark me further in some way. Yet, it had also ultimately brought Joy to me completely. I had left the Hunter teetering at the brink of death. There was still a little further to go and the man I considered a son, took him there viciously, giving only enough back to make the Change begin. We watched as the transformation took place, and the hunger filled him, his eyes widening with horror as he realized what we had done.

"Now, Hunter, taste the dawn, with that hunger in your belly, and that fear in your heart. Find shelter, if you have the strength, or die here knowing you are now that which you have hated the most," Leonard growled at him and I pulled on his arm. The sun was coming quickly, and shelter would not be so easy to find. We hadn't the time to reach their home, or the hotel where Joy and I were staying. We had to find cover. We flew through the streets, climbing in through an open basement window to hide for the day. It was the first day since bringing Joy to me that I spent without her in my arms.

I scarcely slept, the images of Rebeka and Joy mingling in my mind, the faces of Hunters long dead and the poor soul we had left to find his own salvation filling me with fear and dread. Leonard and I spent most of that day sitting and waiting for the sun to set. We spoke some, of the nights when we were together, of the years separating us, but nothing of the events which had just taken place. His deed was perhaps less bloody than mine, less vicious and cruel, yet I could see it weighing on him already. He had never given the gift before, nor taken a life with so much intent. As dark neared, I held his head in my lap and tried to soothe the trouble brewing beneath his dark hair.

"You cannot take it back now. It is best to forget it."

"And leave such a creature to the night?"

"Always so dramatic." I sighed, brushing his hair. "Such a creature will adjust, or perish. It is not for you to sort out."

"You warned me against it, yet didn't stop me. Why?"

I sighed and leaned back against the wall. "I could not make that choice for you. Besides, this Hunter was not as dangerous as mine. His mind seemed sound enough, he should adjust well, once he gets past the anguish of it."

He looked up at me with incredulity in his eyes. I smiled down at him. "I have not always been the prim and proper lady you think me to be, Leonard. Indeed, in our time apart I have been much different than I am today." I sighed, and saw it before me, the life that seemed so distant and surreal. "I too took my revenge on a Hunter this way. It was a century ago ... more than that perhaps. He took from me someone that I loved. It dawned the darkest day in my life. His name was Daniel and I made him one of us in the very confines of the holy mother church before an entire town. I released him into the night, but he never fully left me."

"What happened to him?"

I thought about it, all the times we crossed paths, all of the pain we inflicted upon each other. "Ultimately, he died, while returning to me that which he had taken to begin with." I glanced up to notice the light was fading in the distant window of our hiding place. "Come, let's see if we can't discover how much damage we've done to the local level of hysteria."

When the sun had finally gone enough for comfort, we crawled back through the window and made our careful way back to the church. Moira and Joy were there already. Moira rushed into Leonard's arms, melting into him as if they were indeed one person. Joy's smile was all I needed to feel her relief at our safety. There was no sign of the Hunter, or his dead companions. The church was locked and bolted tightly. There was no word on the streets of the strange deaths and no indication that anyone else knew the truth about us. Someone had done a cleanup job on the whole affair, which indicated to me that this was not a town I cared to stay any longer in. Someone with power knew the truth, someone who was willing to kill, and cover up the blood when they were done. Moira and Leonard chose to move on, to find a new place to explore. For awhile Joy and I traveled with them, sharing stories of our lives, and the people who populated them. It felt nice, comfortable.

It was only months later, in a middle-sized town in Middle America, outside an all-night diner that another piece of my life would fall into place. We had stopped for gasoline and to stretch our legs. Moira and Joy had ventured off into the night to explore the town's square. Leonard was talking with the station attendant. We had caught him just before he had closed for the night. I wandered away, toward the diner, catching the inviting aroma of pot roast on a slight breeze. I didn't truly see him at first, so adept was he at blending into his surroundings.

It brought a smile to my face though when I did, and he smiled in return, holding out his arms to me. I went to him, laughing as he folded me up in his arms. "Ah, Dovan. I had wondered where you'd gotten off to."

He released me and swept his eyes up and down me. "You look as though you've recovered nicely. I was worried about you."

"I've survived." I looked more closely at him, and noticed he seemed older, as if something inside his immortal frame had withered. He hadn't fed in a long time, and ... I could almost feel his ... hurting. "What is it?"

"Justine," He said simply, and I realized she must be gone. "Two years ago."

I touched his hand, trying to offer what comfort I could. He smiled sadly, a cold, distant expression that held no emotion. "I have been waiting here for you ever since."

"For me? What made you think I would come here?"

This time his smile was genuine. "You are here, aren't you?"

"I suppose I am." I smiled too, letting him put his arm around me. "And, not alone. Moira and Leonard are here as well."

"And Joy?" He could sense her still, that faint perfume of her presence drifting our way as we approached the car.

"And Joy," I responded as we reached the others. I made the introductions of Dovan to Moira and Leonard, and Joy smiled and threw her arms around him as if seeing her own grandfather. Dovan invited us all to join him, an offer we accepted graciously. I had not realized how much I missed his quiet, paternal presence.

His home was not exactly the most modest in the town, and once you penetrated the outer appearance, it was far more lavish and opulent than any would assume from the facade. It appeared to be a two-level house, with perhaps five bedrooms, and spacious living quarters, but once inside, and past the middle-class American veneer, the word mansion might have been appropriate.

Six levels extended down from the main floor, housing a library to rival most national archives. The shelves in that library held some of the rarest texts in the world, including some in languages I don't even remember. Journals from various members of the Family, including some of my own, filled one corner, while newspapers, magazines and encyclopedias filled another. Crypt like bedrooms on the bottom most floor showed that we were not his first relatives to spend time with him.

"Justine told me that out of all of my children, you alone would appreciate this place," he told me as we stood alone in the library.

"She would be right." I felt so close to him, and yet distanced by something. It was something he wanted, but was afraid to ask for. I decided not to push.

"I've kept track of Francis since you last left London. I thought you might like to know."

I smiled, surprised, and yet not quite, that he had thought to do such a thing. After all, she was his great-granddaughter, as much as she was my daughter. "Of course I would."

"She is well, as are the children. For a woman her age, she is incredibly well kept, or so the gossip says. Amanda is a proper lady, engaged herself. She has many of your talents, your quick wit. Jesse has entered university. He is studying to be a doctor."

I exhaled sharply. "Has it been so long?" I glanced to Joy. We had last been in London for Jesse's twelfth birthday.

"It has. They miss you." He turned toward me. "You should visit."

"I will, someday soon."

"Promise me?"

I smiled softly. "Of course, I promise."

"Good. Your family is very important."

We were quiet then for a time. He led me to the room where he spent his days. It spoke of him, authoritative and sparse, and yet somehow comforting and home. A painting of Joy and Francis and I hung there above a fireplace. "Justine painted that herself, as a gift to me. It was the last thing she did."

"How did it happen?" I finally asked, not wanting to tread on the obviously painful wound, but genuinely interested in knowing.

"There was an accident, she got hit by one of those vehicles, like yours. She was enough like us that she would have recovered, but they took her to the hospital and left her exposed to daylight. She was enough like us that it killed her slowly." He withdrew a little further into himself. "I was away when it happened. When I made it back, she was nearly gone. There was nothing I could do."

I touched his hand, and we sat silently for a moment. When he stirred, it was to kiss my forehead lightly. "I have sat here, in this room, every day since then waiting for you to come."

I knew then what he wanted, what he had waited for. Our eyes met, and he seemed to ask it without speaking. I nodded slowly, accepting what I knew would be my final role in his life. I climbed up onto the bed beside him, sinking into the banks of pillows that softened his dreams. He came to me, lying against my chest. I folded my arms around him and for a long time I didn't move. My heart slowed, my breathing softened. He stilled beneath my touch, as I raised one hand to gently glide it across his face. "I do adore you, Dovan … Grandfather." I whispered, more into his mind than his ear. His hand touched mine.

He had already gone, in so many ways, but the cursed gift that his own brother had forced upon him held him to this body, compelled him to remain long after his will for it had fled. With no other thought or sound I brought my lips to his neck. My first touch was more a kiss, the second barely more. My teeth were gentle when at last I

Changed, piercing the skin tenderly. I closed my eyes, sipping lightly of the cool blood that was all that was left of him. His mind slipped further and further from me, unlike that of a human dying. My fingers were unconsciously stroking the side of his face, as if to comfort him. My other hand held to his, long after his hand had ceased to hold mine.

I sat then, with his fading body in my arms, feeling his presence fade from the room. When at last I opened my eyes, Joy was there, watching and waiting. The tears came then, tears for everything we had shared, and all that we might have had he remained. She came and held me until they passed. "May we all have so quiet an end, when the end has come," she said softly as we closed and locked the door to that room behind us, leaving little more than dust to mark where he had been.

"Indeed." Was all I could think of to say in return.

The home, with all its secrets, had been left to me, perhaps as he had intended since he had bought it. Joy and I took up residence there, finding an easy place within the quiet town and soft memories. Moira and Leonard stayed a while, but eventually moved on, promising to return from time to time.

I wrote to London, to Francis and Amanda and Jesse. I journeyed back for Amanda's wedding and Jesse's graduation. Francis had aged remarkably well, but time had caught up with her as well.

Dovan had left us a sizeable fortune, the remainder of the Family wealth, with which we continued what he had begun, filling the library with the rarest books available on any market. We emptied out my various storehouses of precious history and secret stashes of valuables from the many decades of my life, sorting through it all and selling what I could stand to part with. As I worked on the perfecting of my life's writings, Joy set about telling the true history of the Vampyre. In the dawning of a new age, I was content to sit out awhile, to let the others play the games of life. Dovan had opened the house to those of the Family who remained, on a few conditions of course. It became a haven, a place where those with the inclination could withdraw from the world at large. Joy and I continued that tradition, trading room and board for tidbits of their life stories, typed on hand-return typewriters or scrawled in leather bound journals.

Someday it might make interesting reading. Forever is a long time, filled with lifeless moments and ridiculous truths. If we are lucky it is punctuated a time or two with wonderful people and incredible adventure. I have come this far, finally understanding my place between the world of man and the dark, between the killer and the mother, between the lover and the demon. For each of us there is an ending, and one day I will find mine ... the day will come when forever will seem impossible to me, as it had for Dovan ... but for now I remain ... forever, Amara....

The End.

About the Author

Natalie Case is a writer and photographer living in the San Francisco Bay Area, though she has called both upstate New York and west Texas home at one point in her life. She is fortunate to do what she loves and love what she does.

Connect with the Author

Natalie can be found on Facebook at: https://www.facebook.com/authornataliejcase and on Twitter at: https://twitter.com/natalie_jc

Made in the USA
Monee, IL
09 January 2024

51479077R00293